# Praise for *Anagram Destiny*

"Through vivid prose that delicately navig
temporary history's most devastating trageares, Grishma Shah crafts
a visceral narrative of strength, vulnerability, and the enduring power
of the human spirit that will resonate with readers everywhere."

**—Veena Rao, author of *The Purple Lotus***

"Aanya and Ayaan are endearing characters who immediately grab
your heart and attention. Yet theirs is more than a simple love story;
woven across continents and decades, it encompasses the real-life
impact of terrorism, the nuances of cultural identity, the arc of grief,
and the possibility that one can reinvent oneself. A book you won't
quickly forget."

**—Jude Berman, author of *The Die* and *The Vow***

"*Anagram Destiny* is a sweeping story of an immigrant family, love,
loss and new beginnings. At once heartbreaking and hopeful, it is a
book to be cherished and contemplated, long after the final chapter."

**—Madi Sinha, author of *At Least You Have Your Health*
and *The White Coat Diaries***

"*Anagram Destiny* is a poignant immigrant story that delves into the
deep-seated pains prompting people to seek refuge in a new land.
Through its vivid storytelling, I was transported to India, experiencing its rich sights, scents, sounds, culture, and architecture from the
comfort of my living room. This novel is a profound exploration of
love and grief, offering a heartfelt and immersive journey that stays
with you after the last page is turned."

**—Beth Biss, author of *Redolent***

"In a complex, often dark, sometimes terrifying world, it is good to know we can take comfort in new love, that the heartaches of adulthood have roots in tender youth, and that there are storytellers, like Grishma Shah, ready to capture both the hard reality of our world and the sweet bonds that hold us together."

**—Alida Winternheimer, author of *A Stone's Throw* and the *Story Works* series**

"Grishma Shah writes an achingly beautiful story of lost love, written in dynamic tension with the unfolding of a new one. Shah writes Aanya's story with wisdom and compassion while deftly guiding us through Indian culture . . . While *Anagram Destiny takes us on a journey through loss and grief, it is ultimately a compelling story of hope and of second chances.*"

**—Joani Elliott, author of *The Audacity of Sara Grayson***

# Anagram Destiny

## A Novel

## Grishma Shah

Published by SparkPress, a BookSparks imprint,
A division of SparkPoint Studio, LLC
Phoenix, Arizona, USA, 85007
www.gosparkpress.com

Published 2024
Printed in the United States of America
Print ISBN: 978-1-68463-258-9
E-ISBN: 978-1-68463-259-6
Library of Congress Control Number: 2024905771

Formatting by Kiran Spees

The publisher has made every reasonable effort to obtain necessary permissions for the inclusion of the song lyrics to *Pal Pal Dil Ke Paas* from the film *Blackmail* (1973) and *Lag Ja Gale* from the film *Woh Kaun Thi* (1964) in this work. In the event that any inadvertent omission or oversight has occurred, the publisher sincerely apologizes and pledges to rectify the situation promptly upon notification. The publisher and author reprint these lyrics with the utmost respect, and welcome resolution with the original copyright holder.

With all my love,
for:

**Amit**
Your Wisdom, My Words

**Ayushi**
Your Passion, My Project

**Alisha**
Your Cuddles, My Comfort

"While the tale of how we suffer, and how we are delighted, and how we may triumph is never new, it always must be heard. There isn't any other tale to tell; it's the only light we've got in all the darkness. . . . And this tale, according to that face, that body, those strong hands on those strings, has another aspect in every country and a new depth in every generation."

James Baldwin
"Sonny's Blues"
1957

# Part I

# 1

# Delhi/Gurgaon
## *2008*

As the plane ascended, bringing a broken New York skyline into view, she couldn't help but think about how this would end. Were they destined for a soft—and safe—landing? Or a metal-grinding, earsplitting crash into the crowds of people below, going about their daily lives, oblivious to the powerful machine roaring above, its ability to destroy a thousand dreams in the span of seconds?

She clasped her hands, closed her eyes, and repeated her favorite mantra three times.

Fourteen hours later, she was shaken awake by a thundering thrash, wheels screeching against a runway. Her palms pressed hard on the front seat, her whole body fighting the velocity of the landing.

Safe—if not soft.

Good enough.

She scanned the rim of stout men from right to left, searching for her name—*nothing*—and then backward, from left to right. *Still nothing!* There was no sign, typed up professionally on thick stock or scribbled carelessly on a whiteboard, reading AANYA or MS. PAREKH or even TECHLOGICALLY.

People hustled all around her, shouting out names, waving to loved ones, struggling with belongings as they navigated the crowd. The air-conditioned chill of the cavernous concourse sent a shiver down her tensing body. Releasing the grip from the luggage trolley, she lifted one hand to her neck, found her silver chain, and grazed it until her fingers reached the solitaire resting between her clavicles. She twirled the single diamond between her fingers, took a deep breath, and released a sigh.

She could do this. This was what she wanted—a new beginning in a new place, a challenge unfettered by the prickling pain of the past. Her touch on the solitaire grounded her on this, her ancestral land, granting her the strength to search the circle of men once again . . . and voila. There he was.

The man reached for her trolley as the echoes of relatives, friends, acquaintances, even strangers, all instantaneous experts—many of whom had not stepped foot on Indian soil for decades—swirled in Aanya's head like a cluster of gnats clogging her resolve: *Be careful not to give your luggage to anyone. Everyone will attack like hawks, trying to offer help and seize your bags. They are all out to get you! Hold on to your belongings. Hold on to your purse. Secure your passport. They know you are a foreigner. They can tell right away. Don't show them dollars. Carry rupees. Don't give the beggars anything; more will follow by the dozens. Be very careful. There will be people everywhere—like, everywhere—buzzing all around you. Try not to look like an outsider, especially like an American.*

"No, no—it's okay. I will get it."

"Please, ma'am," he resisted, giving her a servile nod.

"I can do it. It's fine. Which direction is the car?"

It truly required all her resilience not to dissolve and submit to the kind-eyed man earnestly offering his help.

The driver, glowing white from head to toe in a finely stitched Nehru jacket, surrendered uneasily. He placed the placard—with TECHLOGICALLY and then WELCOME AANYA in large capital letters—into a refined leather bag as he directed her toward the large glass doors.

Aanya, looking more like the porter than the passenger, struggled to clear the trolley over the threshold. The driver caught her eye, seeking approval, before he placed one hand at the edge of the cart handle for a final push over the protruding entryway.

Under the scorching September sun, Aanya stepped onto a pressed-gravel parking lot, regretting her midday arrival. Most international flights into India, shaped by colonial remnants, landed during the cool of the night. Now, her midday choice, a subtle form of resistance to this vestige, felt utterly foolish, *really damn stupid*, she concluded, sweat trickling down her back. She desperately craved the cool of the night and some ice-cold water as her sweaty shirt clung to her body. Perhaps a little help with the unruly trolley on the jagged pavement would have helped, too, she conceded, as the driver, his hands free, led her through the parking lot.

They reached a large SUV, where she cursed herself for not sticking to the prescribed fifty pounds as she struggled to lift her overweight bags into the trunk. The driver observed her once again. Aanya caught his eye and gave him a look that said, *Sorry I have been such a jerk. It's not you; it's me. It is so hot, I am tired and tense, and people were so wrong about how crazy landing in India would be—please, help me!* She couldn't feign tough girl anymore.

"Ma'am, ma'am, give me, give. I will take care," he said, smiling wide.

Aanya surrendered completely, full of remorse for her brash behavior. He gave her a forgiving nod, proceeded to the driver's seat, ignited the engine, blasted the AC, waved her into the surprisingly lavish vehicle, and offered her a bottle of cold water from a foam cooler. Relishing the icy liquid as the blast of cold air tingled her skin, Aanya finally smiled—her very first happy moment in India.

The car slid smoothly down an open tree-lined road as they drove beneath an arched WELCOME TO DELHI sign. She expected the road to deteriorate as they left the airport, but in fact, the opposite came true. The highway expanded into three-lane tracks on either side, one way toward the airport and the other toward the city. Aanya was curious about all that was passing along the side of the road but refrained from questioning the driver.

*Only foreigners talk to drivers, Aanya,* the voices warned, *especially the Americans. Americans want to know everything all the time, immediately—and if something does not sit right, they want to swoop in and fix it, too. The Indians do not talk to drivers, Aanya.*

Luckily, the driver broke the silence.

"You from US, ma'am, correct?"

"Yes, from the United States. How did you know?"

"Your accent, ma'am. Very American," he said with a smile. "What part of America?"

"New York, but I grew up in Georgia." Aanya spoke as though on autodial.

"Geor-gee-yaa," he repeated.

"Yes, that's right. It's in the South; New York is in the North."

"Yes, ma'am, everyone knows New York," he said. "How long is your Gurgaon stay?"

Aanya hesitated.

"I am not sure. I just moved here for work. I don't know how long."

"That is very good, ma'am. Many people, they move to Gurgaon. Many foreigners here now. Every day, more people come and stay here. You from India, ma'am?"

Although she had just answered where she was from, Aanya knew exactly what he was asking: *I know you said you are from New York, ma'am, but you look like one of us—dark hair, skin a shade of light brown, unmistakably from these parts. So, what is the real deal? Let's get to the bottom of this—where are you really from?*

Again, accustomed to the question, Aanya spoke almost robotically, recognizing the irony. Whether she was in New York or New

Delhi, people had the same desire to ascertain her origins, all searching for the right box to tick mark in their heads. *Where do you fit in? Let's figure that out first, so we can all find a comfortable, common space to exist and possibly even move forward.*

"I was born in Georgia, but we—my family is from Gujarat. Actually, my father is from a small village in Gujarat. My mother is Gujarati, but she has never lived there. She was born in Uganda—you know, in Africa."

"Gujarati—nice people and good place, ma'am. It is very good you have come back; welcome home," he said humbly, ignoring the latter part of her statement.

Aanya understood that this was where the world thought she belonged; these were her roots, the original box checked when she was born. Indian, and then later, Indian-American, and this was the ephemeral motherland—but *home?*

"Yes—thank you—it—is good to be—ho-ooome."

Gazing out the window like a goldfish temporarily placed in a clear plastic bag next to its fishbowl, Aanya felt at ease. Comfortable. She could swim and certainly survive, but . . . home? She couldn't quite digest the journey that had brought her here. Never in all her wildest thoughts had she imagined herself relocating halfway across the world for a job opportunity. As a child, when someone asked her, "What do you want to be when you grow up?" she always shrugged her shoulders with an "I don't know," prompting the surveyor to abort mission. She definitely never said, "When I grow up, I want to help the world by strategically introducing technology to make processes, operations, and outcomes more efficient, informative, safer, and more secure for businesses across the globe." Yet, here she was.

Though never one to have a grand vision or a five-year strategic plan, she was myopically driven, always giving a hundred percent to the task at hand. Her talent and work ethic were well known at TechLogically, so when it came time to move beyond back-office work and build a marketplace in India, she was the top choice. She accepted, not because the work would be exciting, but because she felt an unprecedented and unrelenting need to escape New York.

The car curved toward a sign for Gurgaon as shiny, mirrored buildings appeared on the side of the road, along with billboards, massive cranes, and glaring signs for American Express, GE, Microsoft, and DLF. In a different phase of life, Aanya was well versed in current affairs. And though recently she had disengaged—for she could no longer stomach the media's incessant peddling of fear and terror—she was well aware of India's growing importance on the world stage. Yet this, the breathtaking spectacle that was unfolding out the window, dwarfed the headlines. Gurgaon was no small coincidence. It was the manifestation of every "India Rising" *Economist* cover she had so apathetically ignored, she thought, peering upward to gauge the height of a skyscraper on the side of the highway.

Ninety minutes after the estimated half-hour ride, Aanya found herself in one of those large skyscrapers at the front door of her new apartment, the doorman wheeling in her luggage. Before closing the door to behold her glistening new living room, she thanked the doorman profusely, overcompensating for her rash behavior toward the driver earlier.

Directly across from the front door were wall-to-wall, floor-to-ceiling windows overlooking the stream of cars lining the exit ramp they had just descended. At eye level, beyond the glittery jungle of buildings, a hazy horizon peered out from a jagged skyline. The other walls were layered with textured herringbone wallpaper in alternating shades of cream, a fifty-inch flat-screen television, and abstract paintings in traditional beaded framing. Above the TV, a cool breeze from a wall-mounted AC unit swirled the scent of jasmine radiating from an oil diffuser placed on an accent table. A three-seat leather sofa, chic and modern in design, sat atop white marble tiles. Everything in the apartment seemed to be dipped in gloss, eliciting the chicness of picture-perfect modern spaces often found in *Architectural Digest* or *Modern Home*.

The square dining table tucked between the sofa and the kitchen held a leather binder with information on anything and everything you might require in Gurgaon: where to shop, where to eat, where to buy groceries, how to get anything delivered to your home, general safety tips—which upon further examination were only intended for women—and a notably brief history of Gurgaon. All of these followed an opening vignette about the Shalimar Apartments, inaugurated in 2006 and described as "indulgent with modern luxury and a touch of old-world charm," each flat "styled with utmost attention" by a renowned Delhiite designer.

Just as Aanya pulled out a fresh T-shirt and shorts (conveniently packed in her handbag for a quick shower upon arrival), the doorbell rang. The doorman held up a white, cubed pastry box tied with a sophisticated royal blue ribbon, almost like the white ribbon on a Tiffany box.

*Indulgent is right!* she thought.

Aanya accepted the box with a "Thank you." She placed the box on the dining table and admired it for a minute before meticulously untying the ribbon. It was too pretty to throw away, so she placed it on the side, hoping to recycle it for another present. Inside was a gourmet ganache fudge cake drizzled with white chocolate and topped with a fresh strawberry. Taped to the inside flap of the box was an envelope with a small note in a calligraphy font, complete with a royal blue border to match the branding of the packaging.

Dear Aanya,

Welcome to TechLogically, India!
We are excited to have you on board!

*Best wishes,*
*Sid & the TechLogically Team, Gurgaon*

Aanya, feeling flattered by the warm welcome, the shiny accommodations, the impressive buildings, the eager doorman, and the luxurious car with the kind driver, went to the kitchen to gather a plate and utensils. As she sliced into the cake, modish knife in hand, the empty room began to close in on her. She swallowed the lump in her throat, placing a chocolate wedge on her plate as the blast of air from the AC unit cooled her scalp.

Just then, it occurred to her that the space around her was too bare, too desolate, too clean, too clinical, too quiet, and just too lonely for a celebratory welcome. A tear dropped onto the parcel of chocolate atop her spoon. The cake; a celebration, a symbol of her new beginning, a rebirth of sorts, a salute to her career accomplishments—and yet, there was no one to serve a slice to, no one to feed a bite to, no one to shove a bite into her mouth, and no one to smear the buttercream on her cheeks. No one to share all this with, the commemoration of her hard-earned triumphs. She placed the spoon in her mouth, the salty tear still fresh against her palate, realizing she had never felt more alone, not even on her darkest days.

Instinctively, she reached for the solitaire resting between her clavicles, twirling the single diamond between her fingers. In the cozy comfort of her dim-lit New York City apartment, the firmness of her father's reliable arms had wrapped her in warmth as his tears dampened the very shirt she was still wearing. Her mother closed in on them to complete the triad of a perfect farewell family hug, her father's words echoing in her ear. "*Beta,* a solitaire diamond always shines brighter than two, three, or many nestled together. You are proof of that. You shine brighter than a hundred diamonds. You shine bright every day, and we want you always to remember your own strength as you embark on this new adventure by yourself."

Memories of that tender moment during her final hours in New York hardened her enough to grab the leather binder and order pizza from a local chain. By the time it arrived, she had eaten half the cake and was lying groggily on the sofa. She placed the whole pizza box into the fridge. Too spent for a shower or even to walk to the bedroom, she plopped on the cool leather sofa and dozed off, caving to the jet lag.

Up at 4:23 the next morning, by 9:00 a.m., she had brushed her teeth, showered her sweat-laden, plane-infested body, eaten half of the pizza from the fridge, and browsed random TV channels for almost three hours. She caught the tail end of *Jab We Met*, the latest addition to her list of favorite Bollywood movies, and an episode each of *Friends* and *Seinfeld*, back-to-back. She filled the time in between by watching music videos and commercials, finding the Indian advertisements especially amusing.

Midmorning, halfway into another episode of *Friends,* the landline rang. She picked up on the second ring, curious who would have this number aside from the doorman.

"Hey, it's me, Sid," a male voice said. "Welcome to Gurgaon, Aanya!"

"Hi, Sid! Thank you for the welcome cake. It was so thoughtful—and delicious."

"Anytime. Nothing but the best for our newest addition. You sleep okay?"

"Yes, slept like a baby, but been up since four. Jet lag, I guess. Don't mind it, though—can't complain about being in this apartment for sure."

"Well, that's Gurgaon! The whole place is on new money steroids, thanks to the IT boom. Allow me to show you some more of it. I was thinking, if you are up for it, let's grab lunch today, get you acquainted."

"That sounds great."

"Perfect. I can pick you up around noon."

For lunch, Aanya found herself at the far right of a fully air-conditioned indoor piazza surrounded by an excessive number of food stalls—a bit like a food court in an American mall, except this was signature Gurgaon. There was luxury and indulgence all around. The place was upscale, with no signs of grime or grunge, just glistening facades, cushy seating, and shiny floors with an amalgamation of spicy, fishy smells. Among the options available were Japanese, Thai, Tibetan, Malaysian, Italian, Indo-Chinese, all kinds of Indian, of course, and several varieties of pizza—not to be conflated with Italian.

"It is the best place to come if you can't decide what your palate craves or if no one agrees on a cuisine. Hopefully, it will work for you."

"Are you kidding me, Sid? Everything looks and smells fantastic. I think I crave it all," Aanya fibbed, her belly still swollen from the pizza she had downed for breakfast.

Unlike a food court at an American mall and fully yielding to Gurgaon swank, a waiter took their order, placed it at the pertinent stall, and would soon bring them their meals—full service, indeed.

"I am in awe—Gurgaon feels nothing like India," Aanya said, catching a man, about 5'9", with light hair, staring at her from a distance. The man looked inquisitive and a little lost. Aanya tried to ignore him.

"When was the last time you were in India?"

Sid raised an eyebrow, looking like a skeptical teenager. His unruly curls matched his laid-back demeanor. His snug white T-shirt with the TechLogically logo in the pocket corner and a pair of artificially weathered jeans made Aanya feel prudish in her business casual navy slacks and silky white button-down blouse. It seemed everyone around her was trendy, hip, and in their twenties—and she had clearly missed the memo on all things young and cool.

"Sometime in the '90s, but I never left Gujarat—for the most part."

The staring man sat four tables down, beyond Sid's shoulders, with two other men, both foreigners, pale and pink from sunburn. Aanya caught him glancing her way again before consciously looking away.

"Well, things have definitely changed, but rest assured, my friend, the '90s India is not too far away. It's just around the corner. I can take you there one day if you want to reminisce. Trust me, the glamour of Gurgaon gutters quickly."

Beyond Sid's left shoulder and directly in her line of vision, the curious gaze continued to distract Aanya.

"All okay there? Hello?"

Sid waved his hand in front of her.

"Yeah, sorry about that! Was just thinking about something and maybe hitting that jet lag wall."

"Understandable. Will get you back for an afternoon nap soon. So, tell me, how are Ari and gang back in New York?"

"All good. We had a superb farewell party."

Aanya had worked closely with Sid for years, as he was the liaison between the New York clients and the software development team based in India. In the last year or so, Sid, without deliberate effort, had developed a small client base in India and personally persuaded TechLogically's global CEO that they could no longer have just a back-office presence in such a fast-growing economy. TechLogically needed to conquer the Indian market, and to do so, they needed a potent head for business development, poaching Aanya directly from her New York boss, Ari. In India, Aanya's main objective was to acquire a long list of clients, help them understand the need for TechLogically's services, and manage those relationships. Sid, the

Chief Technology Officer, would build out those services with his
team of 158 employees, based mostly in Gurgaon.

"Great. So, not to talk shop too early, but we have a lead. Seems
promising. Thought maybe you could start there."

"That's what I am here for—tell me more."

"It is at the Taj Hotel in Mumbai. We did a small project for one
of the Tata affiliates here in Delhi, and they liked our work. If we bag
the Taj in Mumbai, the rest will follow suit, such as the Taj Delhi and
others throughout India. Not to mention they have a bunch of brands
under their banner. I am sure you know, but the Taj Mumbai is the
flagship hotel, the—"

As Sid spoke, the staring man approached them.

"Excuse me, sorry to be a bother, but I feel like I know you."

The staring man was standing above their table, speaking directly
to Aanya. His tone was soft, genuinely curious.

"I am sorry, maybe you are right, but I can't recall," Aanya said
as she searched his face.

Recognizing the American accent on both sides, the man
scrunched his forehead tight and then released it as if he was struck
by the perfect thought.

"Did you go to Emory, by any chance?" he asked.

"No, but—um, I have friends who did," Aanya responded.

"That's it! I recall you on campus. You were with one of my
friends from freshman year. We lost touch over the years, but he was
always with you—ahhh—what's his name?"

Aanya, feeling a pressing load on her, instinctively sought her
silver chain and turned the solitaire between her fingers before
speaking his name in the softest of tones.

"Ayaan."

"That's right, Ayaan! How could I forget? Such a smart, genuine
guy—how is he doing? Are you still in touch?" The man's face lit up
as he spoke of the memory.

"He's good, I am sure. We haven't spoken in some time, but I'm sure he is fine."

"Well, if you are in touch, tell him I said hi. My name is Ethan."

Aanya, unwilling to delve deeper into the matter, diverted the conversation.

"So, what are you doing here in Gurgaon?"

"Had a few weeks off between jobs, so I took on some volunteer work with Habitat for Humanity. You know the cliché: trying to find myself and all, do something good along the way—what better place than India? We are building some houses about fifty miles from here, but we had the day off, and people kept raving about Gurgaon, so some of us are spending our time off here."

"And you? I'm sorry, I can't recall your name."

"Aanya," she said. "I am here for work. This is my colleague, Sid."

The two men shook hands.

"Well, I don't want to impose on you two any longer, but let me leave you my email; maybe Ayaan and I can get in touch. Do share it with him."

Ethan jotted down his email address on a napkin.

"Good luck with the houses—and finding yourself," Aanya said, slipping the napkin into her purse.

Ethan gave her a bright smile, looking handsome for the first time.

"Thanks. Good luck with your work as well."

Ethan shot both of them a smile before walking back to his table.

"So, anyway, this lead at the Taj—I have heard great things about him. If we can get in the door with him, the rest should be cake. He is our man for sure, Aanya," Sid continued.

"All right, reaching out to him with a proposal offer will be first on my to-do list. You are making my job so easy—keep going."

Their meals arrived: hers a traditional North Indian *chole bhature* with bottled water, and his, a tray of assorted sushi with a Diet Coke.

"I will email you the info, but his name is Abhimanyu," Sid said, picking up a sushi roll with chopsticks. "Now, let's get to the fun stuff."

Sid shot Aanya a mischievous look while downing his sushi.

"So, Ayaan, huh?"

"Sid, let's not. Please."

Aanya's face grew tense and her tone serious, making it clear that Ayaan was not up for discussion.

# 2
# Georgia
## *1983*

The drab white light did not dampen the cacophony of noise in the room. Ms. Voorhees, a youthful teacher still fresh and passionate about teaching the first grade, flickered the lights three times. Even on this, the very first day of school, like Pavlov's dogs, all the toothless smiles instinctively narrowed as their heads rotated to the front of the room—right as the PA system beeped twice, prompting her to respond.

"Yes, how can I help?"

The secretary from the main office started speaking with a southern drawl through the brown box in a cheery voice.

"Hi, Katie, an aaa . . . a . . . A—ya-an was dropped off late. I am having a third grader walk him down."

"Sure," said Ms. Voorhees, "I will keep an eye out."

"Katie," Aanya sounded out in a whisper, and before she could process that "Katie" was Ms. Voorhees's first name, she thought, *aaa . . . a . . . a—ya-an.* Oh, wait, she meant "Aa-yaa-n." *Ayaan was in her class.* She had known this but was so busy meticulously organizing her new supplies in her desk that she didn't notice he hadn't arrived yet.

Weeks earlier, their mothers had opened the letters from the school in unison while on the phone, rejoicing at their common teacher. The two children had grown up in each other's presence, as

15

the two families had a short yet linked immigrant history. One of only a handful of Indian families in a hundred-mile radius, the new arrivals not only found comfort in the familiarity of a common language and homeland but also a mutual need for friendship. Just like their parents, Aanya and Ayaan were a natural fit—having known each other since the day they were born, they craved each other's company, always a bit restless if the other was missing.

Ms. Voorhees fussed over something on the board as the classroom door unlatched, and a little boy with a flawless olive complexion and thick black hair in an impeccably manicured pompadour—a style his mother had obsessed with and perfected, making him late for the first day of first grade—walked into the room.

"Aa-yaa-n," whispered Aanya, and her smile widened just a wee bit as the latecomer plopped into the seat next to her—thanks to Ms. Voorhees assigning desks in alphabetical order by first name.

All the desks had name tags made from colorful construction paper, laminated to sustain the wear and tear of the coming year. On Aanya's desk, stuck on with Scotch tape, was a lime-green paper with blue writing and butterfly stickers all around the word AANYA—and, on his desk, a yellow sign with tractors and bulldozer stickers that read AYAAN in blue marker.

This was the first time in her short life that she had seen his name in writing. Aanya was fascinated by the letters. There was something there, so connected, so clear, but being new at reading, she was unable to decipher it.

Later that day, when they were allotted some free time to color, Aanya took her colored pencils and copied the letters of her name off her tag and the letters of his name off his tag onto a piece of paper. She rewrote it again, and then again, and then one more time. She scrambled and unscrambled the letters until clarity hit her: their names shared the exact same letters in a different order.

She doodled her name again and then connected his to it, sharing the "A" in common. She did it again, this time using the second "N" as the common letter, and again using the "Y" in between her name to finish hers. She turned to him and pointed to her doodling. He stared at it, taking a minute to digest what Aanya had already deciphered.

When he finally figured it out, he took his red colored pencil and put a heart around her last doodle, the one in which they shared a "Y." Aanya giggled. Ayaan followed suit.

Their names, Aanya learned much later in life, were an anagram. Ayaan meant "gift of God," and Aanya meant "inexhaustible." She was too young to understand then that names could become destinies.

# 3
# Mumbai
## *2008*

A confident-looking man stood to the right of a towering, opulent floral arrangement placed atop a grand round table. The arrangement of hibiscus and orchids, centered beneath a magnificently lit bulbous dome, augmented the grandeur of the man's image. She had corresponded with him a handful of times, and surely, this was one of those rare moments when the individual's persona matched their real-life image.

"Hi, I am Aanya; you must be Abhimanyu," she said in her fast-paced American accent, thinking she must use the restroom in this fancy hotel before she left. Sid was right—the glamour of Gurgaon guttered quickly.

"Yes, you have it right! Welcome, Aanya, to the Taj Palace, Mumbai. It is a pleasure to meet you finally."

He reached out a hand, the shake firm, his touch unexpectedly soft. His palm lingered as he held her gaze, smiling profusely.

She turned to the flowers, commenting on their beauty.

"They arrive fresh every few days, flown in from all over India—sometimes the world," he said. "This way to my office. We can meet in there."

While the modern chic of Gurgaon was impressive, here, the luminescent marble floors, the authentic old-world charm—first in the colossal lobby and then down a quaint corridor—radiated charm and magnetism. Light sconces with emerald and ruby stones inlaid in white porcelain lit the pathway. Matching porcelain chandeliers centered beneath domes—shrunken replicas of the large bulbous dome in the main lobby—hung every few feet. Along the hallway, a light fragrance of rose water emanated from the intricately carved marble pedestals, adorned with floating candles and scattered rose petals. Everything was a far cry from what she had expected when Sid described the historic hotel as iconic—the preferred choice for heads of state, international royalty, dignitaries, and Fortune 500 CEOs.

The trendy designers of Delhi might have found the "old-world charm" too much, off-balance with their modern chic, perhaps too ancient and traditional. But she was in awe, feeling as though she was on the set of *Mughal-E-Azam*, an old Hindi film she had loved as a child that captured the *Mughlai* era in India. Her head oscillated slightly as she silently hummed a classic song from the film: *"Jab pyar kiya to darna kya, jab pyar kiya to darna kya"*—the tune about loving without fear flooded her with warm childhood memories.

*If only it were that easy.*

Though his office was plain—a shed-sized box with an old wall clock that ticked loudly, some crown molding, and a laptop connected to a sleek desktop monitor that wholly undermined the grandeur and antiquity just beyond the office door—Abhimanyu, the Director of Events at the Taj Mahal Palace Hotel, played no small role. In any given year, he was in charge of hundreds of meetings, conferences, weddings, parties, and other events.

Aanya sat; Abhimanyu followed and began. He spoke directly, quick to the point: "Why should we use TechLogically's software when we could build our own system in-house? Would volume control pricing? What if a head of state refused to have his entourage barcoded and scanned—what about those that wished to remain anonymous and invisible? What if people copied the barcodes and crashed events? What happens when a scanning machine breaks down? Why do we even need this when things are working just fine?" Yet, she noted a softness in his voice, empathy in his tone, a palpable compassion difficult to find in such a straightforward person. He smiled—a lot—and while he was not in sales, Aanya was convinced he was the reason for return business at the Taj. He had what she called the "L" factor. He was immediately likable.

She answered each question with poise and placidity. "An in-house system would take much longer, and we already have a number of patent filings on the technology that may further delay your development. Any hotel client, whether it is the prince of Saudi Arabia or the entitled son of an Indian politician, can refuse to enlist in the system, but opting in actually protects anonymity, as it is the number, not the name, that retains the guest's data. If the guest still refuses, the hotel may use it internally for back-end operations only. For example, room keys could be coded, but not the guests themselves—yes, barcodes can be copied, but the scanners being used have patent technology built in that red-flags possible counterfeits. A human would be alerted to take additional verification—and do not forget security. I know it is not a major concern as you have in-house measures, but this is an added safety precaution."

Abhimanyu grinned with a satisfied nod, gazing directly into her eyes—and just like that, he made her feel adequate, like that was enough. *She* was enough. *Damn, he was good.*

They agreed on the system's merits and that the technology would benefit heads of state, dignitaries, and conference attendees before they moved on to weddings. Weddings in Mumbai—the center of Bollywood and the duplicitous underworld, with its thousands of invitees per multi-day affair—could easily benefit from the system. A wedding invite with a barcode could exemplify the exclusivity of the invitation, enabling guests to boast about their mounting stature in elite society.

Their back-and-forth on the uses of the technology for weddings lasted some time, and there was intermittent laughter as they mocked the quirks of the Mumbai elites. As the minutes passed, there was a lightness in the air, and Abhimanyu, in an old aunty impression, said, "Look at this, *beta*—let me show you this invitation to so-and-so's son's wedding. It was hand-delivered with a box of dry fruits on top, but look! Look at this; don't mind the dry fruits, just some almond falmond—that, too, from India, not even Afghani. But see this, *beta*, so many people, paparazzi, and street rats trying to crash the wedding; they have put a computer code—you must bring this, get scanned, and then security lets you inside. This is very official and organized, you see; not everyone gets invited to such things. You know we need this nowadays; just too many people up to no good, trying to click pictures and blackmail. Mumbai is just full of those kinds. This is good, I say, good—and you see this; there is a code to scan for every event. I tell you, this is something special—and all do this now, with the dry fruit and all, but to think of this—smart people, I say."

As Abhimanyu, dressed in a sophisticated suit, performed the petulant monologue with merriment, Aanya couldn't help but relax. Her gentle smile escalated to a chuckle and then a wholehearted, body-convulsing laugh, her head perched back, wavy hair falling off her shoulder, the solitaire on her bare neck catching the light.

Mid-laugh, realizing her professionalism had tanked, she covered her mouth with one hand, suppressing her amusement.

He straightened a bit, composed himself, and smiled wide again—a smile that left her feeling confident and professional again.

"So, you are sold on the wedding thing, I see. All jokes aside, I am telling you, if you get the wedding parties on board, Taj will be a pioneer."

"You are absolutely right, Aanya. There is a lot of untapped potential here."

This exchange, though relatively ordinary, left her feeling

extraordinary—significant, as though she were the only person in the world at that very moment, that nothing was more valuable than her and their rather business-as-usual meeting. Most importantly, he made her laugh—and not the fake kind of laugh she did for most clients to keep the mood light and peppy, but a wholehearted, make-the-whole-body-convulse kind of mirth—the kind that was beginning to make her feel slightly uneasy, now that it was over.

"Thank you, Abhimanyu. I really appreciate your time and hope that we can work something out."

The meeting was not so much an opening as, hopefully, a closing. She had flown to Mumbai to meet Abhimanyu in person after several exchanges and a formal proposal offering to streamline the thousands of guests and VIPs that passed through the Taj for conferences, events, weddings, and parties. She had wanted this deal long before she set foot in Mumbai, but now, after meeting Abhimanyu, she wanted to close it even more. The urgency was shooting up her spine with each passing word. She was not sure why, but something about him made her not want but *need* this deal.

"Call me Abhi. Abhimanyu is reserved for my parents, Aanya."

When he spoke her name in the last breath, his eyes smiled candidly into hers before his mouth fully widened to perfectly aligned teeth. She returned a quick, unsure smile before leaning down to pick up her handbag. They walked through the ornate corridor into the grand lobby and stood facing each other again, just as they had an hour ago.

Abhimanyu stared her directly in the eyes and said, "Thank you so much for flying to Mumbai. I think it was worth it. We may have something here."

Aanya lifted her gaze, pretending to admire the grand dome, fiddling with her solitaire, feeling a continuing unease creep through her senses.

"I am glad we may have something. The Taj Mumbai is special, iconic, and absolutely stunning. I am lucky to be working on this project," she said.

Abhimanyu gave her what seemed to be his signature grand smile and turned toward Ram Singh, the doorman, who was dressed in a traditional Maharaja jacket and turban. Ram Singh gave Abhimanyu a salute of understanding and gestured Aanya toward the door.

"Mr. Singh can call a taxi if you need," Abhimanyu said. "It was gre—really great meeting you."

"Same here. Thank you, Abhimanyu, for your time."

As she walked down a small set of stairs toward the main entry-way, she felt a new weight against the lightness of her earlier laughter. Just before she was about to walk out onto the bustling streets of Mumbai, she turned toward the grand foyer table, sitting amidst the magnificent lobby. Abhimanyu stood there, perfectly still, staring at her with a smile. He looked luminous, strikingly handsome, his hair in an impeccably manicured pompadour.

Aanya's smile narrowed instinctively at the realization. All of a sudden, she felt a surge of something she could not fathom until much later that evening. In the tranquil still of the night, as she lay alone on the king-size hotel bed, drenched in guilt.

# 4

# Georgia
## *1988*

Sustained Silent Reading, or SSR, was Ayaan's least favorite period, not because he despised reading—not at all—but because it was so quiet in the classroom that he could hear the buzz of the white tube lights installed in three neat panels above his head. The incessant ringing bothered him so much that he couldn't concentrate even on the most interesting of words.

Adding to the torture, his SSR classroom was positioned in the inner courtyard of a U-shaped school building, giving one side of the classroom a panoramic view of the playground with a flat, square slab of concrete and a wide green field framed by a distant tree-lined fence. Fortunately, the silver lining of that torment was that Ayaan sat in the last row, at the last desk, on the side of the classroom adjacent to the windows.

Each day, the teacher, Mr. Breza, sat at the front of the room with his round glasses and mustache, fully engrossed in Sustained Silent Reading, each book thicker than the last. Mr. Breza, though a scholarly fellow himself, was wholly unconcerned with what Ayaan—or any other kid in the room, for that matter—did as long as the room was pin-drop silent. (Barring the persistent hum of the white lights, of course.)

In fifth grade, SSR was Ayaan's fourth period of the day—the same time that Mrs. Lopez's class had lunch and recess, granting

Ayaan a full thirty-nine minutes to stare at a playground replete with sixth graders. With each passing minute, he grew more envious and eager to join the boys and girls playing foursquare, freeze tag, catch, or even chasing a frog.

On this day, the group of sixth graders was scurrying around aimlessly, playing not much of anything. The only organized game he could decipher was two girls facing each other, rhythmically slapping their palms together in a pattern, singing something that was blotted out by the closed, maybe even soundproof, window. Six other girls crowded around them, trying to learn the song, pattern, and rhythm in what seemed like an advanced version of patty-cake. About nine boys ran around them in chaos while five or six jumped around, horse-played, and wrestled each other without rhyme or reason.

Watching this spectacle each day, Ayaan had concluded that boys his age, or at least the boys in Mrs. Lopez's class, were incapable of playing any systematically organized game unless supervised by an adult or a group of sixth-grade girls. He acknowledged this with the utmost respect, understanding that, on most days, he was one of those boys—unless, of course, his recess overlapped with Aanya's. It did so every two or three weeks, when the school condensed and staggered the periods in some odd formation to adjust for special events such as a pep rally or a school-wide assembly. On those days, he and Aanya would spend the time together, walking up and down the field until their nine overlapped minutes ended. For the remainder of the semi-overlapped recess, he would go back to the boys from his sixth-grade class and join them in a frenzied game of nothingness. On sensical days, the boys would join the girls in an orderly game of red rover; foursquare; red light, green light; or freeze tag, but on most days, they just bounced around here and there like escaped animals from the zoo.

Today, a new set of girls started to practice patty-cake on steroids, clapping their hands neatly in tune with their newly learned rhythm.

Ayaan caught one of the girls who was standing around watching notice a boy calmly standing by her side. The girl had vibrant red hair and a nose full of freckles. The boy had curly brown hair and a pale face. Vigilant of the individual members of the class and their daily playground interactions, Ayaan recognized them but had never noted anything remarkable about the two. The redhead always played on the girls' side, and the pale boy always scampered about—but today, the pale brown-haired boy had stopped his activity and was standing right next to the girl.

The boy bounced up and down, heel to toe, toe to heel, both thumbs hanging in his pants pockets, while the girl, visibly demure, began twiddling her fingers. Then the boy said something to her. All of a sudden, the girl beamed, smiling as though an imminent rain cloud above had just let in the expanse of the sun. The boy smiled back, equally radiant. The two of them stepped just a few feet away from the cluster of their classmates, but no one noticed their retreat— not the girls playing innovative patty-cake, not the unruly boys tackling each other, and definitely not the teacher standing guard, meticulously picking dry hangnails off her cuticles. No one noticed except Ayaan, of course, through his soundproof window view in the last seat at the last desk.

Withdrawn from the crowd, the redheaded girl and the boy continued to converse, both dawning smiles and a gentleness that made Ayaan more and more curious about their conversation. Then the boy reached for the girl's hand, clasped her fingers, and held it for a full three seconds—Ayaan counted. She beamed brighter, and the boy, the brightest. Suddenly, the bell rang, ending both Sustained Silent Reading and the recess theatrics that had enthralled Ayaan. The boy and girl grazed their hands goodbye and joined the line of students walking into the building.

For the rest of the day, Ayaan could not stop thinking about that boy and girl. The way they looked at each other, their short walk together, their bashful smiles, their fingers touching each other. Something about observing the episode unfolding before his eyes had made him both happy and abundantly restless. He thought about it through math, then art, and through his science period. He couldn't figure out why, but he kept going back to the scene, replaying it in his head again and again. There was something about it that made him anxious, almost light-headed.

Finally, right before lunch, as he saw Aanya file out of the cafeteria with her classmates as his class drifted in, it hit him—and it hit him hard, weakening every sensical brain cell he had available. Ayaan was so consumed by the revelation that he forgot to wave "hi" to Aanya.

When he finally realized his mistake and turned around, she shot him a concerned glance. He gave her a thumbs-up—not one thumb, but two. Two thumbs up! What a ridiculously stupid, idiotic, silly gesture to give someone. *Two thumbs up! Idiot.* He spent the rest of the day thinking of the boy and the girl—and now his stupid two thumbs up to Aanya.

After school that afternoon, he finished his homework, then helped his little sister, Aditi—a first grader—with hers, and then the two played a game of hide-and-seek. In the evening, he had an early dinner with his family. When his father, Kishore, needed to fix a leaky faucet in a room at the motel they managed and lived in, off of I-95, Ayaan and Aditi accompanied him, wobbling on the waterbed until their father finished his repair.

During all these activities, Ayaan was okay, distracted by Aditi and his daily routine. He had almost forgotten about the playground scene and forgiven himself for the idiotic two thumbs up. That night, right before he dozed off to sleep, as he stared at the picture of Lord Laxmi hanging in the bedroom he shared with Aditi, it came back to him: the redheaded girl and her luminous smile. The power of the boy in eliciting that smile. Aanya ambling into the cafeteria, distracted by her friends but almost instinctively pausing to wave at him, then turning around, worried, when he failed to respond. Him noticing her, the revelation, and then his idiotic thumbs-up—two thumbs, mind you, elbow high, hands wide, both thumbs sticking straight up from his fist.

*Idiot.*

The next day, during Sustained Silent Reading, Mrs. Lopez's class was running amok again. He saw the redheaded girl playing with her friends and the pale boy with his. Then they both paused momentarily, looked at each other, waved, smiled, and returned to their respective activities. A couple of minutes later, they stopped, waved, and smiled at each other again and then returned to their games.

This loop continued for the rest of the recess. Pause, wave, smile, play. Pause, wave, smile, play. Pause, wave, smile, play. Neither, not once, crossed over to the other, spoke, or held hands, leaving Ayaan wondering why—why were they not talking and holding hands?

Then, just as the bell rang and the class lined up to file indoors, the curly-haired pale boy waited. He paused to see where the redheaded girl would end up in the queue and joined in right behind her. The girl began to giggle, and the boy nervously looked down at his shoes.

Again, no one else noticed this rendezvous, only Ayaan. Although they had not held hands today, to Ayaan, their connection seemed closer, deeper, better, and more satisfying than the day before. This last little bit, the brief moment when the pale boy waited for the redheaded girl to line up so he could join her, his bashfulness, her giggle, the two momentarily recognizing the significance of the other—it made Ayaan happy, leaving him feeling mushy.

Ayaan went through the rest of the day in a distracted but joyful mood. When Aanya crossed him at the cafeteria exit, she waved and smiled. Ayaan, fully conscious, alert, and in complete control of his actions, waved and mouthed a "Hi!" in response, feeling almost proud of not screwing up. *Phew, no two thumbs up!*

Aanya was no stranger. She was a good friend, both inside and outside of school. They had known each other since they were in diapers, and because their families shared proximity, affinity, and of course a common motherland, they saw each other frequently, especially on weekends and holidays. Yet in the last two days, since the SSR scene with the boy and girl, Ayaan had grown much more cognizant of her—and more so, him around her.

While both of them were in the fifth grade, in the same school, Aanya was randomly assigned to team 1A and Ayaan to team 1B, meaning they shared no classes. For the most part, except for the lunchtime crisscross and occasional nine-minute overlap, they only interacted when their families met on weekend evenings for dinner—usually at their homes, both situated on the premises of the two road-side motels their parents owned just miles from each other.

Unaware of when he would get a chance to speak to Aanya again, that Tuesday evening—a day and a half after the SSR scene—he wrote Aanya a note, folded it into a triangle, and tucked it away in his back-pack. The next day, the clouds grew dark around third period, and by fourth, there was a full downpour, leaving Ayaan staring at an empty playground full of puddles. The thirty-nine minutes dragged, as did math, art, and science.

As they lined up for lunch, Ayaan made sure he was at the front of the line. In his left hand was a piece of lined paper, meticulously folded into a triangle with the word "Aanya" across the front. When Aanya appeared amid a cluster of girls, he waved to her and stuck up one finger, indicating that she should wait a minute.

When they crisscrossed, she paused for a split second. He placed the triangle fold in her palm, feeling a tingle when her fingers touched his skin. She gave him a surprised smile. He smiled back nervously.

September 27ᵗʰ, 1988, 6:56 PM

Dear Aanya,
    You know you are one of my best friends, but I have to
tell you something. I think I like you.
    Like, like you, like you.
    Please don't think I am weird. Please. And sorry.


Ayaan


By the end of the day, a hurricane had hit the coast of Florida, and while there would be minimal damage in Georgia, it meant two days' worth of rain. In fourth period on Thursday, Ayaan sat, both bored and nervous. Watching rain can be fascinating, but its charisma paled in comparison to the playground drama. Ayaan wondered how the redheaded girl and pale boy were doing. He wondered if Aanya had read his note.

The thought of her reading the note made him anxious. Did she think he was crazy? Was she now going to avoid him? When would he even get to talk to her? He dragged his feet to math, art, and then science. Not wanting to seem desperate, he placed himself in the lunch line wherever there was space, but as close to the back as possible. He had never been so nervous to see her.

In the cafeteria corridor, he saw her, and the image was to remain perfectly pristine in his mind for decades to come. She wore a frilly red shirt and blue jeans with a pair of tennis shoes. Her wavy hair was up in a side ponytail in a bright red scrunchie, the same shade as her shirt. He waved, his anxiety unable to release a smile. She waved and held up a finger the same way he had done the day before.

When they crossed, he paused. She handed him a triangle piece of paper, folded just as he had. On it, in pink pen, was the letter "A."

September 28th, 1988, 8:56 PM

Dear Ayaan,
    I do not think you are weird at all. You are also my best friend, and I think I maybe like you, like you too . . .
    Sooooo???

    Aanya

The next day, Ayaan handed her a note.

September 29th, 1988, 7:12 PM

Dear Aanya,
    I am so happy. I like your red shirt. It looks pretty on you.
    Soooo—I think I want to hold your hand. That is what we are supposed to do—I am pretty sure.

    Ayaan

That Friday, the rain stopped. The redheaded girl and the pale boy were once again back on the playground. Ayaan watched them, grateful the hurricane had passed and the sun was shining.

Entranced by the two, he watched the girl glancing over at the pale boy. The first time, he did not notice her, too distracted by the boys who had gone fully coo-coo after two days indoors. Finally, he glanced at her, but she missed it as it was her turn on the foursquare box, but just then, she threw the ball, purposely bouncing it hard in a wayward direction toward the boy.

The ball grazed the boy's foot. He looked at it and, just as he was about to pick it up, he saw the redheaded girl's shoes. He looked up and smiled. She smiled back. He handed her the ball. They both paused there for a second, said something to each other, and returned to their respective games.

When the girl's turn ended at foursquare, she went and stood at the corner of the concrete slab. He noticed and walked over to her. They faced each other, both luminescent under the fiery glow of a stifled post-storm sun. She reached out her hand; he touched it.

*TRINGGGGGGGGGGGGGGGG!* The show was over.

It was Friday, a special day. SSR was only twenty-nine minutes. There was a speaker, a say-no-to-drugs type, scheduled to speak at the school assembly that afternoon. By design, the cafeteria was low-capacity so that recess could overlap on the playground but not during the hot lunch. All the classes were compressed and staggered—along with Team 1A's and Team 1B's lunch and recess schedule.

Throughout the next three periods, although they were shortened, Ayaan's anxiety was building. In just over an hour, he would see Aanya for a full nine minutes. He was nervous, his leg shaking and tapping rapidly as he copied the science notes from the blackboard. On this special schedule, Aanya had lunch first, then recess, and Ayaan had recess first, then lunch—so, just as Aanya's class was pushed out to the playground for recess, Ayaan's class was also released outdoors.

Ayaan spotted Aanya quickly, sitting with her friends on a bench, skimming through a copy of *National Geographic*. He walked a little closer and waited for her to look up. She lifted her head, scanning the playground from right to left, squinting her eyes for clarity, spying Ayaan at the very end of her search. She shifted subtly as he inched a bit closer. They met midway between the bench and where he was standing.

"Hi—" Aanya said.

"Hi—" Ayaan replied.

Aanya beamed, smiling as though she were single-handedly responsible for pushing the darkness of the hurricane away, sparkling under the brilliance of the sun. Ayaan smiled back, equally radiant. The two had never been at a loss for words. They had always chattered just like the swarms of kids running around them, prattling endlessly, but today—

"I just want to say . . . umm. I just want to . . . umm . . . you look nice," Ayaan said.

Aanya blushed, twiddling her fingers.

"Umm—thanks. You always look nice, your hair all perfect in that pouf."

There was a long pause. Ayaan stared at his shoes.

"So—is that it?" Aanya said, finally.

Ayaan froze for a few seconds and looked down at his shoes again, his thumbs linked in his pockets.

"You want to hold my hand—you think?" Aanya said.

Ayaan gave her a demure smile. An unrelenting yes.

Her hand shifted slightly, timidly moving toward his—*TRINGGG!* Nine minutes were up.

# 5

# Mumbai
## *2008*

Abhimanyu arrived at the Taj early the next morning, rushing past the opulent lobby and through the corridor, uncharacteristically oblivious to the freshly adorned vases of blush and lavender bouquets, specially ordered to match the theme of the Jain wedding that weekend. There was a flurry of activity at the hotel in anticipation of not only the Jain wedding, the largest of the events, but also the NASSCOM Board of Directors meeting—and, of course, the arrival of the Royal Highness of Malaysia along with his entourage.

Abhimanyu whisked straight past the registration desk, smiling pleasantly at the three women behind it without pausing for chitchat. The women rotated their heads 180 degrees, following his steps from the main entrance, past their desk and to the corridor behind them as if they were ball boys at a tennis match, gawking sternly at the lime-green shape moving across the court. Longing for their usual convivial niceties, they resorted to rapidly clicking away at their keyboards when Abhimanyu overlooked them.

Once in his office, Abhimanyu checked his email, skimming for urgent matters. There were six different emails from the wedding planner for the Jain wedding, all within a three-hour window, requesting a range of dietary and beverage needs, including three bottles of Cristal champagne for the head table at the reception. The planner's next email detailed how the six tables framing the dance floor would be served a lesser-known brand of champagne, preferably Dom Perignon, while the remainder of the grand ballroom would be served an acceptable but slightly more economical brand. She specified that except for the three bottles of Cristal—to be popped as the bride and groom cut the cake—no bottles should be on display. The sparkling champagne flutes should appear magically behind each guest just as the three bottles of Cristal erupted around the cake-cutting couple, tricking the guests into thinking they were indeed sipping Cristal.

The last email, again from the planner, finally had a hint of an apology followed by a clear threat:

*Thanks, Abhi. I understand all these last-minute requests are challenging, but I do appreciate your assistance—especially on the Cristal, which is a special request from the Groom's father. You know how such matters go . . . can't let him down, so let's make it happen.*

Jains—as in the group of people that follow the religion of Jainism and often carry the last name Jain—were decreed not to consume alcohol, Abhimanyu mused. But then again, he quickly acknowledged, nothing about the clientele at the Taj was standard or mainstream. While it was his norm to entertain such requests on a regular basis, it was not the daily reality of millions of Indians, which he reminded himself every time he generously catered to the fastidious requests of each guest.

He loved what he did, but this—the contradiction of it all, the superfluous needs he served versus who he was and where he came from—always unsettled him in a way he was never able to pinpoint. He shook his head and rolled his eyes, forwarding the email to Natasha, the logistical head of food and catering services. Luckily, this was one issue he could push off to the kitchen.

Considering himself free of pressing issues, he relaxed back into his chair, interlaced his fingers behind his head, and stared at the empty seat in front of him. The image of her chuckling, hair slipping off her shoulder as her head tilted back, exposing the length of her neck, lined with an exquisite solitaire (*surely a gift from someone special?*), warmed his soul. That uninhibited mirth—genuine, full, wholesome—made him acknowledge, candidly, that she was *beautiful*, a word he used very judiciously.

The Taj was a revolving door of pretty women. He no longer turned his head or took notice when many such women gave him a positive head-to-toe appraisal. Over the years, the value of external beauty diminished according to the laws of supply and demand at the historic Taj. Too many pretty women on the premises at all times devalued that which was truly beautiful. He had learned through his many female clients and guests that beauty is nothing unless it radiates humility, humbleness, and compassion—a depth he could not unearth in most of the women he chatted up for his work.

Hundreds of well-dressed, attractive women crisscrossed his path on a regular basis, and yes, admittedly, they were very attractive. But they were not *beautiful*. If Aanya were just pretty like one of them, it would have been business as usual. But Aanya, he sensed, was more. She was *beautiful*. Something about her had captivated him, making him thoroughly skittish and amply curious. Based on their exchanges and all she had discussed with him about her work background and experience, she had to be older than she looked. Perhaps she was in her late twenties, even thirties, but she looked like she was twenty-five at the most . . .

He shook his head again, and his whole body followed.

*Get a grip on yourself, Abhi! You have work to do—not to mention you are a grown man with a real job. You don't have time to coo over crushes. Those years are long gone.*

He leaned forward and rang the kitchen for his chai.

Jai promptly brought him his tea, some biscuits, and a piece of buttered toast. It appeared appetizing enough, but Abhimanyu always craved a bit of savory spice and saltiness with his chai, a habit from his morning meals as a child. Nevertheless, because he still found the privilege of breakfast served on a sterling silver tray in the comfort of his very own office unsettling, he graciously accepted whatever was proffered, never making special demands or even flinching in dismay.

When Jai came to pick up the tray an hour later, the toast remained untouched.

"Sir, can I get you something else?"

Abhimanyu looked up from his screen, giving him a sincere smile. Before his breakfast tray was swooped from under him, he grabbed the toast and took an unappetizing bite. Even in the solitude of his office, hidden within the gilded Taj, his mother's saliency on certain matters prevailed: "*Rozi roti*, your daily bread on a plate is a privilege. Leaving it on your plate is nothing short of a sin." Woefully aware of the day-to-day struggles of the non-Cristal drinkers, wasting food, no matter how bland, was not an option.

"No, no, Jayesh, I am quite okay," Abhimanyu said, referring to Jai's real name, not the one printed on his name tag for ease of pronunciation by foreign guests.

"Tomorrow we can try something else, sir," Jayesh said as Abhimanyu took forced bites of his toast.

Abhimanyu, already restless and distracted from the thoughts of her swirling in his head, turned toward Jayesh and said with utmost sincerity, "Jayesh, it is really fine. I don't get hungry in the morning, that is all. No need to worry, *bhaiya*. How is everything going today for you?"

Jayesh smiled, looking flattered.

Abhimanyu's innate ability to make someone feel special and acknowledged, as if their existence really mattered, was well known to Jayesh. He had once told Jayesh under his breath, too low for the others to hear, "Ahh, these biscuits were a special treat in my home. We only got them on Diwali—and that, too, only one packet to be shared by all." Jayesh nodded doubtfully, but Abhimanyu could tell that he appreciated the clandestine moment. The intimacy shared was not only the kind reserved for two equals but two friends—and the reason why whenever Abhimanyu rang the kitchen, Jayesh stopped whatever he was doing and attended to him first.

"All okay, sir; God is good—"

"Jayesh, how long have you been here?"

"Seven months and three days, sir."

"That is very good, Jayesh. You are doing well. Are they going to put you in front of the guests soon?"

"I—I am not sure, sir. At the last review, they said soon, but I need some more practice, sir. Also, English is still a problem, but I am learning. I have some books, and Saara-madam helps me a bit when she can. She brings me her daughter's books to study."

"Ahh—you can practice with me, Jayesh. Always speak to me in English when you can. You just need some practice. You will get there fast—you are doing very well."

Serving the internal staff was part of the training program at the Taj. One could not make mistakes in front of hotel guests, so catering to the staff was a soft launch. Slipups in front of staff were utilized as a learning opportunity, and those involved were encouraged to give constructive feedback. There was no set time for the training program. Usually, it was eighteen months, but some were bumped up quicker, while others were delayed based on their learning curve.

Once he was ready, Jayesh would be placed in the main lobby, where there was face-to-face interaction with guests, but minimal. Then the coffee shop, then the restaurants, and eventually to in-suite butler, attending to every whim of the residing guest. Such positions were reserved for senior staff and only provided to the suite-level guests upon request—and secured payment, of course.

"Have a seat, Jayesh."

Jayesh looked at the seat with confusion.

"It's okay, *bhaiya*, go ahead." Abhimanyu gestured toward the same seat Aanya had been in the day before.

Jayesh sat uncomfortably.

"What do you really want to do, Jayesh? I mean, we can practice English, but what do *you* want?"

"Umm—I am happy, sir. I think I will be able to see guests soon. I do like what I am doing now, sir. Good people here, sir, like Saara-madam and you."

"Yes, indeed, good people, but I do not mean what you want today or tomorrow. Let's say you could do anything in the world—dance, sing, whatever. What would you want to do?"

"Sing, dance, sir? I do not understand, sir."

"I mean—okay, not sing or dance, but what do you enjoy doing? I mean, if you knew for sure you would have a chance to do it, what would you really wish to do?"

"I really don't know, sir. I just need to send money back to Maa, and that is really it."

"You know, Jayesh, I started out like you. I used to serve at the Taj in Nashik, just like you. It is much smaller than this place, but what I did does not change. I did what you do now."

"Really, sir?"

"Yes, Jayesh. Please think about what you want. I do not mean money to send home and the day-to-day. India is changing, Jayesh, and it is changing fast. Understand this. There are new possibilities, ones we did not have the breadth to imagine just a few years ago. Think about what you really want and come tell me when you are ready. You cannot do this forever, and I want you to know, now more than ever, that you have a chance at more than you thought possible. You can dream. It's allowed. Do you understand what I am saying, *bhaiya*?"

Jayesh submitted warmly.

"Thank you, sir, very nice of such a big man like you to talk to

me, to think of us small people. You are too kind," Jayesh said as he
stood up.

"Think about it, Jayesh. We will talk again soon."

Breakfast tray in one hand, Jayesh opened the door and exited, a
glassy glaze of tears threatening to escape.

Abhimanyu's phone rang.

"I cannot do Cristal at that price, Abhi. Tell them it is not possible," Natasha grumbled.

"What is your price, Natasha? We can work it out internally."

"Just tell them to pay for the bottles; service is included. I will
provide them with an invoice. That is, if I can find Cristal in Mumbai
in two days."

"Of course you can find it, Natasha. Overnight it from Singapore
if you have to—you know there is always a way, and we have to find
it."

"Not at that price, Abhi. Please tell them this was not part of the
deal."

"To them, it is always part of the deal, but I will do what I can.
Give me till this afternoon."

"Cristal does not come cheap, and it definitely does not come
free. Remind them that it is Thursday morning, a day before the
first event tomorrow evening. This should have been done months
ago. Convenience—and Cristal—cost money, Abhi. *Cha-ching,
cha-ching.*"

"Okay—give me a little time, but work on finding those three
bottles."

Abhimanyu sighed, surprisingly grateful for the temporary distraction both Natasha and Jayesh had provided.

Turning to his screen, he tried to read a report breaking down
wedding income versus smaller events. Clearly, weddings were the
way to go in Mumbai. The demographics were in their favor: more
than 50 percent of the population was under the age of nineteen, all

to be married between the ripe ages of twenty-one to twenty-nine—
although twenty-nine was pushing it in this country, he admitted.

*Damn, that only gave him a couple of years to find his soulmate.*

Thoughts of her swirled again. *You are a grown man, Abhi! Get a
grip. Soulmates don't just show up in your office for afternoon business
meetings . . . do they? What is wrong with you today?*

He minimized his inbox, revealing a desktop image of a chandelier that hung under the archway leading to the Shangri-La restaurant under the Cinderella staircase in the main lobby. The photo was
taken by a renowned photographer who had visited the hotel and was
widely shared on the internet. It was framed so that the sparkling
crystals of the chandelier were the main focus and not the grand
lobby.

As the crystals shimmered, Abhimanyu was reminded of the
shining solitaire pendant resting salaciously on her bare skin. The
image of her across from him intruded on his peripheral vision. His
mind was simply unable to escape her. He shuddered. *Get a grip!* He
stared at the chair across from him, imagining she was there again.

Then, as if someone had splashed a pitcher of cold water on him,
he turned sharply to his screen and searched his inbox for "Aanya."
The last email she had sent him quickly populated the preview
window, and his eyes shot straight to the end.

*September 24, 2008*

*Hi Abhimanyu,*

*Thank you again for reviewing TechLogically's draft proposal for
the Taj Hotel and agreeing to meet with me. As discussed last week,
I am confirming our meeting. See you in the main lobby of the Taj at
2:00 p.m. tomorrow.*

*I look forward to meeting you and answering your questions.*

*Note: I will be flying into Mumbai tomorrow a.m. Should you*

*need to contact me with any requests/changes, I can be reached on my*
*mobile at (987) 891-9768.*

    *I look forward to meeting you!*
    *Regards,*

*Aanya*
*TechLogically*
*Vice President, Business Development*

". . . mobile at (987) 891-9768"—exactly the line he was searching for. He picked up his cell phone and turned it over in his hand a couple of times before precariously pressing each digit. He took a deep breath as it rang. He never got nervous, but for once, his whole body was shaking.

*What is wrong with you? Relax! It's just a girl.*

On the third ring, she spoke a light "Hello?" and Abhimanyu's whole being melted like a candle in the summer sun.

"Hello—uh—it's Abhi. Hope I am not disturbing you."

"Hi, Abhimanyu—actually, I overslept. Probably should get out of bed and get ready anyway, so no disturbance at all."

Aanya spoke in her usual super-fast American accent, but Abhimanyu could sense a smile in her voice.

"Just Abhi is okay, Aanya, really," he said, imagining her in bed with a T-shirt and shorts. *That's what American girls wear to bed, right?* His only real reference, honesty prevailing, were Monica and Rachel from *Friends*. No one wore nightgowns or proper pajamas in America. Everyone always paraded around in old T-shirts and short-shorts—or so it seemed, at least on the American TV shows he watched.

Abhimanyu felt a trace of shame for letting his imagination run in this direction, but oh gosh, the image of Aanya in a T-shirt and shorts! He shuddered again, trying to shake off the goose bumps.

"So . . ." Aanya hesitated awkwardly. "How are you?"

"I am good—really good—and you? Sleep okay?" Before she could answer, Abhimanyu covered up his "Really good" with, "How long are you in Mumbai?"

Awkward was an understatement for how this conversation was going. *You are a grown man, Abhi, the Director of Events at the Taj. Get a grip!*

"I slept fine—and I am here until this afternoon. I have a four thirty flight to Delhi."

"Well, I must say I'm happy to hear you are not meeting any of our competitors this a.m. I suppose that is good news."

"Does this mean you called to talk business, Abhimanyu?" She paused for a second and added a snide, "Should I come over with the contract?"

"Aanya, I need to run it by a few people, as you know, but as I said, we may have something worthwhile here," he said, tone sorry and serious.

"I know, I'm just kidding, Abhimanyu. Please take your time with it; I am not going anywhere."

"I do hope you are not going anywhere. So, what's the plan for today?"

Wait—did he just say that he hoped she was not going anywhere? *Idiot! So much for staying professional and discreet.*

"I honestly don't know. I haven't been to Mumbai in a long time. Guess I will just walk around and explore."

"You know, I have a really light morning." *The hell with the Cristal at the Jain wedding.* "Maybe I could—perhaps I can show you around? I mean, that is, if you are up for it."

"Really, you have the time for that? I suppose—" There was a long pause. "That would be nice, Abhimanyu."

He felt like correcting her with a "Call me Abhi," but let it go—again.

"Where are you staying? I can pick you up."

"I am at the Orchid, near Marine Drive."

"Ah—that is pretty close, but still with the competition," he joked.

"You have nothing to worry about. Trust me. I can be ready in about an hour. Ring me when you get here."

An hour felt way too long to see her. *Why can't she just come in her American T-shirt and shorts? I really wouldn't mind!*

Embarrassed at himself again, he stopped mid-thought.

"Wait—what do you want to see?"

"Surprise me. I haven't been here in sixteen years, so it's all new to me."

# 6
# Georgia
## *1988*

A yaan scrunched his face and squinted his eyes to make out the image before him. Aanya, whitewashed by the sunlight flooding the entryway, stood before him. The halo behind her was reminiscent of the goddess Laxmi portrait on the calendar that hung in his bedroom. In it, the goddess sits atop a pink lotus flower in a red silk sari, a bright golden glow radiating from behind her head. He had always been captivated by that image, just as he was now by Aanya. He had never seen her in this light, either literally or figuratively.

Her glow, enhanced by the dusk, made the earth scurry under his feet. It was as if he was experiencing an epiphany. She appeared flawless in her pale pink dress paired with matching sandals. Her slightly misaligned teeth, soon to be bound by braces, the budding blemishes of a prepubescent teen, the awkwardness in her "Hi" and subtle *Can you move over so we can come in?* look simply did not register as anything less than divine.

Absorbed by the way her wavy jet-black hair pulled all to one side, gathered on her left shoulder just above her clavicle, he stood still, frozen in the moment. The normally up-in-a-side-ponytail, now side-swept, hair made it look full, luscious, sensual, and—well, he wasn't sure.

He didn't know such words existed—or, more profoundly, that an individual could own those words, could make it so that it seemed if one were to define, say, the word "beautiful," that person's face and only theirs would monopolize the mind. Such words had no meaning for him until Aanya, celestial in her presence, gave them meaning. Long before he recognized their depth—and even longer before he worked up the courage to make a real move—sensations he had no words for would consume the restless nights of this soon-to-be-teenage boy.

"Ayaan, *beta*, move over; let them come inside," Leela, Ayaan's mother, said.

Behind Ayaan, his mother stepped closer to the threshold with Aditi, his little sister, perching her head forcefully on her wrist. Ayaan was nudged to the side as his father, Kishore, gleefully welcomed their friends for the evening.

Aanya's father, Raman-*kaka*, who was standing close behind Aanya, and her mother, Shalu-aunty, stepped inside. Shoes were slipped off at the entryway before crossing the main threshold, but because the day was warm, there were no coats to be collected.

The living-room-turned-check-in-office—or rather, the check-in-office-turned-living-room—had an open oak counter for guest registration on one side, with an attached vestibule and entrance for motel guests. There was another door for personal use on the opposite wall from the check-in desk.

To a stranger, the room's purpose was difficult to decipher, as the quality of the check-in guest, the status of their own guests, and the peculiar moods of their parents determined the room's primary function. The children were often scuttled to the back room if the check-in guests were rowdy and accompanied by underdressed women. Yet the presence of lingering children went unnoticed when tired, middle-aged couples with kids in tow came in to catch a few hours of sleep before making their final descent to Orlando. In the case of Aanya, Raman-*kaka,* and Shalu-aunty, the function was indisputable: they were welcomed in and left to make themselves comfortable in the living room as they deemed fit.

After all, this had been their home first. Long before his parents moved in as the glorified managers (as per their entire village back in India) of the motel, Aanya's parents had occupied it for many years until they, pooling capital from friends near and far, purchased a larger motel down the road. They had vacated this motel, their first home, only four months before Aanya was born—and now the two families lived within a few miles of each other.

As everyone tried to get comfortable, a room key jangled into a bucket atop the registration desk. Kishore waved goodbye to the hotel guest—a man dressed in an oversized suit, his shirt wrinkled, a charred cigarette in hand exiting the vestibule. The man in the suit got into his white Benz, rolled down the window, and savored the last bit of his cigarette.

A tarnished tan-colored car pulled into the parking lot and paused under the canopy next to the white Benz for almost a minute before driving off toward the main road. The occupant of the vehicle was not visible as the angle of the desk obstructed a portion of the driveway.

Two mismatched three-seater sofas with maroon floral designs formed an "L" shape along the walls. A brown curtain, designed to cordon off the registration desk from the sitting area, was now pushed open and hung in the center of the room. In front of the sofas, a folding card table was open and covered with homemade savory Indian snacks and a teapot full of *masala chai*. Leela had prepared a full spread for dinner, inclusive of delectable *rasmalia*, but heavy appetizers were still a must.

Kishore gestured for Raman and Shalu to sit on the bigger sofa before taking a seat next to his wife on the smaller couch. Aanya sat down next to her father, and Ayaan sat next to Aditi, who had plopped herself next to her mother, still snuggling her arm tightly. Comfortable with each other's company and the lack of distractions by motel guests, the families relaxed quickly. The adults exchanged typical pleasantries. They savored the tasty snacks, discussing the pleasant weather and the resulting business it brought down I-95.

"Had no vacancy for two nights in a row—some left in the middle of the night, but I did not know. No time to clean room," Raman said as he nibbled on some *gathia*, made from chickpea flour and deep-fried to perfection.

"Raman-*bhai*, save room—I have some hot *bhajia* coming, not to mention a full dinner," Leela said as she shook Aditi off and walked toward the kitchen to fry corn fritters.

Shalu followed with a clichéd, "Let me help you, Leela. You really should not have fussed so much."

Aditi, Ayaan, and Aanya were at a loss until Kishore urged, "Why don't you kids go play something?" Almost immediately, Ayaan took Aditi's hand and nodded at Aanya. Aanya stood eagerly and the three swiftly escaped the boredom of grown-up chatter.

Behind the office/living room was a small, corridor-like room with just enough space for a futon, on which Kishore slept most days to attend to the bell ringing of late-night arrivals. The space gave way to the kitchen on one side and two adjoining bedrooms on the other. One was Kishore and Leela's bedroom, and the other was for Ayaan and Aditi. The rooms were connected to each other so that one had to go through Kishore and Leela's room to get to the children's room. Both rooms had once been part of the thirty-four-room motel, now reduced to a thirty-two-room occupancy. The door linking the children's room with their parents' remained in place but was rarely shut.

The moms began frying fritters in the kitchen as the fathers set aside the chai and opened a bottle of Black Label whiskey. The children bickered over what they could play, bouncing between bedrooms before settling on Connect Four.

"You can be on my team, Aditi. We'll definitely win," Aanya assured Aditi as they settled on Ayaan's bed.

Aditi agreed cheerfully while Ayaan grimaced uncomfortably. Although he had played all kinds of games with Aanya for as long as he could remember, he felt a discomfort he could not discern. Aditi and Aanya were their normal selves—Aanya playing the big sister role, taking Aditi under her wing, and Aditi soaking up the attention—but what was going on with him? His leg was shaking uncontrollably.

The two girls took turns dropping the round red chips into the yellow stand. Aditi glanced at Aanya every time for assurance before releasing the chip. Aanya always approved, catching the flicker in Ayaan's eye as the chip clanked down.

They persisted for two rounds before Aditi lost interest and went in search of her mother.

"Come on, let's play for real—quick speed round," Aanya said.

Ayaan, caught off guard, reacted only after Aanya had played the first move. Just as he was about to drop his yellow chip, Aanya playfully tapped his hand, forcing the release before he could think it through.

He flinched, not at the coerced move but at her touch. Aanya's supple fingers nudging his hand made him quiver, his body unsettled as goose bumps covered his arms. His heart fluttered. His stomach churned. Everything around him was a blur. She made her moves, uninhibited by his restlessness, not an ounce of distress. How could she carry on like this after they shared those notes, almost held hands? How could she behave as though everything was normal? Like nothing happened on the playground last week?

His uneasiness quickly turned to frustration.

"Come on, kids, get some *bhajia*," Leela echoed as she walked past the bedrooms with a tray of fritters and chutney.

"Just one minute, Aunty! Let's pause until we eat," Aanya said.

As they uncrossed their legs and scuttled across to the edge of the bed, they heard a long, raucous bang, followed by two excruciating screams and Aditi's wail. They ran toward the front office, but Shalu tackled them in the corridor.

"Get in and lock the door," she told them, shoving Aditi in their direction.

Aanya grabbed Aditi's hand and pulled her close. The three of them dashed to the first bedroom, locked the door, and sank to the floor. Aditi wept uncontrollably. Aanya held her tight in her lap, caressing her head.

"It is okay, it is okay—you are fine, baby. It is totally okay, you are fine."

Aanya repeated the words over and over as Ayaan sat next to her, paralyzed except for his shuddering hands. He had never been so frightened.

"Daddy's hurt. There is blood. Go help him, *bhai*," Aditi pleaded with Ayaan.

"What?" Aanya said.

"There was a man with a gun. He hurt Daddy," Aditi spoke through her sobs.

Ayaan pictured his papa's bloodstained body, an image he puzzled together from violent scenes he was accustomed to in Bollywood movies. Shaking, he began to stand. Aanya took his hand and pulled him down.

"You cannot go out there. We have to stay locked in here. My mom said."

"I need to go help my dad."

"I know, but you can't help him right now. You have to stay here. We have to listen."

Ayaan stared at Aanya. The willful, bittersweet nervousness he felt just a few minutes earlier had vanished into uncharted terror. He imagined his father's bloody body again. His face softened, a tear dropped from the corner of his right eye, and then a split second later, another from his left eye.

Aanya shifted Aditi to one side of her lap. She put her other arm around Ayaan, tucked him into the hollow of her shoulder, and squeezed him tight. He began to weep. She squeezed him tighter.

"Everything is going to be okay. I promise. Everything is okay, Ayaan. Your papa is fine," she repeated over and over.

Aditi calmed a little but was still weepy. Aanya wiped Aditi's tears and consoled her some more.

"It's okay, Aditi. Everything is fine. It will all be okay."

Aditi couldn't control the tears, and Ayaan, powerless to help his sister or father, began to sob more profusely.

Aanya squeezed them both a little tighter, under the hollow of her shoulders, stroking their cheeks and drying their tears.

In the front office, Kishore was sprawled out on the floor, the fabric of his green gingham shirt soaked in blood. Leela and Shalu were on either side of him, attempting to control the bleeding from his left arm with the extra sheets and towels they kept for housekeeping. The white of the linens quickly turned crimson as the blood seeped through the parched fabric.

A lanky figure dressed in dark clothing, with a ski mask exposing only the marble of his eyes, held a gloved finger to the trigger of a Glock 17 handgun. Raman, hands trembling, collected the cash from the register and placed it in the key-drop bucket as he negotiated in a calm voice, "No shoot again. We'll give you everything. Do not shoot, please."

He pushed the overflowing bucket across the counter. The shooter, later described by police as "an armed robber, six-foot-one, one hundred and seventy pounds," grabbed the bucket from Raman's hand and dumped the contents into an empty trash bag by his feet. He dropped the hand with the trigger, indicating a closure to the episode. His eyes dropped to Kishore's body and the women on either side of him, zero remorse in his eyes.

"Give me the necklaces," he commanded.

Raman gazed at him, perplexed.

"The women—is that gold? Get me the necklaces. You want me to shoot, man?"

The half-filled *chai* cups and whiskey, along with the partially nibbled *bhajia* scattered on the floor, remained witness to the frantic scene being played out in slow motion for Kishore. He surveyed his wife unhooking the beaded black and gold necklace, her *mangalsutra,* which had sanctified their nuptials. Flashes of the past surfaced. An image of childhood friends and joyous relatives showering them with flower petals among ancient Hindu mantras and melodious *shenhai* brought a narrow smile to his face, reminding him of their first meeting.

Shortly after his arrival in America, Kishore returned to his village in Gujarat for the prospect of an arranged marriage. The US-returned bachelor was in high demand and growing arrogant with the attention, sporting superficiality, rejecting dozens of suitable girls presented to him by those near and far. Too short, too tall, too wide, too dark, too loquacious, too boring, too high-pitched, too eager, too pockmarked, too desperate, too weird, or just too ugly, he protested when the prospect departed.

Leela was the twenty-sixth girl brought to Kishore as a potential marital partner. At first sight, it was a win. She was by far the most beautiful of all the girls presented—literally the fairest of them all, with a light olive tone and hazel eyes most uncommon in the villages of Gujarat. Her jet-black hair and contrasting pale skin had rumors of an ancestral bloodline tainted by the British, Persians, or Moghuls murmuring around Leela. For sure, she was as beautiful as the girl Kishore was crushing on in his advanced calculus class at Georgia Tech.

Within minutes, Kishore requested some private time with her.

When they were alone, Leela finally spoke. She cracked a joke about the absurdity of the so-called private meeting. She assured him that there were about eighteen-and-a-half ears (her great-grandmother was nearly deaf in one ear) glued to the other side of the door and suggested that they make mischievous moaning sounds. Kishore doubted his ability to make such mischief, but he liked the idea. He liked *her*. He liked that she was humorous and bold.

Enamored by her willingness to lighten the seriousness of such a rendezvous, he nervously agreed. So they sat facing each other on the small *charpoy* layered with all the household bedding, to be laid out on the floor each evening for the dozen or so inhabitants of the home.

Kishore was stumped.

Leela began to make some soft sounds and convinced him to imitate her. They made the silliest of moaning sounds, at times sounding like wild animals, knowing full well that eighteen-and-a-half ears were probably glued to the door outside, too startled and shocked to speak or interrupt. Kishore made ridiculous *oooh* and *aaah* noises, sounding in most cases like a monkey gone wild. He had never in his life been persuaded so easily to do something he was so unsure of, something so puerile that the thrill of it made him giddy.

It was then that he understood Leela's special power. On top of being beautiful, full of surprise, and funny, she had the gift of persuasion. He was confident then that if she asked him to jump off a bridge, he would—not because he wanted to, but because she would convince him, aptly and effortlessly, that it was the right thing to do.

With Leela possessing beauty, humor, and a supernatural charm for persuasion, Kishore was sold on her. She had proven to be way better than what her promoters had promised. Ten minutes later, they emerged from the room and obediently consented to the nuptials, both with feigned, demure smiles. They married within a few short days, friends and family showering them in an array of flowers as as Kishore draped the *mangalsutra* around Leela's neck, taking in her face—beautified in hues of red and pink, a mischievous wink in her eye.

Now, as Kishore's eyes slowly shut, Shalu took the necklace from Leela and passed it to Raman, who handed it to the armed robber. The shooter exited and jumped into a beaten-up car. Raman rushed out from behind the registration desk into the vestibule to catch the license plate. It had been removed, so an hour later, when the police asked for a description of the fleeing vehicle, all he could say was, "Light brownish, kind of tan, tarnished and old."

Once the paramedics left, Shalu retrieved the three children from the first bedroom, consoling and contriving half-truths about what had happened.

"Everything is okay. Just a little robbery. He wanted money," she said.

"Where is Daddy?" Aditi asked. "Is he dead?"

"No, no, *beta*, we do not say such things. His arm is hurt. Mummy is taking him to the hospital. He will be very much fine. He is a very strong man."

Ayaan cracked, weeping harder, his body heaving, his leg shaking frantically, his foot tapping hard against the floor. Shielded under the layers of her pale pink dress, Aanya slipped her hand into Ayaan's, interlacing fingers, pressing soft palm against palm. He looked up at her. His leg relaxed and a tiny smile pierced through the tears, making it clear, it was all he needed – her hand in his.

# 7
# Mumbai
## *2008*

As she hung up the phone with Abhimanyu, the quandary of emotions from the night before resurfaced. There she was, snuggled in the same bed, her tiny body staring at a blank white ceiling, feeling light, an intangible, unidentifiable joy. And yet, before she could fully pinpoint its source or embrace the bliss, thoughts of Ayaan drowned her in an abyss of guilt.

She scanned the phone to find the last call received. She couldn't do this. She would call Abhimanyu back and say, "Something urgent came up in Gurgaon and I need to take an earlier flight back."

Just then, her phone rang. It was Jeeni, her only real friend—well, the only one that was not her mother.

"Hello, hello! How is the hustle and bustle of Delhi?"

"It's amazing, but I am in Mumbai at the moment."

"Oh yeah, for the Taj meeting! How did that go?"

"It went well—how is Ria? Is she over the teething? What's her latest antic?"

On calls and in life, Aanya had become skilled at the art of deflection, diverting others toward their own lives instead of hers.

"She is fine, but I am tired of talking about her. Don't get me wrong, you know I love my baby, but jeez, seems like that is all I ever talk about to anyone—babies and motherhood. I need real adult conversation, Aanya. Tell me about what's going on with you. How was the Taj? Let me live vicariously, at least."

"Exquisite, Jeeni, just jaw-dropping. When are you coming to visit? Did you look into your visa requirements?"

"No idea—can't think beyond Ria and the day-to-day. You going to be in Mumbai for a while? I want to hear about what's going on with you. It's the same old here."

Jeeni had long ago caught onto her friend's nonchalance toward her own life.

"Well, okay. Here is something. The guy—I mean the executive—I met at the Taj yesterday just offered to show me around, but I don't think it's right."

"Wait now, I will decide if it's right. So let me ask the most important question: Is—he—cute?"

"He is, kind of—well, he is gorgeous actually, handsome and put together. You know, the whole package . . ."

Aanya imagined him smiling wide, looking luminous, perfect, in the grand lobby of the Taj. *Oh gosh, I need to call him back to cancel.*

"Wait, wait, wait. Did you just say he is 'gorgeous, handsome, and put together'? Aanya Parekh, I haven't heard you talk like that about a guy—or any man, for that matter—in, like, ever. Unless you have doubts it's all a facade and he is really a serial killer, what's not right?"

"Jeeni. He is not that. I just—I don't—I just don't think it's right. Seems more than professional. You know, him showing me around. It's a key would-be client, and I don't want to risk the contract."

There was a time when Aanya had had it all and was less uncertain about such matters. She was the master of her own domain, taking charge when she needed, no matter the situation. Over time, though, afraid that her past preempted her present, Aanya learned to take a back seat with social matters and a front seat professionally.

Now that these two worlds seemed to be colliding, she felt a pressing need to stop it before her present dragged her into the past.

"Okay, so let me get this straight. A gorgeous, hotshot executive from the Taj wants to show you around Mumbai, and you don't want to go because you think it's *not right*? Did I mention that this mom of a sixteen-month-old is living vicariously through you here? Pushing strollers through the suburbs of New Jersey—"

"Jeeni, stop. Your life is perfect and you know it—and you, more than anyone, know how complicated things are for me."

"That is not the point, Aanya. You should go, period! Let's face it—you moved halfway across the world to escape your past. I mean, we can pretend this is all about work—and it is. I am not undermining that. I would never—but it is also so much more than that. You need a fresh start, Aanya, and part of that means you can frolic around Mumbai with a guy who seems to be into you. Just have some fun, even if it's only for a few hours."

"I just don't feel right. It's not professional."

"Oh God, spare me the bullshit, Aanya. There is no way to keep the professional and personal separate, not when it's the only place left to meet people. If it hadn't been for our workplace romance, I wouldn't be married to Jai or have Ria. The rule is that there are no rules. Find love and romance where you can because they are rare— and really, Aanya, we all know what this is about. I am telling you, it's okay for you to see—what's this gorgeous guy's name?"

"Abhimanyu—you can call him Abhi."

"It is okay for you to see Abhi. What I was saying is that it's okay for you to do this without feeling guilty about—*Ayaan*! There, I said it, as straightforward as I can be. No beating around the bush and ignoring the elephant in the room, just the way you like it. Not everyone needs to know about your past, Aanya. You don't need to talk about it—not unless you are ready, that is. Just have some fun. Now, go get your sorry behind up and put on that beautiful Aanya smile and go frolic around Mumbai, guilt-free—because if you don't, I am calling your mother and telling her about your bullshit antics, not Ria's."

"Okay, okay. I will do it—and thanks, Jeeni." Aanya sighed.

"That's what I do—make sure people don't do stupid things like pass up chances to hang out with gorgeous hotshot executives in exciting cities, while I master potty training. You're welcome. Now, go get ready!"

Aanya gazed at herself in the mirror of the ultra-modern bath-room at the Orchid—an homage to some future date in which people would fly cars and eat nutritious pills for each meal—wondering how old she really looked. She searched for traces of fine lines, which in reality were ephemeral, appearing only when she distorted her face so they could artificially materialize. As she attempted to flatten flaws and find faults that didn't exist, she wondered what strangers thought of her. Did young teenagers on the street look at her and think, *Another old lady walking by*? Did all women do this? Did they stare at themselves in a mirror and play a game? "If we asked a hundred strangers ranging in ages from ten to eighty-five"—no, change that to twenty-two to eighty-five. Anyone below twenty-one thinks everyone else is old, so maybe that was a poor gauge.

She started again, in her best game-show-host *Family Feud* voice. "If we asked a hundred strangers, ranging in ages from twenty-two to eighty-five, who had never met you before and had to guess your age on a first impression, what would they say?" Despite their laden credentials, did all women obsess over the futile vanity of their exter-nal beauty? They must, she thought, or else the beauty, fashion, and cosmetics industries would be dead.

Upon further musings in the mirror and ending with a demure smile, she concluded that she did not appear too old, but under the smooth skin and plastered smile, she knew that years of solemnness had etched cracks so deep that no amount of concealer would be enough.

Thank God she did not have the luxury of fretting over her outfit in the same way she did her face. She had only brought two pairs of clothes in a carry-on to Mumbai: the pale-pink pencil skirt and white blouse with matching blazer she wore for their Taj meeting yesterday and an airy pastel-yellow dress for a hot day of solo sightseeing, which she had planned on for today. The dress was one of her favorites as the layers of chiffon rippling around her made her feel bouncy and pretty, ensuring a confidence she so badly needed on a day like this.

Outside the Orchid Hotel, Abhimanyu stood in front of the passenger side of an economical white Tata Indica. His attire was far from casual, black trousers, a crisply ironed white dress shirt, and a matching suit jacket. He was dressed almost identically to the day before except for the missing tie. He appeared the picture of perfection, just as he had been yesterday, standing in the grand lobby adjacent to the round table and floral arrangements, gazing at her as she left the Taj. He opened the passenger door, gesturing her in as if he were the chauffeur to a royal family, guiding a princess into a carriage. She smiled, sliding into her seat.

As he assured her comfort and carefully closed the door, her attention was drawn to his precisely manicured pompadour, parted to the right, unsettling her as she clicked on her seat belt. Swallowing hard, she willed herself to smile. *Am I really doing this?* Unconsciously, she reached for her solitaire and twirled it between her fingers before clasping her hands in prayer atop the layers of chiffon—silently reciting her favorite mantra as Abhimanyu sat beside her, belting himself in.

> *Oṃ bhūr bhuvaḥ svah tatsaviturvareṇyaṃ bhargo devasyadhīmahi dhiyo yo naḥ prachodayāt.*
> *Oṃ bhūr bhuvaḥ svah tatsaviturvareṇyaṃ bhargo devasyadhīmahi dhiyo yo naḥ prachodayāt.*
> *Oṃ bhūr bhuvaḥ svah tatsaviturvareṇyaṃ bhargo devasyadhīmahi dhiyo yo naḥ prachodayāt.*

*(Oh God! Thou art the Giver of Life, Remover of pain and sorrow, the Bestower of happiness. Oh! Creator of the Universe, may we receive thy supreme sin-destroying light, may thee guide our intellect in the right direction.)*

When she had finished, she turned to him. He looked rather large in the seat, like an overgrown teen riding his childhood bicycle. Surely this bite-sized economical car was not designed for men his size. As they pulled out onto the frenzied road along with rickshaws, two-wheelers, cars, bicycles, a bullock cart, dogs, and an occasional cat or cow, Aanya understood that the size of the car was designed for the demands of the overcrowded road and not the breadth of the driver. Now even this compact car vying for space seemed like a behemoth on the incessantly narrowing lanes.

"So, where are we going?" she asked.

Aanya was trying hard not to flinch at what seemed to be ongoing attempts at near misses on the road. The streets of Gurgaon were busy with insurmountable traffic, but usually, it was all cars. Nothing like the streets of Mumbai, which had a distinctive vibe of inclusivity, chaos, and uncertainty. Here, it seemed, everyone was due somewhere *yesterday,* meaning no one was willing to compromise even an inch of pavement beneath them.

"As requested, it is a surprise."

Abhimanyu grinned as he snuck the car between two scooters, cutting off a giant public bus. The bus driver honked profusely but was drowned out by the cacophony of other noises, the least of which was everyone else—including Abhimanyu—honking. Some notably grating sirens did prevail above the rest.

In India, Aanya had learned that customized honks—similar to the choice of ringtones on your cell phone—were a thing. Specialists existed to install honks at an offensive pitch, a notch above the rest, coercing the human ear to listen and cringe with the utmost annoyance. Thankfully, Abhimanyu's car did not have such a honk installed. Unfortunately, every other vehicle on the road that day did.

A tiny little moped carrying two plump women nearly sideswept their car. Aanya subtly clasped her hands a wee bit tighter and closed her eyes for a few seconds.

"Are you okay?"

"Yeah, I guess. Still trying to get used to the driving in India, especially here in Mumbai. Gurgaon seems just a little more controlled—still crazy, but controlled."

Abhimanyu turned to look her straight in the eye.

"Eyes on the road, please, before I have a heart attack!" she squealed.

"Don't worry, Aanya; I have been navigating these roads for a long time. If I don't move aggressively, we won't get anywhere, and I'll have to drive you straight to the airport for your afternoon flight."

Aanya smiled, conceding. Abhimanyu was definitely good at steering through the traffic, but she couldn't help but narrow her lips into a tight squeeze and close her eyes every few seconds.

"So, I take it you do not drive in Gurgaon."

"Nope, TechLogically will not allow me—thank goodness! Something to do with liability and the high rate of road fatalities in India. It does not say that in my contract, I mean the fatality part, but HR hinted at it when I questioned why I cannot officially drive here during my assignment."

"That must be hard. I mean—how do you deal with it? Depending on someone else all the time to take you somewhere?"

"At the risk of sounding very uncool, I have to say I do not get out much. The office is within walking distance of the flat they assigned me. It's just a bunch of expats in the whole building. No one is going anywhere but work, it seems—and no one seems to be driving themselves anywhere, either."

"So, how long are you here?"

"I don't know. At least a year. Depends on if I can make this sale to this really fancy hotel in Mumbai."

He chuckled and his picture-perfect, melt-any-girl's-heart-as-she-falls-backward-with-a-hand-on-her-heart smile surfaced. Aanya felt elated. Her silly joke had made him laugh.

"We are almost there—hang in there. You asked for a surprise."

There was a comfortable silence for the next few minutes as Abhimanyu concentrated on the directions and Aanya feigned equanimity among the utter organized chaos that engulfed their car. She was finally getting a glimpse of the India outside the glamour of Gurgaon—a country on the precipice of something great, seesawing, much like her, between the present and the past.

They both walked through columns of serene stone. The place, a colonnade reminiscent of Roman structures, was empty aside from a young family with two children wandering along the perimeter while their lovestruck parents followed, hand in hand.

"Welcome to one of the most peaceful places in Mumbai," Abhimanyu announced.

"I did not think Mumbai was capable of being peaceful," Aanya said, circling around a column as she grazed her fingers on the earthen stone.

"It really is not, but this time of day, here, is usually good—or maybe just bearable."

"So, you skip work often and bring women here in the middle of the day?" Aanya smirked, raising her eyebrows at him.

"Well, I am sure Natasha, our head of food and catering is hunting me down right now and has forged a plan to murder me, once she gets what she wants of course. So ditching work—work that I am rather passionate about, by the way and that too, in the middle of the day and setting myself up for a beating is not my thing—yet here I am! Make of it what you want."

Aanya blushed, unsure of how to respond.

He gestured her to follow him.

They strolled through columns of carved rustic stones crowned by the mountain above. The place was naturally calming, a breeze flowing through the pillars from the Arabian Sea.

"You know, I have never been here at this time of the day. I come here during the monsoons when no one else dares. I sit here under the canopy and watch the rain drown the city. That is when it is most peaceful," Abhimanyu finally said, breaking the silence.

"Wow, that—that sounds beautiful. I would not have taken you for the poetic type, Mr. Director of Events."

"Me? A poet? Is that a joke!"

Abhimanyu childishly stuck his tongue out, before resting the smile back on his face. Just as Mumbai was incapable of being peaceful, it seemed his smile was powerless given the situation, wholly uncontained.

Abhimanyu paused and turned to Aanya, gazing into her eyes.

"And for the record, to answer your second question, I've never been here with anyone. I've only come alone, and you are right, *so* right, Aanya—Mumbai is way too chaotic. Much like New York, I am assuming. It's almost impossible to escape the chaos and frenzy, except here—for a bit. It's the closest I get to a sense of home."

Aanya's gaze shifted down to his polished shoes. He caught the yellow flurry of her dress reflecting in the shine. Seconds later, she began to wander again. Abhimanyu followed.

"So, where is home?"

"It is a village a few hundred kilometers away, still here in Maharashtra. It's called Bari. I am sure you have never heard of it. My family is still back there."

"Nope, never heard of Bari. I think. I am not exactly well versed on my Indian geography—just the basics. I know where my family is originally from and the major cities. How embarrassing."

"Nothing like that. I bet I know just as little about the States. I know just the big cities and anything they have mentioned on *Friends*. Now, what's more embarrassing?" Abhimanyu raised his eyebrows and grinned. "So, where is your family from?"

"From a small village in Gujarat—Naswadi. Have you heard of it?"

"Actually, I have. We have a recruiting program there."

"What do you mean?"

"The Taj Group has a program in which they recruit students from villages, train them, and place them into our system. The training is from A to Z, and then it's up to you how far you take it. You know, you are looking at a product of the program, Aanya."

"Really, sounds like a much-needed program! I would have never thought you—"

"That I was a village boy? And a poor one, for that matter."

"No, I mean—it's just that you—I mean, you are—well, you are very impressive, Abhi—manyu."

"Thank you. It—it means a lot coming from you."

"Tell me more about the program. I'm fascinated."

With nostalgia in his eyes, he recalled the story.

As a young woman in a humble, crisply ironed white *kurta* spoke of the Taj's history and founding principles, Abhimanyu envisioned himself standing among the historic facade of the banquet hall, serving someone their high tea and biscuits or whatever it was that those people ate with their chai. That was the magnitude of his dreams when a team of Tata recruiters, owners of the Taj Group of Hotels, presented a small vocational training program that would be available to the youngsters of Bari and neighboring villages. The program skipped over Tier One and Tier Two cities and sought its talent in villages, where opportunities were in short supply, wages low, and motivation sky high. Most importantly, the deep sense of loyalty still found in villages was an endangered trait in most cities.

Though well versed in English, the presenter spoke in the local dialect to explain the program. "Tata is looking for good people. Yes, you must be smart, but more importantly, you must be good, very motivated, willing to learn, and show commitment. We will take care of the rest of your training after you are accepted into the program. Of course, it helps if you know a little bit of English, but we can teach you more. We will teach you everything from speaking proper English to making beds, serving tea, and dressing etiquette. We will also train you in computers and systems. You will be able to operate all the different software programs utilized by our chain of hotels. Again, you must be smart, but much more importantly, you have to want this. You need to have the right attitude, as the line is long and the selection exclusive," she said. "But you are all welcome to apply."

Although his education was limited to the government public schools he had attended in Bari and the generic commerce course he had enrolled in thereafter, Abhimanyu was an adequate student. Yes, his grades were average, but he listened with care and always managed to impress his teachers with diligent questions. He had okay marks, some accolades, and many friends. He was as likely to be seen with the principal, headmaster, or professor as he was playing cricket with the neighborhood children, having a *bidi* with his classmates, or chatting up the *mausis* with the latest gossip. At his core, he was an emotionally intelligent being, conversing with utmost attention to anyone and everyone, leaving the receiving party not only in awe of his presence, but feeling the importance of theirs.

In those late teen years, Abhimanyu had mulled over all the quandaries that bounce around in the heads of intelligent, young, and ambitious men entangled in the complexity of a socially stratified and economically immobile society. The recruiting for the Taj

Program fell in sync with his own uncertainty about his future, leaving him little choice but to give it a shot.

Abhimanyu spent that evening filling out the application, gathering the required documents, and practicing his English, most of which was self-taught by watching reruns of American shows like *Friends* and BBC broadcasts. Years of devouring shows in English had made him so good at imitation that he developed a knack for flip-flopping between accents, from American English to British English to Indian English, gradually growing unsure of which one was most authentic to him.

Abhimanyu returned to the recruiter's station the next day, nominally prepared, to find a line winding around an open-air structure. Word of such a training program spreads quickly in a place like Bari, not just in town, but to all the neighboring villages. Marketing the program was a non-issue for the recruiters. However, weeding out the top twenty candidates from a pool of 2,182 was a mind-numbing task.

The Tata recruiters, a middle-aged man and two women in their early thirties, sat behind a seven-foot folding table on a square concrete platform, open on four sides and covered with a thatched roof. The space normally served as the town center, hosting the village *panchayat* meetings, weddings, and festivals. On most days, though, it was just a shaded area where the village folk gathered after an evening amble to catch up on the day's gossip.

Under a blazing sun, Abhimanyu waited patiently in a line at least a hundred feet long, winding around the corner of the platform. No hat, no sunglasses, no sunscreen, just him in the best pair of clothes he could find in his modest wardrobe: a red-and-navy gingham button-down dress shirt and oversized, hand-me-down khakis held up by a belt. Sweat slithered down his back and chest as he watched the three recruiters sift through the submitted documents and arrange them in order.

As the temperatures reached the dread of high noon, the recruiter in the middle chair—one of the two women—seemed increasingly uncomfortable. Abhimanyu observed her carefully. She reached for the glass of water in front of her but then let it go without a sip and continued. Droplets of perspiration formed on her forehead as her face grew more and more pale, yet she continued, a smile concealing her queasiness. She reached for the glass again and examined its crystal-clear contents, then placed it back on the table without taking a sip. She continued, unwilling to break the pattern of reviewing an application, asking a few questions of the young person sitting in front of her, noting specificities, and wishing them well in the selection process before bidding them farewell.

Abhimanyu surveyed the queue, then turned and requested that the young woman behind him hold his spot because he needed to use the facilities. She obliged, and Abhimanyu stepped out of the row of humans snaking around the piazza, walking a quarter of a kilometer to Lalu-*kaka*'s provision kiosk. There, he bought three bottles of ice-cold mineral water and walked back to the pop-up recruiter station. He proceeded to the back of the concrete platform, weaved through the line with a charming smile, and placed a bottle of water in front of each recruiter.

He looked at the woman in the middle with concern in his eyes and said, "I noticed you were not drinking the water from the glass. Please take a sip of this—it is safe, sealed, and clean, I promise!"

The woman smiled, but before she could speak, Abhimanyu continued with a sparkle of humor.

"I would not want you to faint before it's my turn, madam."

The woman, visibly pleased, smiled wide as Abhimanyu strolled back to his place in line.

"No amount of education, training, or preparation," the woman later told him, "could match that level of perspicacity."

That is how Abhimanyu became one of the twenty candidates, or the top 1 percent, selected for the Taj training program that year. The woman's acumen was spot on. Abhimanyu was quintessentially talented at gauging people and discerning their needs before they could even decipher them for themselves. It was a gift indeed, a special power that helped him climb from his original assignment training as a water server at the Taj Hotel in Nashik to the Director of Events at the flagship Taj Mahal Palace Hotel in Mumbai—all within the span of eight years.

"Wow, that's a really impressive story, Abhimanyu, but that makes you, like, what—twenty-four?" Aanya rolled her eyes.

"No, much older, but thank you for the compliment anyway. Enough boring stories about me; are you getting hungry?"

"Kind of—I skipped breakfast, but in all seriousness, your story is amazing and the program sounds fantastic."

"What? I cannot believe you didn't mention that earlier. We could have gone to brunch straightaway—and thank you, by the way."

"This is so much nicer than brunch, Abhimanyu. I'd much rather be here," she said, finally looking into his eyes, leaning in ever so slightly.

Abhimanyu's heart fluttered, and his limbs grew weak. He wanted to reach for the solitaire on Aanya's bare neck, pull her closer to him, place a palm on her cheek, feel her skin against his fingers, and kiss her softly under the refuge of the canopy.

The moment, the time, the place, the sensation—felt oh-so perfect. But, he found himself unable to move, frozen, ironically, by the moment, the time, the place, the sensation, by *her*.

He understood that once the boundary was crossed, especially if it were crossed prematurely, he would never be able to return to this—the perfection that existed just then, the distance of a lifetime spent on two different continents, of childhoods and upbringings in two different worlds, traversed almost instantly without clichéd cultural clashes. It would vanish instantly.

Aanya retreated, dropping her gaze and taking a visibly reluctant step back.

Abhimanyu lifted his eyes and looked out through the pillars, beyond the shore, and into the water surrounding the island. The two children were still playing onshore while their parents looked on with contentment. Without a word, they moved in sync from under the colonnade toward the exit onto the vast shore lining the azure-blue sea.

The moment slipped, but somehow, its sanctity had been permanently preserved—which, in the long view, was profoundly more satisfying.

# 8

# Georgia
*1988*

The day after Kishore was shot, Leela sat by his bedside, watching a nurse carefully dress his wound in the same hospital where both Ayaan and Aditi were born, remembering those early days.

When Leela had first arrived in Georgia, just months after her arranged marriage, she was dismayed. There were no streets paved of gold, but rather porcelain toilet bowls waiting to be shined and bedsheets with cigarette holes to be mended. She had had little time to get to know or understand Kishore in the few days they spent together after their wedding.

Dozens of relatives fluttered about Kishore's home for days after the wedding, going in and out, pretending to offer the newlyweds privacy—only to stay and gossip about the wedding and its minuscule failures, neglecting all that had gone perfectly well in the three-day affair. After all, what good is a plate brimming with twenty-one different delicacies if the *jalebi* is served lukewarm? How could such a grave mistake be condoned?

In those few days, the dawn of their married life together, Kishore had warned Leela that engineering was not his calling and cautioned her of the America void of gold, glitter, and glamour. His plan was not to finish his engineering degree but continue working for Raman-*bhai* until he could afford his own motel.

Upon her arrival, Leela became the good wife, the plus-one in his plan. Together, with love and laughter, they opted for the dollars and drudgery, taking the short route to becoming illegal aliens— letting Kishore's student visa lapse—and the long, hard road to the American Dream.

Somewhere between attending to profusely tattooed men at the front desk and turning over beds every few hours, pea-size love blossomed in Leela's belly. Even with Kishore by her side, it was a lonely pregnancy and a lonelier birth. There was no one to stuff homemade brews and sweets down her rising belly and surely no one to massage her aching back. No one to offer unsolicited advice on the health of the baby and no one to criticize her body and its permutations. No one taunting her at the possibility of a girl and no one rejoicing at the reality of a boy.

During those few days in the hospital after the birth of her son, Leela felt the solitude brought on by the void of close family for the first time in her life. Simply put, there was no one to mother the mother, no one to father a daughter, and no siblings or cousins to share in the joy of a new nephew. How she wished that her whole village would flock to the hospital to coo over her baby while exchanging the latest gossip. How she wanted brothers and sisters and little cousins to run around him while her mother gave her advice that her mother-in-law would spitefully refute.

The privacy so luxuriously granted to her in a single room, void of bickering aunts and *paan*-chewing grandmas, felt unnaturally claustrophobic and dismally sad. Gazing at the pristine white bassinet in the desolate corner of her single room, she failed, for the first time, to find any humor in her isolation, crying her very first tears in America.

When one of the neonatal nurses stopped by to check on her and asked, "Is your family coming to visit? Where is your mama, new mama?" Leela smiled, but the emptiness in her eyes was so translucent that the nurse immediately came over and sat beside her.

"Now, don't you worry, dear. We here are going to take good care of you and your lil' guy. Don't you worry, mama."

Her long southern drawl and wide smile made the words sound even sweeter than they were, making Leela collapse into sobs. The nurse sat with her, caressing her hand and giving soft hugs as needed until Leela regained some composure. Leela caught the nurse's alabaster hands against her darker, browner fingers—which had been the fairest in her village. Suddenly realizing that this was the first time she had touched an American. This was her first interaction, unbuffered by the half-wall of a motel registration desk, with a person who actually belonged to the land she now called home. While she ached for her family, the fact that a non-family member—an American, for that matter—could be so compassionate made the nurse even more angelic in Leela's eyes. That sweet nurse sat with her for a long while and later continued to check in on her at every opportunity.

Indeed, the nurse had not lied—they all did take good care of her. Someone came and checked her vitals regularly and, while not homemade, they gave her painkillers, vitamins, and nutritious, tasteless vegetarian meals. Leela was surprised and relieved to know that there was a special nurse dedicated to teaching her how to breastfeed and another to help her get up, take her to the bathroom, and down the hall for her first walk as a mother. While they were not family, Leela was comforted by their unadulterated care and kindness and was convinced that there was a special place in the reincarnation cycle for these women who attended to her every humiliating discomfort post-labor. By the time she took her newborn son, Ayaan, home three days later, Leela had concluded that these were special people.

Today, as the kind nurse wrapped the last of the bandage around Kishore's arm, the trauma of the preceding day—the thought of losing Kishore, her children crying for their father, removing her *mangalsutra*—all came crashing down on her. And she cried for the second time in America, her new home.

From a distance, Ayaan watched his mother weep. He wanted to get up and comfort her, but before he could, he began to sob.

The next day, Ayaan handed Aanya a note at their lunchtime exchange.

October 3, 1988, 8:12 AM (I am on the bus)

Dear Aanya,

My dad is still in the hospital, as you know, but he is doing better. We went to see him at the hospital Sunday. He looks okay. His arm was being bandaged up. He looked worried, and so did my mom, but they both kept smiling at each other. This reminded me of that boy and girl on the playground during my SSR I was telling you about—I will tell you about them one day. Anyway, my mom keeps telling me that my dad is going to be fine, but I am not sure if she is just saying that to make me and Aditi feel good. Do you know? Did your mom or dad say anything about him? I want him to come home . . . I think Aditi is scared, too, but she seems stronger than me—she was able to laugh when my mom made a joke about the whole thing, which by the way, also made my dad laugh, so mission accomplished, I guess. At least, I thought so, but then when my dad laughed, my mom began to cry, which made me cry, and that made Aditi and my dad cry, too. This made everything sad again . . . Things are very wrong, Aanya. My dad is the crier, in case you did not know (don't tell anyone I told you that). But when my mom cries, things are usually really, really bad. Please tell me if you know anything. I think my mom is lying to me—not in a bad way, but you know, to protect us kind of way.

Aanya, I wanted you to know that I was so, so, so scared on Saturday night; I did not know what to do. I wanted to take care of Aditi and my father and you, and I just couldn't do any of it because I was so freaking frightened. I wanted to tell you that when you hugged me tight, but I couldn't. Then, when you held my hand under your dress, that was the moment I felt like it was all going to be okay. It was so very special for me and made me feel okay all of a sudden. It made me like you . . . like, like you like you even more . . .

Ayaan

PS: You looked really pretty in the pink dress you wore Saturday. I wanted to tell you that when you first walked in, but our parents were around. Okay, fine, even if they were not, I was not sure I would have been able to—anyway, you looked really pretty.

The next day, Aanya handed Ayaan a note.

October 3, 1988, 7:19 PM

Dear Ayaan,

Your dad is really doing good, like really, really. I promise. When my parents got back from the hospital Sunday morning, I asked my mom how Kishore-uncle was, and she said it would take time, but he will make a full recovery. She told me to tell you not to worry, even though she knows we never get time to talk in school. Anyway, I know she is telling the truth because later that day, I overheard my mom and dad talking. They said your father was very lucky that he was shot in the arm and not anywhere else. This is why I think he is really doing good, Ayaan. Don't worry; I would not lie to you about this. I have been listening to my parents talk about it a lot. I heard my dad say that he has this new uncle he knows that he is going to send over for the front desk at your motel so that your mom can spend some more time with your dad at the hospital and when he gets home to recover. That is all I know, but I really think he is good; your mom is not just saying that to make you feel better. I would not lie to you. I promise.

On Saturday, I was super scared, too; I was just pretending not to be, so hugging you (and Aditi) tight made me feel better, too. And by the way, I really wanted to hold your hand. I liked holding it . . . a lot . . . like a lot, a lot.

Aanya

Kishore was released from the hospital four days later with a bandage on his upper left arm. The bullet had grazed his bicep and escaped from the other end. There was pain, a lot of it, but there was no long-term damage—physically, at least.

One week after that, three men, burdened with overweight tool belts, erected drywall on either side of the oak registration desk, leaving a square opening for a bulletproof window with two pocket holes for cash, conversation, and keys.

Nine months later, by the end of fifth grade, the redheaded girl and the pale boy had advanced to spending more time together on the playground. There were days when they would spend the whole recess together, sitting on the concrete slab conversing and holding hands, but mostly just smiling a lot.

One year later, Kishore's mobility fully restored, Leela found herself joking about the whole matter.

Years later, Ayaan's fright from the day dissipated. Unbeknownst to him, his serenity was tied to his mother's humor and his father's normalcy. As his father returned to the bulletproof desk each day, frightful yet determined, Ayaan's terror subsided, and another feeling, pervasive and protracted, crystallized. The elation he felt when Aanya had walked through their front door that day, her gentle fingers wiping his tears dry, the tight embrace alleviating his terror, the pull of her hand on his, her palm soft against his under her pale pink dress—it consumed and sustained him through all of his fears for years to come.

# 9

# Mumbai
## *2008*

That afternoon, after dropping Aanya off at the airport, Abhimanyu strolled back to his office with an inexplicable lightness in his step. He opened the door to a *ding* on his laptop—a pop-up window on his Microsoft Outlook alerting him to "Call home." This alert popped up daily at 3:00 p.m. Abhimanyu was not one to intentionally forget to call home, but on more occasions than could be counted, the unpredictability of his work would divert him to more pressing matters.

On this day, at 3:01, the front desk called.

"Hello, sir, this is Saara. Mr. D'Souza is here at the front desk with me, and he needs to speak with you. He needs to host a Christmas party for 550 guests on December 25 itself. I have told him we have been booked out for more than a year, sir, but he wishes to speak to you directly."

Abhimanyu responded with his standard spiel.

"I already tried that, sir, and he refuses to leave."

"Okay, put him on, Saara.

"Hello, Mr. D'Souza. How are you this fine day, and how can I make it better?" Abhimanyu said.

On the other end of the line, Mr. D'Souza made his plea, explaining the urgency of his social needs.

Abhimanyu responded, speaking intermittently between Mr. D'Souza's petitions.

"Sir, sounds like such a wonderful party, and yes, so many important guests. I will surely try to make it happen for you. You know how important you are to us here at the Taj, and—yes, that is very generous of you, Mr. D'Souza, but as you know very well, in this city, money is not always the problem; it is the space, you see . . .

"Yes, I am aware of who you are, and that is why I am going to talk to my superiors and see what we can do, sir. Surely, we can try to help you.

"No, I am very sorry, Mr. D'Souza. Unfortunately, I cannot have you come down as I have someone in my office. I am sure Saara will assist with anything else you may need, perhaps a cup of refreshing chai or a soft drink. We are at your service, Mr. D'Souza, anything you wish."

Mr. D'Souza handed the phone back to Saara.

"Saara, get him something from the coffee shop; help him calm down a bit."

"I understand, sir; I will surely get him what he needs."

Abhimanyu knew well that Saara had had no choice but to call him and let him handle the situation. The game was well rehearsed on both ends, and she simply played along to placate Mr. D'Souza before an outright scene broke out on the premises of the stately hotel.

"Thanks, Saara. I am sorry you had to be in the middle of this. I appreciate you dealing with it."

With the old Indian middle class drowning in new money, the richer elites were exercising their power relentlessly, exacerbating their influence at every juncture. Abhimanyu understood this well. He was keenly aware of how Mumbai money worked, and though he did not have much experience in other large cities, he assumed things were no different elsewhere. If you wanted something, you threw money at the problem and the people involved, and *voila*—whether it was the sheer desperation of some hard-on-his-luck soul or pure greed, the outcome would favor the one flinging the cash.

Money got you what you needed. It was straightforward, simple, and guaranteed.

Unless, of course, you had the misfortune of dealing with Abhimanyu. If the latter was your luck, as it had been for Mr. D'Souza, then you needed an alternate plan. While Abhimanyu was adept at talking the talk, he never walked the walk. He never caved to the power of money or the influence it wielded. He never gave a client's time or space to another who came and offered more money. Any mention of money was an immediate turn-off for him.

Everyone knew you had to turn some people away, but the fact that he always played the game fairly without preferential treatment to the VIPs' time made him a staff favorite. From the doorman, Ram Singh, who greeted him every morning; to the peon, Jayesh, who served him *chai* a few times a day; to Saara, who could predict his response to a T—they all knew that when the time came, Abhimanyu-sir would be on their side, the right side, fair and square, every time, guaranteed. No negotiation needed.

Of course, Abhimanyu was an anomaly in the larger system. He was part of a growing minority that wanted something better and aspired for something more than the generation before but understood full well that change is sluggish. When a system is so deep in the trenches, with few knowing how to dig out of it, it takes years, decades, and often a generation or two before idealist virtues of fairness materialize. Abhimanyu was a believer, a glitch in the system. When upper management occasionally came down hard on him for slighting VIPs and their fat wallets, he would gently remind them of the lessons *they* had imparted to him during his first few weeks of training.

At his initial introduction to the Taj Group of hotels, his first lesson was on the history of the Taj Palace Hotel. The flagship Taj

Palace was built in 1903 under British rule in defiance by Jamsetji Tata, founder of Tata Industries, after he was turned away from a "whites only" establishment.

Its extravagant Turkish baths and the exclusivity of being the first hotel in Mumbai to have electricity had not impressed Abhimanyu as much as the virtues of an open-door policy. "Customer service is our top priority. Move mountains to help the guests but play fair. All guests are equal, and remember that this hotel was built on the principle of an open-door policy. Turn no one away," they were told over and over until it was ingrained. While impressed with the open and fair policy, there was something deeper at play for Abhimanyu. He played fair not only because he believed in it but because he was a product of it.

Fairness, if not luck, was what had brought him this far.

At 3:09 p.m., the snoozed alert went off again: "Call home."

Abhimanyu picked up his cell phone and dialed the landline to his home in Bari. He knew that his father, home for lunch and an afternoon nap, would have just woken and be waiting for this daily reminder that, although his son had made it to the big city from his small village, his heart was with them—his family, his people. He was still one of them, and he would never forget the people or the place that had made him the well-respected Director of Events at the Taj Palace in Mumbai. For him, the headmaster who had taught him the virtues of a good life, attained through kindness and fairness, and the silent presence of his father carried much greater weight than rubbing shoulders with celebrities and heads of state.

Abhimanyu's father was a farmer. They had a small patch of land, less than two acres, on which they grew vegetables sold at the local market. There were ups and downs, floods and droughts, bears and bulls, killer insects and deadlier pesticides, but through it all, there was always food on the table.

In times of hardship, his father would say, "We may not have much else, but the son of a farmer never goes hungry. The poor in the city, they may go to bed hungry, but the poor in the village, we will always have our *rozi roti*, we will always have our daily bread"— to which his daughter, Abhimanyu's younger sister, Seema, would retort, "Neither does his daughter, Baba." Baba would be quick to reckon, "Yes, yes, *beti*, how can I forget? The daughter of a farmer never goes hungry, either. *Kush* [happy]?" Seema would roll her eyes at the delayed recognition only to meet Abhimanyu's, which assured her he understood that their father's patronizing was no consolation.

An earnest man, Abhimanyu's father had never ventured out of the village or desired to do so. For Baba, glistening city lights could never match the glimmering clarity of a night lit with twinkling stars, nor could they compare to the satisfaction of watching a periwinkle horizon peek through the grand mountains of Bari. Despite his father's contentment and nostalgia for village life, Abhimanyu understood at a young age that the father of a farmer never wanted his son to be a farmer. Even with the provision of a bull cart and farm help, the long days under the raging sun sowing and harvesting were much too arduous, and the uncertainty of the seasons took years off your life.

During good years, there were new clothes, the addition of a small home appliance (maybe even a television), and a day outing or two to the nearest city for a *mela* or a movie, topped off by the most succulent of sweet treats—a *kala khata*–flavored *baraf ka gola*. Indeed, every day of a good, profitable harvest would end with a mouthwatering snow cone for both Seema and him.

Till day, even after years of indulging in the rich, creamy ice creams at the Taj, on summer days, Abhimanyu would step out of the air-conditioned, airbrushed world of the Taj and walk across the street to the edge of the waterfront overlooking the Arabian Sea to an utterly satisfying slurp of a freshly shaved *kala khata* snow cone.

With one eye on his two daughters playing on the soiled pavement nearby, the vendor would spy Abhimanyu at the entrance of the Taj and begin to prep his regular order. While Abhimanyu made his usual small talk with Ram Singh, the doorman, the snow cone vendor would begin manually churning a giant block of ice to generate a ball of shaved ice. The snowball would then be lathered with midnight-blue *kala khata* syrup, penetrating each micro ice crystal with a sweet-and-sour flavoring just as Abhimanyu ambled up, the timing perfect on both ends.

The vendor, whom Abhimanyu just referred to as *Kaka*, the universal and respectful word for "uncle"—precisely, your father's brother—would beam with pride as Abhimanyu carefully slurped with satisfaction. For Abhimanyu, that was and always would be the taste of childhood melded together with the success of a profitable harvest year, and it would easily surpass the richness of any world-renowned buttercream ice cream. The taste of success then and now was exactly the same: a *kala khata*–flavored snow cone served to you by a humble *kaka*, who stood in the sweltering sun, day in and day out, hoping for a profitable year himself.

On not-so-good years, there were hand-me-downs and debts owed to the local money lender, *Munsi-kaka*. Basking in his superiority, *Munsi-kaka's* lips would be tinged maroon, with a bit of betel juice dripping out the corner of his lips as he sifted through a giant ledger.

Watching Baba explain the difficulties of a rough year, *Munsi-kaka*—adroit at ascertaining a borrower's desperation by the distress in their voice, the dampness in their eyes, and the wrinkles forming on their forehead—would gauge the situation with precision. Any sign of a faint wrinkle on the forehead or a dip in tone during the story would result in a 0.1 or 0.2 percentage increase in the lender's already-bloated interest rate. In *Munsi-kaka's* world, desolation and interest rates were directly correlated, irrespective of the person's relationship or good-natured character. Business was business to him, and this particular business was not for the faint of heart, as he was sure to remind you.

Abhimanyu and Seema always warned Baba to remain emotionless, speak little, and avoid eye contact, but unfortunately, Baba had a laughably weak poker face. His despair was tangible not only in his liquefied eyes and the lines on his face but also in his stuttering voice and the stagger in his stroll. Therefore, on particularly bad years, their family was awarded the highest interest rate for the misery brought on by the fickle nature of seasons.

Abhimanyu's mother, a short, round woman, had been married off to Baba when she was fourteen. She considered herself fortunate that Baba turned out to be a good husband, a kind man, and a gentle father. Because Maa, as Abhimanyu and Seema called her, had few choices in her life, she was stern about making sure her children had options.

Early one morning, without Baba's consideration, she had enrolled both her children in the local government school. While she could not help them study, as she herself was illiterate, she made sure to take care of all the ancillaries, allowing her children to focus on studying. She would keep the pencils sharpened, the papers in neat order, and organize their backpacks. The night before examinations, she would stay up late, igniting the lantern and adding fuel as needed so brother and sister could sit tight with books under its glow. The next day, she would wake up earlier than usual to make them a hot breakfast, warm up the water for a bath, and allot extra time for prayers and the lighting of a *diya* and incense for good luck.

Despite her determination, Maa was completely ambiguous about what she wanted her children to be. In her world, dreams and visions were a nonentity. She could not envision a banker, lawyer, doctor, or engineer because she did not have the proficiency, language, or scope to do so. She did not dream big, not in that way. She comprehended that doing so would be a clear mismanagement of expectations.

But while Maa never had a concrete vision or image of what her children were to become, she did have perfect clarity on what she did *not* want her children to become. She knew for sure that Abhimanyu would not become a farmer and that Seema would not marry at the age of fourteen. Simply put, they were not to become their parents. That was unacceptable. For Maa, her children had to do a notch better than their parents. Period.

Consequently, when the phone rang at 3:10 p.m. that afternoon, Abhimanyu could hear his mother swell with pride, understanding deeply that her determination had paid off, her prayers were answered, and her mission accomplished. The reality of what Abhimanyu had achieved was beyond her wildest imagination and foggiest ambiguity—and it was about to get better.

"*Beta*, let me give it to Seema. She has some news to share," Maa said.

"*Bhaiya*, I did it. *We did it!* I just got word—I got into the Taj training program," Seema exclaimed.

"Yes, I knew it! I knew you had it in you, *ben*."

Just what he needed to hear on that frustrating afternoon: a gentle reminder that he played fair because, although there was no such thing as the Indian Dream in the nation's consciousness, somehow he had achieved it—and now his sister would, too.

Fairness worked for him. He was not only the manifestation of the credo on which the Taj Hotel was founded in 1903; he was also the manifestation of an impossible reality, a dream undreamt, and a vision unknown for the generations that preceded him—and the Taj was nothing more than a symbolic representation of it all.

# 10
# Georgia
## *1988–1991*

Despite their budding affection, the childhood duo had the misfortune of never being on the same team throughout their middle school tenure. In seventh grade, Aanya was in 7D while Ayaan was in 7B. In eighth grade, Ayaan was in 8D while Aanya was in 8B. Finally, when they got to high school, none of their classes matched. At one point, Aanya convinced Ayaan that it was intentional, that the school never put the two of them in the same team or class because they wanted to eliminate any confusion that might arise from their anagrammed names.

"Think about it, Ayaan. I mean, our names are so similar, and on top of that, look at us. We would totally screw up all the teachers if we were in the same classes, so they are like, 'Let's keep them as far away from each other as possible; no room for any confusion.'"

"Hello? You are a girl, and I am a boy. Did you miss that? How can they get that confused? I like you and all, Aanya, but that is the stupidest thing I have ever heard—really, it is. I think it's some random lottery thing, and we are just that unlucky."

"They do not know which is the girl's name and which the boy's, or which name belongs to which person, silly. It would be too much effort. Think about it. If I were the principal, I would use the same logic. It gets rid of would-be issues."

"I think it is one hundred percent coincidence, that's all. No one has time to scheme up such plans."

The argument reminded Aanya, once again, of Ayaan's incessant optimism. Ever since they were kids, they had played people-watching games together. They would see a person, a couple, a family, or even a dog or cat, then fabricate elaborate backstories.

Once, when they were eight, Aanya noticed a couple of siblings playing soccer on a playground. "That little boy wants to play, but his sister will not let him because she is bossy and a ball hog," Aanya noted.

"No, she's not bossy. She knows how to play, and she is going to teach him. That's why she has the ball. She is a good big sister," Ayaan countered.

"Why does everyone in your world have to be so good, Ayaan? Stop it. Brothers and sisters fight and steal each other's soccer balls. That's what they do, and that is what is happening over there. She is hogging the ball, and he is trying to figure out how to get it back."

Ayaan, always managing to see the positive in everything, annoyed Aanya so much that she would sometimes quit the story game smack dab in the middle. Sensing her irritation at such a minute, fictitious matter, Ayaan often preemptively gave in. "Okay, okay, I am sorry. You are right; the sister is a ball hog—but I also think she likes to run through open green fields. I think she fights with her mother to put on the most twirly of dresses every morning. Only when you have a frilly dress can you run down the field, swing around in circles, and watch the frock ripple all around."

Even at that early age, Ayaan knew Aanya well enough to know she liked to twirl, especially in her *chanya choli*, a traditional Indian dress with a separate top and a long ankle-length skirt designed just to twirl and make little girls light up with joy as the vibrant colors took flight in a beautiful bulb around them.

Aanya added her piece about how the brother also liked to twirl so his mother would dress him in his sister's church dress, enabling them to play the twirling game together, unknowingly delighting their mother. Their backstories, as always, made both Aanya and Ayaan giggle—as they did now, imagining the boy in his sister's dress and then in traditional Indian *chanya choli.*

"Okay, fine, it's a coincidence," she said.

"You are probably right—it's intentional," he said.

Agreeing the argument was going nowhere and not helping their situation—their very real issue of having no real means to have alone time together—they dropped the subject. However, they did agree on a different matter: they were convinced that their family bonds augmented their problems instead of aiding them.

Over the years, their family gatherings had grown more crowded, with not only more adults but more children joining the ranks. The handful of Indian immigrant families up and down Highway I-95 had swelled from two to more than two dozen. Many of those families spent time at Aanya's home as they trained and moved on to their own business ventures, financed in part by private loans from her parents and anyone else capable of the means.

Though the duo enjoyed their new friends, the abundance of festivities, and a strong sense of community, their time alone as restless teenagers both at school and outside was virtually nil. Consequently, between the fifth and ninth grades, although it did nothing for their raging hormones, they continued to write each other hundreds, maybe thousands, of notes detailing the mundane nuances of their middle-grade lives.

The years dragged, but finally, in first period on the last Tuesday before the end of the ninth grade, Aanya executed a brilliant idea she had had the night before. After class, Aanya dropped a note through the slits of Ayaan's locker, knowing he would stop to refresh his books and pick it up between third and fourth periods.

May 19ᵗʰ, 1992, 9:06 AM (I am so totally bored in this class, help me!)

Listen, Ayaan,

During seventh period, when you have art and I have social studies, ask to go to the bathroom at 1:16 PM (EXACTLY) and meet me in the stairway closest to the bathroom—the one by the courtyard. Do as I say . . . don't question it, and don't really go pee first! Seriously, I know you!

Aanya

That afternoon, at precisely 1:15 p.m., Aanya raised her hand in social studies and requested a hall pass to use the restroom.

Down the hall, with a sweaty palm, Ayaan made the same request, genuinely frightened he may actually have to use the bathroom.

Under the stairway closest to the bathroom and near the courtyard, Aanya waited, apprehensive and eager not only for what she had planned but at the possibility of someone disrupting her plan. She had had the foresight to wear her pale pink dress, the same one from the robbery night in fifth grade. Although snug, it now fit her in all the right places.

At 1:17, she peered out from under the stairway. Ayaan was walking toward her, dressed in blue jeans and a navy polo shirt. He looked curious and a little giddy. She waved him over to her.

"Hi," Ayaan said.

"Hi," Aanya replied.

Right then, before Ayaan could open his mouth again and babble nervously, Aanya leaned into him, closed her eyes, and pressed her lips to his for a full two seconds, as the world beyond them blurred and a moment they had imagined a hundred times over became reality. From all objective angles, their embrace had all the elements of an awkward first kiss, but for them, it was and always would be masked by the pristineness of a long-awaited moment, melded into the euphoria of first love.

When Aanya pulled away, Ayaan, kind of shocked, stood still in awe of her audacity before smiling salaciously. Just then, before she could open her mouth again and babble nervously, he leaned into her, closed his eyes, and pressed his lips against hers—a bit harder this time.

Aanya felt her whole body warm up in an intensity she hadn't known existed. When Ayaan pulled back, she, too, smiled wide—but was feeling a bit sheepish.

"Tomorrow, eighth period, east wing by the gym, 2:09 p.m."

Aanya had thought through their schedules already.

"You are a genius, Aanya, just brilliant," Ayaan said as they both walked back to their classrooms, holding hands until the very last second when they had to part ways.

Three days and six kisses later, summer break started. Within a week, Aanya and her family left for a two-month holiday to India, leaving Ayaan restless in the relentless summer heat.

When Aanya returned in mid-August, they reunited at a crowded gathering at Aanya's home, which was always the center of all social festivities —a sort of hub for all the Indian families at various stages of their immigrant journeys.

"I missed you so much, and since we couldn't meet and mailing a letter would take, like, forever, I wrote you a letter every day, Aanya. It's all in here—my thoroughly boring summer fully detailed for you. You're welcome!" he said, sticking his tongue out at her, while handing her a spiral red notebook.

"No way, I can't believe this. Guess what?"

"What?"

"Take a guess first."

"I don't know . . . as long as you don't tell me you found this really hot guy in your father's village, I don't really care. I mean, I missed you like crazy, Aanya. Like, seriously! You know how boring this little town can be without you? I was just praying there were, like, no boys at all living in this village, or, like, in all of India—I couldn't lose you to a real Indian boy, or I would literally die of boredom for the rest of my life!"

Ayaan smirked.

"Okay then, are you done with the drama? And by the way, there were tons of cute guys in India checking me and my frizzy, unwashed, oily hair out, but you are lucky—this bird's nest up here is reserved just for you!"

Aanya patted her already-smooth hair to calm the strays while sticking her tongue out at him.

"Okay, fine, I'm done! Just tell me," Ayaan said, resisting the urge to tuck a loose hair behind her ear. He was craving any kind of touch, even if it was a piece of her hair, but Aditi, his little sister, was close by on the bed, reading a book to two small children, so he managed to refrain.

Aanya ducked and pulled out a backpack from under her bed. She took out a diary covered in decorative burlap and handed it to Ayaan.

"I wrote you every day, too."

They both smiled at each other, content with their mutual obsession.


The next day, a Sunday, Ayaan sat and read two months' worth of letters detailing Aanya's days in India. She had written down everything for him. She started by telling him about landing in Mumbai in the middle of the night, dragging the family's six bags—expanded to full capacity and loaded to the max weight limit—to a low-grade motel for the night.

The next morning, her father woke early and managed nothing but a whole bucket of cold water in the dingy, yellowed subway tile bathroom, void of a functional water heater. By the time she rose, stiff from a night spent sandwiched between her parents, two complaints had already been lodged with hotel management, and her father was still grumbling.

She didn't need to explain to Ayaan that because her parents ran their own ramshackle motel back in Georgia and their service was always five-star, the moaning had more to do with the stale service than the low-grade accommodations. About thirty minutes after the second complaint, as her father was opening the door to head to the front desk for yet another round of groaning, he found a gaunt boy about half Aanya's age holding a bucket of piping hot water.

Her father's face softened immediately. The boy's bright white smile was nothing short of top-notch service. Her father took the bucket, gently ruffled the boy's hair, and handed him a wad of rupees.

"This is for you, *baccha*, not *sahib*. Treat yourself," he said, smiling warmly.

That morning, the family of three carefully divided the hot water amongst themselves using the two empty buckets already in the bathroom. They adjusted the water temperature by adding cold water and stirring until it was just right for a bath. This proved good practice, as two days later, after an eleven-hour, nausea-inducing car ride, they arrived in Naswadi, her father's native village.

Here, she was allotted one lukewarm bucket for bathing for the next eight weeks, the full duration of their trip. Repeatedly, she was made aware of the water tank on top of her grand-uncle's one-story, two-bedroom home. The water tank was filled once a day at 5:30 a.m. when the nearest city released the taps. The tank would fill to the top, and they had only that amount of water to last the day. The cistern of water would be used for household chores such as cooking, cleaning, mopping, and laundering, along with bodily functions such as bathing and brushing.

Even with all that, a little had to be left in reserve for emergencies, so constant warnings blared as each member approached the bath-room with their stovetop-heated bucket of water. "Don't waste too much water; we have a lot of clothes to wash today . . . Aanya, do you really need to wash your hair today?" With Aanya and her parents in the house, American returnees prone to wastage, the water warnings were more rampant.

On that first day in the Mumbai hotel, inexperienced in effi-ciency, she had carelessly used more than half her lukewarm water before applying soap and shampoo, finding out in due time that she did not have enough warm water to rinse all the foamy bubbles off her body and hair. She ended up washing off the excess with frigid water, shivering and shaking in the process.

By the third day of bucket bathing, she was an expert. On day three, she carefully soaked her whole body with one full tumbler, used half a tumbler to wet leftover dry spots, after which she soaped her whole body and face before rinsing it all off in one go. Midway through the bath, she still had three-quarters of her warm water left, allowing for a luxurious indulgence at the end.

Every two days, when she needed to wash her hair, she applied shampoo right before she soaped her face. She rinsed it all off in one go, holding the oversized tumbler over her head, keeping her eyes shut the whole time. Even though she skipped the conditioner on hair wash days, she still did not have much water left to indulge, gradually prompting her to let more days go between hair washes. Rinse and repeat made no sense. Rinse once (if you are lucky). Period.

She wrote about other things—their visit to the Gateway of India and the elephant caves; the sleeping arrangement in the village, with thick cotton-filled mattresses all along the floor; the *kala khata baraf gola* she savored each evening—but by far, her newfound expertise on what days to wash her hair using just the right amount of water at every stage was clearly her favorite topic.

Somehow, one too many family conversations were about water, and she needed to explain these to Ayaan. "The tank is empty; who is going to wake up at dawn to open the tap? Who will run up to close the tap? Oh no, we left the motor running. The vat overflowed. Why is the cleaning lady using so much water to wash the clothes? She is so wasteful." People all around her went on and on about the water, repeating the same things over and over, and it seemed that no one seemed to tire of it.

Eventually, Aanya concluded that talking about water was like talking about the weather in America. Since the weather stayed more or less the same in Naswadi—hot, hotter, a little rainy, cooler after the rain but still hot, really hot, and so on—no one cared to talk about it. The water situation, on the other hand, was much fussier. Sometimes they ran low. Sometimes the tank overflowed. Sometimes they ran out because someone took an extra bath or used more than their allowance. On occasion, a neighbor came over to borrow a bucket. "We have some extra guests visiting in need, you see," they would say, ignoring the three extra Americans in the lender's home.

Of course, the worst possible situation—Aanya's worst fear on a really hot and dusty day—was no bath at all. When the city did not release the water from the tanks that morning, rumors would roar about a possible drought upstate, widespread bacterial contamination, or a defect at the water dam, but the murmurs subsided when the water runneth over the next morning. On those dreaded days at the mercy of city officials, Aanya wrote, "My hair is disgusting. I smell, and I really, really miss showers. Bucket bathing stinks. Period! You would definitely not be into me right now—trust me, Ayaan. I am a hot mess. Actually, just a mess, not hot . . . okay, fine, hot—hot in like it's 110 degrees here, hot."

Despite its redundancy, Ayaan found it all very interesting and read about every episode with care. The one thing he waited for, the sentiment he sought out in each sentence, in each word and nuance of her day, always came at the very end of each entry: "I miss you a lot.

I wish you were here with me. This would be so much more fun with you here." It was all he needed to know.

Much like Ayaan, Aanya also spent the whole Sunday reading the letters Ayaan had written her. Details about the books he was reading; what he and Aditi did all day to pass the time—helping their parents fold towels and bedsheets, playing on the swing set, making up guessing games, and watching TV, a lot of TV! He described the joy of waking up late and watching cartoons with a bowl of cereal at noon, no school to worry about and no homework to do— undoubtedly, a summer well spent.

And then, at the end of each letter, there would be the one line Aanya craved, the sentiment sought out in each sentence, each word, each nuance of his day—and, just like in her letters, it was always there, at the end of each page. "I miss you so much; I wish you were here with me. All this boring stuff would be so much more fun with you here."

Each entry ended this way with the same words, except the last, written just the night before she had returned. It said, "When we grow up, Aanya, will you marry me, please? A life with you would make every boring thing more bearable!"

# 11
# Gurgaon/Mumbai
## *2008*

As expected, Abhimanyu paid for that morning at the colonnade with Aanya for the rest of the week, retreating to his one-bedroom flat for a few short hours of sleep, a quick shower, and a change of clothes. Over that weekend, he missed going home at all, catching a few cat naps instead in his office and freshening up with a hotel shower between events.

These weeks leading up to Diwali were the busiest time of the year. Amid the Cristal at the Jain wedding and the three wedding crashers that needed to be escorted out by security during the frenzy of the *baraat* (the never-ending cavalcade of the groom's procession), which needed to be skillfully diverted in order for the business elites of Mumbai to roll out the red carpet for the Royal Highness of Malaysia—whose entourage without any advance notice had asked the front desk to extend his stay for three days—Abhimanyu hardly had time to breathe.

The whole hotel had been short-staffed and on edge, leaving Abhimanyu exhausted. Thankfully, he loved nothing more than that—the thrill, the rush, the hustle of making chaos flow calmly. The kick he got after a successful event, the guests praising the seamless execution of it all, made the frenzy and fatigue all worth it. It offered him perpetual stimulation and affixed a permanent smile on his face. He loved the natural high of escalating tension and, more so, the exquisite challenge of seamlessly soothing it out.

On top of the rush, in the last week, there was Aanya, her dark eyes shining at him from under the shade of the colonnade as the ocean breeze cooled his fiery body, the yellow chiffon of her dress fluttering like his heart. Thoughts of her made all the chaotic moments in the last week feel tranquil. While drowning in the urgency of each event, he imagined her and that moment he had let pass, wondering, *Should I have . . . ?*

Amid the frenzy, he thought about calling her—to say hi, hear her voice, imagine her on the other side of the phone, lounging in her T-shirt and shorts, lying on her bed as he worked late into the night. In the end, with one pressing issue after the other, he found no time to call yet sensed, somehow, that she was there with him all along, conversing with him in his thoughts and tricking his psyche into believing that he indeed had spoken to her—that she was right there, with him, an ally, cheering him on as he ran the endless marathon reserved for the Director of Events at the Taj Mumbai, a glamorous title for not-so-glamorous work.

When anything went wrong, he took the blame. He was the one everyone pointed to and screamed at as they leveraged their deep pockets and threatened never to pay, criticizing and complaining at even the tiniest of mishaps. Abhimanyu's main mission remained, always, to ensure that it never got to that point. The two Ps of event management—pleasing and perfection—were his top goals, even if it meant zero sleep, zero time off, and, worst of all, zero time to call Aanya. In his world, work-life balance was a luxury he had no time to contemplate or really care about—until now.

First thing Monday morning, as the weekend mayhem subsided, he called her.

"Hi, Abhimanyu, how are you?"

"Exhausted. We had a very busy weekend, but I am good. So sorry for not calling earlier.

How have you been, Aanya?"

"I am doing okay. Working hard and exploring a little here and there."

"That is wonderful to hear. Well, I have good news and bad news on the business front."

"Start with the bad—always, please."

"Apparently, I did not do a great job of selling TechLogically. The senior management is interested, but they have questions and have agreed to a full presentation."

"That's great! Wonderful news, Abhimanyu. It's a big undertaking. Questions are warranted. I am happy to make a full presentation to them. Now, tell me the bad news."

"Well, that was it."

"Really? That's it?"

Abhimanyu's mind, glad to hear Aanya's excitement, had just puzzled together how asinine his assessment of bad and good news had been. There was no bad news. It was all good news—great news, in fact. Aanya would be coming back to Mumbai, to the Taj, to him. His smile widened.

"I suppose you are right. It is not exactly bad news, it's just—I wanted to be able to make the decision myself. I did not expect the slew of questions. Guess I was a bit annoyed by it—not even sure why, now that I give it some thought."

As he spoke, Abhimanyu realized he had conflated the questions and criticism of TechLogically's proposal with Aanya. Perhaps his subconscious had already concluded that if the project were denied, his chances of seeing Aanya would be nil—or worse, the project's failure was equivalent to Aanya's failure, and that he could not fathom.

Was it? He had not even had a minute to think it through. While he feared the first, was he more concerned with the latter? Aanya could not fail. He was sure of that. She needed to succeed! He shook his head to clear the jumble of thoughts racing through his mind. He needed time to process this, but no matter what he concluded, there was no denying that his uncertainty was somehow personal—rooted in the melding of his professional life with his personal desires, a notion so foreign to him that it made work-life balance look like a good friend.

"So, what are we looking at in terms of a time frame?" Aanya interrupted his thoughts.

"We have weekly status meetings with time reserved for new agenda items every Tuesday at 9:00 a.m. sharp. There is room on the agenda tomorrow—it's pretty tight. You think you can make it?"

"There is a Delhi–Mumbai at 5:30 a.m., but I guess it's better to come this evening. The fog here has been so unpredictable, and I wouldn't want to be delayed or canceled. I am checking flights as we speak, and I think I can make the 6:00 p.m. this evening."

"Great, let's plan to have dinner tonight," Abhimanyu blurted out, grateful that Mondays were the slowest in the world of event planning.

"Dinner?" Aanya hesitated.

"Yes, it will give us some time to catch up, and I can fill you in before the a.m. meeting."

"Umm, true. That would be helpful. Okay, let's do it."

"Thank you, Aanya. Looking forward to having you back in Mumbai."

Abhimanyu waited under the portico of the Orchid Hotel for Aanya to appear just as she had once before. He was restless, hands shaking slightly, as she emerged from the revolving door atop the stairs.

This time, she wore a more sophisticated dress—straight-cut, V-neck, long-sleeved and black, classy yet sensual, with the length resting just above her knees, and flat espadrilles laced up her shins. Her hair, all pulled to the front, rested on her left shoulder. A few wisps in wavy curls touched the edge of her silver chain. The trademark solitaire, centered between her exposed clavicles, made him sigh in submission. His professionalism was about to go through some rigorous testing.

He wondered, again, about her age. *She looks young. She couldn't be more than twenty-eight. Could she?* While he wanted to not care about her age, it perplexed him, not because he knew for sure that she was older—that he could handle—but more so because he couldn't figure out why this smart, successful, beautiful *older* woman was single. Was he missing something, or was he simply afraid she was out of his league?

*Wait,* was *she even single?* Maybe she did have someone special in her life—even a husband. Maybe that special someone had gifted her that enticing solitaire. *Damn, what if she isn't single? This is, after all, a business dinner.*

The thought made him melancholy and left him wondering what the heck he was doing here on a Monday night, blending his personal wants, or whatever it was he was feeling, with his thus-far very professional work-work balance. *Stop. Stop. Stop!* He resolved not to think about all this and just ask her. He was a grown man, for God's sake. He should be straightforward. *Well, maybe when the time is right.*

As she neared, he sighed again. *This woman is going to be the end of me.* He circled the hood of the car, beating the bellboy to open the door for her. She thanked him with a generous smile, slipping into her seat.

"So, where would you like to go?" he said as he settled in the driver's seat.

"You were so good with the surprise thing, I thought let's try that again—no pressure, of course, Abhimanyu," she teased.

"Hmm . . . you are a tough client, Aanya. Believe it or not, I am not hiding any more secret sweet spots—not in Mumbai, at least."

"But you do know the perfect place to take me, right?"

Abhimanyu liked that Aanya was in a cheerful, almost flirty, mood.

"Well, maybe. You said you loved Indian, so that makes it a little easier. I know the perfect place to take you for dinner. It's not as charming as our colonnade escape—there will be no warm ocean breeze—but we will have food, not go hungry like last time, and we may even get to see the ocean. Let's see."

Abhimanyu turned toward her, catching a glimpse of her eyes shining bright. She brought with her a calming scent he could not pinpoint, but it had the lightness of a sweet-smelling floral shampoo and not the overpowering perfume that preceded the women he normally engaged with at the Taj.

She gave him a genuine smile.

The air lightened.

His heart warmed, fluttered, skipped a beat, and did all those things hearts do when there is a palpable moment of harmony.

They repeated again the interplay in which she flinched at every moving object on the road while he tried hard to play it safe, attempting to placate her with slow interceptions and smooth turns. He turned the radio on to calm her even further and possibly distract her from the frenzy that so quickly engulfed their car. A well-known classic Bollywood song, "*Pal Pal Dil Ke Paas*," played its second verse. They both listened in silence.

*Har shyam, aankhon per, tera anchal lahariye*
   (Each evening, upon my eyes, your sari flutters)
*Har raat, yaadon ki baaraat, le aaye*
   (Each night, it brings procession of sweet memories)
*Main saans leta hoon, teri khushboo aati hai,*
   (Each breath I take, I inhale your fragrance,)
*Ek maheka maheka sa, paigham latee hai,*
   (And each aroma brings with it a sweet message,)
*Mere dil kee dhadkan bhi, tere geet gaati hai.*
   (Even the beat of my heart, sings songs of you.)

"I love this song," she said softly when the verse finished, sounding instantly solemn.

"Me, too. The lyrics are flawless. Wouldn't you say?"

Aanya nodded as Abhimanyu wistfully hummed the chorus.

*Pal pal dil ke paas tum rahatee ho, jeewan mithhee pyaas ye kahatee ho.*
(Every moment, every second, you remain close to my heart, bringing with it a sweet thirst for life.)

They both listened to the final verse in silence.

Abhimanyu was so tuned in to the lyrics, each word an embodiment of his state of being for the last ten days, that he didn't notice Aanya's smile disappear as she stared into empty space, suddenly impassive to the chaos around them, growing more and more distant with each word, vanishing into her own world as the sweet melody filled the air. When he finally turned to see why she was so quiet, he noticed her press her forefingers to the solitaire, blinking rapidly. She then interlaced her hands in prayer atop the black fabric of her dress. Her brightness had dimmed.

"All okay, Aanya?"

"Yeah—fine. It's just such a beautiful song; it makes me a little sentimental. That's all," she said, ever so softly, eyes wet, a tear threatening to escape.

Abhimanyu retreated, letting it go, sensing her need for solitude.

# 12
# Georgia
## *1992*

Ayaan sat between his mother and father in a lemon-stained room with a bright dandelion border along the top. The decor had preceded his parents, Kishore and Leela—and most likely Aanya's parents, Raman and Shalu, too. It must have been put in by the original owner of the motel, who had built this live-in suite with a kitchen for his own residence.

The October sun, spread brightly across a portion of the clear plastic tablecloth, gave no indication of the pending autumn. One length of the table was pushed against a wall to save space in the galley kitchen tucked at the back end of their residence. Four chairs were lined up along the three other edges—one each for Kishore, Leela, Ayaan, and his sister, Aditi. Two folding chairs were squeezed upright in the space between the refrigerator and the load-bearing walls, and two more folding chairs were tucked on the other side of the fridge, forming a barrier between the turmeric-stained stove and the double-door fridge. It was a tight space, but they managed, on occasion, to cluster as many as eight people at the table, all getting roughly a twelve-inch span to maneuver their food and spread their elbows. While the kitchen was dated and cramped, Leela kept it immaculately clean, wiping down the stove each night and mopping the embossed linoleum floor each morning, making the space feel newer than it was.

This Saturday morning, instead of sleeping in, Ayaan was picking at freshly cooked *poha*, his favorite breakfast, and nursing a tepid cup of *masala chai*. Being a typical teen on this matter, he was not an early riser, but by 7:30 a.m. that morning, he had made it clear to his parents that this was no ordinary day.

Ayaan had risen at 6:45 a.m., brushed, showered, perfected his signature coiffure—an ebbing pompadour—and was seated at the Parekhs' kitchen table clad in a crisp dress shirt and khaki trousers. Now a budding sophomore in high school, the night before, he had the foresight to prep for this morning.

The previous evening, after dinner, he had rummaged through the crammed closet shared by his entire family to find the only dress shirt he owned, bought two years ago in a size too big for his eighth-grade graduation ceremony and not worn since. He then laid out a four-fold bedsheet, retrieved from a stack piled high in their now bulletproof living room, at the corner of his bed. He spread his baby-blue shirt on top of the crisp white sheet and began smoothing out the wrinkles with meticulous precision, ensuring not to miss even a sliver of a wrinkle from every possible angle.

Half way into doing the same with his khaki trousers, he had grown aware of his mother surveying him from the door frame, surely cooking up a plan to mock him about how fastidious he was being about his appearance (something he reserved only for his hair, a habit that admittedly his mother had instilled), but he didn't care. He needed to make sure he looked his best, so the pending ridicule was worth it. Fortunately, instead of calling him out or offering to help, his mother patiently watched and offered to make him his favorite breakfast of *poha* the next morning—his sixteenth birthday.

When finished, Ayaan laid his pressed clothes out on the dresser and got ready for bed, forcing a reluctant Aditi, now a tween, to turn off the lights early on that Friday night.

"There is no way I am going to bed this early on a Friday night. It's not a school night. It's not fair."

"Please just turn off the lights first, Aditi. I am asking nicely."

"Not until you tell me why you are being so weird, *bhai*," Aditi negotiated, referring to him lovingly as "brother" instead of by his name.

Ayaan knew this fight was futile.

"Okay, fine, turn the lights off and get in bed. I will tell you, we don't need the lights to talk."

Aditi turned off the lights, put her head down on her pillow, and waited for Ayaan to tell her the mystery. For the next thirty minutes, in a dark room lit by just the moonlight slipping through the pulled shades, the two rehearsed and perfected the lines Ayaan would perform the next day—much to Aditi's satisfaction but not Ayaan's. He had a restless night and lay awake in bed for hours before he was able to fall asleep.

In the morning, he woke well before the alarm clock buzzed and scampered around the room softly, in slow movements, in an effort not to awaken his sister. Though, she would hear the story for years to come, in multiple versions, with multiple variations, and begin to think that she, in fact, had witnessed the whole morning, ultimately developing her own version, one she would share on a very special day.

"Ayaan, *beta*, why are you all dressed up so early in the morning?" Leela asked as Ayaan sipped his chai.

"Mama, I need to do something important. Can you or Papa drive me?"

"Only if you tell us what it is, Ayaan. You look really nice this morning, by the way. Happy birthday, *beta*! That shirt fits you just right now."

Ayaan hesitated, not because he was embarrassed, but because he wanted to choose his just-turned-sixteen-year-old words wisely and speak confidently. He did not want to be discounted by his parents as an impulsive, irrational teen, despite its imminence.

"I am going to go over and ask Raman-*kaka* for Aanya's hand in marriage," he said sharply.

Kishore refrained from a very obvious chuckle, signaled by a drip of chai escaping the corner of his lips. Leela kicked Kishore under the breakfast table, nudging him to keep it together. While his parents were aware of Ayaan's mega crush on Aanya and Aanya's mega crush on Ayaan, neither of them suspected anything more than that for the time being.

Their affection was palpable, it was sweet puppy love, and they hoped it would last, but both sets of parents, despite their skyrocketing hopes, remained rather pragmatic. They were just children, after all. They had a long road ahead, with college and maybe graduate studies—and though it seemed like Ayaan and Aanya's mutual admiration was everlasting, one never knew, especially with teenagers.

"*Beta*, that is . . ." Kishore took a loud slurp of his tea in order to gather his words. "That is, umm—a very noble thing to do, but you and Aanya, *beta* . . . It is very sweet, but you two need some time. I am sure Raman-*bhai* will say the same thing. Aanya is too young, *beta*, as are you. This is not something you need to be concerned about now. You should focus on your studies and enjoy being with your friends."

Kishore sounded genuine, but the right side of his mouth smirked, disclosing his amusement.

"Papa, come on! I don't mean like we will get married now, but like when we are twenty-one or twenty-two, right after I finish college. I know I have to finish college and settle down and stuff—then we will get married," Ayaan retorted.

"So what is the rush, *beta*? I mean the rush today. Can't this wait a few years?" Leela asked, a tinge of ridicule in her voice.

"I knew it," Ayaan said under his breath as he took a sip of his now-cold chai. "This is why I didn't want to tell you both before. Can you just drive me there? Please! You—you just will not get it. I *love* Aanya, like love her, love her—the real stuff, like in all those Hindi movies. I will always love her, and I want to marry her. I would do it today, but it's not legal, and I think we should both finish high school and even college. That would be the smart thing. In any case, I need to get permission from Raman-*kaka*—the sooner, the better."

"Have you gotten permission from Aanya?" Leela asked, sounding very serious.

Ayaan may have blushed, but it was often difficult to detect on his skin tone. Though he had his mother's light skin with the tiniest tinge of tan, his glossy, gelled-up, jet-black hair made him appear even lighter than Leela. Indeed, when his sister was not around, the contrast of light skin with dark hair made his teachers think he was Italian, although his features were distinctly not.

"Trust me, Mummy, I know what I am doing."

Despite his obvious infatuation, Ayaan was unwilling to reveal any personal matters between himself and Aanya. Surely, he was not one to kiss and tell—especially when it came to Aanya, his future wife. Anyway, who tells their parents these things? *Eeeeek!*

"All we are saying, *beta*, is that Aanya should know what you are about to do. It's only fair to her." Kishore spoke up, finally with a bit more composure; no *chai* left as a distraction.

"She has a clue, Dad."

"A clue, *beta*? That does not sound right. We cannot drive you over there, to one of our dearest friends' home, so that you can ask their one and only beloved daughter—who is barely sixteen—for her hand in marriage. Sounds completely insane *beta*; try to understand," he said.

Aditi sauntered into the kitchen, rubbing her eyes, and settled into her mother's lap, snuggling her head into her mother's chest.

"I think you should let him go," Aditi said.

"Do you even know what we are talking about?" Kishore asked his precocious child.

"Of course I do; *bhai* practiced his speech with me last night. I helped him get it just right—it needed work," Aditi said, all-knowing.

Kishore and Leela rolled their eyes at each other. How did they raise such a smart-aleck child? It must be the American influence from school. Children in India didn't get involved in adult matters, nor did they speak their opinion so freely as their youngest did. No one had asked her what she thought of the matter, yet she felt at liberty to offer her judgment. *How?* They both ignored her.

"Ayaan, I am sorry. I cannot drive you," Kishore reiterated. "I understand your feelings, but you need to slow down a little. I cannot let you embarrass yourself over there."

"If you don't drive me, I will walk! It's only like three or four miles."

Ayaan was being uncharacteristically stubborn, something normally expected of Aditi. She had prepped him well.

"It is almost five miles straight down I-95. We cannot let you just walk along the highway. It's a death trap with all those big trucks," Leela said.

The atmosphere in the room had turned from lighthearted amusement to condemnation.

Determined but respectful, Ayaan's voice softened a bit—*time for a new approach.*

"Pleeeeeease, Papa—I know what I am doing. Try to understand. I just need a ride."

Ayaan purposefully used "Papa" instead of "Dad," which Aditi easily defaulted to, knowing his father softened to it much more easily.

"Did you brush your teeth?" Leela asked Aditi.

"Yes, I brushed and washed my face," Aditi said with a whiny twang as shifted to her own chair.

Unsure of how to proceed with Ayaan, Leela got up to make Aditi a glass of Ovaltine.

The jaundice-colored rotary phone that hung on the wall above the dining table rang. This was the personal line, so there was no chance of it being a disgruntled guest demanding fresh towels, clean sheets, or a switch of the adult content, which needed turning over every few hours from a central transmitter in the front office.

Leela picked up on the third ring, allowing her enough time to dissolve the last teeny bits of Ovaltine into the creamy milk before sliding it over to Aditi.

"Hello," Leela said in her artificially deep phone voice.

"Hello, *kem cho*," said Shalu.

The conversation continued in a colloquial Gujarati as Ayaan's ears stood up in alert. His main goal, of course, was to find out what Aanya was up to. Was she sitting next to her mother at their kitchen table, unable to consume her breakfast like he was? Was her stomach too weak because her body was still shaken from their unruly kiss the day before? Was she still snuggled up in bed, floating lightly amidst the clouds? Was she thinking about how to get on the phone and wish him a happy birthday without her mother suspecting anything more than a friendly salutation? Was she planning out precisely how they could parse out a few precious moments alone under the guise of an urgent school project or family-friendly dinner get-together?

He did not expect, of course, for her to surprise him or plan something special for his birthday—they did not have such liberties in their households. They both understood and accepted that their feelings, while suspected by their parents, could not be expressed overtly like their American peers, at least not for some time to come. They would not share ice cream sundaes on Friday afternoons at the local eatery; they would not attend school dances or be each other's dates for homecoming; and, of course, while they could go to each other's homes for dinner, family in tow, they would never hold hands or even sit in close proximity in the company of their parents. They didn't even talk on the phone unless it was school-related.

The nonexistence of casual dating—or dating for that matter—was a universal truth in their world, and they were well in tune with their reality. Neither Aanya nor Ayaan was phased by this. They conceded to it, much like their parents had accepted the way they were treated differently in the country they called home, a universally accepted norm that baffled only Aditi.

"Some things just are the way they are, *beta*," her father had said when Aditi questioned why her teacher spoke to her father in a slow, condescending voice as if her father were mentally challenged.

"Aditi is doing good in school, Mr. . . . Mr. Parekh. She is progressing well for, you know—she is one of the smartest kids in the class. Good for her. Her English is very good, too," Mrs. Jones had offered almost as a condolence when she met Kishore at the last parent-teacher conference.

Aditi wished her father would tell Mrs. Jones that she was born in America, held American citizenship, and, much more importantly, to his utter dismay, spoke better English—her first written language—than she did Gujarati. She wanted her teacher to know that her dad had lived in this country, had woken up from a deep slumber on his futon in the wee hours of the morning to attend to insatiable drug and sex addicts, all so he could make a better life for his "doing really good" daughter. But, in the end, like always, her father said none of those things.

Instead, he politely asked, "When are the major exams? Is Aditi ready for them?"

"We don't have major exams, just projects throughout the year. There is one state-run test. I am sure Aditi did okay on it. It doesn't count for anything, anyway," Mrs. Jones said, frowning at Aditi, while shuffling through some papers. In the event that her father did not speak English, Mrs. Jones had allowed Aditi to remain in the room during the parent-teacher conference.

"Ahh! Here. It seems Aditi is in the ninetieth percentile for English," she said haphazardly as if it were the first time she had seen it.

"Thank you," Kishore said as he looked at the paper imprinted with a bell shape on a graph.

On the ride home that day, Aditi was direct.

"Daddy, why was she talking to you like that? That is not how she normally talks. She was off."

"What do you mean, *beta*?"

"She was so slow, like—I don't know. What did she mean, 'progressing well for—*you know*'?"

"Nothing like that, Aditi. It is just the way things are. She wanted to make sure I understood, that's all."

A few years later, Aditi understood that her father had accepted deeply that it was all about expectations, and he, her mother, Raman-*kaka*, Shalu-aunty—and, undoubtedly, the hundreds of thousands of Indian American immigrants sprinkled across the country in motels and 7-Elevens, in gas stations and dry cleaners, in assembly lines and warehouses—expected nothing more than to work hard, twice or even three times as hard, as their neighbors to survive and build a future for their children. That was the one and only goal. They were indeed immigrants, brown tones in a spectrum of light hues, keeping their heads bowed low so their children could one day lift theirs high.

"It's a slow and steady rise to the prize, and managing one's expectations changes everything, you see. It enables you to work harder and succeed without questioning your worth," Kishore explained to Aditi.

Back in the yellow kitchen smelling of frying oil and *poha*, Leela hung up the phone and turned to Ayaan, who knew exactly what was coming because he had eavesdropped on his mom's conservation with dog ears.

"Raman-*bhai* and Shalu have invited us to dinner tonight. They said it would be a nice excuse to celebrate Ayaan's birthday," Leela announced.

Ayaan blushed again, his whole being relaxed at the thought of being in close proximity to Aanya tonight, on his sixteenth birthday.

"So maybe your question for Raman-*kaka* can wait until tonight, *beta*—but please, take the day to really think about this. You just turned sixteen; you have—"

"Okay, Papa. I can wait, and I will think about it. Happy?" Ayaan said, smiling.

"Raman-*bhai* said he has someone to work the front desk tonight. His name is Devan-*bhai*. He will come over around five this evening," Leela added.

Ayaan finished his *poha*, elated that Aanya had worked her magic. She had to be behind this. She had always been the clever one about these things. She had come through on her promise. Somehow, she had cajoled her mother to invite them to dinner, making his birthday wish to see her that day come true.

Ayaan ran through the number of hours he would need to wait until he would see her again. Ten and a half!

# 13

# Mumbai
## *2008*

As expected, the Arabian, a restaurant on the second floor of a glass building, had panoramic views of the Arabian Sea. They sat on a table adjacent to the wall-sized windows, the sunset outside producing a spectrum of gold and saffron on the horizon, casting a warm iridescent glow on the occupants inside.

Captivated by the dusk, Aanya spoke as she gazed out the window. "You succeeded once again, Abhimanyu. This is breathtaking."

"Well, not so fast, Aanya. In my opinion, you cannot judge a restaurant by its views. Let's wait and see if you like the food, shall we?"

Aanya conceded with a warm smile.

They ordered a bottle of white wine, both independently calculating that a bottle would be more economical than a few individual glasses.

A pristinely dressed waiter uncorked the wine and poured them each a generous portion. They lifted the glasses in sync and cheered.

"To the beautiful, secret sweet spots hidden amid the madness of Mumbai," Aanya said.

"Hmm . . . no. To you, Aanya, for gracing Mumbai with your—um—presence."

Abhimanyu stumbled, switching the word "beauty" to "presence" in an effort not to sound desperate—or just plain cheesy. He couldn't decide, but he was confident he had just managed to do both effortlessly.

Aanya's eyes sparkled in response, and her narrow mouth, tinged with mauve lip gloss, widened to a flattered smile. Before the moment turned awkward, her eyes quickly meandered around the spacious restaurant. It was rather quiet for the locale and view.

"Pretty quiet—maybe because it's Monday night, or worse, the food is terrible," Aanya joked.

"Let's hope for the best," he said, raising crossed fingers in the air.

"So, what do you recommend, Abhimanyu?"

Abhimanyu lowered the menu, smirked, and raised his eyebrows. His face transformed into that of a young boy caught sneaking in some cookies past bedtime. On cue, a flap of hair fell from his finely combed pompadour pouf onto his forehead, deepening his youthful appearance. Abhimanyu swept the hair back to its precise position and spoke with a smile.

"Well, that would require me to have tried this place before, so a confession is in order—it is my very first time here. On top of that, I cannot take credit for finding it, either. Our concierge, Varun, recommended it because it has great views and, well, hopefully, decent food. So, sorry, not much of a secret sweet spot. I am pretty sure every last Taj tourist who's tired of our own restaurants is sent here. My apologies, Aanya, but picking out restaurants or even going out like this is not my thing."

Aanya's eyebrows flared with an *Are you kidding me?* look.

Abhimanyu appreciated the girlishness of the gesture, which cast frivolity on her that seemed to ebb and flow much too freely. He smirked and continued to speak.

"Sorry, I know this sounds hard to believe, but I don't get a lot of time to go out, Aanya. I am at work all the time—I mean *all* the time—and because there are multiple events almost every evening, I never really leave the Taj. Most days, I am lucky to make it home for some sleep and a shower.

"Sometimes I do not even get time for that—like this last weekend. I spent the whole weekend on-site and showered in the gym locker room. I guess you can say I don't have much of a life. I know it sounds a little pathetic, but honestly, I don't have any regrets. Growing up, I could have never imagined any of this—sitting at a fancy seaside restaurant with—"

Abhimanyu looked down and swirled his wineglass, searching for the right words. "What I am saying is, I love what I do and am very grateful for the work, but I must admit, Aanya, you have a special knack for making me drop what I love and escape for a bit. This makes twice in the span of a few short days."

Abhimanyu looked into her eyes blissfully.

Aanya blushed, looking like she was sinking into uncharted territory. She sipped her wine.

"I get it. I am a bit of a workaholic myself. I have gotten better in the last few years, but there was a time when I worked nights, weekends, holidays—pretty much all the time. I mean, it was to the point where the janitors took pity on me, urging me to go home. Anyway, I have cut back recently."

"So you must love what you do and have no life, or you have no life because you love what you do. Must be one or the other, like a chicken-and-egg kind of thing, no?" Abhimanyu said.

"Well—more the latter. I did not have much of a life, so I worked all the time. Lately, I am trying to step back and smell the roses, dance in the rain, bask in the sunshine—you know, all the good stuff. 'Trying' is the key word, I suppose. I mean, I did technically move halfway across the world for work, so I am not sure how that is going."

Abhimanyu, perplexed, read an uneasiness in her softening tone. The lightness was ebbing as rapidly as it had flowed a few minutes ago, making her age almost instantly, casting a dark shadow on an otherwise happy existence—just like it had on the car ride over. He couldn't stomach making her feel that uncomfortable again, so he quickly diverted the topic.

"So, were you born in the States?"

"Yes, American Born, *not* Confused, and Desi," Aanya answered, referencing a popular acronym, ABCD (American Born Confused Desi), used to refer to first-generation Indian immigrants coming of age in America who were supposedly experiencing an identity crisis.

"You definitely don't seem confused. Trust me, I have seen my fair share of ABCDs at the Taj. There is a lot of 'I gotta find my roots while I sip martinis in the lap of luxury in Mumbai.' A sort of coming home but never really going home, if you know what I mean. No offense."

"None taken, and I am happy to report I don't fall into that category. In a way, I was brought up so connected to my roots that I never felt a need to search for them. I guess that is what happens in a small town where your parents know every other Indian family in a hundred-mile radius—it builds a community that kind of shoves your roots down your throat. Not that I am complaining. I am so grateful for not being lost or confused. I have always known exactly where and what my roots are, thanks to my parents."

"Small town? I thought you were from the big city—New York?"

"Well, I lived in New York for about seven years before shifting here, but I grew up on the premises of a roadside motel—*nothing* like the Taj, mind you. It's in a little town in Georgia, down South. That is where I was born and raised. My parents own a small motel—well, it used to be small. They recently renovated and made it a brand name. In any case, I spent my whole childhood running around the open-air corridors of the old truck-stop motel until I went off to college."

"What was that like, living at a motel?"

"Perfect. I never thought about it like living at a motel—it was home. I don't think I could have had a happier childhood."

"That's always nice to hear. I kind of live at a hotel now, and trust me, it feels nothing like home. Anyway, were your parents born in the States, too?"

"No, my dad was born in Naswadi, Gujarat, and my mom in Kampala, Uganda."

"Really! That is interesting—and how did they come to be?"

Aanya was glowing now. Parents and childhood were clearly a light topic.

"Their story is the kind of love you can write a book about. It has hearty triumphs and tribulations, and, of course, a once-in-a-lifetime kind of love spanning countries and continents."

"I am intrigued! Tell me more."

And so Aanya shared the story her parents had told her throughout her childhood.


At twenty-one, on a hot Kampala day, Aanya's father, Raman, spotted her mother, Shalu, haggling with the shopkeeper about the proposed price for the sacks of tea leaves loaded on a trolley behind her. The temperamental bargaining was a testament to the deadly sun, the dry earth, and the incessantly rising temperatures.

Her mother was feisty, animated, and determined to get her way. Her prominent features—pointed nose, almond eyes, sleek olive skin with jet-black hair in two waist-length braids—kindled a sense of home in her father. She was one of theirs, Indian for sure, but her narrow lips blurting out Swahili so effortlessly made her feel foreign.

"Can I help you with something?" Shalu howled at Raman with a swift jerk of her head.

Raman turned his head to see who she was talking to. The empty space next to him left him baffled. Noting his confusion, Shalu snickered and landed on a wide smile. She squinted her eyes and repeated her words, this time softly and in Gujarati, his native tongue.

*"Tane koi madat kari saku?"*

In a blink, the language, not the words, bridged generations and geography. His eyes lifted with a genuine smile, but he was unable to speak. He stood tall and rugged, melting on the inside. She repeated her words, this time slower. He responded by shaking his head in a soft no. Just then, he had nothing more to say, but he returned to the same spot each day and waited until he found the courage to tell her he had fallen for her.

For Raman—homesick and seared bronze from the hours wrestling the sun, muscles toned and tight from lifting sacks of cargo for twelve hours a day—her five words, spoken in a language that felt like home, proved to be the respite of a lifetime. From a young age, he had been shuffled from one relative to another after his parents passed from malaria. When he turned twenty-one, just six months before, Raman's patriarch uncle had coerced him into a job opportunity, claiming it to be the chance at something. With no prospects lined up in his native land, Raman found himself on a crowded ship, violently seasick, on a journey from India to Uganda.

Here, he loaded and unloaded cargo onto trucks bound for the Kenyan seaport. His days started at dawn and ended long after dusk. Day in and day out, his morale declined and his confidence waned, but, having little choice, he persevered, hoping that one day, hard work would lead him out of the bondage of backbreaking labor.

Shalu, on the other hand, was third-generation Indian Ugandan. Her great-grandparents had been hauled to Uganda from India as indentured servants in the late 1800s; both countries were then under British rule. Through troubles and toil unknown to Shalu, they triumphed. By the time Shalu was born in 1953, they owned more than thirty acres of tea plantations, and her childhood was spent roaming her family's plantations, feeling the tea leaves between her fingers, taste-testing the quality of the tart green leaves each harvest.

Though she had never been to India, Shalu grew up eating *daal*, *baath*, *roti*, and curries simmered in turmeric, cumin, and coriander powder. She wore *salwar kameez* and, on occasion, a *sari* as she prayed at the *mandir* in her home—a shrine with Lord Krishna in his classic flute pose with Radha by his side. She lit *diyas* on Diwali and decorated their front porch with *rangoli*. Traditions distilled by the three generations that came before her were still part of Shalu's everyday life. She was entrenched in the culture of a country she had never stepped foot in but was spoken of with deep reverence in her home.

Shalu introduced Raman to the beauty of Uganda, its landscape with its serene fields and hills, its diversified culture, and the history of Indian migrants in the country.

Raman, in turn, told her stories of the real India—not the one her grandparents had left, but one that Raman called home. He told Shalu about his village, tucked away in the state of Gujarat, and about his friends and family, also farmers, but ones that struggled each year to stay afloat, borrowing money and burrowing in debt to make ends meet. He told her about his school days, filled with friends that studied little and wandered more. Village living in which a hoard of boys and girls would walk to the sandy banks of the local river to eat snow cones, peanuts, and sweets as they relished the sun surrendering to a rising tide. He spoke with nostalgia, missing home more and more with each passing word. He missed his friends, his brothers and cousins, even his uncle.

Through Raman, Shalu fantasized about the wonders of India, a romanticized rural life, and empathized with Raman's passionate love for roots, his family, his birthplace, his home.

An immensely hard worker and a natural giver, Raman never complained to Shalu about the weight he loaded onto trucks or the shambles he slept in each night, instead pushing himself harder each day to be worthy of her stature. "Don't do it for me; I am madly in love with you already. I will marry you right now if you will have me," Shalu always said, watching him struggle through his days.

After months of bitter homesickness, she had become his light, a reason to wake up, a motivation to push forward in an otherwise bleak existence.

Determined to be more financially stable before he would meet her parents or even think of making Shalu his wife, Raman pushed harder and harder each day. Eighteen months after their chance encounter, when Raman was finally in slightly better living quarters and a pay grade above the last, Shalu convinced him to meet her family.

Struck by Raman's propensity toward hard work and the stories he carried from home, Shalu's father found in Raman a manifestation of his family's nostalgia for the motherland. Raman's small acts of kindness, such as pulling a chair out for Shalu, helping Shalu's grandmother up the stairs, and loading the sacks of tea leaves onto the trolley, had Shalu's family charmed. Most of all, Raman's affinity and affection for Shalu had grown so deep and so rooted that Shalu's aunts, uncles, and cousins all grew to love Raman and cheered him forward. Nonetheless, Raman refused to marry Shalu until he was settled and comfortable in his ability to provide the best possible life. She had known nothing less, and so their courtship continued until a reckless dictator brought an axe to the prosperity Shalu's family had enjoyed for decades.

In 1972, when President Idi Amin mandated an exile of all Indian Ugandans from his country, Shalu witnessed the unimaginable. The regime confiscated the land her family had cultivated for generations, the fields she had roamed her whole life, and her childhood home replete with sweet memories. Within months, her aunts, uncles, cousins, siblings, friends, everyone—the whole Indian community her father had so proudly shepherded—fled to Kenya, the United Kingdom, Canada, India, or anywhere they could find refuge. Worst of all, Raman was forced to return to Gujarat.

Ultimately, on a late August afternoon in 1972, Shalu's father found himself sprawled on his knees, two machine guns and a machete pointing at him in the courtyard of their home, which was nestled among thirty acres of family land. Shalu would never forget the image, nor his passion-filled words as the men threatened her father's life.

"I am not leaving. This is my home! You can shoot, slice, and dice me, but I am not going, you bastards. Look at that sea of green! My grandfather planted every last seed. Every single one! It was barren, totally barren, until my family dug their hands deep into the rough soil, scorpions biting their fingers while the British bastards kicked and spat on their heads. This is my land, and my blood will flow proudly through its roots, deep into the land, my land. So go ahead. Just shoot!"

The standoff lasted days, with Shalu and her mother imprisoned in their home. The patrols would leave each night and return the next morning, only to find Shalu's father guarding his land. On the fourth night, after the patrols had left, Shalu spoke in a hushed voice, trembling with fear.

"Papa, I know this is our home, it is *my* home, it always has been my home, but I am scared, really scared. I cannot lose you, Papa. So please, I know I am asking you for the world, but please, Papa, let's just go. We need to get out of here. We can build a home somewhere else. Please, Papa. Please. Raman's left. He is gone. I can't lose you, too."

As was often the case, his daughter was his greatest weakness as well as his greatest strength. Papa surrendered the next day. He could not refuse Shalu, not when his wife was also pleading for the same thing. Later that week, they boarded a plane for England with nothing more than three suitcases.

"Eventually, my mom found her way from England to America, built up from scratch, and saved. Years later, somehow, she arranged for

my father to join her," Aanya concluded. "That part is a little complicated. Maybe a story for another day."

"And what happened to your grandparents? Did they ever return
to Uganda?" Abhimanyu asked.

A dim inquisitiveness came over Aanya's face as if she were processing the question for the first time.

"My mom tells me that the psychological turmoil of losing their
home in Uganda haunted their physical health for years. They slowly
withered and sadly passed a few months before I was born. I never
had a chance to meet them, and they never had a chance to go back
home to Uganda. My mother, she always talks about her childhood in
Uganda, but the life after exile . . . the thought makes her solemn, so
I don't bring it up much. I can't even imagine how hard it must have
been for her and my grandparents to be thrown out like that from
their home, their land. Losing everything they knew."

"I am sorry, Aanya. I can't imagine it, either, but your grandparents sound very courageous, and your parents' story—it's heart-
warming, so romantic, don't you think? I mean, reconnecting like
that on a totally different continent after years. How beautiful."

"Agreed. They were so determined and brave, and if you want
romantic, you should see them now—still the same, so, like, *so* in
love." Aanya rolled her eyes and stuck out her tongue, feigning
disgust.

Abhimanyu smiled warmly, not only because he believed so
much in that once-in-a-lifetime kind of love but also because he
could tell Aanya did, too. She was on a topic she loved: her parents.
Her face was fresh, animated, and her mood was light once again.

"So, if I have this correct, your mother moved the earth so your
father could join her in the promised land, America, the land of
dreams. They made the dream come true, and a few years later, here
you are back in India—that, too, to grow your career. Strange, no?"

"Sign of the times, Mr. Abhimanyu. And by the way, it's more than a few years—more like decades. I am thirty-one. And it seems to me you watch way too many movies."

"Thirty-one!" Abhimanyu looked shocked.

"Don't look at me like I belong in a nursing home. It's not that old."

"I am so sorry, it's not. It's just that you don't look—anyway, it doesn't matter, and I am totally guilty of the latter. I basically learned English by watching American shows, movies, and the BBC. Between that and the clientele at the Taj, I may indeed have a completely misconstrued understanding of the world, fully fabricated by Hollywood, Bollywood, and the ultra-rich."

"I am right there with you. Most of my knowledge of India comes from very old Bollywood movies, zealous parents who did a very good job at instilling roots, and uncles and aunties who haven't been here in decades. Each day, I am learning that this is not their India, nor is it the India of Bollywood. It's a place misunderstood by so many.

"But wait, back to this age thing for a second, how old are you? Please do not say twenty-four, just—don't—say—twenty-four!"

"I won't because I am twenty-seven."

Aanya furrowed her eyebrows.

"So you are mister young hotshot executive, aren't you?"

"Takes one to know one, right, Miss VP of Business Development?"

They both chuckled and cheered their wineglasses again.

"Here's to workaholics shooting up the corporate ladder," Aanya said.

"Because they have absolutely no life," Abhimanyu concurred.

"Curious—what brought you to New York, Aanya? Why not stay in Georgia? Sounds like you are a small-town kind of girl."

"Work, mostly. Probably the same reason you are in Mumbai and not Bari—it's where the jobs are." Aanya looked down, fiddling with her food.

She continued to chat about her childhood and upbringing,

mentioning her move to New York for TechLogically only in passing. Despite her lowered inhibitions from the wine, Abhimanyu still sensed a trace of reticence in her tone. She was visibly struggling at times to fill in the growing gaps in the quick synopsis of her life story. The glow on her face continued to ebb and flow, like traces of the sun peering through a set of half-shut Venetian blinds, making Abhimanyu teeter on and off of topics based on his reading.

In spite of this, their dinner conversation continued naturally, well beyond the sunset on the Arabian Sea. Their exchanges were pleasant, playful, and smooth, without any strain or forced effort. Abhimanyu was a chatterbox, perhaps a prequalification for his line of work. He was quick to close the silences with anecdotes from his experiences at the Taj interlaced with stories of his childhood in Bari, making sure Aanya felt comfortable at each juncture.

Much to Abhimanyu's relief, the food was delicious, and the wine flowed freely, calming nerves with each sip. As the dinner came to a close, Abhimanyu not only wanted more time with Aanya, he needed time for the wine to wear off before he could drive again. While he had treaded lightly thus far, expressing his adoration with subtle compliments, his desperation made him bolder.

"I know a great place we can get dessert. You up for a short walk?"

Aanya looked down at her watch, indicating her concern at how late it was getting. She gave him an apologetic smile and turned toward the sea. It was completely dark, with just the halo of streetlights glowing as the frenzy of people seaside went about their business. Aanya caught Abhimanyu's reflection in the glass. He caught her gaze, and they both held it, unable to look away.

She smiled at his reflection in the window and nodded a yes, visibly succumbing to the tender moment.

Abhimanyu beamed, slowly shutting his eyes with a silent *Thank you.*

# 14
# Georgia
## *2001*

A grand bouquet, mostly bright white lilies accented by stargazers, was delivered to suite 400. Inside the mini greeting card attached to the arrangement was a note written in pencil on blue-lined, loose-leaf paper folded into a triangle.

July 4, 2001, 5:45 AM

Dear Aanya,

24 years since the day we met . . .

19 years since our first day of first grade . . .

13 years since we held hands for the first time . . .

11 years since our first kiss . . .

10 years since I first asked you to marry me . . .

9 years since I asked your father for your hand in marriage . . .

4 years since I proposed with a real ring . . .

. . . and finally, the wait is over!

Today, I get to marry you . . . the only girl I have ever liked, like like-liked!

Happy wedding day, Aanya!!!

I can't wait to see you as my bride.

With all my love,

Ayaan

# 15
# Mumbai
## *2008*

They walked across the street from the restaurant and onto the
footpath bordering the Arabian Sea.

"You know this place is called the Queen's Necklace? If you look
at it from a distance, it loops around, and at night, when the lights
are on, it reminds one of a glimmering necklace. It's best seen from
an aerial view, but you can catch it on the ground at certain angles."

Abhimanyu explained this as they strolled down the dimly
lit path, tepid breezes sieving between them. As they walked past
families huddled in torn blankets and worn-out clothing setting up
their ocean-side suites for the night, a row of high-end luxury shops
stretched across the road in the background, featuring everything
from Armani to Louis Vuitton. Both of them looked upward, not
down, allowing the street residents of Mumbai their much-needed
privacy. It was not ignorance, but the opposite, a small offering of
dignity in an otherwise prying world. After all, the party of two was
strolling on *their* streets, trespassing through *their* makeshift homes.

They were both in sync on this matter without exchanging a
glimpse or word of concurrence. Rarely did Abhimanyu find this
level of humility among visitors to India, especially Americans.
Almost all the tourists he mingled with at the Taj, especially the
Indian Americans, pitied beyond comprehension, trying embar-
rassingly hard to assist these families by pulling out swaths of large

bills—assuming not only the families' failures at large but judging the government's inadequacies in addressing the issue.

"How could anyone let this happen?" they would say—even as they stood in front of the Taj—missing the irony. Abhimanyu never knew how to respond, as he never had a definite answer. What he did know was that it was much too complex and complicated to explain—their judgment, not the situation—and so he would feign an acknowledgment of understanding and smile politely.

They, the street dwellers of Mumbai, did need money; of course they did. But here, at the end of an arduous, heating draining day, they craved dignity, even an ounce of it, as they prayed for a safe night and dreamt of a hopeful tomorrow. Abhimanyu understood this deeply and was surprised Aanya did not gawk and goo at the swaths of people lying down for the night. She ambled by his side, head up, looking beyond the huddled families, not with arrogance, but in empathy. This small gesture deepened Abhimanyu's admiration for her. He turned his face to her and gave her an *I like you—like, like you like you—even more* smile as he breathed a sigh of submission.

Twenty minutes and half the Queen's Necklace later, they were at *Kaka's baraf ka gola* stand, the one across from the Taj—the taste of success.

"I promise you will not get sick from this, Aanya. I have known *Kaka* here for years, he uses only filtered water and is clean as can be. You up for it? No pressure, of course. Can't have you sick for our 9:00 a.m.!"

Aanya responded with an insatiable smile.

"It's one of my favorite treats in India. I couldn't resist even if I tried—even if it meant I was sick to my stomach for our 9:00 a.m. I had this every day as a kid visiting Naswadi. It brings back fond memories."

*Kaka* gave Aanya a humble smile. Any friend of Abhimanyu's— and that, too, a special friend—was a special guest for him. While

*Kaka* prepped, Abhimanyu had a genuine conversation with him about his family and the business, offering *Kaka* what he craved most—visibility. In return, *Kaka* made them both only his very best *golas* and handed them over as if offering a blessing of lifelong happiness. Undoubtedly, all of *Kaka's* good wishes for the presumed couple were tightly packed into his signature flavored ice cones.

The two stepped toward the seawall to enjoy the dessert and the breeze. Abhimanyu watched as Aanya slurped the last bits of her snowball, lips tainted purple with black currant juice. The reflective sparkle of the solitaire blinded him for a second, flashing him a tease.

"Your necklace, Aanya, it is . . . beautiful. It really suits you," Abhimanyu said, failing to mention that he had been wanting to link it between his fingers, pull her close, and taste the sourness of the plum syrup dyeing her lips.

Aanya placed her forefingers on the solitaire protectively, childishly licking remnants of the syrup off her lips.

Between the wine and breezy seaside walk, Abhimanyu had very little control left, but still, he knew better—much better. He took a step back and turned to the sea.

"Thank you. It's a gift from my parents—it means a lot to me."

Abhimanyu sighed a breath of relief, widening his smile. *A gift from her parents! That is sweet.* He could handle that. Throughout the evening, there had been no mention of anyone significant in her life except her parents. No mention of siblings, a boyfriend, or a husband. *Thank God.*

Abhimanyu thought about asking her the question more directly but hesitated. Either he was not ready to face reality should the answer be anything less than what he desired, or he worried that Aanya would be offended. *You think I would just be frolicking around Mumbai with you if I already had someone special in my life?*

Would she? He had known her no more than four weeks; had seen her three times in total. At times, he felt such questions were futile. The tenderness between them was palpable. Yet he feared the danger in his presumptions.

*What if I am wrong?*

Abhimanyu dropped Aanya off at her hotel, waiting under the portico and waving goodbye until she ascended the stairs, stepped into the lobby, and the doorman released the door behind her. Just then, Aanya turned back, smiled gently, and waved goodbye from behind the glass.

*I'm not wrong!*

Abhimanyu's whole body warmed as he ran through the number of hours before he could see her again: ten and a half.

At the head of a sleek modern conference table, intensely contrasting the majestic ambience just beyond the double-paneled mahogany doors of the room, Aanya stood dressed in a sharp black knee-length pencil skirt with a matching blazer over a baby-blue silk blouse.

From the opposite end of the table, Abhimanyu watched her effortlessly mesmerize the room with TechLogically's capacity to streamline the hundreds of visitors at weddings, conferences, meetings, and special events at the Taj, making everyone ponder the idiocy of not having such a system in place already.

"It is not just a matter of analytics, providing the conference clients with accurate data on attendees and their interests, but also about security at large for celebrity-sprinkled weddings and the like. Giving couples and their families the comfort of knowing that their special day and all the events around it are safe from media, crashers, and vagabonds is a service that will gain demand quickly. As weddings grow grander, both fans and foes have become more extreme, and the media more aggressive," Aanya concluded.

The gazing heads around the table, most of them men, nodded in agreement as she made a final, articulate push for TechLogically's services. Knowing the intricacies of her product and client base along with TechLogically's accomplishments in the space worldwide, she spoke confidently, persuading the room—Abhimanyu was sure—to jump on board before their competitors beat them to it.

Abhimanyu, enamored yet restless, sensed a feeling he could not decode. While he understood her charisma, he could not digest all the eyes in the room entranced by her words, her presentation, her presence. It was not that he wanted her to fail; of course not. He wanted her to kill it, get 'em good, just as she was doing—but this process, all eyes centered on her, unsettled him. It made her feel so distant, like a stranger.

He wanted her to himself, alone, in places where time and space stood still and moments were reserved for the two of them. Maybe back at the colonnade, or at the Arabian, or even on the street slurping a succulent *gola*—anywhere but here! He needed the nodding heads to understand that she was exceptional, really, really extraordinary, and that all of them bobbing their heads and smiling needed to stop ogling.

*God damn it, stop staring. She is taken!* Abhimanyu took a deep breath and tried to relax back in his chair.

*Wait,* was *she taken?*

*Kind of . . . no, not really, but I am working on it.*

*Am I?*

*Kind of.*

Abhimanyu felt even more unsettled. This feeling, the potency of it, it needed—well, he wasn't sure, but it sure as heck did not need this level of jealousy. This was not acceptable and completely out of character. He took a deep breath and counted to ten.

Jayesh (aka Jai) entered the conference room. Again, like a fly on the wall, he served those seated around the table their choice of tea, coffee, or chai while his new trainee followed close behind him and offered a choice of croissant, muffin, or biscuits. When the serving duo reached Abhimanyu, he was startled back from his reverie to reality. Jayesh's trainee followed close behind him as Abhimanyu whispered to Jayesh, "Looks like you will not be serving us too much longer."

A humble smile relaxed Jayesh's face.

A round of applause once again interrupted Abhimanyu's trance. He stood up and formally thanked Aanya for her presentation, ending with a note on next steps and a possible timeline for a concrete decision. She gracefully thanked them, shaking hands with the general manager to the right of her and a few others at her end of the table. Abhimanyu retreated to his reverie, admiring her from a distance.

"That was superbly well done. I think you got this," Abhimanyu said as they left the meeting.

Aanya dipped her fingers in each one of the marble vessels full of rosewater lining the antiquated corridor.

"If you do not mind, Aanya, let's take the service elevator back to my office. It's faster."

"Sure, that's fine." Aanya smirked, flicking the last bit of water on his face.

They stepped into a deep yet narrow elevator with stainless steel walls, void of character. Before they could settle, the elevator dinged, forcing the about-to-close doors open. Without pause, a floor-to-ceiling food cart pushed its way into the vestibule. View hindered by the slits of shelves lined with tiramisu and earthen bowls of custard, the cart pusher thrust forward without hesitation.

Abhimanyu stepped back as far as he could, granting Aanya some space before the cart crashed into her. The cart operator thrust the cart a bit farther, carving out a thin space for himself to the front of the delicacies, facing the doors. Before the cart could settle in place, Aanya, facing the exit, turned quickly in a last-ditch effort not to press her behind into Abhimanyu, who instinctively pressed himself against the back wall until he could not move any farther.

The two were left contracted in the back of the elevator, face-to-face, with no space to move. The cart locked into place as the door dinged to a close. To allow her more space than the half an inch left between them, Abhimanyu made a failed attempt to push himself farther back against the wall. Aanya followed suit in the opposite direction, pressing her back into the cart. The proximity had Abhimanyu's head a hair above Aanya's nose.

He looked down at her face, noting the solitaire peeking out from under the V of the baby-blue silk blouse.

"I am sorry, bad idea on my part," Abhimanyu whispered, trying respectfully not to let any part of his body make contact with hers.

"It's not your fault—and I am not sure I am sorry," she whispered.

Abhimanyu gazed into her eyes, dark with an ever-so-thin layer of mystery. She took a prolonged blink. He felt as though she were trying hard to forget something, pushing back a memory or a thought so powerful that it could break walls and flood tears down her cheeks. When she opened her eyes, she sighed in relief as though she had beaten a demon and survived.

*This is it*, he thought. If there was ever a moment he was going to make a move, this was it.

*Ding!* The elevator stopped. The cart exited, and as it turned the corner, the man pushing it came into plain view.

*Jayesh.*

When Jayesh noticed that he had squeezed *his* sir and madam into the tight space, he laced his hands together in apology.

"I am sorry, sir. I—I—I did not see . . . Please forgive me, so sorry," he said in what seemed like a profusely feigned apology, the grin at the corner of his mouth giving away its insincerity.

Abhimanyu gave him a forgiving nod, topped by a narrow smile, winking to secretly thank him for his mistake.

The elevator slid shut, leaving them alone in the emptied space. Neither moved into the open. They stood, hypnotized by each other, as if an invisible cart were still cramping their space. A million thoughts raced through Abhimanyu's head in the course of seconds.

She was a professional colleague. He was at work. *She* was at work. If this went wrong, everything could go wrong—the possible contract, her work, his work. Was he wrong in reading that she, too, was attracted to him? Would she think this had been his plan all along, to get her stuck super close to him on an elevator? Well, it was not; it was not at all his plan! All he wanted was to walk her back to his office to grab her stuff, have a delightful conversation like they always did, stall her as much as he could, and . . . well, that was it. He honestly did not have it in him for anything more than that, yet here he was.

There was no plan, but being this close to her was stupendously intoxicating. When it came to her, things just happened as though they were meant to be—no pressure, no games, no guesswork. Just the right feeling leading the way. Every moment he spent with her needed not to end. It needed to exist eternally.

Of course, he had wanted her to himself, but he had not expected this—and granted, this was better than any plan. He had her not only to himself but close to him. He needed to do this.

She was thirty-one—thirty-one! His mother, God bless the woman, would definitely have issues with an older woman—and work! *Arr!* Damn professionalism! *I really shouldn't do this*, his mind incessantly reasoned, but his heart and body relentlessly fought every possible piece of logic he pieced together in a matter of seconds.

*I really should not do this.*

Just then, when he had finally convinced himself to retract, Aanya gave him a beatific smile and took a baby step in, closing the tiny gap between them, liquefying every cell in his body, drowning all remnants of reason. That was all he needed. A tiny, baby step forward.

He leaned in, and their lips linked together the way two lovers instinctively interlace their fingers in a dark alley. His right palm seized the nape of her neck, softly caressing her cheeks with his thumb. She placed a gentle hand on his cheeks. He reciprocated by wrapping his arm tight around her waist. Yearning, fervor, tenderness, passion—everything melded together in a moment of perfection as the stainless-steel box and everything outside of it receded into a cloud of euphoria.

*Ding!* The elevator stopped, jarring them back to reality. They stepped off and walked toward Abhimanyu's office, both in sync with each other's steps, a tinge of guilty indulgence evident in their stride.

Aanya nibbled her bottom lip.

Abhimanyu swirled his tongue over his lips, ensuring there was no evidence of her lips left behind.

As they approached Abhimanyu's office, Natasha came into view.

"What took you guys so long?" Natasha said, slaying their mood.

"Took the service elevator—it was slower than usual, though," Abhimanyu said, thoroughly annoyed.

"That was good stuff, Aanya. Your presentation was interesting, and I have some ideas on how to use the technology with food services should we move forward," Natasha said pleasantly.

Abhimanyu scoffed.

"Thanks, always open to suggestions," Aanya responded.

"Abhi, we need to run through the logistics of the pharma conference this week. I need solid numbers for each meal and setup details. You have been so MIA lately, I had to come stalk you—like seriously, where have you been?"

*Damn it, Natasha! Can I get some space, please?*

"I am here twenty-four seven, Natasha, you know that, and you have my mobile. Can I have a minute, please?" Abhimanyu said, glancing over at Aanya, feeling his whole being surrender in her presence.

"It's fine. I can just grab my stuff and be on my way. You two carry on."

Abhimanyu darted Aanya a look. *Natasha is no one, and no, please, don't go. Not now!*

Aanya ignored him and turned to the office door. She looked flustered. Her face had the distressed look he had caught in the elevator right before they—the prolonged blink. It seemed the demons were back.

Aanya waited for Abhimanyu to open his office door.

Once inside, Aanya grabbed her belongings, placing her sunglasses on her head. Natasha hovered like a mosquito.

"Thanks for everything, both of you."

"Aanya, I have time. Just wait just a few minutes, please," Abhimanyu pleaded.

"I really need to go. I fly out today. Let's touch base soon."

"Aanya, are you okay? Seriously?"

"I am fine. I need to go, I am—I am sorry."

"Let me walk you out and hail you a taxi."

"No, it's fine. I can ask Ram Singh. You carry on."

Aanya fled with a sense of urgency that Abhimanyu felt deep down in his gut. *Something is wrong. Did I just screw this up?*

"Damn—what's with you two?"

"Nothing, Natasha. Let's get this over with."

Abhimanyu was fuming at her interference. He had no patience for her—not right now.

Fifteen minutes later, Natasha exited Abhimanyu's office and he immediately called Aanya.

"Hey, it's me, Abhi—I mean, Abhimanyu. I just wanted to talk to you. You left so quickly. I—what happened in the elevator, I hope it was okay. I hope *you* are okay. Anyway, please just call me."

He left a voicemail and flipped the phone closed. He stared at the silver framing of the phone, waiting for the black screen on top to light up with a response. *Nothing!*

Later that day, absolutely restless and unproductive, he sent her a text.

*Worried about you. Please call or just let me know you are okay. Please.*

Aanya replied, *I am okay. Thank you for everything today. I have a flight to catch. Will let you know when I reach Delhi.*

*Can we talk for a minute—please, Aanya!*

Thankfully, his phone rang.

"Hi, Abhimanyu."

"Hi. It is so good to hear your voice. I—I am so concerned. Did I just screw up, Aanya? I am sorry. It's the last thing I want. To mess up with you and make you upset like this. Are you okay? You seemed so—so out of it, so distressed when you left."

"Listen to me, Abhimanyu, you didn't do anything wrong. It's just that—I am thirty-one, almost thirty-two, and—"

"I know that, Aanya. Who cares? I surely don't. Age can't be the reason you ran off like that. There must be something else to it. I could see it on your face."

"You are right, Abhimanyu. It's more than age. It's the weight it carries, and I—well, I cannot get into it now. The plane is already boarded, but I promise to call you and fill you in—well, I will tell you what I can. I really need to go for now. The flight attendant is giving me dirty looks. Just trust me; we can talk about it later."

"Trust is not the issue, Aanya. Of course I trust you. It's more than that. I am worried about you. You—you had this look when you left. You aren't okay, or you aren't okay with what happened, at least—and if that's true, I owe you an apology."

"You don't need to apologize. You didn't act alone, I am guilty as well. If anyone needs to worry about doing something wrong, it's me—but I can't get into it right now. I need to go. I am getting more dirty looks here."

Her voice began to quiver. "Can we talk later, please?" she said softly.

He knew she was crying, but he also got a feeling that this wasn't something he could resolve quickly, not now, at least.

"Have a safe flight back, Aanya, and please take care of yourself. Whatever it is, it will be okay. Trust me—and please do not cry. I can't bear the thought, especially when I can't be of help—or worse, I am the cause."

"You are not the cause. Let's just talk later, please," she said in the softest of tones.

Abhimanyu conceded, forlorn and frustrated, understanding for the first time why so many romantic movies end with despondent lovers running to the airport to stop flights. That was all he wanted to do—run to the airport and stop her from leaving.

As the plane took off, Aanya stared out the window, tears rolling down her cheeks. The city of Mumbai was big buildings in the foreground and the slums of Dharavi at a distance, like two pictures displayed side by side, one being the before and the other an after. Every time she sat on a plane, she could not help but think about how this would end—with a safe and gentle landing or a tumultuous crash, possibly into the crowds of people below, going about their everyday lives, oblivious to the powerful machine that roars above.

Subtly, she clasped her hands together right above her knees and prayed—for an uneventful flight, for forgiveness, for all the unknowns her future held, for everything and nothing at the same time. She repeated her favorite mantra three times.

*Oṃ bhūr bhuvaḥ svaḥ tatsaviturvareṇyaṃ bhargo devasyadhīmahi dhiyo yo naḥ prachodayāt.*

*Oṃ bhūr bhuvaḥ svaḥ tatsaviturvareṇyaṃ bhargo devasyadhīmahi dhiyo yo naḥ prachodayāt.*

*Oṃ bhūr bhuvaḥ svaḥ tatsaviturvareṇyaṃ bhargo devasyadhīmahi dhiyo yo naḥ prachodayāt.*

That evening, Aanya called Abhimanyu and began telling him her truth. Indeed, there had been a grander love story than her parents'— it was hers!

# Part II

# 16

# New York

## *2001*

*Ding!* Two lethargic doors split open to a robotic voice saying, "Floor seventeen."

Ayaan strode out and scanned the etched glass signage mounted on a rectangular piece of mahogany and nailed to a pewter-colored wall, giving it a classy yet modern edge. It listed TECHLOGICALLY with an arrow pointing to the left and APM FINANCIAL SOLUTIONS with an arrow pointing to the right. To the right and left of him were two oversized glass double doors with frosted stripes. Ayaan stepped to the left and swung open one of the doors.

What seemed like hundreds of rows of equally spaced cubicles with heads bopping out had Ayaan at a total loss. No receptionist was in sight, and the security guard that checked him in at the ground level had only requested the name of the company before directing him to the set of elevator banks servicing the seventeenth floor.

Unaccustomed to such an environment, Ayaan never considered asking for directions upon reaching the floor. Instead, he systematically began walking up and down the rows, bright white lilies in hand. Everyone was so engrossed in their computer monitors that few noticed or cared as he weaved through the first three rows of cubicles.

At the end of the fourth row, just as he was doubting if he had the right floor, building, or company, she gleamed under the light of a computer screen. He stared at her for a few seconds, taking in the rare glimpse he got into her work persona. As usual, her wavy black hair was pulled onto her left shoulder, fingers frantic on the keyboard, eyes locked on the monitor. She had her glasses on, which she never wore at home. It made her look like a typically geeky, tech-type math nerd, yet absolutely adorable at the same time.

On her monitor, two windows were open. One was clearly her email software, that much Ayaan could decipher in this tech-savvy world he knew little of, and the other was a black box with some alien green characters blinking on it. Beyond the screen, tacked to the cubicle, were some pictures of them at various ages and stages, along with a tear-off calendar, confirming he had the right date: September 4, 2001.

Ayaan fake-cleared his throat just enough to draw her attention. She turned her head, and on cue, Ayaan whispered, almost mouthed, "Happy two-month anniversary, wifey." Then he swiftly got down on one knee, partly to be cute and partly to hide himself within the cubicle's walls. He whispered again, "Can I have the honor of taking my wife of two months to a celebratory lunch?"

Aanya's initial shock melted into humility. Her face brightened at the sight of Ayaan on his knees. Smiling through hushed words, she whispered, slightly embarrassed, "Thank you, happy anniversary to you, too, silly. I must be the luckiest girl on the planet." She winked and gave him two thumbs up, imitating him as a child.

An audience of onlookers from neighboring cubicles responded with gasps and a synchronous "Awwww."

"Go, Aanya, go," said Julia, Aanya's cubicle neighbor and go-to work friend. "I will cover—get out of here, lovebirds, before I die of cuteness overload."

"Thanks, Julia, I owe you one."

Aanya gently lifted the flowers from Ayaan's hand and inhaled their scent. Lilies, especially white ones, had grown to be her favorite. Every third day since they had moved to New York City, Ayaan made sure Aanya woke up to fresh lilies on her nightstand. The elderly Chinese American man who ran the corner flower shop by their apartment—whom Ayaan affectionately called Mr. Miyagi—made it a point to save the freshest bouquet for Ayaan now that he had a regular customer.

Keeping a conscious distance from each other, they walked through the rows of cubicles as nosy employees peered out of their gray cubicles, mirroring the faces of prisoners envying the release of a cellmate.

To their delight, the elevator was empty when they entered. Once inside, they both immediately searched for each other's hands. Ayaan turned to her, cupped her face with his open palm, gazed briefly into her dark eyes before kissing her baby-pink lips. When the elevator *dinged*, they reluctantly pulled away and stepped to the back of the vestibule, letting others fill the space. They kept their hands entwined behind the crowd, locking eyes and beaming at each other with adoration.

Ayaan mouthed, "Happy anniversary—I love you," and Ayana squeezed his hand tight in response.

Upon exiting the building, the late summer sun struck their eyes, making them both squint and tear up in discomfort as their sight adjusted. Having only conjured up the plans late that morning, Ayaan had not thought through anything beyond the office surprise, so Aanya recommended a cozy corner café with outdoor seating options.

They easily found a table shaded by the building itself, as most of the lunch-goers had opted for direct sunlight. The couple always found this to be a natural convenience in the city. While others scurried toward the sunlit seats to work on their last tans of the season, the two of them obediently and effortlessly followed decades of parental conditioning, convinced that even a ray of vitamin D, while good for you, would make you hideously unattractive.

"Bad news: I have to work tonight, baby; sorry." Ayaan dropped the update within seconds of sitting down. "I know we had plans to have dinner together, but I got called in—a few of the others are sick, some sort of stomach bug they all caught at the same food truck. I thought the least I could do was have lunch with you, but I promise, I will make it up to you."

"Really, babe, you are kidding, right? It's fine! Surviving two months of marriage is not a big deal. Can we at least make it to two years before we go crazy over celebrations? Besides, I don't have any-thing up my sleeve, so please spare me the agony of living up to your adorable, over the top antics." Aanya smirked sarcastically.

Ayaan's face dropped in feigned disappointment.

"Oh well, too late for that!" He said.

"I have to say though, this is a great surprise. Finally seeing you in the middle of the day is a treat. You look good in the natural light," she said.

"Well, too bad I can't say the same for you. The sun doesn't suit you as well. You, my dear, definitely look better in the dark—no glasses, tiny shorts, hair all wild, that is kind of your thing. In the dark, you shine and you roar—and, well, you know the rest." He winked salaciously.

Aanya's jaw dropped.

"Aaa—yaan. Please, there are people around."

Ayaan was charmed by this airy embarrassment. How could his wife, a girl he had known since kindergarten and been in love with as long as he could recollect, be so abashed by his superbly unscan-dalous comment, especially one she had prompted? This is what he loved about her.

After their two-month anniversary lunch, neither Ayaan nor Aanya was awake in their apartment at the same time until the following Saturday morning. Much like their middle school mismatch, their

schedules had been incongruous since moving to New York a few
weeks ago.

Ayaan was off to med school classes, followed by studying during
the daytime and moonlighting as an EMT in the evenings. Most
nights, he got in around midnight, washed off, and silently rolled
into bed next to Aanya. Watching her sleep, he relished her beatific
smile, caressed her soft cheeks, and dozed off within minutes, a sleep
induced not only by incessantly exhausting days but more so by the
peace he gathered knowing Aanya was always by his side.

Strained by the mental focus required of a first-year med student
and drained both physically and emotionally with the vigor required
of an EMT—witnessing disturbing disruptions caused by a stroke, a
slipped foot, or a freak accident in an otherwise ordinary and usually
happy existence—Aanya was his daily respite from it all. From the
torture of his pathology lecture to the haunting sound of a mother
wailing for her unconscious child, an uneventful moment with her
brought him rejuvenating solace. Just watching her for a minute
before his eyes involuntarily shut brought him the calm he so badly
needed for a restful sleep and another challenging day ahead.

Most mornings, Aanya woke at 7:00 a.m. and was gone long
before he woke up. Depending on his class schedule, Ayaan usually
slept in for another hour at least and left around 9:30 a.m. or later. On
non-class days, he was more lax but still followed a disciplined study
schedule at the university library. If he unintentionally did wake
in the mornings before Aanya left, they would spend a few price-
less moments together snuggling quietly, playing with each other's
hands, and discussing nothing in particular, just simple pillow talk.
On occasion, when they weren't too tired, they would catch up on the
years of intimacy lost to mismatched schedules.

On rare mornings when their schedules did coincide, Aanya
made a habit of sneaking up behind Ayaan in the bathroom while he
worked on his hair. She would walk to the steamy mirror and write

their names in the same way she had in first grade, sharing the "Y." Ayaan would finish it off and draw a heart around it, just like he had with the red pencil as a little boy.

Then Aanya would wrap her arms around him from behind while they both stared at each other in the mirror and say, "No wonder you were late on the first day of first grade. Must have taken you forever to poof your hair just right!" She would take a deep breath, inhale the sweet smell of a fresh shower amalgamated with his intoxicating cologne, and wildly ruffle his meticulously manicured pompadour. She would watch in victory as his mouth dropped in despair, then flee the scene before he could react. Despite the dash of annoyance in having to contour his hair again, Ayaan would smile a wee bit wider in the mirror, his face centered in the heart he had drawn.

That morning, the Saturday after their anniversary lunch, was one such occasion. The couple finally found each other in the same space, awake and energized. Having the morning off, they both slept in and lay in bed, snuggling, for at least an hour before rolling out at 10:00 a.m.

For brunch, Aanya made *masala chai* while Ayaan made omelets. They ate together and caught up on the week with little novelty or gravity to the conversation. Aanya told Ayaan about Julia's crush of the week, a finance guy on the fourteenth floor who happened to take the elevator at the same time as her each day. Aanya was convinced Julia was timing her arrival at work for this little rendezvous, but Julia, a hopeless romantic, denied the allegation, claiming it was all serendipity.

Ayaan, trying hard not to weigh down the mood, spoke little of the cases he faced as an EMT. Aanya was always happy to hear about them, but the conversation often left them at a loss, feeling helpless and bogged down by the gravity of the events, the unpredictability of life, and the sheer sadness of it all. It reminded them, unwillingly, of the night Ayaan's father was shot.

So that morning, Ayaan consciously chose to complain about one of his professors, a brilliant man and accomplished doctor who, for the life of him, could not teach. Ayaan had resorted to teaching himself the nuances of a pathology report to be tested on Monday, confirming that with the exam pending and evenings booked on ambulances, he wouldn't have any time for Aanya that weekend.

"Honestly, babe. I basically need to teach myself all the content, which means I will be studying every minute I get. It's a total waste of your weekend if you hang around here—not to mention you can be a huge distraction when I am studying," he said, smiling flirtatiously. "You should spend the weekend with your cousins in Jersey."

In actuality, Aanya had no cousins or extended family in the United States. To the best of Ayaan's knowledge, her real aunts, uncles, and cousins, whom she barely knew, were spread across Kenya, South Africa, and India. It was hard to tell, as Shalu-aunty, or Mom—something Ayaan was still adjusting to calling her—rarely spoke of her family across the world.

"You sure?"

"Absolutely. In fact, having you around will make me feel guilty all weekend for studying. I'd rather you had some fun on your own."

"Hmm—you are right. I have not seen the girls since the wedding. I should pay them a visit. It's always a good time with them. It will give me something to do—and you time to study."

Though Aanya knew few, if any blood relatives, she did know a lot of people that served as her extended family. Many of these family friends she met growing up in Georgia, people her mother and father had spent countless years getting settled into a foreign nation. Growing up, Aanya's home was like a halfway house. Every person from all over her father's village and within a thirty-mile radius was welcome to stay with them as long as needed. They housed anyone and everyone that needed a short-term place to stay while they found a job at a local factory, convenience store, or motel. While she was thoroughly irritated with it at the time, growing jealous of the attention they demanded—especially from Ayaan—more recently, Aanya had begun to appreciate the innate kindness her parents extended to every family needing their help.

When Aanya was about fifteen, one such family was making their rounds at their home. They had two daughters, one fourteen and the other sixteen. As part of their ceremonial initiation into American life, Aanya was in charge of showing them the ropes at school—high school, that is.

"Lucky me!" she whined.

Having no option in the matter, Aanya adjusted, understanding that this was what her parents did and fighting it was futile. Fortunately, Jaya, fourteen, and Jeeni, sixteen, would not be in her grade. Jaya would be entering ninth grade and Jeeni eleventh grade, and luckily, Aanya was a sophomore, smack dab in the middle of the two, which reduced her duties to getting the girls on the bus, showing them to their homerooms, and getting them back on the bus. Everything in between was their problem.

Thinking back to her attitude now, Aanya felt like one of those super mean high school girls. When Jeeni sought advice on changing in the gym locker room in front of all those girls, Aanya lied, "Just do it; just change. There is no method."

In reality, there was a method, the goal of which was, of course, to minimize bodily exposure. Aanya knew it well: You first had to have your shirt swallow your arms. You then pulled up the shirt and kept it on your neck while you put on your new shirt over it and slid in your arms. Lastly, you removed your old shirt from underneath, over the head. This technique ensured that none of the other girls had the opportunity to see your awkward adolescent growth and compare notes, especially on your conspicuous brown skin with overgrown black hair.

A few days after she asked Aanya for help, Jeeni, in the most genuine manner possible, offered to show her the method. "Aanya, I have been secretly watching the *goris*, and I can show you how they do it." Aanya rolled her eyes while Jeeni proceeded to demonstrate with an extra shirt in the room the three girls now shared.

All these years later, Aanya wondered, *Why the heck was I so mean and selfish? What made me so much damn cooler than the kids that were fresh off the boat? Was it really because Ayaan gave some attention to Jeeni? How stupid of me to be jealous!*

Thanks to karma, the joke was on Aanya. No matter how aloof Aanya behaved toward Jaya and Jeeni, especially in the school hallways, they always responded with a smile. The girls were kind—absolutely angelic, in fact. Aanya always felt envy, jealousy, and guilt all at the same time when she compared some of her selfish deeds to theirs.

In those early years, they acclimated to the school—high school, that is—effortlessly. By the time Jaya graduated four years later, she was shortlisted to be homecoming queen and valedictorian. The fact that none of them were allowed to go to homecoming, or any dance for that matter, was a moot point. The point was that Jaya and Jeeni somehow managed their adolescent years—those unsure, awkward, tough ones, and that, too, in a new country—without a hiccup, like some sort of superhumans.

The family, including their mother, Renu-aunty, their father, Devan-uncle, and the girls, lived with Aanya's family for almost fifteen months before moving to manage a nearby motel. Some years later, the family bought a convenience store in New Jersey and settled there.

Admittedly, though Jeeni and Jaya could have gotten into any Ivy League school and moved away from home but for financial reasons, the girls opted for a state school, both on full scholarships. As was the norm in their community, their parents had accumulated large sums of private debt, borrowing from friends and family in order to buy the convenience store. The girls, wise beyond their years, understood their inherent responsibilities in repaying those debts.

Though she was initially dismayed, over those years, Aanya grew very fond of the girls, reconciling her bad behavior with a recipro-cated friendship. Jeeni had studied finance and was now working in NYC, while Jaya studied pharmacy and was working in Jersey City. They both lived at home with their parents in central Jersey, and Aanya hadn't seen them since the girls were bridesmaids at their wedding two months back.

With the girls being who they were, Aanya needed no formal notice; no dates penciled in months in advance. All she had to do was call and say, "Hey, I am going to take the train over." Without a blink, Jeeni and Jaya would seamlessly fold her into whatever plans they had for the weekend.

This was the superpower Aanya's father had developed by being who he was: a giver, a caretaker, a natural mentor, and a supporter of all who wished to find a home in a new land. He had deep-rooted friendships sprinkled across the United States at motels, convenience stores, and gas stations. It turns out that debts incurred during an immigrant journey are never forgotten and always returned, more than tenfold, in loyalty that far surpasses bloodlines and generations. Thanks to her parents' generosity, Aanya had a big extended family she could count on all up and down the East Coast. Ones, she can easily count for some weekend fun.

When Ayaan returned from the library that Sunday night at 11:00 p.m., Aanya was already knocked out. She had returned earlier that evening, exhausted from a fun-filled weekend with the girls, including an old-fashioned slumber party on Saturday night. Within minutes, Ayaan took his place next to her and cuddled in close. She felt him caressing her cheek, so she rolled over and scooched her body into his.

"I missed you," she whispered.

"I missed you more," he said, squeezing her tight.

The next day, late afternoon, he called her.

"How was your exam?" Aanya asked.

"It sucked! I am just glad it's done. I am going to go home, nap, and then study for the next one."

"Stop! I am sure you aced it—and you definitely deserve a nap."

"We'll see! Honestly, I don't wanna stress about it anymore. It's out of my hands. Anyway, listen, come home on time. I will finally be home on a weeknight, and I want to spend some time with you—missed you all weekend!"

"Yeah! You're not working tonight? Awesome! I will leave at five on the dot. About dinner—should I pick up something?"

"No, we will figure it out. Just get home."

"Can't wait. Love you."

"Love you more."

"No, I love you more! Bye."

Ten seconds later, Aanya's phone beeped.

*"I love you times infinity—I win."*

When she entered the apartment that Monday evening, the savory aroma of turmeric, red chili powder, cumin, and *garam masala* simmering over chickpeas overpowered the crystal bowl of potpourri left on the two-person dining table in their snug Upper West Side apartment. This was the first weeknight Ayaan had had off since their two-month anniversary last Tuesday.

Knowing Aanya would despise going to an upscale restaurant only to be cramped into a tiny table in the corner and be served even tinier portions, he cooked her favorite dish, *chole bhature.* (Actually, he had bought the *naan* from the store in the absence of his *bhature*-making skills and was attempting to master the curry for the *chole* as per his mom's instructions.)

"I told you I would make it up to you," Ayaan said, smiling whimsically.

She placed her handbag on the table and ambled over to him. He was facing the stove, so she reached around him from behind and gave him a big bear hug.

"You are crazy, you know that. I already married you; you can stop all this above-and-beyond stuff." She kissed him softly on the neck. "Too bad for you; there is no getting rid of me, sweetie."

That evening, they had a romantic candlelit dinner, slow-danced to their favorite Hindi classics, and teased each other with soft kisses for hours before retreating to the intensity of the bedroom. Though delayed, it was a perfect evening, a beautiful celebration of their two-month marriage and the lifelong love that had preceded it.

# 17
# Georgia
## *2001*

Aditi copied the solution for the last equation verbatim from the whiteboard. It was only the third day of her analytic geometry and calculus class and she was officially lost. Pleased the period was coming to a close, she neatly slipped the textbook into her backpack, took off her glasses, and walked toward the exit.

Since only freshmen were stuck taking painful 8:00 a.m. classes, the Quad, lush with grass, was nearly empty at 9:16 a.m. New to campus, Aditi was still learning the layout and pondered whether crossing the Quad was really the shortest distance to the cafeteria. Despite being exposed to and immersed in American norms her whole life, Aditi was still overwhelmed by the campus and all its happenings. She could not at all fathom how, thirty-seven years ago, her father, Kishore, had navigated the same terrain as a foreigner.

In August of 1974, when her father first arrived and witnessed girls lying out in bikinis, soaking in the sun on the open Quad, he was convinced he had ended up at the wrong address. Surely, this had all been a silly mistake. He had never seen a woman in her underwear before, let alone four of them, giggling and rubbing suntan lotion on each other. The four girls in scanty swimsuits, lying on their bellies, flailing their bare legs back and forth, made Kishore's blood surge in all the wrong places. His minuscule grandmother's underwear, which he had unwillingly seen drying on the clothesline, surely consisted of more fabric than all the clothing on these four bodies combined.

Instinctively, he closed his eyes and placed a hand on his forehead to obstruct his vision further, murmured an apology audible only to himself, and fled the scene. Half expecting to be punished for witnessing the forbidden in broad daylight, he scurried back to his dorm room, forgoing his lunch and anticipating a rapturous knock on the door from the moral police. Tomorrow he would find an alternate route to the cafeteria. There must be a way to bypass the Quad and its scurry of salacious activity.

From that day on, Kishore avoided all paths that were routed through the Quad until about mid-November, when he mentioned this absurdity to another foreign student on campus named Deepak. He had befriended Deepak not because he liked him but because he was from a village in Gujarat not too far from his own.

"Let's not go that way," Kishore said.

"But why? It is a much shorter route," Deepak said.

"I just don't want to take that path," Kishore said firmly.

"*Arreyaar*, fine, we will not take it, but you must tell me why."

"Umm . . . hmm . . . there are always half-naked girls there. It makes me . . . *uncomfortable*."

Deepak was dead silent for ten seconds, hinting at empathy, before he broke into uncontained laughter, slapping his knees and dropping to the floor.

Kishore gave him a sincere look of disappointment. *Some friend you are, you . . . you . . .* Unable to think of the appropriate curse word in English, he did the next best thing—he found the most derogatory word he could think of in his native Gujarati and spit it out at him.

"Okay, okay. Sorry, *yaar*. Take it easy. What if I guarantee you no girls in bikinis? Will you go that route?" Deepak asked.

"Yes, but how can you promise me that?"

"Because, idiot, it is November. If you need a jacket to keep warm, I assure you that there is no one in bikinis out on the Quad."

Deepak shook his head in disbelief.

"Some man you are, avoiding the chance to catch foreign beauties on the Quad."

"Shut up and let's go," Kishore said, wondering why he was friends with this jerk.

Upon inspection of the lawns—a slow and thorough scan as he walked—Kishore lifted his self-imposed ban on the Quad crossing routes, opening up once again the shortest distance between his dorm and every other place on campus.

That morning, Aditi decided to cross the Quad diagonally to reach the dining hall, passing the open lawn her father had avoided for months. She often got nostalgic over such matters. She felt a pang of pride thinking about her father's courage. What strength it must have taken to leave a community where everyone knew your name, not to mention every nuance of your life, to one in which you were a complete stranger. Maybe that is why green card holders in America are called "immigrant aliens"—the migration feels like landing on a new planet.

When she had decided to study engineering at Georgia Tech, it was partly to finish what her father had started. As a child, she heard over and over how hard it was to be in graduate school and work at Raman-*kaka*'s motel at the same time, how her dad liked to learn but did not have the time to both study and survive in a new country. Until about three years ago, she only got tidbits of the story here and there, suffixed at the end of a scolding or prefixed by, "You have no idea how hard it was for us."

As children, through eavesdropping and overhearing conversations they cared little for, Ayaan and Aditi understood that their father had come to the US from his village in India on a student visa for graduate school at Georgia Tech. They had puzzled together that he had gone back at some point and had an arranged marriage with their mother. Later, around the time Aditi was five, her parents and Raman-*kaka* became the beneficiaries of President Reagan's amnesty for three million undocumented immigrants, a deed that still made Reagan a fan favorite in their households.

Aditi, keen on such matters, also piecemealed together the unspoken family debt they owed to Raman-*bhai*, whom Ayaan and she had lovingly called Raman-*kaka* until a couple of months ago, when Ayaan began calling him Dad. Raman-uncle was the one who had helped her father in every imaginable way to establish himself in the United States. Although Raman-*kaka* himself never hinted at such altruism or took any credit to date for his good deeds, it was for this reason, Aditi reasoned, that she never heard a negative word about Raman-*kaka*, Shalu-aunty, or their daughter and her new sister-in-law, Aanya.

Even when her mother disagreed with Shalu-aunty on the wedding date and discrepancies arose over how and which century-old Hindu wedding traditions to embrace and which to conveniently discard, her mother played it safe, modestly agreeing to rituals unknown to her or her family.

"Sure, Shalu, if that is how your family does it, it is fine with us. Anything is okay with us as long as the children are happy," Leela always said with a genuine smile, though even Aditi had to admit that Shalu-aunty, having no real family to consult, was pretty easygoing on such matters.

Since Aditi never made it to breakfast before her 8:00 a.m. mornings, she decided to grab a quick meal before her 10:15 Introduction to Microeconomics class. At 9:19, as she waited for her turn at the coffee station, her phone rang in her backpack. She ignored it. She could not hold a phone in one hand and assemble her coffee with the other, especially before she had actually had her morning coffee, so she decided it was best to sit down and check her phone while she was eating. The phone stopped ringing.

Twelve seconds later, it rang again. It had to be Mom or Dad, but they usually didn't call her this early in the morning. Normally, they waited until after five or six in the evening for their daily catch-up call. She unzipped her backpack, pulled out the phone, and answered. She knew it was her father from the caller ID on the screen.

"Hi, Dad, what's up? Everything okay? Why are you calling me so early?"

"Where are you? Are you watching the TV?" her father questioned her in one breath.

"No, I just finished a class and am getting breakfast."

In the background, on the other end of the phone, her mother was frantically asking for a play-by-play of the answers, leaving Aditi wondering why her mother hadn't called herself.

"There is something going on in New York, *beta*. We just talked to *bhaiya*. He is fine, but he does not know where Aanya is. Where does she work, Aditi? Do you know what building Aanya works in?"

"What do you mean something happened? I don't get it."

"A plane hit a building. The tall building. Is that where Aanya works?"

"You mean the Empire State Building? What are you talking about? Every building in New York is tall."

*Had Dad officially lost it?*

"Aditi, I don't know. It is on TV. Just get to a TV. A plane hit a building in New York. We spoke to Ayaan. He is okay, but I don't know—he does not know where Aanya is, and he hung up with us so he could call her. The TV says it is a building in downtown. Where is that, Aditi?"

"I am not really sure, Dad."

"Let me try to call her. I will call you right back."

Just as Aditi hung up, she became unnervingly alarmed by phones ringing all around her, one after the other, in mish-mashed ringtones like melodies in a relay race. All around her, faces crunched, eyebrows lifted, and mouths dropped as other confused, shocked *You have finally lost it, Mom!* expressions abounded. It seemed her father was not the only one watching TV. He was not the only one overreacting, losing it. All the parents had gone nuts, all at the same time.

She skipped the coffee and walked over to an open table. She sat down and called Aanya. The phone rang four times before it went to voicemail. She heard the others around her chatting, picking up calls, and having unusual, uneasy conversations. She did not know what to do next. A plane hitting a building sounded like her dad was hallucinating, but her father never hallucinated. He was always straightforward, direct, and unequivocal in every action as if it was based on a well-calculated formula. He was never one to lose it.

The temperature in the room rose with every ringtone, every word. With each syllable uttered and bite taken, the room seemed to close in tighter. She dialed her father back.

"Hi, Dad. I tried Aanya. She is not picking up her phone, but I am sure she is fine."

"*Beta*, please go to your dorm room," Kishore pleaded.

"I have a class in a few minutes, Dad."

"*Beta*, just go to your room, and please turn the TV on—forget the class for today."

Forget class? *Who are you, and what have you done with my dad?* Aditi was tempted to ask, but her father sounded panicked, and she could hear her mother breathing heavily in the background, sounding vulnerable.

More than her parents' behavior, something else was tormenting Aditi. *Downtown?* She had no idea where downtown was, but she had a hazy recollection of Aanya saying she worked downtown and they lived uptown. Having been to New York only once—and only under thorough guidance by her brother and sister-in-law—the references to uptown, midtown, downtown, or lower and upper sides were irrelevant pieces of information that had no meaning in Aditi's world. When she had heard the words on her trip to New York City over the summer, she had discarded them as information she had no use for long-term. All she needed to do was follow her brother and Aanya around—they knew what they were doing.

Aditi got up and walked out of the dining hall.

In the foyer, at the entryway to the dining hall, a swarm of students, along with some professors, were crowded in absolute silence. CNN was always running on a small TV hung in the corner. Aditi stopped to watch. There was an image of a tall building billowing smoke.

Aditi felt a surge of tears. She recognized the building—that was the building Aanya had taken her into to use the restroom. That was it! Aanya had a security pass to that building, and after a ferry ride around the Statue of Liberty, which left them in some park, Aditi desperately needed a bathroom.

"Just hold it a few minutes, Aditi. It's New York. Hard to find a clean bathroom; any bathroom really," Aanya had warned before taking the elevator to the seventeenth floor of that building so they could use the restroom and check out Aanya's cubicle. Ayaan had passed on the bathroom stop and offered to go wait in a long, winding Mr. Softie ice cream line instead.

As the revelation crystallized, Aditi stepped back from the TV, turned around, and sprinted toward her dorm room. She frantically scanned her security card at the main entrance of her residential hall. Tears rolled down her cheeks as if she had just trudged through a rainstorm.

The elevator always took forever and had too many people, so she ran up the stairs to her dorm room to avoid the lag and other students. She sat on her bed and scanned her phone for Ayaan's number.

It rang twice before she heard three short beeps and the call dropped. She tried again—straight to voicemail. She called again—this time, two beeps and the call dropped. The anxiety was swelling in her body. She did not want to call her father back without any news, but then her phone rang and it was her dad.

"Where are you, *beta*?"

Aditi took a deep breath before answering. She tried to sound calm in order not to give away the revelation she had a few minutes ago.

"I am in my room, Dad. I am fine. Did you hear from Ayaan again?"

"No, *beta*, the phone is not working properly. You try."

"Okay, okay—let me call you back after I try."

Before she could hang up, her father blurted out, "*Beta*, where does Aanya work in New York? Do you know anything about her job?"

Aditi swallowed hard.

"She works downtown, Papa. I don't know—that is what *bhaiya* and Aanya always say, that she works downtown and they live uptown, but I don't really know what it all means."

Aditi purposely used "Papa" to soften the blow. She knew he preferred it. It was what Ayaan always called him.

"Okay, okay—stay in your room and keep trying to call them. We will do the same—call us if you reach them."

Aditi hung up and called Aanya. It went straight to voicemail. She tried again—straight to voicemail. She called Ayaan; it beeped four times and dropped her call.

She started texting.

*Bhai, are you okay? Please let us know.*

She started typing again, this time to Aanya.

*Are you guys okay? Please tell me you are okay.*

Aditi paced around the room. She had been too distracted to

turn on the TV. She frantically searched and found the remote near her pillow. She and her roommate had been watching *Late Night with Conan O'Brien as* they dozed off the night before, so the channel was NBC.

Newscasters were on the screen with the word "Live" on the top right. The image was of a smoking building. Aditi was mesmerized. It felt like a very distant place. Then the screen switched to people running away from the building on the ground. Aditi watched in shock until she realized she needed to search for Aanya in the crowd of people. Too late. It switched back to the newscasters.

She could not recall the channel number for CNN. They never watched it. Instead, she flipped one channel up to Fox News. The same smoking building. Then she flipped one more. People were talking to a cameraman, disheveled, confused. She looked for Aanya in the background. Nothing.

She paced some more.

Her phone beeped. It was a text from her roommate, Emily.

*Doesn't your brother live in New York? Are you watching the news—is he okay?*

Aditi ignored it. She dialed Ayaan. It rang once.

"Hello," he said in the softest of voices. Aditi had never heard him speak with so much tenderness.

"*Bhai*—are you okay?"

She tried to sound calm but failed.

"I am okay—I can't reach Aanya, Aditi. I can't reach her. I don't know where she is. I need to go to keep my line open. Bye."

Aditi knew he was weeping. There was only one other time in her life she had seen her brother cry. It was the night her father was shot in the arm and a few days after, and that was it, never again—until just now.

"*Bhaiya*, wait, where are you?"

"I am in the ambulance."

"I love you, *bha—*"

Three beeps and the call dropped. She called back. This time, she could only hear a bunch of muffled signals.

She texted him.

*Bhai. I love you—don't worry, Aanya will be fine.*

The tears began to flow again, and the anxiety made her pace in circles between the two twin beds. She wiped tears and grabbed the hair above her temples, realizing she needed to call her dad.

"Papa, I just spoke with Ayaan; he is okay."

"—and Aanya?"

"She—she is—he cannot reach her yet, Papa."

Her voice cracked hard, and she pulled the phone away from her mouth to make sure he could not hear the sobs in her voice.

"Where is Ayaan?"

"He—he—he was in an ambulance."

"Ambulance?"

The word had no meaning until her father said it in that tone.

Aditi hadn't registered the word "ambulance." *Ayaan was in an ambulance. He was in an ambulance. He was in an ambulance!* It sunk in. Was he working that morning? He never worked mornings! Why was he working?

"*Beta*, where was he going?"

"I don't know, Papa."

"Was he hurt?"

*Hurt? Why would he be hurt? He was working.*

"I think he is just working, Papa."

"Now?"

Just then, Aditi looked up at the television. Level after level, the smoking building collapsed like dominoes on top of each other. There was absolute silence. She knew her father was watching the same exact scene on the other side of the phone. In the background, her mother gasped.

Her father broke his silence.

"*Beta*, are you there?"

Aditi sobbed uncontrollably, unable to speak, as her father repeated over and over again, "It's okay, *beta*, it's okay. Be calm. All is okay; everything is okay. It's okay, *beta*, it's okay. It's okay, *beta*, it's okay."

After several sobs, Aditi finally gathered the strength and spoke.

"Papa, Aanya works in that building."

# 18

# Georgia
## *2001*

Kishore glared at the distant scene on the tube TV mounted to the wall. Aditi's sobs were now steady and audible on the other end, her voice echoing in his ear: "Papa, Aanya works in that building."

He was unable to process the words or the sounds. He simply stared at the screen, unable to fathom the imagery. The space around him grew so cavernous that no one could reach him. Leela was in Kishore's view, but Kishore saw nothing but her mouth moving and her body shaking frantically. The vacuum around him was too vast for her to traverse.

Just then, an old-fashioned *ding-dong* doorbell jolted him to the present. The pitch of the chimes was set intentionally loud to awaken Kishore for late-night check-ins. He handed the phone over to Leela, his head low, unable to make eye contact as he walked to the registration desk.

"I need a room for a few hours. How much?"

The voice behind the window was quick and concise.

From the periphery of his eye, Kishore noted a tractor-trailer outside. The trucker had probably driven all night and needed some rest, unaware of what was happening on TV screens around the nation.

"Room available, $59 for four hours, $99 for longer or a full night," Kishore said robotically.

It was not a busy time of the day, month, or year. Firstly, it was

9:30 a.m. By now, the day truckers had caught a good night's sleep and left early that morning, the night drivers would continue a little longer before taking a break, and none of the hourly customers would show up before lunch. Kishore processed all of this mechanically within seconds, worked out the formula, and projected feasible numbers.

The driver at the window looked at him skeptically. Kishore could not tell if the price was too high or too low, so he remained silent.

"Four hours, but if I need longer, I will come by and give you the rest—the night for $79."

Kishore nodded, took the $59 in cash, and handed him the key without an ounce of his characteristic haggling or negotiation.

"Listen, are you okay, man? You look like you are going to puke. You need some water or something?" The driver asked.

Kishore forced a narrow, closed-mouth smile.

"All okay, sir. Have a good stay."

The man reached for his wallet, pulled out a $100 bill, and slipped it under the glass pane. "Keep it, man. You folk work hard. I know it. Not sure what is up with you, but I hope it helps," he said, slipping out before Kishore could react.

Kishore turned to Leela, still on the phone. She looked alarmed but unmoved. Had Aditi not told her what she had told him? Was his daughter weeping, and Leela did not understand why? It was as if he and his wife were in two different universes. He was shaken, sharply stirred, like a volcano about to burst, and she—she was solely a mother, defiant and determined to stay strong for a daughter convinced of the worst. Or had Aditi not told her?

"Aanya is fine, *beta*, calm down. It is just a crazy, very crazy plane accident. She is fine. Please have some water, *beta*. It will help," Leela consoled Aditi.

So convincing was Leela in her tone that even Kishore felt a little more at ease as they locked eyes. At once, reading each other's minds as married couples often do, they both knew the next step.

"Aditi, *beta*, drink some water, stay in your room. I will call you back in a few minutes."

Leela pressed the off button and held the handset up to Kishore. He timidly shook his head no, with a *Please, you do it* gaze. Leela grinned and brought the phone closer to herself. She pressed a series of numbers and waited.

"Raman-*bhai*, it is Leela-*ben*." She defaulted to their native Gujarati.

"Ahh. Leela-*ben*, *kem cho*."

Raman-*bhai* was full of delight. You see, Raman-*bhai* did not watch the news, and when indeed he did consume news, it was always a day old. He was quaint that way. He preferred his information in print. The only television Raman-*bhai* ever sat through was classic Hindi movies that spanned the second half of the last century—and only because after twenty-seven years of being married to Shalu, a die-hard Amitabh Bachchan fan, there was no escaping the icon.

Raman-*bhai* was a restless being. Sitting in one spot to consume a sitcom or a drama for thirty minutes or an hour made his body uneasy. He would much rather organize invoices or the catchall drawer, go for a walk around the open-air corridors of the motel for the umpteenth time, or simply vacuum the industrial-grade carpet in the main lobby. He would happily fix a leaky faucet, turn over a room himself, or run the laundry full of dirty towels and sheets before tuning into any kind of entertainment.

When Kishore had stared at Leela with his *Please, you do it* eyes, it was for this very reason. Kishore understood all too well, as did Leela, that they would be the ones explaining the most bizarre information they had ever heard to their newest family members: "Listen, good morning, wanted to let you know the building your daughter— and, oh yes, our new daughter-in-law—works in just crumbled to the ground after an airplane struck it this morning. It sounds too uncanny. Something made up, like a really bad joke, but it's not. Turn on the TV, and you will see the scene repeated over and over. We are trying, but we cannot get ahold of your daughter. Our son seems fine, though."

They would surely think their daughter's in-laws, their dearest friends, had lost it overnight. What a silly joke to play, they would chuckle, forgiving them easily for such cruel ill-intentioned humor.

"Raman-*bhai*, you have to turn the TV on. Something is going on in New York. The children—"

Leela's voice quivered.

"What is going on, Leela-*ben*?"

The motherly equanimity in Leela's demeanor earlier quickly dissipated.

"There was this accident in New York. A plane hit a building—and then it fell."

"What? Did you talk to the children?"

"Kishore spoke with Ayaan this morning, and he is okay. Aditi also spoke with Ayaan a little later—he was fine—and . . ."

Leela's voice tapered off.

"Leela-*ben*, what about Aanya?"

There was silence on the phone.

"Leela-*ben*, are you there?"

Leela's resilience melted as she murmured, "Raman-*bhai*, we have been unable to contact Aanya—that building—"

Raman-*bhai* hung up before she could finish.

Immediately, Raman signaled his wife to turn the TV on and dialed his daughter's cell number. It rang four times before it went to voice-mail. Standing in front of their thirty-inch tube television mounted to the vertex of their living room ceiling, Raman and Shalu glared at a clip of a building falling like dominoes. The screen repeated images of a plane hitting a tall building. It then cut to a clip of another plane hitting the building behind it, and then cut to a building collapsing, like a house of cards.

Raman and Shalu both continued calling Aanya alternating between the landline and cell. No Answer. In between calls, they called Ayaan's cell phone a few times, only to receive muffled signals.

Raman refused to panic, but was spiraling quickly. Why had Leela spoken only of their son and not his daughter. The children had always been considered as one, inseparable, referred to as "Aanya-Ayaan" or "they." There was no Ayaan without Aanya, and no Aanya without Ayaan. They shared a love found only in fairy tales but more profound than that. The ubiquity of the pair was their only reality— the children were a single entity, separated only by the fact that they existed in two different bodies. Their unity was a universal truth. To speak of one without the other agonized Raman to the core. The fact that Leela had said, "He is okay," pierced Raman to his core.

Raman took a deep breath and thought sensibly about the chances of Aanya being in that building or at that spot at the very moment. *The chances were slim, right? New York City is a big place; she could be in any of the thousands of buildings in New York at the time, nowhere near the one or two buildings that collapsed on the screen. She could be home, or on the subway, or getting coffee. The rolling headlines said it all happened before 9:00 a.m. She doesn't work before then.*

At 10:20 a.m., the doorbell rang. Not the *ding-dong* doorbell for motel customers, but the simple, short *ding* reserved for personal guests at the back of the office. Raman opened the door to find Leela and Kishore. He was still irritated but relieved to see them. Their daughter's in-laws, the parents of the boy that meant the world to her, and their best friends were there. That had to count for something.

The four of them stood together, not knowing what to do next. Raman-*bhai* stepped aside after a moment, no words spoken. They all sat in the small living room with a three-seater sofa and two chairs as they stared at the TV. Raman had the landline in his hand, Shalu the

Nokia cell phone, and Leela held their cell phone. All three phones dialed Aanya's and Ayaan's numbers, one after the other.

In between, Aditi called.

"Maybe we are all clogging their phone lines."

Her tone was uncharacteristically empathetic as if she knew she might possibly be the only child these four parents had left.

"—let me try for five minutes, please. Just me. I'll call you back," Aditi said.

Leela communicated to the others that Aditi was trying. The others kept their phones to the side. The constant commotion on the TV filled the room like white noise. No one spoke a word for what seemed like hours, yet it had only been seventeen minutes since that doorbell dinged.

Leela, the most optimistic of the four, broke the silence.

"Nothing has happened to any one of them. Our children are fine. They are probably just having trouble with their phones like we are, with so much going on."

Kishore sat quietly, unwilling to kill her optimism, yet the guilt turned him into a shivering mannequin. The possibility of knowing their son was probably okay, yet their dear friends' daughter, their new daughter-in-law, might have died in the building made him intensely sick.

Kishore had held on tight to the piece of news long enough. The weeping murmur of Aditi's confidence echoed, again and again, in his head: "Papa, Aanya works in that building." He could no longer betray his dear friend, the one he affectionately called brother, so he cleared his throat and whispered, "Aditi thinks Aanya works in that building."

# 19

# Georgia
*2001*

That Tuesday afternoon, September 11, 2001, after all flights had been grounded, the quartet of parents began driving to New York. Despite her insistence on joining them, the grown-ups pushed back, and Aditi remained on campus at Georgia Tech. A day later, despite all her efforts at trying to remain calm and rest—deep breathing, counting sheep, recalling positive thoughts, meditating, just breathing—Aditi could not sleep. As she faced the wall and wept silently into her pillow, concealed whispers made her tighten.

"No, Mom, she is Indian—that is very different than—" Emily said.

Aditi couldn't hear the other side of the conversation, but it was easy enough to decipher. Aditi could imagine Emily's mother, whom she had met only once, saying in her sweet southern lilt, "But they did this, dear. They just took a plane and blew up a building—you don't know what these folks are up to. You gotta get out of there, sugar plum, trust your mama. These folks—they're all the same, dear. Nuts, I tell you! I gotta do my job and protect you."

"It's not all the same, Mama, trust me, there is a difference. She was born here. Her family is from India. She is Hindu. Like, it's a totally different religion in a totally different part of the world. And even if she was Muslim, that doesn't mean that—Mama, you met her parents—stop being crazy. I am *not* requesting a roommate change, not over this."

Emily sounded sincere, making Aditi's tense body loosen just a little.

In early summer, when Aditi had first called her assigned roommate upon receiving the match, she expected a southern drawl and some inane questions about how to pronounce "Aditi" followed by "My aunt went to this Ashram in India last summer; she is totally into meditation and prayer."

Instead, much to her relief, Emily surprised her. Although she was from Kentucky and had only been to neighboring states on occasion, Emily exuded a sense of awareness. It was hard to pinpoint, but something about her saying, "Hey, so good to hear from you, and I hope you are as nervous about this as I am," made Aditi feel as though they were going to be okay.

They spoke of logistics, arrival schedules, orientation, and household wares: "You bring a hair dryer, and I will bring the TV. You bring some DVDs, and I'll bring a couple of board games. I will bring the trash can and you some garbage bags." They discussed linens and laundry baskets, flip-flops for the yucky communal shower they had heard rumors about, and maybe a bean bag they could share. Lastly, they decided to check out the dorm room first before committing to more decor, such as artwork or a rug.

That day, when Aditi hung up, her mother's look was enough for Aditi to respond with, "She seems really nice. I think we will get along. I have to bring the TV and some other small stuff. I thought a TV would be easy for us." There were always TVs on rotation at their motel—some broken, some repaired by her father, some replaced, while others stayed trashed. The commitment to a TV was the one thing she knew her parents would have no issue with, as it was sensible thinking on her part. They would shine with pride at Aditi's pragmatism.

Leela tried a more direct approach.

"So, where is she from, *beta*?"

Aditi knew the *How did it go?* look was not intended for a logistics update, so she got straight to the point.

"She is from Kentucky. She was born and raised there. She is white, Mom, like really white-white, but she seems nice, and she didn't ask me anything about my name or where I am from, which makes her okay in my book. She is also planning to study engineering, and it seems a lot of the female engineering majors are assigned to our building. Emily heard that from someone she knows there already."

Leela smiled at her daughter, attempting not to break her spirit, but she was not happy. Leela was hoping Aditi would magically be assigned an Indian roommate, someone Aditi could relate to more and be a good influence to keep her on the right track—someone whose parents Leela could understand with ease and speak to directly should the need arise.

On move-in day, despite Aditi's attempt at nonchalance and to her own surprise, her first impression was, *Wow, could this girl get any whiter?* Emily had long, straight Valley Girl hair with just the right amount of wave at the bottom, as if it had been styled at a salon that very morning. She was light in her step, as if walking on clouds, and no matter what she said, it sounded fluffy and euphoric.

Emily reminded Aditi of Reese Witherspoon in *Legally Blonde*, a movie she had watched with Ayaan and Aanya while in New York that summer. Elle Woods and Emily could have easily traded spots. Lucky for Emily, Aditi loved Elle's character in *Legally Blonde*, and lucky for Aditi, Emily indeed was genuinely nice—and, more than that, she was worldly. Aditi liked her immediately, and Emily reciprocated.

The two shared not only a room but many firsts on campus. They stuck together at orientation and the freshman mixer and even had their first drink together at a frat party. They both were the type to tread lightly, cautiously, grounded in a way that meant they did not overdo anything yet missed out on nothing.

Despite being in a minority of girls studying engineering on campus, they had no classes together. The student body was huge, and the campus even more ginormous, so it was impossible to run into anyone twice without seeking them out intentionally. On different trajectories during the day, Aditi and Emily tried to catch up for dinner every evening before heading back to their rooms, studying into the night, or watching TV until they could no longer keep their eyes open.

They were a good match, bringing out the best in each other, the kind of positive influence parents wish for as their babies leave the nest and embark into a world of temptation and freedom. In fact, though she did not know it, Emily was exactly what Aditi's mother had sought in a roommate for her daughter—a kind, smart, worldly girl, a history buff that nailed *Jeopardy!* questions and had a strong head on her shoulders.

As Aditi secretly listened to Emily's conversation that night, she wondered how well she really knew Emily.

Without warning, Aditi sneezed loudly. Emily turned, light from the desk lamp spotlighting the fear on her face.

"I need to go right now, Mama; call you back."

Emily rotated her office chair to face her roommate. Aditi didn't care that Emily could see she'd been weeping.

"I am so sorry, Aditi. I didn't mean to wake you, and, umm ... my mom, she doesn't know stuff like this. She grew up in a small town, never went to college, and hardly reads. What happened today—it's hard for her to process. I mean, it's hard for *us* to process, so you can imagine ...

"She thinks everyone like you—I mean, anyone who looks like you—is the same. I mean, I am pretty sure she doesn't know all Indians are not Muslims, or that you are Indian and Hindu, and all the conflict stuff between Hindus and Muslims. You know I know all this stuff because I love world history, but she—she is a good person, Aditi. She just doesn't get the whole thing, you know? She's just scared. She honestly didn't mean anything bad, and neither did I."

Aditi slowly sat up in her bed, eyes bloodshot and puffy. Her body was exhausted, her mind numb.

"It's okay, don't worry about it. My mom is the same way. She also grew up in a small town and has lived a pretty isolated life here in America, surrounded by others like her. If things were different, I am sure she would react like your mom did.

"Call your mom back. I totally get it."

The truth was, Aditi didn't totally get it. She never had. In all her years, she had never felt anything less than equal to the likes of Emily. But tonight, there was a revelation. Thanks to a plane hitting a building, she finally understood what "progressing very well for— you know" meant: for being an outsider, for being brown, for being a foreigner, for not belonging to this country—and now for, you know, being a terrorist. That is what Mrs. Jones had meant!

How stupid had she been all this time? Her father's constant acceptance of second best, only to fight twice as hard, finally made sense. *Expect less and accept more.* Her father was right! It really didn't matter who you were. What mattered was how you appeared. Perception mattered. The color of your skin mattered —whether you liked it or not.

Her parents were right all along. It didn't matter that she and Emily could have been the same person in different bodies. What mattered was that her body was tainted brown, and from that day forward, that alone was enough to make her a terrorist—or, worse, un-American.

Emily stood up and wrapped her arms around Aditi. She held her tight and tried hard to be there for her, but this would not change Aditi's new reality. Nothing would.

Later that month, within weeks of 9/11, Aditi moved back home—not because this would secretly make Emily's mother happy, which it did, but because her parents, Kishore and Leela, needed her, their only remaining child, by their side.

# 20

# New York
## *2001*

Aanya's mother stood at the door of the bedroom, watching Aanya scribble in a spiral notebook. Aanya's face went from resilient, to distressed, to solemn. Profuse tears began to flow down her cheeks.

October 1, 2001

I met with a grief counselor at work today. She said that writing my feelings down at times like this helps. I read somewhere else that you should write it and then burn the paper; it helps more.

I don't know what I am going to do with this paper yet. All I know is if you were here, I would not need to write anything. I would just tell you all of it, detail by gritty detail. All the crazy feelings I have been having. I would tell you every horrifying emotion. The big things and the little ones and everything in between—and you, you, Ayaan, would pull me close, hold me tight, really tight, until all of my worries and anxieties evaporated into thin air, just like that! The magic of you, my Ayaan.

I didn't want to go to counseling, but HR made it mandatory for everyone to go at least once, and my mom and dad, both of whom have been staying with me, also thought it would help. Mind you, everyone in HR is gone, Ayaan, everyone, so I don't know who is actually making us go to counseling. All the HR people were in the office by 8 AM on 9/11 for their annual team-building retreat.

Speaking of, there is also no TechLogically office, Ayaan! It's GONE. I haven't been to work since, but I know work is a mess. I had to go to Jersey City to meet the counselor. They have rented some space there. Everything is in disarray. There are no notes or records or anything about our clients. We have nothing! We don't know what we are doing.

Julia is gone! Sweet, sweet Julia, Ayaan. She was on the PATH on her way in. Does that mean her crush is gone, too? He must be. I know she timed her arrival to match his. I hope she is with him. I really do! I hope the two of them took the elevator up to heaven together. I can see Julia blushing all the way up!

Of the fifty-eight people that worked on my floor at TechLogically, thirty-six are gone. That is almost everyone. Our CEO is alive. He was in India with the CFO and CTO. He called me with condolences. It was nice of him. He was genuine, but none of it helps, Ayaan—none of it. I DON'T NEED CONDOLENCES! I NEED YOU! WHERE ARE YOU?

Are you out there? Where? It has been three weeks since I saw your beautiful, bright smile. I want to see your face first thing in the morning and last thing before I go to bed. I am nothing without you. JUST COME HOME already! Please, please, please, baby, just come home. This is enough already!

I will make you your favorite, pav bhaji, just the way you like it, with the slices of lemon and onions cut super thin and the bread loaded with butter. I will cook and also do the dishes. I will take care of everything you hate, and I promise I will not even complain about it. I will put on the light-blue dress, your favorite, the one I wore when you proposed (I mean the real proposal, not all the will-you-marry-mes growing up). We will put on the mixtape I made you in high school, the one with our favorite classic songs, and we will dance all night long, just like we did in my dorm room the day before finals my freshman year. We will sway to classic Kishore and Lata hits and end with some '90s stuff, the same way the mixtape flows. It will be the perfect night, Ayaan. Pav bhaji, our favorite songs, and you and me, just us!

In the morning, we will go for a walk in Central Park and watch the little kids learn how to ride their bikes with the training wheels. We will look at their parents swelling with pride and imagine our future children.

Ayaan, please, please, please, come home, baby. I can't do this without you. I can't imagine a future—our future—without you.

"Almost done, *beta*?" Shalu interrupted, resolving not to cry.

Aanya looked up from the writing.

"It's not helping, so I guess yes. I am done."

Aanya looked as broken as she felt.

Shalu walked in and sat at the edge of the bed. She did not bother wiping Aanya's tears. She wanted her daughter to cry, to get out all the pain. Bottling up her feelings would only make matters worse. Shalu understood this too well, more than Aanya would ever know.

When Aanya mentioned the grief counselor meeting, Shalu insisted she go. She hadn't had such luxuries in her time of need. That morning, not only did she and Raman make sure Aanya got out of bed on time, they drove her to the session and waited outside the room until she finished, but Aanya spent no more than twenty minutes in there.

"Hungry, *beta*?" Shalu asked as she shifted closer to her daughter to push a tendril of hair behind her ear.

"Not really."

"Well, you have no choice, not when it comes to eating. Your dad is waiting for you."

Aanya sighed deeply, closed the notebook, and handed it to her mother.

"You can read it if you want."

"It is okay, *beta*, I understand."

Shalu said a silent prayer. She willed God to simply erode her daughter's pain, to pass her agony on to her. When parents witness their child suffering from a headache, a fever, or a scraped knee, they can help heal the pain. They can ease the throbbing discomfort away with some Advil. They can sanitize the scar and wrap a bandage, but this—God, this was too cruel. There was no pill, no poultice, no cure, no remedy. Not even time could reconcile this tragic loss. Her daughter's grief was permanent; no one knew this better than her.

For a second, Shalu considered telling her daughter the truth about what happened to her grandparents after their exile from Uganda.

When the three of them had arrived in England and started from scratch, Shalu worked as kitchen help, cleaner, and cook—anything to keep her parents from having to resort to the same arduous work.

Late one evening, when she returned to the paint-chipped, one-room apartment she shared with her parents, she found her mother and father flat on the floor, crumpled note in hand.

*Our dear daughter, Shalu,*

*This is not and will never be home. Here, we are nothing more than a burden to you. We are sorry we cannot carry on like this. Please find Raman and marry him. Call Aunty Sarla. She has something for you.*

*With all our love,*

*Mummy and Papa*

It was her father's handwriting, not her mother's. She traced her fingers over the words, trying to feel his despair as her tears soaked the paper and smeared the ink, and it was then that Shalu broke. Not when Raman had been given little choice but to flee to India, not when she said goodbye to classmates she had known since kindergarten, not when she fussed over what part of her childhood was worthy of packing in her allocated suitcase; not when she touched the tart tea leaves for the last time, plucking one to place in a book; not even when she said goodbye to her aunts, uncles, and grandparents, all of whom had fled to Kenya early in the exile when they still had time to close out bank accounts and ship belongings. Not until right there, when her parents, white bubbles still foaming at their mouths, abandoned her in a foreign land with nothing but remorse and guilt for forcing them to leave Uganda—that was the moment Shalu broke. At that moment, the nightmare of losing everything, all at once, rushed in and crushed her like a tsunami.

It took decades for Shalu to understand that it was not poverty or the loss of wealth that had made her father wither, slowly bringing her mother down with him, but the loss of his only home in a country that had refused him that right. For years, Shalu struggled with the guilt of making her father leave the plantation—his land, his home, his country. She should have let his blood flow through the roots of the tea plantations as he wished, and he would have died a happy man, a martyr fighting for his homeland, to be remembered and relished by all those exiled by Amin. Instead, she let her father wilt and die a no one, on foreign soil, bubbling at the mouth, with his wife, loyal to the end, sprawled out beside him, leaving his only daughter catatonic from the guilt.

Aunty Sarla sent not only the few hundred dollars her father had saved for her before leaving Uganda but much more than that, securing the future of a niece she considered a daughter in honor of a brother she had failed to keep safe. Through her darkest days, when Shalu, just twenty-one, set off for America alone, having burned her parents' funeral pyres side by side, Raman was her only lingering light. Without the hope of one day reuniting with Raman, who had fled to India, she would surely have taken the path her parents had chosen.

On a dark night on the shores of New York, they reunited after Raman snuck off a ship he worked on as a deckhand with the intention of never returning. They married at a Hindu temple in Queens, with only the priest as a witness, and moved to Georgia with the promise of work. There, slowly, Raman began to mend Shalu, carefully picking up each shattered piece of the feisty, confident woman he had once known. Yet it was not until years later that the young woman he had fallen for so easily emerged again, thanks to the joyful birth of their daughter, Aanya.

Perhaps sharing this would help Aanya understand that her mother had also witnessed days and months, even years, without any sight of light yet somehow managed to come out of it okay—but Shalu thought better of it. She didn't want to risk shocking her with such news, not now, at least. More so, one's own grief cannot cancel that of another's—but because Ayaan was her light as Raman had been hers, she couldn't help but fear the worst.

She rubbed the small of her daughter's back and gave her the narrowest smile of hope.

"This grief is yours and yours alone. I know. Write as much as you can as long as it helps, *beta*, but promise me—and I mean really promise me, *beta*—that you will never give up, that you will always choose to fight, to live, even though right now it feels like there is nothing to live for. Fighting is a choice, and I need you to keep fighting, to choose life. I promise you it will be okay. Not anytime soon, but one day, it will have been worth the fight. It will be worth it to live. Promise me."

Aanya squeezed her mother's hand, affirming her promise, and turned to place the notebook on her nightstand, taking a long, hard look at the wilting white lilies, the last of Ayaan's gifts, fighting to hold on to the last bit of life.

# 21

# New York

*November 4, 2001*

Happy four-month anniversary, Ayaan! What's the special plan? Let me guess: you are surprising me by coming home! This was all some master plan of yours so that you could make an over-the-top, grand gesture—right? Please, baby, tell me I am right! I so want to be right!

Everyone wants to have a memorial service for you, Ayaan. Mom, Dad, even your mom and dad. They all feel I need closure, that <u>we</u> need closure. That they need closure. That you need closure—that you need the Hindu sacred blessings so you can have peace and pass with ease to your next life. They feel a service where we say a proper goodbye to you will help me, help them, help us all. BUT I HAVE NO PROOF. I HAVE NO PROOF THAT YOU ARE DEAD!

I have been calling the missing persons hotline every day, twice a day, asking about you. Today, Miriam, the lady at the hotline, asked softly, "Do you have someone to talk to, sweetheart? Can I get you a number? Talking helps. Please try calling this number I give you, sweetie."

I told her I talk to people all the time.

When I called again in the afternoon, I am sure Miriam

was breaking some professional rule because she said, "Aanya, honey, can I meet you for coffee? We can just talk. It can help. It really can. Trust me."

"I am okay, but thank you. It is very kind of you to offer."

I hung up after that. I heard her voice quiver when she said, "Take care of yourself. Bye, sweetheart."

She does not need to cry for me, Ayaan. It is you that is missing, not me. I will find you. I know.

Anyway, the point is, I was not lying, Ayaan. I _do_ have someone to talk to—I have you! Right? You are out there . . .

Remember the old Hindi movies we used to watch? The ones where someone gets into an accident, loses their memory, or has amnesia or something crazy? What if that is you? What if you just got hit with some falling debris and lost your memory, and you are out there somewhere—lost, confused, don't even know who you are? How can you come home if you can't remember our home address or the directions to it or that you have a home and even a wife? That's right—a wife.

You can't come home if you can't remember anything, right? I know this sounds bad, but I want something to hit you in the head, hard! I hope something hits you again and it triggers your memory so that, slowly, you will remember your name. Someone will ask you who you are, and you will say, "I am Ayaan, that's spelled A-Y-A-A-N," and as you spell it, your subconscious will connect your "A"s to my "A"s, your "Y" to my "Y," and your "N" to my "N." Aanya's "N"—your love, your soulmate, your wife now of four full months.

Your brain will struggle a little, but slowly, it will populate, puzzle all the pieces together—our home, our address, our life. You will find your way home, to our home.

Everyone is being extra nice to me. Very supportive.

They will not leave me alone. My mom is in the next room, making me some rotli. I have lost some weight. They are all afraid, Ayaan. They are all afraid I am going crazy, but I am not crazy, baby. I just, I just—I should have—but, Ayaan, you should not have gone into a burning building! I love you, but how could you do that? That was just stupid. I was not in there, and even if I was—you shouldn't have done that! Do you understand that you do NOT run into burning buildings?

Okay, stop. I am so sorry! I am so sorry! This is not helping. I am really sorry, baby. I was not calling you stupid. I am not angry at you. Well, maybe just a little. It is just that if you hadn't gone in, Ayaan, it would all be okay. We could still be us—laughing and loving like we have all our lives.

Please come back, baby. There is no Aanya without Ayaan, remember? We—WE, meaning you and I—agreed to that.

You lied, Ayaan. YOU LIED, YOU LIED, YOU LIED.

You suck, Ayaan!


PS: Your turn for the last word.

# 22
# Georgia

November 30, 2001

Happy birthday, Ayaan! This is the first birthday in nine years on which you will not have to propose to me because, for the first time on your birthday, I am already your wife!

Happy 25th! You did it—we are married! I am Mrs. Aanya Ayaan Parekh! That is going to confuse people a lot more. Don't you think?

I am home, like home-home, in Georgia. I thought it would be best to be here for your birthday. Aditi bought a cake to celebrate. She insisted we celebrate your life, but when we gathered around your kitchen table and tried to sing you happy birthday, no one, not even Aditi, could hold it together. It was the saddest happy birthday song I have ever heard. No one could celebrate or take a bite of the cake, not even me. We all just cried into the cake.

I am sorry, Ayaan. I tried. I really did, but I couldn't be happy on your birthday. I couldn't hold it together, not even for our parents.

Your parents, Ayaan, they are in bad shape. Leela-mom, she is not able to make fun of this—for the first time in her life, she cannot find the humor, Ayaan. She is speechless.

without her jokes, none of us are laughing. Her whole world has stopped laughing. She has stopped laughing.

Please come back, Ayaan, so your mom can laugh again. So that she can make us all laugh again, help us see the lighter side of everything—maybe even this.

I am sorry, but I can't do this alone. I can't help them by myself. I wish it was me and not you. You would be better at this—maybe they wish that, too. Why you and not me? It should have been me!

I should have texted you, Ayaan. I should have let you know I was not even in the building. This is all my fault. Your parents' pain is unbearable to watch. Your dad is way worse than after the time he was shot. Even my parents are at a loss on how to help.

The four of them—our parents, Ayaan—just sit in silence. They have no words left. I don't know who they are, and I don't know how to find them. Please come back, Ayaan, if not for me, then for them—your parents, our parents. Please!

# 23
# New Jersey

December 11, 2001

I caved, Ayaan! Today we had a memorial service for you.
It was in New Jersey. Jeeni, Jaya, Renu-aunty, and Devan-
uncle planned everything. I mean everything. I don't know
what any of us would do without them. We cleared your last
rites with a long pooja by the Maharaj, the same priest that
married us. Had he lied when he bestowed our marriage with
the blessings of a thousand saints? Maybe, just maybe, he
forgot a mantra or two, the one that guarantees a long,
happy married life . . . maybe an aunty or two didn't mean
it when they whispered, "Akhand saubhagyavati bhawan"
into my ear. Maybe someone screwed up a word or two when
they were asked to repeat, "May you always be the one whose
husband is alive; may you remain safe from the curse of wid-
owhood" in Sanskrit. Because if they did it right, if they all
genuinely warded off all the evils on our wedding day, then
. . . how?

The pooja was finished before the service was opened
to the public at the advertised time. I don't know how it all
came together, Ayaan. I didn't even know it was advertised. I
just know a lot of people were there.

Thousands of people came, Ayaan! THOUSANDS! There was no room to walk or move in the space. There were all the people that came to our wedding and even those we invited but did not come. There were people we fought with Mom and Dad to cut from the guest list—600-plus people at a wedding is just stupid, we said, but they all came, Ayaan, even the ones we dismissed. They all came today! Dressed in white saris, salwar kameez, and kurtas, rows and rows of people chanted, "Hey, Ram; hey, Ram," as they bid you a peaceful farewell.

I stood there for hours in a receiving line, next to my mom and dad and your mom and dad and Aditi, hugging, shaking hands, being held, watching throngs of tearful, swollen faces mouth, "I am so sorry . . . We are so sorry . . . It's just so tragic. Take care of yourself, beta . . ."

"Ayaan was in my pathology class. He helped me study. I will miss him. We will all miss him. He was always so helpful . . ."

"We are sorry; I am sorry. So sorry for your loss."

"Muslims have gone mad, and we can't believe this happened, beta. So sorry. Such a terrible thing to happen to such a good person. Take care of yourself."

"Ayaan was the first on-site when I had my stroke."

"He helped when my baby was choking."

"Ayaan was the first to come in that morning when all hands were on deck."

"Ayaan would have gone into the building to help no matter what," someone said; I don't know who.

Mr. Miyagi was there. "You don't know me, but Ayaan bought white lilies for you from my shop every week. I always saved the best for him; for you. Such a sweet, handsome boy. God bless his soul," he said when he handed me the freshest of white lilies, exactly like the ones you give me. You were right; he does look exactly like Mr. Miyagi from The Karate Kid.

Your dean, your professors, and your classmates were all there. Our landlord, Mr. Ramos, was there. There were mayors and councilmen and leaders of the Indian American community. There was an imam or two from the local mosques, which had all our uncles and aunties roaring with whispers. There was a signed letter from the White House with the signature of George W. Bush at the bottom. Jeeni had it framed and placed it next to the condolence book.

I stood there, Ayaan. I just stood there for hours as all the people you have touched—and maybe even those you never met—prayed for you to rest in peace and sang your praises. They called you a hero again and again, and I thought, who needs a hero, Ayaan? Who the F needs a hero when they can have you? Who are these people, Ayaan? Who are they? Do they even know you?

Do they know you cry when you see your mom cry? (By the way, you would have cried a lot today—I mean a lot, a lot.)

Do they know you like your toast lightly brown, edges cut, and loaded with butter? Do they know your left nostril is smaller than your right? Do they know you have a cute little birthmark on the back of your ear? Do they know you sleep with socks on even in the middle of summer when it is ninety degrees?

Do they know you say a small prayer every time an ambulance whisks by?

Do they know that when the cashier asks for a donation at checkout, you always say, "Yes, one dollar, please!"

Do they know that if given a choice between folding the laundry and doing the dishes, you will always pick dishes because you hate folding laundry?

Do they know you are scared of mice and that zebra stripes make you dizzy? (weirdo!)

Do they know you loudly slurp your chai simply to annoy me? ME—your wife!

Do they know you make love with a passion found only in erotica novels? Do they know, Ayaan, that there has never been anyone else but you for me and me for you . . . that we are just one being born to different mothers?

Do they know it was not "only" a two-month marriage ("Thank goodness," they whispered, "no poor kids to worry about") but the bond of a lifetime? Do they?

Do they know that when you were twelve, you started crushing on a girl so hard that you asked her to marry you on the fifth-grade playground—and then again, sixteen more times?

Do they know I am that girl, Ayaan? I am that girl . . .

They don't know, Ayaan. They just don't, because if they did know you at all . . . if they knew the way you hold me so tight, absorbing all the pain in one squeeze, they would never say goodbye to you. They would never give up! They would search for you, night and day, and keep searching in the piles of rubble and dust until you emerged, miraculously surviving it all. They would make a documentary about your bravery, about how you survived three months in a small gap, caved under concrete, eating bugs or something crazy like that.

Maybe you and a vending machine got enclosed in the same cavity, and you meticulously planned out the chronology of your meals. First, a Snickers bar each day, then the chips, from your most favorite to least: Doritos to the yucky barbeque flavors. You would save the peanut butter crackers for last in hopes of being found before it came to those disgusting fake cheese crackers.

Then, one day, a big dog would sniff around, bark once, then twice, and then prolifically. People from all around would dig and dig and dig until the dog stopped barking and you miraculously emerged! Emaciated but ALIVE.

At the end of the Oscar-winning documentary, they would interview your loved ones, and I, your wife, Aanya Ayaan Parekh, would gloat and tell them how I NEVER gave up. Never ever. I never for once believed that you were dead! I never bid you a final farewell! Not like these cowards!

# 24
# New York
## *2002*

Late afternoon on a Sunday, Jeeni drove smoothly down the highway with Aanya in the passenger seat of her Honda Civic. They were headed to Manhattan to have dinner at a cozy new Mexican restaurant before Jeeni dropped Aanya off at her apartment on the Upper West Side.

They were both relaxed, tuned into the Bollywood radio station, which was blaring annoying ads about jewelry stores with real 24-karat gold, low-rate mortgages, and opportunities for business ownership. The radio jockey came back on with exasperating chatter filling valuable airtime. *Just play a damn song already!* They both rolled their eyes at each other, in sync with their irritation.

"Here is a very special request for a very special couple celebrating their fifth wedding anniversary. A classic all-time favorite for you retro lovers," the radio jockey squealed before a pristine melody filled the space. Jeeni recognized the song a millisecond before a soft male voice caroled:

*Pal pal dil ke paas*
*Tum rahati ho*
*Jivan mithi pyaas*
*Ye kahati ho*

Jeeni immediately reached for the tuner to switch the station. Aanya gently pulled her hand away.

"Leave it, it's okay."

Aanya spoke softly but with conviction.

Jeeni rested her hand back on the steering wheel, gave Aanya a thin *I am so sorry* smile, and let the song play.

It was a classic '70s song from the Bollywood film *Blackmail.* The melody was soft, and the lyrics were romantically poetic—simple yet profound. As adolescents, any effort to translate the lyrics as they often did with so many of their favorites were disappointing. Unlike them—this, the music they had inherited from their immigrant parents, was imbibed with beauty and nuance unsuitable for migration to a new language. The amalgamation of Sanskrit and Urdu, derived from Persian and Arabic, yielded prose so exquisite, so deep, it was impossible to capture its immaculate intensity and slippery sophistication in the sharp stiffness of English syntax.

In seconds, without warning, tears flowed down Aanya's face.

In the blurriness of her tears, Ayaan's face, flawless at every imaginable level, was tilted down to her. He was holding her safely, one arm on her shoulder, the other on her bare waist just above her lilac *lenga,* studded with delicate rhinestones in intricate *mehndi* designs. Her wavy hair in full curls was pulled all to the left and adorned by a shimmering barrette clasped to the right. In a shade of darker lavender, her *dupatta,* pinned to her right shoulder, was spread translucently across her arm, veiling Ayaan's left side as she rested her palm on his shoulder.

Ayaan, in a tailored tuxedo with a lilac cummerbund and bow tie and crowned with his signature pompadour, sparkled with the broadest of smiles under the spotlight following their dance. Seated behind them at a long head table trimmed by white lilies, Raman, Shalu, Kishore, Leela, and Aditi admired the couple.

To the right of them was a three-tiered wedding cake topped by a figurine in which the groom was wearing a *sherwani* and the bride a traditional red wedding *lenga*. So annoyed was Aditi that no such topper readily existed on the open market that she had made this her top pet project for months, ultimately hand-crafting the idols so they perfectly matched her brother and Aanya in their wedding couture.

In the dim light of the ballroom, there were tables full of family and friends, some genuinely admiring the glowing couple and wishing them a lifetime of happiness while others sneered with envy.

Gazing straight into her watery eyes, Ayaan mouthed the lyrics:

*Pal pal dil ke paas tum rehti ho*
*Jeevan meethi pyaas yeh kehti ho*
*Pal pal dil ke paas tum rehti ho*

*Har shyam aankhon par*
*Tera aanchal lehraye*
*Har raat yaadon ki*
*Baarat le aaye*
*Maein saans leta hoon*
*Teri khushboo aati hai*
*Ek mehka mehka sa*
*Paigham laati hai*
*Meri dil ki dhadkan bhi*
*Tere geet gaati hai*
*Pal pal dil ke paas tum rehti ho*

*Kal tujhko dekha tha*
*Maine apne aangan mein*
*Jaise keh rahi thi tum*
*Mujhe bandhlo bandhan mein*
*Yeh kaisa rishta hai*

*Yeh kaise sapne hai*
*Begane hokar bhi*
*Kyun lagte apne hai*
*Mein soch mein rehta hu*
*Dar dar ke kehta hu*
*Pal pal dil ke paas tum rehti ho*

*Tum sochogi kyon itna*
*Maein tumse pyaar karoon*
*Tum samjhogi deewana*
*Maein bhi iqraar karoon*
*Dewaanon ki yeh baatein*
*Deewane jaante hain*
*Jalne mei kya mazaa hai*
*Parwane jaante hain*
*Tum yunhi jalate rehna*
*Aa aakar khwabon mein*
*Pal pal dil ke paas tum rehti ho*

He sang, unabashed by the hundreds of eyes peering at them as they swayed to the mellifluous music. Aanya softened further at every word, euphoric tears flowing down her cheeks. He wiped them gently, nodding a playful *No crying, missy!* warning before his own eyes prickled with tears. He blinked them back, causing her blissful smile to widen even further. They danced into their own abyss until the music subsided, letting go only when the last magical note had dropped, childhood soulmates celebrating the sanctity of their love, dancing into their marriage.

Jeeni pulled the car onto the shoulder of the highway, grabbed a stray napkin, and wiped away Aanya's tears. She positioned her body closer to Aanya and put an arm around her friend's shoulder, giving her a tight hug in spite of the gearshift jabbing her thigh. The song ended, and the squeaky radio jockey came back on. Jeeni quickly pushed the radio off.

"I am so sorry, Aanya. I am just so sorry."

Aanya continued to sob. She was inconsolable, so Jeeni sat there holding her as tightly as she could, pressing Aanya's head onto her right shoulder, offering an endless supply of silent comfort. The car shook every few seconds as vehicles flew past them at sixty-five miles an hour, but they just sat there as the sky went from azure to hues of orange and ruby, understanding that time was trivial at a moment like this. When the sky was on the cusp of landing on a midnight blue, Aanya lifted her head up from Jeeni's shoulder.

"Thank you so much, Jeeni. I am sorry. I think we can go."

Jeeni gave her the biggest fake smile she could conjure up and proclaimed, "Okay, missy! You ready for some rice and beans? I promise it's just what you need!"

Aanya chuckled subtly as they pulled back onto the highway.

Since the weather was warm, they opted for an outdoor table. While snug, it still provided a little more elbow room than the space inside. It was a dark evening, but a string of lights strewn together in a criss-cross canopy provided the ambience of a fiesta.

Jeeni opened the menu.

"I think a margarita is in order, don't you?"

"Sure, you pick."

Aanya put down her menu. Jeeni ordered the margaritas and looked at Aanya. There was a moment of awkward silence.

"So . . . you want to talk about it, Aanya, or pretend it never happened? Your call, totally."

"I don't know, Jeeni, it's just so hard. I don't even know. Just when I think I am doing okay, I totally lose it like that."

"Okay, so we are talking about it—good. Listen, I understand it is super hard, Aanya. I cannot even—I am so sorry."

"It is not your fault," Aanya said.

"The song. I mean, I didn't know what to do. Sorry for trying to turn it off. It was stupid of me. I was just trying to—you know, not trigger something. Epic fail, I suppose."

"I know you had the best of intentions, Jeeni. You always do. But it's really, really hard, and I am dealing. I really am. But it seems like everyone around me is walking on ice. They are trying not to bring him up. My coworkers avoid talking about their boyfriends and husbands. My boss the other day flipped a newspaper over right in front of me because the headline said something about Saudi Arabia or something. So it's not you. People think that somehow something they do or say will remind me of him or what happened to him—"

Jeeni nodded in understanding.

"—but the reality is, Jeeni, I cannot be reminded of him because he is always here with me. I think about him all the time. The moments with me—our last words, our first-grade meeting, our letters from grade school, our first kiss—the small moments, the big moments, everything in between. Our whole lives, Jeeni, we were never separated. Our lives were connected. No one can remind me of him because he is a part of me—it's not just our song, or a headline, or someone else being happy and in love. The crazy idea that I have somehow, even for a moment, forgotten, and you will remind me? That is not how it works. He is just here. No one has the power to take him away or remind me of him because he's with me all the time."

Jeeni reached out her hand across the table, touched Aanya's fist, and squeezed it.

"I want people to know—you are not walking on ice. It cracked and shattered, and it will not be whole again ever, so don't pretend like everything is normal and hide truths from me. Just do what you would normally do, and I will deal with it—I *am* dealing with it. Aren't I?"

Aanya began to tear up.

"I am sorry." Jeeni sighed. "I mean, I am not sorry for the song, but—just . . . everything. It's not fair. I have only known you and Ayaan as one, and even I can't bear the thought of you and him—I mean you alone. I can't begin to imagine your anguish."

"Thanks, Jeeni. All I was saying is—let's not act like everything is okay in order not to bring up the topic. To me, it's not a topic. It's . . . me. It is every part of my being. I mean, I am the first one to admit, I have no idea how to live without him. I don't even know who I am without him, but I guess I will need to learn. I will somehow need to deal and discover what it's like to be Aanya without the Ayaan."

"I get it." Jeeni frowned.

"I wish others would. You know, the other day, I walked into the pantry at work, and these two girls—they just stopped talking and then restarted about the coffee or some bullshit. One of them is having her bridal shower this weekend. I am happy for her; I wanted her to know that. She can talk about it—her happiness will not augment my heartache. The pain is already at maximum capacity, and I am not here to take away from anyone else's happiness. Trust me."

"I understand—or at least I am trying to. I guess we are all trying to somehow make this easier for you, to help however we can, but we don't know how, and we end up doing stupid things."

"Thank you. There is no formula, I guess. Even I don't know how to help myself, but I know you are doing all you can, Jeeni, and I appreciate that. I really do."

The waiter brought over two brimming margaritas.

Aanya picked up her glass and offered a cheers to Jeeni.

"Thank you for today. You are a really good friend—the best! Actually, you are just a very good person, Jeeni. I am sorry I was such an ass to you when you first moved to America."

Jeeni chuckled.

"Yeah, you were pretty mean, dear. I mean, don't get me wrong—I would have been that mean, too, if I had a hot boyfriend at fourteen, but still. Two wrongs don't make a right."

Aanya laughed.

She actually laughed for a whole four seconds as a mariachi band began to play at their table. The two friends looked at each other with content smiles as they downed the margaritas.

Later that night, Aanya walked into her empty apartment. As she passed the sofa, she envisioned her father sitting on the couch next to her while she sobbed, emaciated and broken; her mother sitting on a chair pulled over from the dining table.

"*Beta*, we are just saying, please think about it. This apartment. Everything here will remind you of him. We are not saying forget him. That is not possible. We know better than that. Ayaan was like our son—but you need to consider moving out of here. You need change," her dad reasoned, but Aanya wasn't processing.

Her mother stepped in.

"Maybe you can come back to Georgia for some time. Be with us. You need people around, *beta*."

Aanya glanced at her mother and sighed.

"I can't, Mama. I have work—and trust me, Georgia will be way worse. Everything there will remind me of him—all our memories. All that time together growing up."

Aanya was right: Georgia was infused with way more memories than New York or this apartment they had lived in for only six weeks.

Shalu didn't press further. Aanya would need the distraction of work, but leaving her here alone was not viable.

"Okay, *beta*. Let's keep the apartment. Let's do what makes you most comfortable right now."

Recalling the conversation, Aanya made a note to call her parents in the morning.

Slightly tipsy from the margaritas, she took off her shoes and lined them up next to his loafers. She placed her keys on a tray next to a framed picture of her and Ayaan in high school. While they had hundreds of more beautiful photos together, this awkward adolescent photo was the one Ayaan loved. In the shot, she wore her pale pink dress; and him, his navy-blue polo shirt—the same clothes they wore the day they shared their first kiss.

In fact, it had been taken by the yearbook photographer on that brilliant-idea day, right as they got on their school buses. The photographer, a friend of Ayaan's, had shared the photo with him, but at the time, Ayaan hadn't shared it with Aanya. Instead, on her twenty-first birthday, he gifted her the framed photo, confirming in the process that he would always be the better gift giver.

In the bedroom, she took off her earrings and bracelet, placing them next to his cologne on the dresser. In the bathroom, she brushed her teeth and placed her toothbrush next to his on a vanity tray containing his comb and hair gel, used every morning to perfect his pompadour. In the mirror that she refused to wipe clean, she could make out the faint remnants of their anagrammed names with "Happy two months, hubby!" written beneath it. On the bed—nine months, five days, and fourteen hours after she had kissed his serenely sleeping face for the very last time—she rested her head on his pillow in a pool of her tears; his white lilies, now dry and brittle, dead on her nightstand.

# 25
# New York
*2002*

Under a bright blue sky full of promise gathered an audience, mourning in misery. Aanya, Aditi, Leela, and Kishore sat side by side in the second row of a pop-up auditorium at Ground Zero. Family members of those who had lost loved ones on 9/11 were invited to this, the one-year anniversary of the tragic day. Due to limited seating, Raman and Shalu were not invited but were given an option to watch the remote stream in an auditorium nearby. They opted not to come. Aanya understood. If she had not married Ayaan last summer, would she be here? Would she have been invited?

Special guests, one by one, read the names and ages of those lost on September 11, 2001. As Ayaan's name neared, Aanya caught Kishore-uncle's leg shaking, his foot tapping frantically. She looked up at him, his face still youthful but worn, trying hard not break down.

An image came to her from a picture Ayaan had once shown her of Kishore-uncle's ceremonial farewell from India, full of applause, tears, and excitement, captured on the one camera owned by the most prosperous family in his village. In the middle of this, the only picture taken on that day, adorned in thick red and white flower garlands, was Kishore-uncle, eyes dazed, in black blazer, white shirt, tie, and matching slacks. Around him were his mother, eyes damp, in a white *sari* with gray print; his father, eyes cold, in a white *kurta*; his three

sisters, eyes giddy, in traditional ankle-length skirts and blouses covered with white *dupattas*; and both his paternal and maternal grandparents, eyes proud, matching the wardrobe of his parents. In the
suitcase beside his feet, the only thing of value, according to Ayaan,
was a handful of audio cassettes, including the soundtrack from the
Hindi film *Blackmail*, with the song *"Pal Pal Dil Ke Paas Tum Rahati
Ho,"* sung by the legendary Kishore Kumar. Behind them all was a
vintage train, with signage in both English and Hindi, bound for
Mumbai, where he would catch his flight to America.

Kishore, then twenty-one, came to Georgia Tech to study engineering, but in reality, he was not much of a scholar. In fact, he had a
very vague idea of what engineers did. Chemical, civil, electrical, and
mechanical were all words he had been intrigued by during a quick
briefing by a rather intelligent fellow, a native visiting his village
back in India with a foreign degree and the fanciest brown leather
wing-tipped shoes Kishore had ever seen. The fellow's charm, wit,
and decadent wardrobe had the villagers soaring with pride. One of
theirs had made it abroad—and not just in England or South Africa,
but America!

The bar was set, and it was set sky high. A path had been paved; a
new road had opened—one that everyone, given the limited options
within the village, was eager to try at least once. Kishore jumped on
board. Though thoroughly bluffed, his intelligence and confidence
paid off because by some wild luck of the draw, on a treacherous
monsoon day, he was handed papers embossed with a red seal by
the American Embassy in Mumbai, confirming his student visa to
America.

Shortly upon his arrival in America, Kishore was overwhelmed
not only by the sheer level of academic rigor required to stay afloat on
campus but also by the debauchery available at this so-called prestigious technical institution. The daytime bikini parade on the Quad

was just the beginning, he learned. Kishore was unable to decipher how young men and women smart enough to be admitted to this college, paying large sums of tuition in *dollars*, could drink to the point of unconscious embarrassment from Thursday to Sunday and then leisurely amble into class fully alert on Monday morning, ready to conquer Greek letters in formulas.

This was not at all what Kishore had envisioned as esteemed. He expected to walk onto a campus with boys and girls dressed in a semi-uniform-like fashion: girls in below-the-knee dresses and boys in slacks, button-down shirts, and sweater vests, books at their side, engaging in intellectual conversation, just like he had seen in the one brochure the native-foreign engineer had circulated throughout the village. The enlarged picture at the American Embassy in Mumbai advertising the student visa option—with the boys in maroon blazers and girls in glasses and polka-dotted A-line dresses—seemed to be from an alternate era altogether.

Eventually, Kishore was able to walk through the Quad with some trepidation, even when girls in bikinis were sunbathing. However, he simply could not reconcile the prestige with the partying. The two could not coexist for him, and the fact that they did, right before his eyes, fascinated him. The same attractive girl he had seen smoking and inebriated in a sloth-like state on Saturday night was also the smartest girl in his Monday morning advanced calculus class. He had observed her time and again—she would raise her hand, walk to the blackboard, scribble some numbers and letters, and sit back down with eased satisfaction. Maybe there was something in the cigarettes or the alcohol she consumed that made her smarter than the rest.

Perplexed, he decided to investigate the matter further.

With no one to guard, judge, and hold him accountable, gradu-ate school in America was a welcomed liberation. At first, Kishore's adventures were always perfunctory in nature, as his own culpability made him incapable of being an indulgent participant. He defaulted to becoming a valiant observer, joining Deepak for a night out given the opportunity to be a spectator, a fly on the wall, a researcher taking diligent notes only to unveil a well-kept conspiracy theory: sex, drugs, and alcohol aren't going to kill you, and if in fact they do, the sin will surely not reincarnate you into a cockroach. As he experimented with the sins, everything ingrained in Kishore about morality, principles, and good virtues vanished into the puff of smoke he so satisfactorily exhaled.

But with excursions came expenses. When Kishore mentioned the need for money in an airmail letter that took two months to reach his father—an earnest man employed his whole life by a not-so-earnest boss at the state electricity board of Gujarat—Kishore was sent the phone number of an old friend of a friend's friend, Raman-*bhai*. The number came in a threefold robin-blue airmail envelope, bordered by alternating red and navy-blue rhombuses, in which Kishore's mother, sisters, and grandmother filled every last millimeter with words, writing sideways along the edges of the paper so as not to waste a single cell of space.

Kishore called the number and, within days, was working for Raman-*bhai*. It was work he was not used to and far from glamorous. He started with turning over the rooms of a thirty-four-room motel off I-95, making beds, vacuuming, wiping down dressers, nightstands, and, yes, cleaning toilets and showers. He despised the work, finding it degrading at times, but he appreciated the dollars, and he soon had extra funds to support his futile habits of hanging around the university with the less ambitious campus crowd.

Working off-hours at the motel, he studied just enough to get by and hold on to his student visa. Again, the work was demeaning, but the money was decent. Between the rigor of graduate-level engineering classes, milling around with friends, and work, the work began to appeal to Kishore more and more. The more he worked, the more money he made. The more time he spent off-campus at the motel, the more money he made; the more he made, the more he wanted to work.

For once, it was a simple formula that made sense to Kishore—no Greek letters, Xs, or Ys involved. On one side: the more he worked, the more money he made; the harder he worked, the more money he made; the longer he worked, the more money he made. On the other side: the more he read, studied, and mused over complicated mathematical formulas, the worse he did and the less motivated he became. Soon, the solution was evident.

In Raman-*bhai*, Kishore saw his future. Work hard, really, really hard, the kind of hard where you are cleaning thirty-four toilets and turning over thirty-four filthy rooms reeking of alcohol, marijuana, and sex within hours and still running the oak-lined registration desk like a boss—that he could do. In a nation where he was invisible, working hard while holding his head low granted him the audacity to dream the American Dream so that, one day, his son could lift his head high and be visible. Then, just as he was about to reach that goal, it all came crashing down—literally—on his son, who endured the nightmare of a nation.

Kishore-uncle's leg shook more frantically, his foot tapping harder with each passing name. Aanya turned to him, gave him a warm smile, and squeezed his hand, holding it tight, calming his leg. She couldn't help thinking about holding Ayaan's hand the day Kishore-uncle was shot, comforting him in the very same way.

On the stage, the mayor introduced a middle-aged woman whose husband, a firefighter, had died in Tower One. She continued to read names. Six names in:

"Ayaan Kishore Parekh, twenty-four."

Kishore-uncle began to weep, audible sobs, and instantly Aanya hated that woman. She hated her for saying her husband's name out loud, for announcing to the world that Ayaan Kishore Parekh—a devoted husband, a kind brother, and the greatest of sons—was dead. She hated her! She hated her for putting a rubber stamp on the finality of their reality—a future without Ayaan.

# Part III

# 26

# New York
## *2004*

The one window, backing up to the apartment building next door, allowed for little light even on a sunny day. So, of course, the dark clouds today—in anticipation of a snowy February weekend—called for all three lamps, one on each nightstand and the third on the dresser, to be switched on, carpeting Aanya's bedroom with a haze of yellow gloom.

"What do you want to do with this, Aanya?"

Aditi pulled out a decorative box from the closet, printed with lavender-and-magenta paisley and embellished with gold-plated hinges.

Aanya seized the box from Aditi and nudged her to the bed.

"Come here, sit."

Aanya lifted the lid off the box. In it were dozens of paper triangles, folded from loose-leaf paper, white with light-blue lines, along with a couple of notebooks, one spiral red and the other decorated in burlap. On the exposed side of the triangles were little doodles in different-colored ink. There were some with bubble hearts in red ink and others with an emboldened "A+A." One in particular had two stick figures holding hands, a boy with no distinct clothing and a girl with a wedge-shaped skirt and stringy shoulder-length hair grazing her polka-dot shirt.

One note had a simple flower, brown in the center, with six yellow circles around it. Two petals, also sketched as circles, were on the ground below it by the stem. In super-tiny letters next to the flower, it said, "He loves me, he loves me not." The doodles were elementary, childlike, and categorically cute, making Aditi smile unwillingly.

At the bottom of the box was a pile of greeting cards, but only the top one was visible. It said "Aanya and Ayaan" on it, and the "Y" in their names was shared, with one name written perpendicular to the other. Around the names, there was a heart—the image was a duplicate of the one Ayaan and Aanya had drawn together in the first grade.

"These are all the notes Ayaan and I wrote back and forth in school—every single one. We would pass them to each other in class or drop them in each other's lockers between classes. Sometimes, we would exchange them in the halls when we had a few minutes to catch up."

"Oh my gosh, how damn cute! You saved them all." Aditi made a puppy-dog face with wide eyes and a pitying frown. "I remember folding the notes in this way, Aanya, into little triangles and asking classmates to pass them around, but this is next-level stuff. You have hundreds of them here—with the doodles and the meticulous lettering, they are works of art."

Aditi winked at Aanya but suddenly felt malaise—perhaps a pang of bitterness. As long as she could remember, Aanya had always been the center of her brother's life. Yes, he was *her* brother, and their relationship was good—solid, in fact—but she had nothing like what Aanya had with him. She definitely didn't have the permanence of mementos like this—not one thing in his own words for her, something special between the two of them that she could hold in her hand, caress, touch, read again and again. All she had were elusive memories of a childhood spent running between motel rooms and playing hide-and-seek, Connect Four, and—oh wait, a flash of something, and then she saw it clearly—the Game of Life, with a handmade birthday card that read, "Happy birthday, Aditi, officially you owe me one. From Ayaan, Papa, and Mummy."

On Aditi's tenth birthday, Ayaan had convinced their parents to buy her a birthday gift. This was not the norm in their household. They celebrated birthdays lightly, with a favorite dish and maybe a humble, homemade cake, but there were no cards, gifts, balloons, or parties. While birthdays felt special, they were usually no-frills affairs—though Aditi's tenth birthday was different.

When she turned ten, she received the Game of Life, a board game. Aditi was in the fourth grade then and had played the game regularly during recess for about three months. After the students finished lunch, they were given twenty minutes each day for free play. They could venture outside on the field or opt to remain in the cafeteria and take advantage of the games, puzzles, and crafting supplies on the shelf next to the industrial kitchen.

Consciously avoiding the Georgia sun as advised by her mother, Aditi always opted for the indoors. Even at that early age, Aditi (through muted comments and her own observations) was aware that her complexion was the darkest in her family, even darker than her father's. Her brother had inherited their mother's olive complexion, while the genes of her paternal grandfather—who happened to be three shades browner than her father—had navigated their way to her. Conscious of her complexion, Aditi at first avoided outdoor recess, even when her friends begged her to play outside. Over time, though, she continued to stay inside for a different reason: staying in meant she could play the Game of Life with the introverts.

Ayaan knew about this–not the avoiding sun part, but the staying in and playing games part—because Aditi prattled on about it endlessly. "*Bhai*, there is this little plastic car—I always pick blue—and you move it along the board, and you get a little spike for getting married and each kid you have. You get to go to college, and there is this white circle thing you spin. It's like the coolest thing. It's so much fun with the little people spikes and all. I wish we had it so we could play! I had two kids today, and Lizzy had one—we did not get to finish, but we are going to start at the same place tomorrow. Lizzy said it was okay to do that. We can just set it up from the middle—do you think that is allowed, or is she making up the rules, *bhai*? Which she may be doing because she is, like, way ahead of me in the game."

On the morning of Aditi's tenth birthday, Leela, Kishore, and Ayaan presented the Game of Life to Aditi at the breakfast table with Ayaan's handmade birthday card. Aditi literally cried with joy. Brother and sister played the game for the rest of the day, stopping only when their mini plastic cars could hold no more children and they had become too rich and accomplished to continue. Aditi later found out that Ayaan had expended much energy on the the whole thing by taking advantage of their mother feeling a bit emotional about her baby growing up and had persuaded her to drive to Kmart and purchase the game at an overpriced $9.99.

Even though her brother loved her and had, in fact, proved it by playing Life with her incessantly even when he was exhaustively bored of it, Aditi had always felt secondary. She had never given this much thought, but now that he was gone, she resented Aanya slightly for being his number one—for preoccupying much of her brother's time, and for having all these handwritten, tangible, meaningful relics. His love, his words, for her to hold and read over and over and over again.

Jealousy quickly crept up Aditi's throat as she wished for that treasured Game of Life and homemade birthday card. *Where were they now?* Why hadn't she taken care of them? Why had she not savored each and every thing he ever gave her, did for her . . . ?

"I wish I had spent more time with him, Aanya. I feel like we could have done so much more together."

Aditi surprised herself with her own transparency as Aanya's face scrunched up, perplexed.

"I mean, you got so much time with him, and you have all this stuff. Notes you can read again and again proclaiming his love for you. I have nothing like this. Nothing I can hold, just to feel his love, his presence, that he was indeed real—that I had a brother. It kind of makes me jealous."

Aanya pursed her lips. "I am sorry. I didn't—I never stopped to think it would bother you."

"It didn't bother me at all, not all this time, but now—I guess I didn't know his time was limited, and I should—" Aditi closed her eyes, forcing the tears back. "I should have made more of an effort to, you know, hang out with him more, just brother and sister. I took him for granted and assumed he would always be there for me because he always *was* there. I love him so much. I wish I had actually told him that more often, but I usually didn't. We didn't do that in our family—you know how it is, but now . . . I wish so bad I'd told him regularly."

Aanya stood up and moved to Aditi's side of the bed. She sat next to her, put her arms around her, and gave her a warm embrace. Aditi softly rested her head on Aanya's shoulder.

"He loved you, too—so much, Aditi. Trust me, I know. I know you don't have all this memorabilia, but you don't need all this to know he loved you. You both had a great relationship, and he was so proud of you. If he knew that you were considering med school to live out his legacy, he would be gloating—his face would literally glow with pride."

Aditi turned towards Aanya and peered into her eyes.. ..

"But you know what he would also say, right? Do what you want and not what he wanted. You know that, right, sweetie? He loved you for you, not for what you do for him now. You know that, right?" Aanya said.

"I know, but I am kind of good at all the sciences, and I do like it. Anyway, who knows if I will get into med school—let's not get ahead of ourselves."

Aditi stilled and gave Aanya an apologetic smile.

"I am so sorry, Aanya. I didn't mean anything bad by, you know—what I said. I am just missing him so much, and it came out the wrong way."

"I know. Don't worry about a thing—and you are *so* getting into med school, smarty pants. Who are we kidding here? I just want you to know that he was *your* brother, and he will always be. You are the one living out his dreams. I, on the other hand, am just a hot mess—trust me."

Aanya looked around the bedroom and sighed.

"I can't even manage to pack up his things without having a nervous breakdown."

Upon Aanya's request, Aditi had come to help her clear out Ayaan's things from the apartment.

As Aanya lethargically moved toward an acceptance of her reality, she was incapable of managing both her psychological state and the simple practicality that the situation required. What should she do with his stuff?

A host of articles on grieving advised her to "keep what is significant and sentimental and let the other stuff go. It's just stuff." It sounded reasonable enough, but Aanya was inept, of course, at making such distinctions. Nothing was just stuff. It all had a story, a significance, a sentimentality, or a charming, humorous, and loving memory attached to it. Most of Ayaan's possessions were already back in Georgia, safely tucked away in boxes in the attic or neatly piled in the back of a closet. Everything of his here, in this apartment, was a vestige of *their* story, of their two months of life together as husband and wife, making it all indispensable.

A week after their wedding, they had moved in with a few

suitcases and a box of memories, yet half the closet was still lined with his clothes, and the rest of his possessions were still scattered around the apartment. Most days, Aanya coveted it all. Staring at his side of the closet, imagining him in the button-down baby-blue shirt he wore on their two-month anniversary, smiling with gratification at the *chole bhature* he had prepared for her with all his love.

That anniversary evening, she had unbuttoned the same blue shirt one by one, teasing him with each move, with long drawn-out kisses as they slow-danced to their favorite Hindi classics. Eventually, it heated up, and the shirt found its way to the floor. The next morning, Aanya picked it up and inhaled the passion-laden scent before laying it down on Ayaan's nightstand.

She had stared at the shirt through dazed, blurry eyes, just lying there on the mahogany table for days, weeks, after, before she finally let her mother hang it back up. On occasion, she would still put the cotton fabric against her cheek and take a deep inhale, absorbing the remnants of his scent and the intimacy they shared on their very last night together.

On top of the closet shelf were their wedding trousseaus: his a beige *sherwani* trimmed with maroon embroidery and hers the same maroon all over with a beige *dupatta*. They were protected in a large fabric sachet, untouched since they were packed away the day after their nuptials. She often thought about donating the contents in the fabric package, but she hesitated.

What if wearing it was a bad omen? Was she igniting a dark and tragic fate for the couple destined for such misleadingly colorful garments sparkling with life? Should the clothes just be tossed, like *stuff*, in the trash so they could do no harm to anyone else? Clearly, such decisions were beyond her abilities, hence Aditi was commissioned and sent on behalf of her parents to help Aanya clear out Ayaan's belongings.

The plan was to take Ayaan's clothes and other belongings back to Georgia, save them until the family's next vacation to India, and donate them to those in need. Since Aanya was static in her decisions, she had concurred with the plan, wondering all along if she should stick a widow's warning in the wedding trousseau: "WARNING: Wear at your own risk, as adorning yourselves with the enclosed may cause hazard to your marriage. The past predicates that while love and marriage may thrive, the bride or groom may be doomed with an early demise, possibly by crazy people convinced that driving planes into buildings, killing thousands in the name of God, earns them martyrdom." Perhaps the poor kismet of an otherwise idyllic couple, glittering in the moonlight in hues of scarlet, could be averted by her simple warning.

"So, what do you want to do with the box? We definitely cannot donate it," Aditi joked, holding a handful of triangle notes in her hand.

Aanya reached into the box and picked out the triangle with the itty-bitty writing and the flower petals dwindling to the ground. She could not recall the contents of the note but knew these notes were always innocent enough. She opened it carefully, untucking the fold so the paper could unravel.

On top of the page, the date and time were in blue ink, as they always were on all their notes. Aanya began reading out loud.

*November 24, 1992. 9:23 PM*

*Hi Ayaan,*

*I am just going to go ahead and say this! I have been thinking about this all weekend. I saw how you were helping Jeeni with her English homework last Thursday. You practically wrote the whole damn essay for her. HELLO! SHE CAN SPEAK ENGLISH. She is a smart girl. There was no need for you to be soooo extra helpful. You are such a Goody Two-shoes—and by the way, you touched her hand like four times and her shoulder once. What the heck? If you like her so much, just tell me! I can handle it! I will be furious with you* and probably hate you forever, but I refuse to be number two. I will be happy to let you go. You got that?

Still yours and still pretty angry three days later,


Aanya


"Wow, I had totally forgotten about that. Boy, did I have issues!" Aanya rolled her eyes.

"Well, I get it! I guess no one likes being number two." Aditi grinned. "Did Jeeni know about this—your totally unwarranted jealousy?"

"I am sure she had a clue. I was kind of a you-know-what to her for a while there—and about this, I am pretty sure Ayaan did something over the top to convince me that he did nothing wrong and it was all in my head."

"Hello? He really *didn't* do anything wrong—definitely in your head!" Aditi reminded her as they both chuckled.

"You are so right, Aditi. He was the best—he honestly didn't know how to do wrong."

"Yup, *bhai* was always the good one, and I the black sheep—like, literally."

"Please, missy, you are absolutely gorgeous, and you know it—and black sheep don't get straight As in college! So let's get back to the good stuff; wanna read more?"

"Of course, this is so much fun. I get to learn how not-perfect you are. Angry Aanya is just what I need to snap out of my jealous mode," Aditi joked.

November 25, 1992. 9:54 AM


My Dear Aanya,

YOU ARE KIDDING ME, RIGHT? I would apologize, but I

cannot because I did NOTHING WRONG. Only guilty people say sorry.

In any case, I have a surprise for you this weekend—my birthday, of course! After this weekend, you will never question my love for you again! By the way, you better have a good gift for me!

Yours, and still very much innocent of any alleged crime, especially adultery.


Ayaan

PS: Oh, wait! Adultery would imply that you and I have—you know, like, actually been together, so I can really not be guilty there, can I, missy? Don't worry; will wait as long as it takes, my love!


Aditi blushed at the postscript. Aanya quickly folded it up and slipped it back before any questions ensued about the latter. Luckily, most of the notes contained very little about the couple's intimacy, so, one by one, the two of them—once friends, then sisters-in-law, and now friends again—sat on the plush down comforter and read the contents of hundreds of the little triangles.

Aditi felt even more jealous. In note after note, their affection, the purity, the innocence of their love was so implicit, it did not need any declaration. It was palpable in each ordinary word inscribed:

"I got a B+ on the lab work—can you believe it? I think Mr. Bara just hates me . . ."

"I think Mira is applying to Emory, but Steve is not. You think her parents know about them? Someone's about to be in trouble."

"I think they know we snuck out to the movies last week. My mom asked me to see the project we were working on. I said I left it at your house. Anyway, my mom is going to invite you guys to dinner Saturday. I can't wait to see you. What should I wear? You pick."

Throughout the afternoon, Aanya and Aditi reveled in the trivialities of grades and gossip, teachers and teenagers, quizzes and colleges—and, of course, love and marriage. They laughed deeply until the early evening. Then, to avoid the bitter cold and still-projected twelve inches of snow, they ordered pizza, shared a bottle of white wine, and went back to the bedroom to continue packing.

Thanks to the vino, they were giddy and ripe with emotions. They spent the evening mostly in silence, folding Ayaan's shirts from the closet one by one. There was an occasional "I like this shirt" or "This color suited him well" in somber voices. Tears flowed freely—on and off, with little warning—from both sets of eyes. They cried deeply that night, making up for the laughter that afternoon, concurring that the Indian proverb their parents had repeated to them over and over as children must be true: "Don't laugh too much, or you will cry twice as hard later."

The weight pushed them into both lethargy and unspoken urgency: *Let's get this packing done so we can be free of this emotional baggage tomorrow.* At 1:00 a.m., they lined up the five file-sized boxes and one suitcase by the front door and resigned their physically taxed and emotionally exhausted bodies to the king-size bed.

The next morning, they slept in, woke up refreshed, and brunched with homemade green pepper and onion omelets. Avoiding the still-predicted winter storm, which had yet to release a single snowflake, they spent the afternoon watching classic Hindi movies and snacking on pints of Ben and Jerry's. Finally, after waiting all day for the never-arriving snow, they gave up and stepped out for a meal. At dinner, they decided libations were in order, not only to lighten the weight of the previous day but to celebrate their friendship and Ayaan. They managed successfully to celebrate it all, stumbling home a few hours later.

The next day, President's Day, Aditi double-parked her car in front of Aanya's building. With the help of the landlord, Mr. Ramos, the three of them made three total trips—four flights up and down the walk-up—to load Aditi's trunk with the boxes and suitcase.

As the sun peeked between buildings and the cold nipped at their toes, emotions heightened, the two held each other tight in a prolonged embrace.

"It's a long drive; you should get going."

Aanya finally nudged Aditi out of her arms, tears prickling both their eyes.

"I know. Wish you were coming with me."

"Me, too. Take care of yourself—and remember, you never were or will be second."

Aditi smiled. "Thanks, Aanya. You take care of yourself, too."

By midafternoon, off I-95 somewhere in Virginia, Aditi craved food, coffee, and a bladder break. She exited the highway at the next ramp. As the amber light turned red, she hit the brakes and waited, catching in the rearview mirror a white car curving onto the exit ramp behind her. The white SUV she had caught at a safe distance pulled up next to her in a flash.

A man in his mid-thirties, pale yet sunburned to a fleshy pink, in a worn-out black T-shirt with disheveled, dirty blond hair, rolled down his window. Aditi, assuming he needed directions, opened the passenger window. As the glass descended slowly, the man's mouth opened in a loud roar.

"Learn to drive, you fucking terrorist, or go home!"

The light turned green, and the white SUV sped away.

Aditi, paralyzed for a moment, regained consciousness, then turned left and left again to revert back onto I-95, thinking, *But my brother is—!*

# 27
# New York
## *2005*

Aanya ignored his slightly open mouth as he chewed on the bruschetta, focusing instead on taking a sip of her pungent red wine. She detested red wine but had accepted a glass, thinking it not only polite but absolutely necessary to get through the evening. The cramped, dimly lit restaurant was BYOB, and Neel, her date for the evening, was thoughtful enough to bring a bottle—that, too, in an ornate, silver-leafed gift bag designed just for wine. *Thank God!* She needed that wine, as she had promised herself she would give this evening her hundred percent.

Neel's deep-set brown eyes hid behind jet-black hair that slipped easily onto his forehead. Every few minutes, he swept his hair aside with manicured hands, exposing thick, perfectly arched, professionally threaded eyebrows.

"So, Aanya, how do you like living on the Upper West Side?"

Aanya took another sip of her wine, tried hard not to grimace at its bitter taste, and smiled.

"It's fine, sometimes a little too perfect, but I don't spend a lot of time there, so I'm not sure I can answer that question fairly. I am mostly at work and usually just go home to sleep."

Aanya voiced no apparent discontent, hinting that was how she preferred it.

"You sound like a workaholic. Can I pour you another glass?"

Aanya polished off her glass, avoided a sour face, and extended the empty glass to Neel.

"I enjoy what I do, so it doesn't seem like I am working."

"Ahh, I see. Well, I must find me a job like that."

She smirked. Finally, the wine was kicking in.

"So corporate law is not treating you right, I am guessing?"

It was a typical, highly crowded New York City restaurant: too many people, too little space, and tables so close together that you either had to whisper your conversation up close or fight the instrumental music humming through the speakers, intended to grant some privacy to each conversation.

Aanya found herself either getting too close to Neel so he could hear what she was saying or backing up and speaking loudly to supersede the white noise and humdrum conversations of other patrons. This choice, along with the proximity of the couple next to them, made the whole situation absolutely agonizing. To top it off, the restaurant decided to dim the lights even further, as though with each passing minute, they had to make a concerted effort to set some kind of mood.

*Give your hundred percent, Aanya*, she reminded herself.

Ignoring the dimming, Neel continued.

"It's interesting work, but not work I wake up and get excited about. It's work I get up and run to because it's a pressure cooker about to explode—always some impending crisis and fire to put out. Sometimes, I'm up at five in the morning because my BlackBerry is just blowing up—"

Neel's face grimaced a little as the last two words carelessly slipped out: *blowing up*. Aanya didn't flinch.

"I mean, I really despise the BlackBerry; it's a curse! I can't seem to get away from work because of it."

"Sounds very intense. Do you get some time on the weekends, away from it all?"

"Yes, sometimes, when I intentionally disengage from work. That's when I go home to visit my parents in Long Island—other times, I grab dinner or drinks with some friends. I like to work out, so sometimes I hit the gym, and on nice days, I try to do some running on Riverside. It's been too cold lately, so I try my best to get to the gym. What about you? You get a little time away from work?"

Aanya took a sip of wine, then chased it with a sliced olive sitting atop a piece of bruschetta. Her index finger hung in the air slightly in front of her mouth so that Neel understood to wait until she had swallowed the olive. She was buying time, trying to make sure her answer was not too canned.

"I do pretty much the same thing. Hang out with some friends, have dinner, drinks, go for a run—and, on occasion, I work on weekends."

The words came out so cookie-cutter from her mouth that even she believed them to be true. Whether it was the truth or not, she wanted it to be true, so she stuck to the old adage: tell a lie long enough, and it will become your reality.

Besides, it was easier than explaining why she was the only one at the office most Saturday afternoons, finishing up projects long before their deadlines, picking up the slack for coworkers on vacations and personal leaves, thoroughly pissing off the ones that had any sense of work-life balance in the process. She failed to mention that she would go home most nights, eat milk and cereal, and go to bed.

On weekends, she would always walk home as it took up more time: making unnecessary stops, sitting on benches, and getting lost in her thoughts for hours until, all of a sudden, her phone would ring or ping with a text—or her fingers would lose all sensation during the frigid winter months.

In those moments, she would take the call—usually, it was her mother, Aditi, or her father, maybe Jeeni or Jaya. Sometimes it was Kishore-uncle or Leela-aunty, but those had lessened in recent years.

In all honesty, it was all the people who knew her well and cared for her deeply, but it was never the one person she still longed for—it was never *him*, and it never would be.

Through those calls, Aanya had become skilled at the art of non-conversation—always asking others questions that required long answers while giving simple, closed, one-word responses herself.

"How are you doing, Aanya? Did you work today?" Aditi would inquire in the lightest of tones.

"Yes, but only a couple of hours; I have a deadline coming this week," Aanya would answer swiftly before turning it around.

"How did your exam go the other day, Aditi? Did you get it back?"

Aditi was now a first-year med student at Emory, living at home. She had tried living there for the first semester but could not fully engage in campus life, nor did she really care to, so she shifted back home. When she told her parents that she couldn't concentrate on the work and was moving back home the next semester, Kishore and Leela tried to cajole her into staying there, giving it another shot, but deep down, even they wanted her home.

The magnetic pull of her parents was so strong that campus life did not stand a chance compared to the bond they shared as a family. The three of them, tucked away in their motel off I-95, felt safest at home together. Though years had passed, there they could hide, mourn, grieve, and live in their own ways, not needing to explain anything to anyone.

"It went really well. Aced it."

"I had no doubt. And how is everything else—your parents?"

Aanya always asked about Leela and Kishore and Aditi understood why—the weight of surviving their son (and her brother) never stopped pulling Aanya down.

"They are okay—the usual."

Aditi would continue, apprising Aanya on the latest, which mostly consisted of studying and home life and the idiosyncrasies of motel guests, something only Aanya could understand, having shared the same upbringing. The pleasantries were exchanged every two to three days, and although they were mundane conversations, they both found deep-seated comfort in hearing each other's voice and the normalcy of a routine catch-up.

With dinner ordered, Neel and Aanya continued with the routine back-and-forth, wrestling with the noise, clamor, and crowd with each word. All too superficially, they exchanged a bit about what they had studied in college, acquaintances they had in common, their upbringing, and their tethered roots to the motherland.

The banality of the date and the routine conversation did not seem to faze Neel. It felt as if he was accustomed to this—drink some wine, have dinner, chat a little, and see if something clicks. If not, try it again another day, with another date or two, and wait for the infamous click.

Dating, it seemed, was much like adjusting to mediocre music. It may not sound great at first, but replaying it over and over as they do on the radio somehow makes it sound better over time—even when the tune remains unchanged. You had to be in it to win it, playing and replaying, listening over and over, hoping that one day the notes would harmonize, and something would just click.

Aanya could not think of anything more agonizing. She had known nothing *but* the click. In fact, she had known much more than that: she had known the kind of love found only once in a lifetime, and she was convinced her chance had passed—literally.

Throughout the evening, neither crossed a line. Neel probably because he was unsure what the boundary was, and Aanya because at some point—she didn't know exactly when—she gave up on the *give it your hundred percent.*

Aware of the growing horde in the vestibule between the main door and the faux-plastic entry temporarily in place to keep the cold out, they both passed on dessert. The usual anticipated end of the date was thoroughly uneventful. They pushed through the line of people waiting to be seated, and since there was no warm, gooey, kiss-me-please feeling, they ended with an awkward handshake and polite goodbyes.

Neel may not have been an interesting date, but Aanya was impressed by what a gentleman he was when he helped her slip on her coat and offered to hail a cab. Pushing no boundaries and making no moves, he was not slick, nor a total oddball. He was genuine, decent-looking, accomplished, and, by all measures, an excellent catch. All of this made Aanya even more remorseful, as she could not formulate one honest, legitimate rationale for why she did not want to see him again.

She decided to walk the twenty-three blocks and two avenues home, partly because she liked the crisp late-fall air and, more importantly, because it granted her a sense of normalcy. As usual, she would make random stops, sit on benches, or stand and people watch from a peaceful spot. She recalled the backstories she and Ayaan would develop, their sweet eight-year-old imaginary world in which anything was possible—a southern boy with hazel eyes, red hair, and freckles could twirl in *chanya choli* until his heart burst with glee while the two of them fell out of the swings from uncontrollable laughter. The cheerful memory brought a smile to Aanya's face as she walked down Fifth Avenue.

She passed a couple holding hands tightly as the woman buried her head into her husband's or boyfriend's chest. They were both gorgeous, dressed to impress, down to the shoes. The woman wore a pink-lemonade pea coat and the man a fitted military-style wool jacket—the kind of couple you would expect to walk down Fifth Avenue in New York City arm-in-arm, impeccable in taste and magnificence. If someone were to snap a photograph of them and edit the ruckus of the city out of it, leaving only the Hermés windows behind them visible, Hermés would save enough on models and marketing to feed an island nation or two.

Aanya began developing their backstory. He was from the Midwest, and came to the big city to become an actor but took a white-collar job to pay the bills. Before long, the money was too good, and after meeting the love of his life—a southern girl working her way up to sous chef at a top restaurant in the city—he no longer cared for acting.

Married? No, but soon. He would propose after he got permission from her father—a good old-fashioned guy who did not desire much more than a serene family life.

Essentially, Aanya envisioned a life opposite of what the Hermés models glorified. No luxurious lofts in the city with million-dollar views, no daily happy hours at the city's finest, no sunbathing on yacht decks or over-the-top vacations at private villas in Italy. Her not-so-Hermés couple preferred cozy, fireplace-lit movie nights in an unknown, unassuming blue-collar suburb.

Before deciding how many children they would have, she was distracted by street-side honking and profanities between a yellow taxi and a livery cab driver. She lost her train of thought, but as the Hermés couple with the not-so-Hermés life passed her, she smiled subtly, appreciating their uninhibited moment. Nothing made her happier than the bliss of a moment, untouched, untainted, unacknowledged by the harshness and impermanence of reality.

To her surprise, her imagined backstories had grown increasingly optimistic over time. She smiled again, wider and more visible this time. Ayaan would have been proud of her progress.

Aanya entered her apartment to find her mother watching a rerun of *Seinfeld*. Shalu spent less time with Aanya these days, dropping in every four or five weeks and staying for a week. When this had first started, Aanya was irritated with the attention and inconvenience of the visit, but as with all matters, she adjusted, grew accustomed, and developed a fondness for her mother's visits.

Her parents had more time now. Though they still owned three motels down in Georgia and lived on-premises at one of them (the one where Aanya had grown up), they were doing much less when it came to the day-to-day management. Most of it was now done by some hired long-distance family, friends of friends, usually new arrivals to the country looking for their piece of the American pie. Never the kind to pull the ladder out from under them, her parents always found new and innovative ways to make the newcomers feel at home.

Through the decades, they had advocated and helped dozens of families navigate their lives in America. With each passing year, Aanya appreciated more and more the time she had spent sharing her room with infants, rowdy children, and teens, all temporary residents until they found some work, built some savings, and could afford to live on their own. Her parents always assisted with applications to local factories, phone calls, and private loans. It seemed to Aanya that her parents felt it their personal responsibility to steer every Gujarati immigrant they remotely knew to find the American Dream, which ideally meant owning their own business one day.

More recently, after her mother had revealed the full story of what happened to her grandparents, Aanya better understood her motivation for such generosity. Watching Shalu lose her childhood home in Uganda and then her parents as a result, Raman also never wanted anyone to experience the pain of not having a home—not if he could help it. So, together, he and his wife had made it their personal mission to help anyone they could—even if it meant their daughter grew up sharing her modest room, toys, and childhood with a steady stream of so-called family.

*   *

One time, when Aanya was nine, her father's uncle's son (or something like that), his wife, and their five-year-old son were staying with them. While Aanya was at school, the five-year-old cut short the hair of Aanya's one and only Barbie doll.

Shalu expected Aanya to be furious and waited for the reaction when she returned from school. She placed the doll with her distorted haircut on their plastic-covered kitchen table, where the five-year-old boy, visibly scared, was having milk and cereal. Nine-year-old Aanya's face dropped as soon as she noticed it. She looked at the little boy and grimaced before meeting her mother's eyes and giving her a mock *I am fine, Mom* smile. When she walked to the TV, Shalu didn't stop her or push her after-school snack of warm *roti* and *dahi* upon her. She let her daughter go.

Aanya watched an episode of *The Flintstones* followed by an episode of *The Jetsons* in silence. At the end of the second episode, exactly fifty-eight minutes later, Shalu called her to the table for her *roti* and *dahi*. Aanya ate quietly. When she finished, she went to the scared five-year-old boy and colored rainbows with him in a tattered old coloring book.

This was quintessential Aanya, Shalu had learned. When someone stepped on her nine-year-old daughter's toes, so to speak, she shut up and moved on, even if she was furious. There was no wailing, crying, or complaining. There was just the silence of her hurt, anger, sorrow, bitterness, jealousy, offense, and, ultimately, reconciliation in a tightly sealed package of resilience, waiting to dissipate over an escapist TV show or a good novel.

Over time, Shalu had also accepted that grown adults deal with triumphs and tribulations the same way they did as children. Personalities are born and rarely waver. Aanya's resilience was evident in her overwhelming acceptance of the ordinary each and every day. Aanya embraced work; she went on occasional dates, she visited and granted visits from family members, she made beautifully polite conversation, and, although muted, she laughed and danced at weddings, pretending that everything was fine.

As she walked home from her date, Aanya was aware that her mother was home, but she also knew that she would not be waiting for her. Her mother understood that she liked to walk and would come home when she was ready, irrespective of what transpired that evening with Neel. Her mother had gotten better at giving her space.

When Aanya walked through the door that night, Shalu momentarily muted the TV.

Aanya gave her a mock *I am fine, Mom* smile.

Even though the mother in Shalu wanted Aanya to find pure bliss again, prayed for a miraculous date with Neel, and craved every detail of the evening, she refrained from saying a word. Instead, she waved her to the couch.

Aanya removed her shoes and slung her jacket over the coat rack before sinking herself down on the couch and tucking her head into the hollow of her mother's shoulder. Shalu unmuted the TV, and they both continued to watch *Seinfeld*. Resilience and pure love tightly packaged on the couch without a word exchanged, with the nothingness of *Seinfeld* as the great escape.

# 28
# New York
## *2008*

It was only 8:00 a.m., yet her building basked in the golden glow of sunlight and the pavement baked under her feet.

"Hi, guys, remember me?" Aanya asked warmly as she dug around for the keys with one hand and wiped the perspiration off her forehead with the sleeve of the other—failing, after a morning jog, to look presentable for the immaculate couple standing at the entryway to her building.

The girl, perhaps in her mid-twenties, with sleek black shoulder-length hair, and her significant other, clean-shaven and crisp, stood with class as if they had just wrapped up a country club brunch. Her navy linen sundress with white accessories and his navy shorts with a crisp white button-down linen shirt created the picture of put-together, color-coordinated perfection.

A few weeks back, when the couple had toured the building, Mr. Ramos had paused to introduce them to Aanya as she returned from work. Aanya welcomed them graciously to the building and invited them over for a drink should they want to check out her apartment or have questions about the neighborhood.

"Of course we remember! It's Aa . . . Ah . . . definitely something with an 'A' . . . I am sorry," the girl said.

"It's Aanya. Indian, of course, means 'inexhaustible' in Sanskrit. Well, at least according to the internet." She failed to mention that the anagrammed male version, Ayaan, meant "God's gift," a pathway to the sun. *Did names determine destinies?*

"That's really pretty—your name and the meaning," the girl said.

"Thanks. So you guys decided to go with this building?"

"Yes, we love the building, the neighborhood, and the apartment. We are just popping in to sign the lease."

"Great news; welcome! When are you planning to move in?"

The girl made eye contact with her other half and smiled demurely before speaking.

"Well, we just got married on the Fourth of July and are so excited about moving in, but it seems the place will not be available until September. We are going to stay with his parents until then."

"Fourth of July! An Independence Day wedding—that's beautiful!"

An enigmatic, soul-warming glow surfaced on Aanya's face. For a second, she considered sharing that her wedding anniversary was also on the same day but then abstained. She had learned through one too many unpleasant experiences that the story, *her* story, always hung in the air like a bad stench, dampening the liveliest of spirits, tongue-tying people into knots with no smooth transitions to avail themselves. Comic relief never seemed appropriate, irrespective of the comedian or the punch line. It was always too soon, too fresh, too raw.

Putting this bright-eyed couple, brimming with newlywed bliss, through that level of discomfort would not just burst their bubble; it would shatter them. Averting such malice, Aanya silently recited her favorite mantra as she keyed the door open, wishing the date would be more auspicious for them than it had been for her. Positivity and prayer, with no guarantees, were the best she could offer.

"Congratulations, that is wonderful! You guys will really like it here. It is a great neighborhood, and everyone in the building is friendly. Most have been here for years."

As the three of them entered, Aanya noted that the couple was incapable of keeping a straight face. Their smiles were etched onto their faces as if someone were permanently photographing them and they were willingly saying cheese.

"The landlord's office is inside his apartment, as you may know, in 1B."

Aanya pointed them in that direction as she put two quote fingers up for the word "office."

"Thank you," they said in unison.

Almost midway up the first set of stairs, Aanya paused. She leaned over the railing and said, "Umm, I think I am moving out. Not sure when yet, but in the next few weeks. No obligation, but you are welcome to my furniture if you want."

"Oh, really, you are moving? That is too bad. Would you mind if we came by later to check it out? We can't afford new furniture after paying the rent here," the girl said, eyebrows raised, smile intact.

"—and don't forget that big, fat Indian wedding," her husband said in his first solo performance.

"Sure, I am home for a few hours. You know where I live—4B. Come on by when you are done."

"If you don't mind me asking, where are you moving?"

"Well, it's all kind of happening as we speak, but I think I am moving to India. I have an opportunity there through my work, and I just decided I am going to go for it."

"Wow, that is amazing! I so need to get back to India," responded the girl.

"Well, you are always welcome to visit once I settle in," Aanya said preemptively before waving goodbye.

Something about the couple resonated with Aanya, something that made her insides smile as if the three relative strangers had been friends for life. Maybe it was the fact that he had never let her hand go. From the moment she noticed them at the front of her building until they disappeared into Mr. Ramos's office, his hand had remained intertwined with hers, palm touching palm as if glued together for life. Maybe it was the way he looked at her when he joked about the wedding costs, as if it was worth the last penny he had as long as it made her happy. Or maybe it was the fact that, despite their country club facade, they, like her and Ayaan, were desi—presumably children of immigrants, reaping their parents' sacrifices as they embarked on the American Dream.

Whatever it was, the thought of their brimming newlywed smiles starting their married life in this historic building made her sigh nostalgically, solidified her resolve, and brightened her already enlightening morning.

Aanya settled into the love seat of her poorly lit living room with a cup of hot chai, ready to call her parents. She had big news to share.

"Hi, Mama."

"Hi, *beta*, how are you?"

Shalu's voice was perky, almost in its normal state. She was spending much less time in New York these days, visiting every three or four months so she and her daughter could spend the week together cooking, shopping, catching up on gossip, and watching television. Shalu's last visit was in February, around Valentine's Day, and it was now nearly mid-July. Aanya felt like it had been forever since she had rested her head on her mother's lap while her mother twiddled her fingers through her free-flowing hair, caressing her face softly as they watched the latest Bollywood movies, cozied up on the couch.

"That feels so nice, Mama; I love when you play with my hair," Aanya always said.

Shalu, who was always overwhelmingly gratified that her small act brought the happiness her child so much deserved, would continue until Aanya fell asleep. Though Shalu missed her daughter immensely, she was much less worried than she had been in the years soon after. Slowly and steadily, she had begun to see her daughter revitalize.

Aanya was regularly going out with coworkers for happy hour drinks, followed by a casual dinner. She was jogging routinely and taking a variety of classes in rotation: kickboxing, yoga, spin, and Pilates. Her daughter explained to her that "Pilates is just like yoga, but not really—there is equipment involved," and "Spin is just a fancy way of saying a stationary bike, but the class fluctuates in rhythm and intensity." Yoga needed no explanation, and kickboxing could be speculated.

Aanya had also garnered new interest in learning the recipes of her favorite childhood meals, mastering traditional Gujarati dishes like *dal dhokli* and *khaman*. She often invited her spin class buddies over to try out her meals, apprising them of the benefits of certain spices and confirming that the dishes were healthy.

Still at TechLogically, Aanya was working arduously but much less—trying, it seemed, to find some sort of balance between work and play. Her daughter no longer brought her laptop home with a pile of papers on the weekend, and she failed at times to make it to the office by 7:30 a.m., basking instead in the light of a morning jog along the Hudson. She would stop to watch the large cruise ships sail by, waving back at the children on deck who were intensely flailing their arms, attempting to gain the attention of those onshore.

Shalu was acutely aware of all this because she and her daughter conversed on the phone every day—either while Aanya jogged, on Aanya's lunch break, or right before Aanya went to bed. Whenever one or other had a spare moment, they would ring each other to chat. Sometimes the calls would end abruptly with Shalu tending to a needy hotel guest or because Aanya had to go underground for the subway. At other times, the calls would last from five minutes to five hours.

The conversations were much too ordinary, the routine banter about day-to-day happenings, but in those mundane exchanges, Shalu found deep solace. The normalcy of Aanya's bellyaching after a joke her coworker cracked, or the poor luck of being served the worst stale coffee on a particular morning only to be saved by the luck of discovering a delectable, sauce-dripping falafel from a new food truck later that day, was all Shalu needed to hear to know her daughter was doing okay.

"You have to try this place when you come, Mama. The falafels are to die for—so much better than Renu-aunty's, but please don't tell her, of course." Jeeni's mom, Renu-aunty, was known for her Indian fusion falafels, the gold standard in their circle of family friends. No one, including Aanya, who adored her, dared to challenge her home-made tahini sauce—or worse, hurt her feelings about it.

With each passing day, Aanya reported a tiny bit more about her return to a new norm. On weekends, Aanya occasionally babysat Jeeni's one-year-old daughter, urging Jeeni and Jai, her husband, to come into the city for date nights. Aanya found bliss in holding the infant in her arms for hours at a time, snuggling Ria close and inhaling the aroma of a new baby slathered in baby lotion.

When Jeeni would call to check in on her baby, Aanya would tell the couple to stay out later and add a show or movie to the date. "You hardly ever get out, Jeeni. It's only 9:00 p.m. This is your big night out; you can't be done already! Go do something crazy—live it up."

Not knowing what else to do, Jeeni and Jai, on pleasant days, would stroll all the way from a restaurant in Chelsea to Aanya's apartment, granting Aanya another sixty to ninety minutes with their angel. Even after the delay, Aanya and Ria had a secret pact to stall their goodbyes as long as possible—first with a soiled diaper, which Aanya despised but accepted with the territory, followed by hunger pangs, and lastly, a wail audible throughout the building.

Aanya loved baby Ria, and Ria reciprocated, weeping and clutching Aanya's hair when Mommy and Daddy arrived to take her home.

All this Shalu knew, each insignificant little detail, because Aanya kept her apprised of all things big and small. Shalu listened with utmost attention, understanding that with each intricate detail, her daughter was reconciling and healing. The light of her daughter's strength was poking through with every ordinary act she embraced. After years of dimness, the clarity was luminous.

"I have something to tell you guys. Is Dad there? Put me on speaker, Mama."

"Really? What is it?" Shalu said.

"Mom, put Dad on speaker first."

"Okay, okay, *beta*, he is here—the speaker is on."

Raman lowered the morning paper, which he was causally perusing while sipping his chai.

"Okay, we are both here."

"Hi, *beta*." Aanya's father confirmed his presence.

"Hi, Dad. Okay, ready? Please try not to overreact, but I was asked to move to India for work. There is a great opportunity, and I am thinking of maybe taking it."

Aanya understood that while her decision had already been made, it could not be presented as such to her parents. She thought it best to propose it as an idea and not a definite, granting them the needed time to absorb, vet, and respond.

"What do you mean, *beta*?" her father asked.

"There's a role in Gurgaon, India, and Ari thinks I would be a perfect fit."

"You can't live in India, *beta*; you don't know . . . how—" Shalu said.

"TechLogically wants a market presence in India, and they want me to lead the sales team. It's kind of a big deal and exciting. Don't you think?"

"Gurgo . . . ?"

"Mama, it's like the new business-tech capital of India, kind of like Bangalore. Gurgaon, right outside Delhi. I was telling you about it, like, a while ago. Don't you remember all the colleagues I have working there? The call centers and tech companies and whatnot—remember?"

While her father knew of the place from his habitual read of the *New York Times* each morning, her mother less so. Aanya could imagine her parents in sync questioning her whole proposal in silence with just their facial gestures.

"The housing and stuff will be taken care of before I get there—I think! We didn't talk about that yet. Ari just asked me to think about the possibility this weekend. He thinks knowing the language and culture will help me tremendously."

Aanya sounded excited—*alive.*

"Okay, *beta*. It sounds okay, I guess. Maybe worth finding out more. I do keep reading about India in the papers. Bangalore, Hyderabad, and Gurgaon. But you need to find out more, ask for details. Is this temporary, or will you be relocated for—"

Aanya felt her father's voice sink at the thought of his only daughter permanently moving thousands of miles away. It didn't matter that it was India, his native land, his first home that he had so longingly missed in his early days in Uganda and then America. This was about his daughter, her comfort, and his desire to have her as close to him as possible.

"I'm not sure. I definitely don't want to commit to it forever. Don't worry, Dad. Let me talk to Ari Monday and at least tell him I am interested."

Aanya assured them.

"Just think about it a little bit, *beta*, like Ari suggested. It is a big decision, and I am sure there is no rush," her mother said.

"I will, Mama. Let's talk again later—I need to go now. I need a shower, bad. I stink."

Aanya flipped the phone closed and leaned her head back onto the love seat.

On the jog that morning, as she ran through the idea that Ari, her long-term boss and mentor, had presented to her the day before, she was surprisingly drawn to it. Her career was doing okay—great, actually. Three promotions in seven years, not bad. But it wasn't the work—it was her. It was her banal existence. It felt like her life in New York had stagnated, taken its course. People were getting married, having babies, buying homes in the suburbs, and she—she was still in the same place, both in time and space, where her life had collapsed—literally.

She had picked up the pieces here and there, a little at a time, but now it was all static. It was as if she were watching everyone else wave goodbye from the deck of a moving cruise ship while she stood still onshore each morning, unmoved. Her life had plateaued, and undeniably, she needed a challenge, a new beginning, a fresh start, a small hill to scale so she could see the other side.

She needed to leave the life in which everyone knew her name, her history, and her tragic story and go to a place where no one knew anything. The idea of such a rebirth was invigorating, full of life, and most importantly, possible in a new land on the other side of the planet.

*Yes, that is it!* That was exactly what she needed—a move to India, she concluded that morning, as the children on the cruise ship once again waved goodbye to her while she stood stagnant onshore.

# 29

# New York
## *2008*

Ari had reserved a private room with one long table. Aanya sat in the middle with four helium balloons floating above her chair. One read "Bon voyage," another "Best wishes," the third "We will miss you," and the last "Farewell," with a silly animated red cat waving her paw goodbye.

Light semi-classical Hindustani music played in the background. *Papad* layered with tomatoes, onions, ground cumin, and red chili pepper lined the table at intervals. Either end of the table had a bottle of wine in a bucket of ice—both white. The room was sparsely lit with Moroccan light fixtures. A waiter of South Asian descent with a light mustache and costume turban came around and filled their water glasses every few minutes, the frequency depending on how well the palate handled the chili-seasoned *papad*.

To the right of Aanya was Aditi and her fiancé, Neev, a first-year resident in med school, followed by her parents, Jeeni, Jaya, Renu-aunty, Devan-uncle, Kishore-uncle, and Leela-aunty, respectively, sitting across from each other. Jai had stayed home with his baby girl, Ria.

Directly across from Aanya was Ari. To the right of Ari was the TechLogically team that Aanya had been a part of since July 2001. They were not all the same faces. Most had disappeared into the cloud of dust and smoke on that tragic day, somewhere on the PATH, subway, elevator, escalator, street, conference room, or their desks. No one knew for sure. These were all deductions made by loved ones to console the soul, based on the last point of contact, desperate calls, text messages, voicemails, and 911 recordings, painful digital remnants in an analog world.

The surviving TechLogically employees, including Ari's team—consisting of Aanya, Samantha, and Oscar—had relocated to Jersey City for almost two years until TechLogically recovered and rented new space in midtown. In those early days, though all four of them showed up to work, sometimes even on weekends, they all understood that there was very little work to occupy them. Sitting on the industrial gray carpet, sun shining through the glass panels, empty cardboard file boxes all around them, they often just stared into the void. There was nothing left, it seemed, except the four of them.

No one knew what to do or where to start, so they started from scratch. Gradually, together, they dug through files and reports sent over from other offices, scraped together numbers and details that had vanished in the haze. Recalling clients' names from memory, looking up their numbers, and saying, "We lost all our data, and we need your help recovering it. Sorry, there will be a delay in our delivery, and we understand if you decide to take your services elsewhere, but we would really appreciate the chance to serve you again." The four of them sat at bare, clutter-free desks, repeating the same message over and over.

To their amazement, their over-the-top, demanding, and at times just plain difficult clients turned supple overnight. People on the other side of the phone did not hang up on them or put them on hold. Instead, they were kind and compassionate, granting them the necessary details, extension, and empathy that TechLogically needed so desperately to survive, revive, and rebuild. Somehow, in the wake of the tragedy, they witnessed a city renowned for its tough, on-the-go attitude slow down and become nimble, placid, and gentle.

It was as if the whole city and all its people were recovering as one, making life at TechLogically bearable.

Sheltered by the shadow of a shared calamity, the four of them—Ari, Aanya, Samantha, and Oscar—built an indestructible bond. In those early days, they stared out the glass windows at the vacant skyline where their office had once stood on the other side of the Hudson and prayed for their vanished colleagues and their families as they held each other tight and cried.

After a long day of cold calls, the four would order takeout and sit together on unoccupied desks—sometimes in silence, at other times with a box of tissues, and on rare occasions with giggles—as they reminisced about the quirks of their deceased coworkers. They missed them all: Julia's crush of the month, Sai's smelly fish, and even Gayle's loudmouthed earsplitting laugh. The four had lost good friends, family, and the most amazing colleagues. They all grieved and suffered, not only from survivor's guilt but the duty and obligation to carry on the legacies of those they had lost.

Despite their losses, they had all somehow triumphed together, and they reckoned this was the reason that, despite their well-sought-after talents, all four of them were still at TechLogically. Undoubtedly, they were TechLogically's greatest success story—the four of them still together, sitting at the table.

Aanya's resplendent face was reflective of not only her perseverance but of Ari, Samantha, and Oscar's victories. They were going to miss Aanya. Without her late nights and weekends in the office during the recovery years, they all would have been disparate and dispersed. It was Aanya who had suffered the greatest loss, yet her diligence, her presence, her persistence, and her sheer will to show up had helped them garner the strength they needed to trudge toward the light —and show up for her. They were here because, despite all that had happened, she was always there. They took pride in this team because here they were, seven years later, together—the survivors.

Ari raised his glass for a toast. The chatter silenced, and all eyes were on him.

"Thank you, everyone, for coming. As you know, this is a bittersweet moment, especially for me and, I am sure, Oscar and Samantha. We have known and worked with Aanya since she started with TechLogically in July 2001.

"Yup, that's right, *that* 2001.

"Everyone at TechLogically knows Aanya as the workaholic go-getter. No joke—clients call and ask for her by name, insisting that they met her at happy hour, she promised them TechLogically would be life-changing for their business, and they needed to know more. There is no doubt she is a TechLogically all-star, definitely no doubt of that, but—"

Ari lightened his tone a notch.

"—there is another side to Aanya that I have had the pleasure to know. She is truly an extraordinary human being. Life has dealt her some very difficult cards, but she has played the hand with strength, dignity, and honor. I am so proud of her professional accomplishments, which are many, but I am so much prouder of her personal triumphs—and for that, I thank and cheer her."

"Thank you, Aanya, for everything! We are all here because you were there."

He looked her directly in the eye.

"I think you know what I mean. I—we—will miss you more than you know."

Ari's eyes glazed over with tears.

Others around the table clapped, oohed, and ahhed.

Aanya blushed, pushing back her own sniffles.

"Aanya's turn," Jaya shouted.

Aanya smiled at her and raised a glass.

"First of all, thank you, Ari, for those kind words. We have definitely been through a lot—and you are right: we have done okay.

Thank you for everything, including this opportunity abroad. I never imagined myself working in India, but I suppose it is a new era. I am going to miss this team so much.

"Oscar, Samantha, Ari—no words can describe what we have shared together. Thank you for being there for me, all of you. It has been a long journey, as you know, and you guys have been there every step of the way. I, too, can say I am here because you were there. Thank you so much for that. You know what you all mean to me."

Aanya's voice began to crack as she blinked back tears. Oscar and Samantha followed suit. Ari extended the cloth napkin to his eyes. After a brief pause, Aanya pushed on.

"Okay then, let's move on! You all have had enough of sappy Aanya all your lives. I guess all I am saying is thank you for being my New York family. Thank you for the long chats over coffee, the happy hour laughter, and the client gossip. Thank you, Ari, for inviting my family to this wonderful farewell. I couldn't have asked for anything more—"

Aanya's eyes circled the table before landing on Kishore, Leela, and Aditi, who were all smiling wholeheartedly. She gave all three a genuine smile, pausing to look each one in the eye. No one knew better the superpower it took to smile through the pain. They were doing well—she was proud of them and was confident that Ayaan would be, too.

Aanya continued.

"You know, I'm close to very few people in my life, and you, Ari, have managed to bring them all together in the same room. I could not ask for a sweeter bon voyage. Mom, Dad, Aditi, Jeeni, Jaya, Kishore-uncle, Leela-aunty, Renu-aunty, Devan-uncle—you guys are my everything. Thank you all for carrying me when I could no longer bear to walk. I have no idea how I'm going to handle this without all of you, but I'm not going to bother thinking about it because I expect you all to come visit me, like, ASAP. I'll be waiting! I've been haggling with TechLogically for a two-bedroom just so you all can crash with me."

She winked at Ari as everyone applauded.

# 30
# New York
## *2008*

To the left of the crown-molded doorframe, a navy-blue tote rested against two oversized pieces of luggage. The remainder of the apartment was bare, aside from a scattering of dust bunnies. Two PhD candidates moving into university apartments had picked up the butterscotch microfiber love seat and the console table. Goodwill had picked up the king-size mattress and bed frame. The landlord was storing the mahogany dining table for two and the espresso dresser—stained by the deteriorating alloy at the bottom of Ayaan's cologne bottle—in the cellar, to be moved to the picture-perfect newlyweds' apartment a few weeks later.

Shalu took a final walkthrough to make sure nothing had been forgotten as Raman used the restroom.

"The taxi will be here in fifteen minutes," Aanya reported from the kitchen as she grabbed the last water bottle in the fridge.

Raman entered the living room just as Shalu wrapped up her walkthrough. Raman eyed her for clearance. Unlike his wife, who traversed the 870 miles between New York City and Georgia on a daily basis, Raman had felt the expanse between him and his daughter deepen inch by small inch with each passing day, month, and year. Shalu habitually shared almost everything with her husband in passing as they combed through the invoices at the front desk, at the breakfast table slurping their chai, or on brief walks around their property. Indeed, Raman was not bothered by the fact that his daughter had grown closer to her mother over the years, but there were times when he wished the translucent wall that had developed between him and his daughter would give way.

Shalu, and even Aanya for that matter, understood the implicit nature of Raman's love. It was unquestionable, indisputable, both imperative and conclusive, but he only spoke to his daughter maybe once, at most, twice a week. They tended to catch up on the big stuff, like the virtues of Hillary versus Obama, as opposed to the latest in desi couture and fusion combinations of Indian and Mexican food that Aanya insisted Shalu must try.

As a father, Raman had found it much easier to demonstrate affection toward Aanya when she lived at home, growing up under the same roof. His love was conveyed in daily exchanges that added up little by little to a heightened bond.

When she was a child, on sluggish Sunday afternoons, Raman would sit next to Aanya and read the paper. He would pass her the comics, and they would laugh together—not at the hilarity, but the lack of it. They failed to comprehend why a lazy orange cat, Garfield, living out a mundane existence was so funny. Dilbert's office humor was unintelligible to them until Aanya joined TechLogically.

"Dad, I get it now, I think. It's kind of funny, the office humor. It's not so off from the real thing," Aanya said once before, trying to explain. Having never worked anywhere but motels off I-95, the comedy still eluded Raman.

When Aanya was a bit older and reading the whole paper, they would raise their eyebrows together at the ridiculous headlines that were commonplace in American newspapers, cogitating over the question: Was this really all the news fit to print?

They would agree that sea turtles flown from Boston to Florida on a chartered plane after they were injured in a storm, while absurd and deserving of an "only in America" label, was a cute story. In America, some very fortunate animals—not the ones in slaughterhouses, of course—were certainly treated better than most humans around the world. They appreciated both the irony and humanity in such headlines as "Ice Skater Whacks Another in the Leg to Secure Win." This was less charming and placed in the "crazy people in America" category, while Monica Lewinsky was classified as "let's pretend neither one of us read that headline." Their discussions on the mystery behind JonBenét Ramsey, a six-year-old girl found dead in her family home in Colorado, occupied them for months. In due time, they concluded that they would never know the truth, but both believed that the family was behind it somehow.

On mornings when Shalu slept in, Raman would make Aanya a cup of *chai* and they would sit in silence, dipping their Parle-G biscuits with precision, laughing out loud as the soggy cookie plopped downward, splattering the chai. Perfecting the allotted time for the biscuit to be dipped in the *chai* was a learned skill indeed, they concluded.

After breakfast, Aanya often tagged along as Raman assessed the damage to a room after an overnight party, usually by a group of teenagers or overgrown adults. Raman would quickly peruse the room before Aanya entered behind him, making sure there was nothing to be censored. Used condoms, dirty magazines, or maybe a syringe or two would be picked up before she was allowed to enter.

In the beginning, when Aanya was about nine, he did this subtly, distracting Aanya at the door. "Go run and get me some extra AA batteries; the remote in this room is overdue for a change," or "A light bulb is out in the lamp, go grab one from the office," Raman would say.

By the time Aanya was twelve, she knew his tricks. In anticipation, when they were about to approach a room, she would slow down, stagger her steps, tie her shoelaces, pick at a thread on her T-shirt, or redo her side ponytail, consciously granting her father ample time to screen the room and dispose of any adult material.

Together, they would rate the damage to the room on a scale of one to ten, with ten being "Let's bring in the professionals (aka Mom)," or one to nine, "We can handle this on our own in about an hour, two or max." Over time, they developed unwritten rules for the cleanup. Aanya would grab a contractor-size trash bag, put on some disposable gloves, and start picking up all the trash. Raman did not start wearing disposable gloves until Aanya pushed him to when she was eleven.

"Dad, there are a lot of germs and diseases that people bring in. Just do it; wear gloves. It is better to be safe than sorry," she explained.

Impressed by her levelheaded approach, Raman took a pair from the supply cart and started his share of the work, undoing all the bedding and gathering the towels, which Shalu and he would launder together. Aanya would spray all the surfaces with Glass Plus while her father wiped them down. Aanya would vacuum while her father sanitized the bathrooms.

Raman had always connected with his daughter in this manner: by cleaning rooms, going grocery shopping together, or driving to the Home Depot to find a valve for a fifty-year-old faucet. Their deep bond was built slowly and steadily over routine maintenance, daily chores, and outrageous headlines until, of course, on September 12, 2001, the *New York Times* front page read: "U.S Attacked: Hijacked Jets Destroy Twin Towers and Hit Pentagon in Day of Terror." On that day, Raman couldn't bond with his daughter over the most outrageous headline of them all.

With Aanya in New York, Raman had found it hard to demonstrate his affection in recent years. While they conversed about local and national news, it wasn't substantial, mainly because Aanya had gradually extricated herself from the details of current affairs—much to her father's understanding.

*    *

Raman and his daughter never talked much about the ordinary, but over time, they were also unable to talk about the extraordinary. They did not talk about love, loss, despair, or the future. Raman didn't know how, and Aanya found it difficult—yet their love was palpable.

Raman prayed diligently for Aanya every morning. He stood in front of their small wooden shrine, filled to capacity with deities of Krishna, baby Krishna, Radha leaning against Krishna with a flute, and jasmine-scented incense with a flaming *diya*. The Hindu gods inside the sandalwood temple glowed as Raman closed his eyes, joined his palms, and moved his lips.

Each time, he had one fundamental prayer. It was simple: He prayed for his daughter's happiness. He prayed that she would find joy again—in waking up in the morning, in taking a walk, in having a meal, in witnessing a flower blossom. He prayed, and he prayed, and he prayed. Unable to express it to her directly, he asked God to lighten her burden—for her to have a good cup of coffee today, a light day at work, a savory falafel, and a cheerful conversation.

He hoped her clients would not demean her work and that the strangers on the subway would be kind to her, offering a seat to his precious daughter after a long day. He wished they would somehow know that she had already suffered enough and would not agonize her by making her stand for the twenty-minute train ride. He prayed, again and again: please do not burden her with any of life's other tribulations; just let her find joy—simple, day-to-day cheer.

Through his prayers, he said sorry to her. *Sorry for what happened, my child. Sorry I am not able to help; sorry that you have endured the pain of a lifetime in your short time on earth. Sorry that Ayaan, the only boy you ever loved . . . died—that, too, so tragically.*

*But also, thank you, Ayaan. Thank you for showing my daughter what real love is. For this, I am forever grateful to you. Because of you, I know she will never settle for anything less, never compromise, and only accept love when it's as pure and loyal as your love for her. Thank you, God, for granting my daughter the chance to be so loved, in that way, by such a genuine, caring human being.*

Deep down, he wished for her to find new love because he, like Shalu, believed she deserved to love again.

Now, as he watched his daughter fret over last-minute checks, Raman silently repeated his simple prayer. *Let her find happiness, joy, and peace no matter where she goes. Let her be happy.*

Shalu rested a hand on his shoulder, signaling him to speak.

"Aanya, *beta*," Raman said, "we have something for you."

Aanya came and stood in front of them.

"Really? I have no space left, guys, seriously."

"It doesn't require space, *beta*; relax," Shalu said.

Raman pulled out a small maroon velvet box from his pocket.

Aanya drew her head back with surprise.

Though it was her idea, Shalu had insisted Raman present the gift. She knew there were very few opportunities for him to bond with his daughter, and, in an effort to bridge the expanse that had grown between him and Aanya, she pushed him to take the initiative. After all, it was all his prayers that were coming to fruition. He should have the honor.

Raman opened the box toward Aanya. A diamond solitaire on a sterling silver chain reflected the light and twinkled at Aanya. She gasped.

"Guys, are you kidding me? You didn't have to—"

"We know, *beta*," Raman interrupted. "We wanted to—we wanted to give you something, that's all."

Aanya took the box and examined the contents closely.

"It's breathtaking, just beautiful. I love it."

She unhooked the chain and positioned it on her neck. Her father helped her clasp the back.

"Looks perfect!" Shalu said.

"*Beta*, a solitaire diamond always shines brighter than two, three, or many nestled together. You are proof of that. You shine brighter than a hundred diamonds. You shine bright every day, and we want you always to remember your own strength as you embark on this new adventure by yourself," her father said as his eyes filled.

Aanya stepped in close, went up on tiptoe, and put her arms around her father. He held her tight, his tears dampening her shirt. Feeling left out, her mother put one arm around each of them. They brought her in and squeezed tight, completing the triad of a perfect farewell family hug.

# Part IV

# 31

# Mumbai
## *2008*

Abhimanyu stood to the right of the towering white lily arrangement, just as he had the first time Aanya met him. But this time, his presence paled in comparison to the stunning woman standing arm-in-arm next to him. Aanya pressed her fingers against the solitaire shimmering beneath the folds of her *sari and* smiled wholeheartedly.

When the young woman unhooked her arm and strolled toward her, a meticulously pleated crimson silk *sari* flowed like a fiery wave as stacks of gold bangles twinkled under the luminescent chandelier.

"You must be Aanya; Abhi has told me all about you! You look fantastic; I love your *sari*," the woman said all in one smooth breath.

Aanya was dressed in a vintage royal blue chiffon *sari* bordered by silver *zari*.

As Abhimanyu snuck up behind the woman, Aanya gave him a wary smile.

Abhimanyu held her gaze for a second, drawing her attention to the white lilies commissioned just for her, before circling his eyes back to her. He gave a prolonged blink and smiled wide.

Aanya blushed, softening in an instant.

"I see she needs no introduction, but in any case, Aanya, this is my sister, Seema—and, Seema, this is Aanya."

The two women greeted each other with a pseudo kiss on each cheek.

Jayesh walked over and proffered all three a tray full of mini water bottles and flute glasses filled with fresh watermelon juice. Abhimanyu offered a bottle of water to Aanya and his sister before turning back to Jayesh.

"So, when did this happen?"

"Today is my first day, sir."

"That is wonderful, Jayesh! I knew you had it in you—proud of you, my friend, but we will miss you back there. Do pay us a visit sometime and remember what I told you—think big!"

"Thank you, sir. You helped me so much, always talking to me and giving me courage. You are a very good sir. I will not forget. I will come see you. My promise, sir, always."

Jayesh rested his free hand on his heart in a show of humility.

When Abhimanyu returned his attention to the two women, chattering away as though they were long-lost friends, Aanya deciphered a tinge of both admiration and pride on his face. Aanya understood why. Seema had made it into the same recruiting program as him, beating out the growing competition in small towns and villages across the country. She was now a few weeks into the eighteen-month training program at the Taj in Nashik, just a few hundred miles away from Mumbai.

Being the eager trainee, she had not taken Diwali off, staying on-site instead to learn and serve as necessitated during the busiest time of the year. In return, her manager rewarded her with a few extra days off after the busy season. With no time off to visit her, Abhimanyu insisted she come visit him in Mumbai. This would give her the opportunity to shadow him around the flagship Taj and give brother and sister some time to catch up.

In addition, the Taj had entered into phase one of its contract with TechLogically. Aanya would be on-site for the next week, observing and taking diligent notes on the events at the Taj, keeping tabs on the possible entry and exit points of visitors, guests, and clients so that TechLogically could better capture the movements on the property to streamline and secure future events. The rest of the team, including Sid, would join Aanya in a few days to begin mapping out the hardware, software, and programming needs.

Aanya had requested to shadow a wedding and all its ancillary events to gauge the nuances that TechLogically would ultimately need to address while seamlessly keeping the hypersensitive egos of both wedding parties intact. Abhimanyu had explained to Aanya that attendance at their corporate events would be rather easy to digitize, as the attendees were usually pre-registered and identification was required to gain entry.

The challenge would remain weddings. The wedding events—both pre- and post—were numerous and continued to grow in breadth and decadence, with each event growing comparatively more difficult to control. Though ancillary events were still manageable, as all guests entered and exited the premises around the same time, the actual wedding—specifically the *baraat*, or the groom's procession, usually consisting of hundreds of people dancing their way onto the property—was the biggest loophole.

Thanks to age-old traditions, the procession carried leverage and expected nothing but the utmost respect, hospitality, and convenience when being received by the bride's family. Sensitivities ran high during this formal rendezvous of the two sides. A scandal erupting from probing queries from the bride's side on the legitimacy of the *baraatis*, the groom's guests, was to be avoided at all costs. With no one auditing who belonged to which side of the wedding party, the *baraat* was an opportune time for wedding crashers to meander onto the property, forcing security to regularly kick out wedding crashers—who were often undercover media, obsessed fans, con artists, and vagrants.

Tonight, the Sharma wedding had its opening event, the *sangeet*, a night of live music and dance, followed by a wedding in the morning and a formal reception in the evening.

"If I may interrupt, ladies, let's focus on the task at hand. Follow me."

Abhimanyu led Aanya and Seema up the grand stairs and onto an elevator that landed in a ballroom, a medium-sized space designed for a few hundred people. At the elevators, they ran into Natasha, draped in a hand-loomed cream Varanasi *sari*, trimmed with a red and gold border, designed especially for Taj staff.

"Looks like it is going to be a long night, Abhi. We have got some serious dancers on the floor. They just asked to delay dinner until nine thirty."

"Of course, they did. Did you expect anything less from this bunch?" Abhimanyu furrowed his eyebrows. "Should I inform the breakdown team? They will need to be on board later than scheduled."

"Yes, please. That would help me tremendously, as I still have some prep left tonight for the 10:00 a.m. *baraat*. Looks like an all-nighter for us."

Natasha turned toward the two women.

"Natasha, you remember Aanya and my sister, Seema?"

"Yes, of course. How are you, ladies?"

The four exchanged pleasantries replete with compliments for the splendor they adorned.

In the ballroom, Abhimanyu pointed out the intricacies of the setup to Aanya and Seema. The cadre of Taj staff moved seamlessly among the hundreds of guests as they managed the flow of drinks, food, and music. There were live singers and a backup DJ to ensure there was no break in the festivities.

As the three moved about the *sangeet*, the bride caught up with Abhimanyu, gave him a big bear hug, and gleamed.

"It's perfect, Abhi. I can't thank you enough. I could not have imagined it better! I mean, did you see the marigold balls up there? You have some serious patience for antics like mine. Thank you so much!"

The bride lifted her head to admire the rounds of orange and yellow marigolds hung twenty feet from the ceiling, placed precisely two feet apart, matching the centerpieces on each table. The raining marigolds were designed to complement the bride's lemon-yellow *lenga* embellished with orange and gold threadwork.

"You are so very welcome. I am happy to hear it meets your standard. If there is anything else we can do, you know where to find me."

"Thank you, Abhi. After tonight, I know everything will be more than perfect tomorrow. I am just in awe tonight. Thanks again!"

The bride twirled to take it all in. Halfway in, she was abruptly pulled back onto the overflowing dance floor.

Abhimanyu continued to point out small details here and there to Aanya and Seema, chatting briefly with each staff member he encountered, reveling in the tiny intricacies of their life as if he were their closest friend.

A couple of hours in, the live singers took a short break and the DJ took over. The crowd grew rowdier, and Seema drifted off behind Natasha, offering to stitch a small tear in a *dupatta* that had snagged under the guest's own stiletto heels.

Abhimanyu and Aanya watched the jubilations from the back corner of the ballroom, close to one of the three entryways but keeping a distance from the disco lights, DJ, and chaos. From the dark periphery, they both observed the exuberant dance floor. Two bulky young men lifted the bride high toward the marigolds as her hands flew up into the air. The next instant, the groom was up, right next to her, and the couple laced their fingers together and swung awkwardly in the air. Below them were ringlets of blissful faces, jumping up and down, swinging to the beat, intoxicated by the aura of love, libations, song, music, family, and good friends celebrating the union of two families. The heart-thumping music and the euphoric ambience had

Aanya's feet tapping and body swaying rhythmically to the beat as she mouthed the words to a popular Bollywood party song.

"Looks like someone is getting in the mood to dance." Abhimanyu smiled coyly at her.

"This whole thing—it's so perfect. The bride and groom are ecstatic, the families are having a blast, the food and drinks are flowing, and those singers are amazing! My God—how can you not get up and dance to those soulful voices? It's perfect, just like the bride said—truly beautiful. It's such a happy place for all. It must be very satisfying to know you play such a big part in pulling all this together, Abhimanyu. I can understand why you love what you do."

Abhimanyu turned to Aanya and gazed at her as if the brilliance of the dance floor was right there in front of him. He had not seen her in weeks, not since their rendezvous in the passion-lit elevator, and this was their first real moment alone. He ached to feel her close to him, maybe touch her face, graze her bare arms, hold her hand ever so softly in his.

"It's really special, isn't it? Gives me this—umm—"

"Natural high, like it's all worthwhile—all the long, hard hours," Aanya chimed in.

"That is exactly right, Aanya. It's an absolute natural high. It's what keeps me going"—thinking of her, not his work, as he said the words.

Abruptly, he took a step back, giving her a comforting smile as his soul sank at the gravity of what might be compressing her heart. *Was it her and Ayaan that she was seeing on the dance floor?*

In the weeks prior, in laboring installments over late-night calls, Aanya had woven together the emotional roller coaster of her past life. Day by day, phone call by phone call, Aanya had brought to life an old newsreel from a distant land, from a different time, that had played on an old tube TV sitting on a crate in Abhimanyu's village home. Piece by heartbroken piece, Aanya's loss, the yearning, the sense of pain and disorientation left behind by 9/11, had become his new reality. He listened to every echo of elation at the mention of Ayaan's name, the whispers about what may have happened to him, and the grief-stricken sobs for days, months, and years thereafter.

He felt her anguish and loneliness burrow deep within his heart. If he could, he would bring Ayaan back just to see what that level of happiness looked like on her face. He would willingly let this woman he was so helplessly falling in love with go because it was crystal clear that Ayaan had been her whole world—and always would be.

Resurrection, unfortunately, was not one of Abhimanyu's many powers, so he focused on the gifts he did have: he listened and listened and then listened some more. When Aanya could no longer speak through the pain, Abhimanyu made wholehearted attempts at consolation and comic relief. He rattled on about his own frivolous love life—there was this girl who had proclaimed to be in love with him throughout his teens, whom he had knowingly ignored for years. Finally, when he reciprocated—delayed and somewhat coerced—he discovered her love was vacuous. Within weeks of his departure from Bari for the Taj training program, she had found a new infatuation in a neighboring village and married him immediately.

"I suspect she has about half a dozen little ones scurrying about by now. Thank God I escaped that train wreck," he joked. The hint of laughter echoing on the other end of the phone was enough for him to continue rambling about an upbringing so simple, an adolescence so innocent, it mirrored Aanya's—minus a childhood love, of course.

At every twist and jagged turn, Aanya was serious and straightforward, warning him she was not who he thought. He was young and baggage free, while she was older, not just in age but in tonnage. She was a weighed-down widow—that, too, a broken one, barely pieced together in the aftermath of the rubble. It was not just that she had been married for a short time but that she had been married to someone she had loved her whole life, possibly since they were in diapers. She had only known one love her whole life, and she had never gotten over him—even worse, she was responsible for his death. She didn't know who or what she could be without Ayaan and had never wanted to know—until maybe now. It was complicated. *She* was complicated, and she believed, deep down, that Abhimanyu deserved better, way better—someone perfect, more whole, less damaged.

She had explained to him that all these years, it seemed that her life story, in some version or other, always preceded her. She had never had the opportunity to present her story before it was preempted by pity. Sharing her past with him, a complete newcomer, felt as if she finally had control over her story and how it was presented—perhaps even how it was perceived, so that she could somehow supersede the rumors before the "Oh, you poor thing" looks sunk deep and conversations treaded lightly. As grueling as it was, telling her own story felt like a forgone right she didn't know she had. Finally, for the first time ever, she had told someone about the text she had failed to send Ayaan that morning. The text she believed could that have saved his life?

At every painstaking pause in her story, Abhimanyu wanted to reach through the phone and wrap her in the security of his arms, make promises of safety he would provide under circumstances he could not control. He wanted to convince her that she was wrong about it all. It was not her fault.

The music softened in the ballroom as couples leaned in for a slow dance. Abhimanyu turned toward Aanya and moved in a bit closer. Under the sheerness of her chiffon *sari*, her solitaire necklace sparkled at the V of her neck. Matching stud earrings caught the light just above her puff-sleeved silk blouse as her elegant chignon exposed the nape of her neck. Its softness under the touch of his palm, the feel of her lips on his in the elevator, her sunlit glow on the banks of the Arabian Sea—it all brought a shiver to Abhimanyu's spine.

"You look absolutely stunning, Aanya. Absolutely gorgeous. I mean, I don't have enough words—"

As Aanya lifted her head toward him, he felt an unruly piece of hair from his perfect pompadour flutter under the blast of air pumping from the vents above. With lucidity on his face, he gazed at her, giving her a tender, warm smile— a smile that could easily permeate and melt the whole the room.

"Please don't look at me like that, Abhimanyu."

"Like what—?" Abhimanyu questioned, eyes widening.

"Like, you know—that," Aanya said tenderly.

Abhimanyu inched in closer, close enough to catch her perfume—something floral, like jasmine mingled with the smell of a freshly unfolded *sari*, a scent he recognized from the handful of times his mother had unrolled her special-occasion *sari* from their *Godrej* armoire.

"Like—like I am so madly in love with you, Aanya? Like that?" he whispered.

Aanya's eyes grew wide. She opened her mouth but could not speak. She paused for a split second before trying again.

"This is really hard for me. Try to understand."

"Really hard because you see yourself and Ayaan up there dancing like that at your wedding reception? Or hard because it's me?"

"Ayaan and me, up there? No—I stopped dreaming that dream a long time ago."

"Well, that's a relief." Abhimanyu smiled. "So, it's me. Well, that is good news. Me—that is an easier fix. I can work on that."

"That's part of the problem, Abhimanyu. You don't need any work. You are too perfect already—way too perfect. You deserve better."

Abhimanyu sighed at the irony in her words. *No, you deserve better.*

"Fortunately, Aanya, I get to decide what I deserve, not you—and what I feel for you, Aanya, is unshakable. There's nothing I have been surer of in my entire life than the feelings I have for you—and I assure you that even if you return an ounce of what I feel, that will be enough. I'm not saying forget him, Aanya. I will never be Ayaan, nor do I wish to be. But maybe, just maybe, I could be the next best thing. Wouldn't he want that for you? "

"Abhimanyu, please try and understand. It's so very complicated for me," Aanya pleaded.

"Actually, Aanya, it's not. It's rather simple. I want you to try, to give this a chance. You deserve love again, and I have nothing but that for you. I am not asking for much in return. Just a chance."

Aanya gazed at him, inhaled deeply, and sighed, tears puddling in her eyes.

"Don't you get it, Abhimanyu? He is gone. He is gone because of *me*. I could have saved him with just one text. He ran into a burning building for *me*—and I couldn't even text him," she said softly.

Abhimanyu tossed his head back and closed his eyes for a second as he thought about taking her in his arms, wrapping her in his embrace so he could absorb years and layers of pain and displaced guilt. He wanted to dig a path to her heart and somehow stop the tears from flowing forever. But he couldn't. This was not the time or the place.

When he opened his eyes, just over Aanya's shoulder, Abhimanyu could see his sister ambling toward them. He warned Aanya with a comforting smile, eyes gesturing in Seema's direction. He caught Aanya blinking back tears as she forced a smile, and turned back toward the dance floor.

Abhimanyu took a deep breath, pursed his lips, and willed himself to take a step back. Just as he did, hidden from Seema's view, he gently caressed Aanya's arm back and forth. They couldn't finish this conversation right now, but he wanted to remind her that his gentleness and understanding would always be there for her.

"Natasha is sending down dinner for us to your office, Abhi. I may have mentioned that I was starving," Seema said with a witty smile. "You're both welcome. Please tell me you are hungry, because the food is on its way and my stomach is grumbling louder than this music."

"You hungry, Aanya, or you want to enjoy the festivities some more?" Abhimanyu asked.

"Let's go and eat. We can always come back after dinner. I am sure these party animals will still be going strong," Aanya said.

The three of them took the service exit from the back of the ballroom onto the elevator. Downstairs, they passed through the quaint corridors and slipped into Abhimanyu's office, situated in the hallway behind the front desk. Seema immediately started clearing the desk to make space for the arrival of their dinner trays, while behind her, in silence, Abhimanyu, obviously restless, admired Aanya, who looked awestruck by the bouquet of lilies on his desk.

Suddenly, there were brassy rumbling sounds, like a string of firecrackers so earsplitting, it felt like they were going off in their heads. They all froze.

Outside, in the grandiose lobby of the Taj Palace Hotel in Mumbai, blood pooled around Jayesh's neck as the wounds across his chest clenched bullets and relaxed his pink flesh. One minute, Jayesh existed, and then, the next, he simply did not.

On that day, November 26, 2008, his first day serving the prestigious guests of the Taj Mahal Palace hotel in Mumbai, Jayesh Mahanar Joshi, the young man that had never dared to dream, who was never disillusioned by the fancy of the imagination, a man that had never sought a life beyond the menial day-to-day, a man invisible in a nation of one billion, had finally found the audacity to dream, to become visible—only to endure the nightmare of a nation.

# 32

# Mumbai
## *2008*

Abhimanyu forced Aanya and Seema to the ground.

"Wait here. Don't move until I come back," Abhimanyu whispered as he creaked his office door open.

Rapid thunder-like sounds rumbled in his ear as he searched the end of the hallway. His eyes froze upon a puddle of blood with an arm lying across it. The face was hidden behind the wall, but Abhimanyu recognized the rainbow twine around the wrist. Saara—murdered so brutally, so instantly, so coldheartedly, that she didn't even have time to clutch the cross on her neck to pray for the protection of her craft-loving, friendship-bracelet-making daughter. Abhimanyu clenched his stomach. *God bless her soul and give her child the needed strength.*

Hearing more rounds of sequential gunfire, Abhimanyu caught a glimpse of a man with a backpack and a large artillery-style machine gun drawn to his chest stepping over Saara's body. Shaken, Abhimanyu swung around and slipped back into his office. He sighed deeply to compose himself, but the terror shaking his body hid nothing. He locked to door behind him and switched off the lights. In the darkness, he found his way to the ground next to Aanya and Seema.

"It's some kind of shootout. There is a man with a machine gun. I can only see one guy, but I think there must be more based on all this noise," Abhimanyu whispered as he found his way to the ground.

There, he rested his back against the wall and put his arms around Aanya and Seema, enabling them to naturally sink their heads into the hollow of his shoulders on either side of him.

"I think they got Saara—and maybe others in the lobby."

Abhimanyu spoke with a quiver in his voice as he squeezed the two women closer to him. His breath heavy and heart thumping as tears rolled down his cheeks. Just as he was about to reach for Aanya's hand under the fold of her *sari*, Aanya slipped out from under his grip.

"We can't sit around. We have to do something now! We have to warn the others—now!"

Aanya was right! Abhimanyu swiftly wiped his tears, swallowed his shock, and called Natasha from his mobile.

"Natasha! Put the ballroom on lockdown. Now! Evacuate everyone through the service exit right away. We are not safe. I repeat, we are *not* safe!"

"What!"

"Those sounds were not leftover Diwali or wedding firecrackers. They were gunshots, Natasha. There are gunmen in the hotel. Our hotel! I don't know how many, but more than one for sure. Where are you right now?"

"I am at the back end of the service exit."

"Listen to me. Shut the music, shut the lights, and lock down the main entrances to the ballroom, now. Get everyone out of there—through the service exit, through the back doors and out to the back alley, or just find some kind of safe hiding space—but do not go through the main lobby! I repeat, *no one* should be allowed in the main lobby! Get everyone out of the ballroom immediately. Natasha, are you understanding me?"

"I got it, Abhi; trust me on this. I can hear the shots."

Abhimanyu hung up and dialed the general manager.

"Sir, where are you?"

"I am off-site—and I know already, Abhi. Something is happening in Mumbai. I am on my way."

"Sir, there are gunmen in our main lobby. It's a massive shootout. There is blood and at . . . at least one body. Do not come to the property. Call the police; send help. Just don't come onto the property right now," Abhimanyu pleaded.

"Where are you, Abhi?"

"I am in my office, sir. There are gunmen right outside by the registration. I can still hear the firing. It's nonstop. I am making calls to secure the events. Is your family on the sixth floor, sir?"

"Yes, Abhi, they are. But that shouldn't be your worry—handle the events. That's your territory. I am on my way."

"You can't come here, sir, not right now!"

"I am coming, Abhi. Handle what you can—I am doing what I can."

"Okay, sir—but do not use the main entrance! The back alley may be best; I am not sure. I have very little to go by."

"Got it—be careful, Abhi!"

Abhimanyu continued the calls. One by one, he demanded that every event and restaurant manager in charge find safety for their guests. Once he had finished with the managers, he called every staff member's number he had stored on his phone. To his surprise, most of the staff listened aptly, had already done what he proposed, or began immediately. They didn't question the absurdity of what he was saying or his over-the-top commands. This was Abhimanyu-sir, after all. He'd never given them a reason to doubt him. He was always on their side.

Between calls, he caught the time on his cell phone:12:47 a.m. The date beneath read 27-11-2008.

In the distance, they could hear the sting of firecracker sounds—not continuously, but intermittent, sometimes just one, six, or a dozen in a row every few minutes, sometimes within seconds. All three slid underneath the desk, away from the door, and closer to the back wall. Aanya grabbed the laptop and started looking up numbers. She sent about a dozen pleas for help via text and email to various outlets —all the police stations in the area, the security office with in the Taj, the security offices at the Orchid—while Seema texted her personal contacts and Abhi pushed ahead with colleagues. Lastly, Aanya called Sid, who informed them that based on breaking news reports, something terrible was brewing in Mumbai—mainly that there was a shootout at the main train terminal.

"Just call or text everyone you know in Mumbai. Tell them to get to a safe place or stay put if they are safe. Tell them to call their loved ones and inform them of their whereabouts. No one should go looking for anyone else. Trust me on this," Aanya reiterated.

In the darkness, Abhimanyu gently rubbed the small of Aanya's back, reassuring her that he understood both her words and her anguish.

*It wasn't your fault. Your text wouldn't have saved him.*

Abhimanyu called all the people he could not reach the first time around—Ram Singh, the doorman; Varun, the concierge; and his dear friend Jayesh. As their phones rang incessantly, he feared the worst.

By the time he was done with his calls, Aanya sat in shock, sunken in a corner, tears dripping down her cheeks, hands wrapped around her knees, shivering with fright. As Abhimanyu tried to reach for her, jarringly, the whole floor shook as if it were an earthquake. Simultaneously, they heard an explosion and a loud clamor as bits of debris crashed against the walls. The sliver of light seeping from under the door went dark in seconds and then, everything was quiet again.

Abhimanyu found his way to Aanya and placed himself next to her. He put his arms around her and tucked her head into his chest, squeezing her tightly, absorbing the shock, the fear, the pain. She wept silently, dampening his crisp white shirt. He pulled her even closer, found her soft hand beneath the fold of her *sari*, interlaced his fingers with hers, pressed his palm into hers, and squeezed as tightly as he could, resting his head against the wall.

"Everything is okay, Aanya; everything is going to be okay. I am here with you. I won't let anything happen to you," he consoled her, stroking her cheeks, wiping away the tears.

Unnerved by the explosion, Seema popped out from under the desk and found her brother in the darkness. Abhimanyu placed his free arm around his sister. Pushed up against the wall, the three of them sat in shock, unsure what to do until a musky, dusty smell crept in through the vents. Smoke, for sure.

Abhimanyu shifted to get on his feet.

"We need to get out of here—and we need to get the guests out," he said.

"We will come with you," Aanya said softly.

"Yes, we are coming, *bhaiya*," Seema said.

"No, we all can't be at risk like that. Let me first go check on the situation."

"Let me go, too, please—" Seema said.

"Neither one of you knows the property like I do, especially the service exits. We don't have time to discuss this. Please let me go. Put your phones on silent. I will text or call you. Stay on the floor, low to the ground."

Seema, a profile against the glow of a phone screen, surrendered. Abhimanyu gave her a kiss on the forehead.

He turned to Aanya.

"Everything is okay, Aanya, everything is going to be okay. I won't let anything happen to you," he repeated.

Though he could not find her eyes in the darkness, he could feel Aanya was still shaken and for a second, imagine what she was thinking: *It's not me I am worried about—it's you. What about you,*

*Abhimanyu? Can you promise me that you will be okay? That every-thing is going to be fine with you? That nothing will happen to you? Can you promise me that you will always be fine, you will always come home, and you won't disappear into a cloud of smoke? Can you prom-ise me you won't be a hero? Can you? Because I can tell you this: I don't want to be fine, not without you, not anymore.*

He searched for her hand, pulled it close to him, and let it rest on his heart for a second. Then, he pressed the backs of her damp fingers against his tear-salted mouth in a simple apology, sealed with a soft kiss that said, *Although I want nothing more, I am sorry, Aanya. I cannot promise you that—I cannot promise you that nothing will happen to me, that I will be fine, that I will come back, that I will not forever disappear into the cloud of smoke behind me. I just can't promise that—but I can promise that nothing will push me harder to try than you. I wouldn't put you through that—not again. Remember, nothing is your fault.*

In the dark, Aanya closed her eyes. No matter how hard she tried, she couldn't help thinking of that day. All she could have done, should have done.

One text and he would be alive—*right?*

# 33
# New York
## *2001*

At 7:15 a.m. on September 11, 2001, Aanya's phone buzzed. It was a message from her new boss, Ari.

*Morning meeting moved to client's office; same time as planned. See you there.*

Aanya smiled. The commute to midtown was twenty-five minutes shorter than her usual downtown. She snuggled in tighter with Ayaan, grateful for the extra cuddle time. Finally, at 8:03, Aanya pulled herself out of bed and tiptoed to the bathroom. As the shower warmed her body, she basked in the afterglow of their delayed yet perfect two-month anniversary celebration the night before. They had delicious *chole bhature*, prepared by Ayaan, followed by slow dancing in the living room to the melodious voice of Lata Mangeshkar to one of his favorite songs.

*Lag jaa gale ke phir yeh haseen raath ho na ho*
*Shaayad phir is janam mey mulaaqat ho na ho*
*Hum ko mile hai aaj yeh ghadiyaan naseeb se*
*Jee bhar ke dekh leejiye hum ko kareeb se*
*Phir aap ke naseeb mey yeh baat ho na ho*
*Paas aayie ke hum nahin aayenge baar baar*
*Baahein gale mein daal ke hum ro le zaar zaar*
*Aankon se phir yeh pyaar ki barsaath ho na ho*
*Lag jaa gale ke phir yeh haseen raath ho na ho*

Embrace me, for who knows if this beautiful night will ever
    come again
Maybe, in this life, we may never have the good fortune to
    meet again
Fate has given us these few moments
You can look at me from up close, as much as you wish
Your fate may never have this opportunity again
Come closer, I will not return again and again
Let me wrap my arms around your neck and cry for a long
    time
My eyes may never shed such a shower of love again
Embrace me, for this beautiful evening may not come again

Aanya hummed the song, feeling a deep sensation in the pit of her stomach as she revered the gentle kisses on her forehead, eyes, and lips, their feet oscillating to the soft beat. They had held each other close, dancing and kissing long into the night until they could no longer bear the splinter of distance between them, retreating to the bedroom to make love before resigning themselves to each other's arms for a good night's sleep. The thoughts warmed her to her core.

Wrapping herself in a towel, she placed a finger on the steamed mirror and wrote their names, sharing the "Y" just as they always had. Underneath, she wrote, "Happy two months, hubby."

At 8:29, she kissed Ayaan, still in bed, on the cheek. He found her hand and kissed the back with a groggy, "Love you, have a great day," and fell back into a deep sleep.

At 8:33, Aanya stepped out to a beautiful, sun-kissed day.

At 9:06, Ayaan's cell rang. By the time he woke from the depths of his dreams and picked up, he had missed the call. Immediately, it rang again.

"Ayaan, it's Jacob. We need all hands on deck, now."

"What—why?"

"I don't know that much. There is a plane in a building some-where—that's what the chief said. Sounds nuts. I just know he wants all hands on deck, like now."

"I'll come down there ASAP."

Ayaan jumped out of bed. In the bathroom, while brushing his teeth, he made out the remnants of the message Aanya had left for him on the mirror. He smiled nostalgically and instinctively fingered a heart around their names.

At 9:17, Ayaan's cell rang. It was his father, Kishore. Ayaan told his papa he was fine and that Aanya had already left for work.

At 9:18, Ayaan called Aanya. It went to voicemail. He didn't leave one.

By 9:21, Ayaan was at his EMT station, just a five-minute walk from their apartment, loaded onto the back of an ambulance. Jacob sat across from him, ready with a debrief. The radio, faint in the background, was tuned to NPR, as always.

"A plane hit a building. They said it is one of the towers at the World Trade Center—you know the building?" Jacob asked.

"Are you sure? A plane. Is this a joke?"

Just as he was processing the absurdity of a plane hitting a build-ing, Ayaan's brain went into overdrive. *Where does Aanya work? What is the name of the building? It's TechLogically, that's for sure; what's the building? Is it—it's the—*

"Sorry, man. Give me a minute," Ayaan said.

At 9:23, Ayaan pulled out his cell phone and called Aanya again. It went to voicemail immediately. He followed up with a text.

*Are you okay? Where are you—what building do you work in—some crazy stuff going on.*

"You okay?" Jacob asked.

"Aanya works downtown—I was there last week, but I can't remember the building name. She's not picking up."

Ayaan's right foot was restlessly tapping the floor, shaking profusely. He fiddled with the phone.

"Keep trying—we will be there soon, though. Don't worry, man, I am sure she's fine."

At 9:25, Ayaan dialed Aanya again. This time, the phone randomly beeped and emitted muffled noises. He followed up with another text.

*Hey baby. Love you—worried. Just text back and let me know you are okay, please.*

At 9:45, Ayaan's phone beeped with a text.

*Bhai, are you okay? Please let us know.*

Too distracted, Ayaan did not text Aditi back.

The ambulance moved quickly for most of the route, but as they neared Lower Manhattan, it slowed. There were no windows in the back of the ambulance, so neither Ayaan nor Jacob caught the scene outside.

Jodi, the driver, warned them through the walkie-talkie, "Boys, trying to cut some corners, hold tight. It's a mess out here—people all over the streets. It's not looking good. Listen to this, boys, just listen to this—"

She blared the volume on the radio.

Two people were speaking: one was on the phone, and the other was at the NPR studio. They were conversing about two buildings, both hit by planes on the upper levels of the World Trade Center buildings. Jacob and Ayaan glared at each other, shaking their heads in disbelief.

*Aanya's building, what was the name?* Ayaan's leg started shaking more fervently, and his foot taps accelerated. *The floor—it was seventeen. The security guard last Tuesday, typing away frantically, gave me a visitor sticker. It read seventeenth floor for sure.*

At 9:49, Ayaan's phone rang.

"Hello," Ayaan said with so much tenderness.

"*Bhai*—are you okay?"

"I am okay—I can't reach Aanya, Aditi—I can't reach her. I need to go to keep my line open; bye."

"*Bhai*, where are you?"

"I am in the ambulance."

"I love you, bha—"

There were beeps, and the call dropped. He was holding back tears.

At 9:51, the ambulance came to a stop. Jodi opened the back door, and the two men jumped out into a panic of people. Jodi had managed to bring them right into the action in a special area reserved for emergency vehicles.

"Where do we start?" Jacob asked.

"Waiting for orders, give me a minute; sounds like confusion all around," Jodi said.

Ayaan looked around at the frenzy of people, searching for something but not knowing what. Through a tunnel of buildings, he could see the smoke billowing from one of the towers. At the periphery of his vision, he recognized the corner café where he and Aanya had their surprise anniversary lunch a week ago, giving him an instant orientation.

"I am sorry, guys. I gotta check on something—just channel me the orders."

Ayaan bolted in the direction of Aanya's building, fighting his way against waves of people scurrying, panicked, bewildered—frightened.

At 9:41, there was a knock on the conference room door in an office building in midtown, followed by an elderly woman walking in and whispering something to the man at the head of the table. The graying, sharply suited man shook his head in disbelief.

"Sorry to interrupt, but there seems to be an emergency downtown. Are you guys in the World Trade buildings?"

"Yes, we are," Ari responded.

"I think we need to take a break and maybe check out the news. There were some planes that crashed into your building downtown. I think—um, sounds impossible, but we should break."

The team from TechLogically—Ari, Aanya, Samantha, and Oscar—looked at each other for direction. The three remaining individuals in the room from the client end waited for further orders from their aging boss. None of them seemed truly alarmed, only confused about their next steps. The information was too absurd to process in a logical manner.

Finally, the woman who had delivered the message—officially the executive assistant to the man in charge—broke the awkward glances.

"We have a TV in the larger conference room. I think you all need to see what is going on—it is probably best if we remain confined to our offices. The security head for the building is already following up and checking on our protocols. I am waiting for him to call back with further instructions. I would advise you to please check up and check in with your colleagues and loved ones. I will be happy to assist you should you need to use our landlines," the woman commanded calmly, as though she had managed man-made disasters her whole life.

The whole group, including her boss, immediately scrambled to pick up their belongings and followed the woman out the door. As they walked, Aanya fished around for her cell phone and turned it on. TechLogically's unofficial policy was that all cell phones needed to be silent, off, and put away during meetings. Ari was a stickler for this rule, especially at client-facing meetings.

Aanya, never having any reason to have her cell on, always turned it off and kept it in her purse. It took almost a minute for her phone to turn on. When it did, it alerted her to a series of messages, both voice and texts.

The latest text message had been received at 9:45 from Aditi.

*Are you okay? Please tell me you are okay.*

Aanya grew concerned but wanted to finish checking her messages before responding. There were at least two dozen texts or calls from Aditi, Jeeni, Jaya, Mr. Ramos, and a hodgepodge of others, along with several from Ayaan.

Aanya's heart pounded with fear.

At 9:47, Aanya called Ayaan. She received a series of static noises and hung up.

At 9:48, Aanya called Julia's office number. She did not pick up. She tried her cell—no answer.

Aanya turned to Ari. "Julia is not picking up."

"I just called in—Natalie picked up, and it seems we are too low on the seventeenth to have been impacted. The orders are to stay put, but there seems to be a lot of chaos and confusion. Some people have left, and others are staying, it seems. She wasn't very clear—and hung up quickly," Ari responded.

Aanya, completely terrified, had no idea how to respond. She gave him a wry smile and went back to her phone.

At 9:49, while staring at images of the smoke-billowing towers from the conference room in midtown, Aanya called Ayaan again. She received a busy signal.

At 9:50, Aanya sent Ayaan a text message.

*I am totally fine, baby—don't worry. I love you.*

She hit the green button on her phone, but due to a delay in transmission, it vanished, like so many others that day.

At 9:51, Aanya called the landline at her parents' motel, only to receive a busy signal.

At 9:52, Aanya called her parents' cell phone, but her phone was acting up. By now, she was continually getting static and beeps and was unable to get through to anyone. Frantic, she continued to send text messages.

* *

At 9:53, Ayaan entered the South Tower of the World Trade Center and dashed upward against the throngs of people coming down. Amid the unprecedented, un-protocoled chaos both inside and out, Ayaan encountered several police officers, but no one stopped him—probably because he was in his EMT uniform.

At 9:54, Ayaan heard chatter on his walkie-talkie confirming that Jodi and Jacob, by order of their chief, were at the foot of the South Tower, oxygen tanks in tow, breathing life into a twenty-one-year-old intern who was suffering from severe smoke inhalation.

At 9:55, Ayaan was on the seventeenth floor of the South Tower, staring at his wife's cubicle. There was a collage of memories pinned to her carrel. There was a picture of them when they were ten, smiling profusely, with Aditi's bunny ears peeking out from behind them. There was a picture of himself and Aanya at their high school graduation, wearing white caps and gowns. There were a series of pictures from trips that they had taken with their friends and parents. There was a picture in which Ayaan, twenty-one, was on his knees on the fifth-grade playground, velvet box in hand, ready to officially propose.

Lastly, there was a picture of them at their wedding. Ayaan recalled receiving this single teaser photo via email just the week before from the professional photographer, who had yet to deliver their wedding albums. It was a printout, grainy on office paper, hand-cropped by his wife to fit the collage. Ayaan vividly recalled the precise moment captured in the photograph.

All around, there was a burst of color—garlands of red and white roses hung from the cream and gold *mandap*. To Ayaan's side sat Aditi in an emerald-green *sari*, hair up in an elegant French twist, shimmering in a vintage *kundan* necklace. His parents—Leela glowing in a gold and blue *sari* and Kishore in a matching blue *sherwani*—stood behind him, impatiently waiting for the unveiling of the bride.

Perpendicular to him, seated on low settees, were Shalu-aunty and Raman-uncle, ready to perform the *kanyadaan*, the ritual of giving away their daughter with ancient Sanskrit mantras and traditions distilled by the pragmatism of a thousand generations. In the background, blurred, was the banquet hall—part of a new hotel jointly owned by Raman-uncle and his father, filled with hundreds of families who called the length and periphery of I-95 home, all bound by the same journey, each on their own shaky ship, sailing a new wave of rough waters to the American Dream.

Dressed in a beige and gold *sherwani* with maroon trim, Ayaan was unconsciously shaking his right leg and tapping his foot as he sat in an ornate throne-like chair. In front of him, Jeeni and Jaya held up a trimmed red fabric straight across Aanya's face, shielding her from the groom.

Aanya, in maroon *chanya choli*, was adorned with a gold and beige *dupatta* spread across the crown of her head. The name "Ayaan" was hidden in the intricate mehndi design that extended from Aanya's twiddling fingertips to her palms and up her forearms.

When the priest directed Jeeni and Jaya to drop the veil, Ayaan closed his eyes and took a deep breath. When he slowly lifted his eyelids, Aanya, his long-awaited bride, more radiant than ever, gave him a beatific smile. Ayaan's smile widened in return and he mouthed, "You look beautiful."

At 9:56, Ayaan's phone rang.

"Hi—it's me; I am totally fine. Don't worry, baby."

"Oh, good! I am so happy to hear your voice. Where are you, Aanya?"

"I'm in midtown—I had a client meeting this morning."

"Oh—I'm—"

Within seconds of their first words, Ayaan began running down the stairs.

"Where are you—why do you sound so out of breath?"

"I—uh, I'm in your building. I was checking on you."

"*What?* Ayaan, get out of there. I am not in there; please, get out—right now!"

"I had to come down here for work anyway—and I couldn't get ahold of you, so—"

"Ayaan . . . please get out of there, now! Please!"

Aanya was sobbing.

"I'm almost out, don't worry! I love you!"

"I love you, too—call me as soon as you are outside and safe. Focus, Ayaan!"

At 9:58, Ayaan was almost to the third floor when, amid the wave of people trying to make the descent, he spotted a woman, charred with smoke, stumbling and struggling with each step. Ayaan granted her the support she required by offering the strength of his left shoulder. The woman, grateful, wrapped her right arm around Ayaan, and together, they pushed forward, slow and steady.

At 9:59, as Aanya, Aditi, Kishore, Leela, and millions of others gaped at their television screens, awestruck with disbelief, the 107 stories of the South Tower of the World Trade Center collapsed, floor by floor, like a stack of dominoes onto Ayaan's kindhearted soul, granting him zero time to clasp his hands and pray for the safety and well-being of his beautiful wife.

# 34

# Mumbai
## *2008*

"Don't go, Ayaan, please—don't leave me."

Seema turned to Aanya amid the darkness of Abhimanyu's office.

"Aanya, Aanya—are you okay?"

"Ayaan."

"Aanya—are you okay?" Seema asked, a notch louder this time, with a hand gently shaking her shoulder.

Aanya lifted her head up and awakened to her reality.

"Oh, Seema. I'm sorry. I'm fine—I think I dozed off for a bit."

"No worries, I think I did, too. It's dark; we're hungry and exhausted—it's bound to happen."

Aanya found her phone and flipped it open. There were several missed calls. She scanned them quickly to ascribe priority.

"I have a text from Abhimanyu. It says he is safe and with Natasha. My parents called a few times—I need to call them back."

"You should. They must have heard the news by now—and Abhi let me know he is okay, too."

Instinctively, Aanya calculated the time difference in her head. It was 5:17 in the morning in Mumbai, making it evening in Georgia. Aanya dialed her mother.

"Hello? Where are you, *beta*?"

"I'm in Mumbai, Mama."

"Where in Mumbai? Something is happening there at the Taj. It is all over the news here. Everyone's been calling us worried about you—please tell me you are not at the Taj, *beta*, please."

"Mama, please calm down. I am safe. I came back to my hotel last night—I am at the Orchid."

Aanya couldn't imagine wringing her parents through the truth.

"Oh, I am so happy to hear that, *beta*. Don't leave your hotel! There is something going on at the Taj. CNN keeps reporting that it's under siege. There are hostages trapped in the hotel. There were bomb blasts. The hotel is on fire, and God knows what else. I hope your friend there is okay—what's his name?"

"You mean Abhimanyu. He should be fine, but I will call him just in case."

Irrespective of how close Aanya was to her mother, she hadn't yet told her about how close she and Abhimanyu had gotten, mentioning him only in passing as a work client.

"Okay, *beta*. Do not leave your hotel! Mumbai is under siege. The footage looks like hell. Are you able to watch all this on TV there, Aanya?"

Shalu was growing skeptical. Given her past, Aanya was too unnaturally calm and controlled.

"I was watching, Mama, but I'm trying not to—you know. It was getting too hard for me, so I turned the news off. I didn't want to panic. But don't worry, I am safe, and I will not leave the hotel."

"Okay, *beta*, I understand. It's probably better if you keep all the bad news off. Stay in your room, lock it, and watch some old movies or something—keep your mind on song and dance. We'll call you again soon."

"I will, Mama. I love you—and Dad. Tell him I love him, too."

In the distance, the two women heard the same gunfire they had intermittently all night. With each jolt of the rapid gunshots, Aanya was brought back to consciousness, triggering the same drill: First, message Abhimanyu an *Okay?* Then, check on Seema, and lastly, repeat her favorite mantra. This was not only to placate herself but to pray for Abhimanyu's safety.

As if on cue, it worked every time, because Abhimanyu always texted back with a quick, *Safe, still in the same place. I am fine, we are fine, we will get out of here. I meant what I said earlier. Madly in love with you, Aanya.*

Then, in sequence, Seema was updated, *Take care sis. You can handle this, I know. Stay locked, low, and quiet!* Neither Seema nor Aanya shared the details of their correspondence, but they did confer on his safety— and that his position had not changed in hours. He had made it to the service area behind the ballroom and was trying to help people hide in storage areas and escape one by one through the back exits.

On the outside, as the iconic Taj burned and Mumbai unraveled, the time spent inside Abhimanyu's office felt far from chaotic. It had been nearly six hours since they had entered the office in search of dinner and heard the first round of gunfire. The battery-operated wall clock ticked loudly, making the seconds feel like hours. From the information they had received from those on the outside, they knew Mumbai was under some kind of terror threat and the Taj had been taken over by terrorists. The nighttime explosion—a bomb blast near the renowned bulbous dome—had set part of the hotel on fire. Fortunately, the smoke seeping through the cracks had steadied overnight, allowing them to breathe without coughing.

In the pre-dawn hours, Aanya had escaped to more harrowing places in her mind, but now it was early morning, and neither she nor Seema could sleep. So the two women, nearly strangers, sat close to each other against the wall near the door and held hands as needed, giving each other a *We are going to be fine, everything is fine* squeeze with each new shot heard.

"Aanya, can I tell you something, honestly?"

"Of course, Seema, why would you—?"

"I know! *Bhai* told me about your past. I don't know everything in detail, but I know. When he told me, I couldn't really imagine what it must be like, but here we are—and the thought of Abhi out there, us in here, all the unknown—it's terrifying! I am so sorry you have to go through this all over again. How are you doing? Like, really doing—?"

"It's not your fault, Seema, and I am doing the best I can. So, what exactly did your brother tell you?"

"Well, I think he told me more about himself than you. My brother, Aanya, he's not the type to mess around. I think it's a small-town thing. When we fall, we fall hard—there is this kind of loyalty you don't find in the cities. And he has fallen for you. I am not sure exactly why, but I think he told me because he's afraid . . ."

"Afraid?"

"Yes, afraid of the fights he will have to put up. You know, Aanya—my brother, he is not perfect, trust me, I know, but he comes damn close. We come from a small village, and Abhi is basically the town hero, the most eligible bachelor around. He literally has a queue of women—well, girls, really—waiting for him back home, but he doesn't care for all that. He wants *you*—I know—and that's going to be a real struggle with my parents and family. I am pretty sure he confided in me to get me on his side. He is going to need an ally in his fight. Which, by the way, is working, as you can tell . . ."

"They're right, Seema, aren't they? Don't forget, I come from the same culture, a tiny little community of Gujaratis, most of whom have deemed me bad luck—unworthy of marriage or remarriage, I guess, or even love. That's what I have been trying to explain to your brother. Your parents, your family—they are not wrong! He deserves better, the best—someone more perfect, like him—not me, a widow with all this bad luck and baggage. Your parents really aren't wrong."

"*Bad luck?* What my family thinks—what he deserves? Is that what's holding you back? You are kidding, right, Aanya? I guess you can take a girl out of India, but you can't take India out of the girl! Is it really 2008?

"Listen to me, Aanya, you are not bad luck. That's bullshit, and I wouldn't have figured you as someone who would fall for that. If you think Abhi deserves better from some wholesome family kind of perspective, you have completely misread him. Abhi is utterly in love with you, Aanya, and the thing he is most afraid of is not my parents and what they will think—not at all. What scares him most, makes him shake in the knees, is the thought of you never reciprocating. What he *deserves* is you. So the real question is—where do you stand?"

"Seema . . . it's complicated."

"How, exactly?"

"Ayaan and I—we were childhood sweethearts. We had known each other since we were in diapers. Our parents were best friends— they still are. We naturally fell in love over the years, and then, just like that, two months into our marriage—he was gone. I never knew who I was without him. Sometimes, I feel I still don't. And on top of all that, it's my fault. He ran into a burning building to save me, and I could have stopped him with a simple text."

"I understand, Aanya, and I am so sorry—but listen to me. We can't go back and change the past. It's done. You have to forgive yourself. You know, if I died here today, I would want my love to move on—I even told him that last night. I would want him to be loved like I love him again—it would make me happy up there, or wherever it is we all end up.

"I'm taking a wild guess here, but I am thinking Ayaan would want the same for you: he would want you to love genuinely and be loved back in the same way. I think you know this already, but it doesn't get more real and intense than my brother. Loyalty is kind of his thing. You know, when he saw you walk in yesterday, he couldn't take his eyes off you. I have never seen him like that—he is so enamored by you. You must know that, Aanya! For him, you are it."

Aanya smiled in the dark as she imagined Abhimanyu's face gazing at her in the ballroom the previous evening, looking . . . like someone who was madly in love with her.

"Also, it's been seven years. Look at you, Aanya, you are amazing! You *do* know who you are without him. You were selected to fly halfway across the world because you are that good, that damn amazing, at your job! You accomplished all that on your own—*after* you lost the love of your life so tragically. You still triumphed."

"Thanks, Seema. You know, we all put up a good facade when we have to. It's not been easy, trust me."

Seema squeezed Aanya's hand before caressing her thumb against the pulp of Aanya's warm palm. Much like her brother, Seema was intuitive. She had a skill not only for making people divulge without inhibition but also for making them feel as though it was all going to be fine—that they would somehow, with their magical healing power, make it all right again. It was a rare gift this family possessed—one that Aanya craved.

There was a palpable silence for some time.

Seema squeezed Aanya's hand tight. Seconds later, Aanya heard Seema weeping. Aanya took her in her arms and gave her a comforting snuggle.

"It's okay, Seema, we're going to get out of here. You are not dying, and your boyfriend is not moving on—not before I meet him, at least. And, since we are on the topic, who is this special someone?" Aanya said, attempting to lighten the mood.

Seema straightened up and tried to gather herself. By now, they could make out each other's profiles as the daylight had hit the crevices of the hotel, and a sliver of it was sneaking back from under the door.

Seema took a deep breath.

"*Bhaiya* does not know, so please—this stays between us. Promise?"

Aanya squeezed her hand in response.

"He is in the same training program. We met on the first day and just . . . clicked. I was planning to tell *bhai* on this trip, but I haven't found the right time."

"Your secret is safe with me—and I am sure he will be very happy for you, Seema, when you do tell him. I am serious—I look forward to meeting him. He is one lucky guy."

Beyond the door, in the hotel lobby, they heard heavy footsteps and several rounds of gunfire.

"Let's get under the desk," Aanya said, pulling Seema's hand toward her.

There, under the desk, too frightened to speak, they snuggled in silence for almost two hours.

Around 8:09 a.m., there were three hard knocks at the door.

"Police, open up."

The two women froze in fear. There was another hard knock, three times again.

"Police, it's safe. Please open the door," a harsh voice said, in Hindi this time.

"I believe them," Seema whispered. "The accent. Only Mumbai locals, especially the working class, speak Hindi in that dialect."

Aanya nodded her approval. Seema slipped out from under the desk and gently opened the door.

It *was* the police! During their first attempt, the special forces had secured the lobby of the Taj. While the terrorists still held hostages in other parts of the hotel, especially the rooms and suites in the tower, Seema and Aanya were escorted out of the Taj.

Aanya staggered behind Seema through the blood-laden carnage of the Taj Mahal Palace Hotel. The white lilies atop the center table were strewn over shattered glass next to cold bodies and baggage.

They recognized some faces: Saara and Varun, Jayesh and Ram Singh—the true martyrs. It was apparent that no one in the lobby had stood a remote chance of survival during the initial rampage.

Minutes later, the two women found themselves among the first people to be rescued from the Taj on the morning of November 27, 2008. As soon as their eyes adjusted to the radiant Mumbai sun, they texted Abhimanyu again. No response. There had been no update in more than two hours, not since the last round of gunfire and the subsequent rattle of footsteps in the lobby.

They continued to scan the crowd as they were questioned by the police, thoroughly sharing everything they could recall. When they were no longer needed, the police insisted that the women return somewhere safe.

For a second, Aanya considered a thought. Perhaps she could bring Seema to the Orchid, just down the road, and return later—but, she quickly realized, this was not the time to sit on the sidelines, not when Abhimanyu was involved. So they resisted, demanding to stay on-site, intent that they would not leave before they found him.

The police did not force the issue but pushed them to the periphery, behind the ad hoc barracks. There, Aanya sat at the edge of the footpath and watched as the smoke billowed from the magnificent dome. It was a moment of déjà vu—her sitting, staring, helpless, as the smoke rose and chaos ensued. Her mind played out scenes—the Taj collapsing like the Twin Towers, one giant bulbous dome on top of the miniature ones, gobbling those inside, while survivors and loved ones, mothers and fathers, daughters and sons, brothers and sisters, husbands and wives, childhood sweethearts and their best friends died a horrific death.

Tears flooded her eyes.

Seema wrapped an arm around her and held her tight.

The touch startled Aanya. She grabbed her phone and texted frantically.

*We're outside of the Taj. Not in your office. Don't go looking for us. We are safe. Don't try to find us.*

Simple words, right? That was all that had stood between Ayaan's life and death. If she had just whispered in his ear that morning, "Few extra minutes of snuggle time, babe. My meeting was moved to midtown," or a quick unintrusive text if she did not want to waken his worn body: *Hey, going to be in midtown this morning, love you.*

For days, months, and years, she had played out the events of that morning—the morning of his death. A bright, sunny morning, full of promise, yet she had let him falter. All she had to do was let him know, right? Tell him she wasn't in her downtown office. That was it. If only she could have let him know, he would have been spared that moment, that time, those extra few minutes in the building.

What Aanya didn't know, and never would, was that a text would not have saved him. Ayaan's life and death had not been dependent on a text. Ayaan was the kind to stop and help a woman in need, period. And if he hadn't found himself in that situation, he was the kind—just like his friends Jodi and Jacob—to be at the foot of the South Tower, attending to the wounded.

The moment of death can't be turned around by an action or inaction. It is bound by a series of synchronous events stretching across the expanse of a lifetime, and that expanse is under no one's control.

Dusk was nearing. Seema went in search of food while Aanya still sat on the footpath of the Arabian Sea. Suddenly, there was a tap on her shoulder. Aanya turned to find the compassionate face of the *golawala*, the snow cone *kaka*. He handed her some *chana*, held in a cone made of old newspaper.

Aanya smiled and accepted. She couldn't refuse his gentle offering.

"*Ghar chali ja beti, mein dehk luga.*" ("Go home, my child, I will keep a lookout here.")

Aanya shook her head no, and he gave an understanding sigh. It was beginning to get dark. The hostages were still inside, and there was no word from Abhimanyu. Seema returned with some snacks. *Kaka* offered them *roti* from his *tiffin*. While they were connected by the larger tragedy unfolding before them, their true connection was one kindhearted man. On this matter, Abhimanyu was no different than Ayaan, and it was this—his heroism—that scared Aanya the most.

The activity just beyond the barracks slowed but did not halt. Twenty-four hours since the first casualty at the Taj, and there was still no sign of an end. Hundreds remained inside as the gunmen raided rooms, seeking out as many foreigners as possible. Close to midnight, Seema convinced Aanya that sitting there all night was not going to change anything. *Kaka* assured them that he would lay out his shawl, rest on the footpath, and keep them apprised.

On the king-size bed, fresh from a shower and nibbling on room service, Aanya watched the rolling newsreel of the coverage.

Gunfire, bombs, deaths, rescues—repeat.

Text, text, text.

No response.

Aanya called her mother again, this time not lying that she was at the Orchid. Seema did the same, feigning her brother's safety as Ma listened in disbelief. They tried shutting off the news to sleep, but neither slept.

By seven the next morning, they were back at their spot on the footpath. *Kaka* was waiting for them with two cups of hot chai but no updates.

The siege lasted another day, with slivers of hope. There were incessant confirmed and unconfirmed reports of gunfire after gunfire, explosion after explosion, deaths, bodies, and rescues—ten here, two there, fifty through the back—but no word from Abhimanyu.

Not tuned to the news, Aanya only knew what she saw. Special agents, police, and media all playing an intense game of rescue—submerged by gunfire, deaths, explosions, death, death, gunfire, death, rescue, death, escape, death. *No word from him.* Aanya imagined his wounded, bloodstained body amid hundreds of others in the corridor behind the ballroom, *sangeet* guests in their best couture smashed against the wall. Years of mass shootings in schools in America, yet it was here in India that she was witnessing the worst. When the thoughts made her weep and gulp for air, she intuitively began her mantras in her head.

*Kaka*, committed to his father-figure role, offered some water and consolation.

"He's safe, *beti*; God is protecting him; trust God. He will fix everything. This will all be over soon."

Aanya couldn't pinpoint what it was that was breaking her—the horrific events unfolding before her or the idea of losing Abhi. Just when she was beginning to forgive herself for the mistake she had made on that Tuesday morning in September, causing her to lose Ayaan, here she was, thrust into the same pain again. The sobs made her gasp helplessly for air.

*Kaka* placed a gentle hand on her shoulder and spoke softly: "*Beti, ro mut, dhonde lange, himmat rakh.*" ("My daughter, do not cry—we will find him, stay strong.")

The siege carried through another day and persisted into the night. Again, at midnight, at *Kaka*'s insistence, the women took another short respite at the Orchid. They didn't exchange many words, but they had an understanding, the kind shared when the safety of a loved one is in jeopardy.

When they returned to the footpath a little after dawn the next morning, November 29, 2008, seeking the latest eyewitness updates from *Kaka*, the scene around the Taj had escalated into mayhem. Hundreds of people were crying, mourning, celebrating, and searching.

That morning, after a night of intermittent fire and heavy explosions, the Indian special forces finally conquered, captured, or killed most of the terrorists, taking control of the Taj. The gunmen—a bunch of kids no more than twenty or twenty-one, brainwashed to kill and/or be killed in the name of God—had managed to unleash the greatest nightmare Mumbai had ever seen.

All of a sudden, across the street, in the middle of the barricaded crowd, Aanya spotted a brightly dressed girl in a yellow-and-orange *lenga*—the bride!

Aanya bolted to her, grabbed her arm, and pleaded, "Have you seen Abhi? You know, *the* Abhi—the one who helped you plan? Have you seen him?"

"No, not since it started, when he and Natasha helped us to a safe hiding space. Natasha is fine. She helped us stay safe the whole time—we are all alive because of her. She saved us all, but Abhi left after some time to take care of others, and I haven't seen him since. Is he—oh God—"

The bride swallowed bittersweet tears as Aanya gave her a defeated smile.

Having split from *Kaka* and Seema, Aanya continued to scan and search not only the faces of those alive but also the line of bodies being pulled out on stretchers. Momentarily paralyzed, she searched for Abhi's socks and shoes at the end of every stretcher, draped in white. She scanned and searched hundreds of faces wandering amid chaos and barricades, but to no avail. The people, the police, the emergency responders, the onlookers, the reporters, and the media—they were all closing in on her.

Her body began to heave, unable to handle it all. *No, not again!* She fought for air, sobbing uncontrollably, caving to the ground in the middle of the crowd, arms wrapped around her knees. Weeping like a baby.

*Not again—God—please—not again.*

Amid the crowd, someone noticed her on the ground, shaking and sobbing. The person sat down next to her, tapping her lightly on the shoulder. She was so consumed by her loss that she did not feel the finger.

The person tried again, tapping her a second time, slightly more pronounced. She reluctantly lifted her head—face swollen, eyes red, hair disheveled, the solitaire peeking out between her elbows.

"You look more beautiful, more perfect, than you ever have before—and I will always be madly in love with you."

# Epilogue
# Mumbai

*November 30, 2016, 12:03 AM*

It's been some time since I last wrote, but there's something about today, your fortieth birthday, that made me want to connect with you. We were much too young, Ayaan, to ever contemplate death or what we'd wish for the other person in such a case, but at the very least, I owe you this . . .

When Abhi entered my life, after seven long and challenging years, I felt alive again. The thought of losing him, like I lost you, opened my eyes to all that I could have missed out on—all over again. Abhi is a good person, Ayaan. A kind, grand gestures type, just like you—you would like him. We married a year after we met, and now we both work at the Taj. He is the General Manager and I am the Director of Safety and Security. We have two children, Julia and Jai, and much of my life is centered around them. I took them to New York earlier this year. It's been fifteen years already. Can you believe it? I told them all about you. They found your name at the memorial. They asked how I knew you, but they are much too young to understand the depth of our love. One day, when they are ready, I will tell them the whole story. It's important for them to know.

For now, I want you to know, I am happy. Happier than I could have ever imagined I would be after I lost you. My life is good, truly good. I don't know why, but something deep down tells me that is what you would want. For me to be happy and live my life. I know that is what I would want for you.

My parents are still there in Georgia, close to yours, and their friendship is solid. I am happy they stayed friends, despite the circumstances. Last year, all four of them came to Mumbai and I had the best time showing them around. It made me reminisce all our family vacations growing up. We all missed you in our own ways, though we did not speak of it much.

All in all, we are all doing okay and I can only hope you are as well—wherever you may be. Sometimes, I wonder, Ayaan, what you would look like now, at forty—If you would still have that manicured pompadour? Where we would be? How many kids we would have. What our kids would look like? You deserved so much more, Ayaan—so much more than what life handed you.

In our next lives, may I be fortunate enough to give you the future we once dreamed of and so rightly deserve.

Cheers to you, Ayaan. Happy Birthday!

I love you and always will,


Aanya

# Historical Context

## 9/11 Attacks

On the morning of Tuesday, September 11, 2001, a series of four coordinated terrorist attacks by the Islamic terrorist group Al-Qaeda against the United States resulted in close to three thousand fatalities. Four passenger planes were hijacked by nineteen terrorists. Two of the planes crashed into the North and South Towers, respectively, of the World Trade Center complex in Lower Manhattan, New York City. Within one hour and forty-two minutes, both 110-story towers collapsed. Debris and the resulting fires caused a partial or complete collapse of all other buildings in the World Trade Center complex. The third plane crashed into the Pentagon, while the fourth plane crashed into a field in Stonycreek Township, Pennsylvania, after passengers diverted the hijackers.

## 26/11 Attacks

On the evening of Wednesday, November 26, 2008, a series of coordinated terrorist attacks by the Islamic terrorist group Lashkar-e-Taiba against India resulted in 174 fatalities. The attacks occurred across Mumbai at multiple sites, including the Chhatrapati Shivaji Terminus, Mumbai Chabad House, the Oberoi Trident, and the Taj Palace and Tower, along with a number of other sites. While most sites were secured by the Mumbai police and security forces within a day, the Taj attack lasted for three days. The attacks at the Taj Palace Hotel began late on the evening of November 26 with a massacre, subsequent explosions, and a fire. Hostages were held with intermittent rescues and escapes during the three-day siege, which ended on the morning of November 29, 2008, after a special operation by India's National Security team.

# Gujarati/Hindi Glossary

| | |
|---|---|
| *Arrre yaar* | Slang meaning, "Oh, friend." |
| *Baba* | A term used to refer to one's father in some parts of India. |
| *Banarsi* | Products from the state of Banaras (also known as Varanasi) in India. It is especially known for its silk *saris*. |
| *Baraat* | The groom's procession in a traditional Indian (usually Hindu) wedding. |
| *Baraatis* | Guests from the groom's side at a wedding. |
| *Ben* | A suffix meaning "sister" commonly added to first names as a sign of respect. |
| *Beta* | Term of endearment for a child, usually a boy, but used fairly universally for both a boy or a girl. |
| *Beti* | Term of endearment for a child, usually a girl. |
| *Bhagwan* | Literally translates to "God." |
| *Bhai* | Literally means "brother"; commonly added as a suffix to first names as a sign of respect. |
| *Bhaiya* | Used to refer to one's own brother, a variation of the word *bhai*, meaning "brother." |
| *Bhajia* | Deep-fried fritters; a common snack item made with a variety of ingredients such as corn, spinach, potatoes, onions, etc. |
| *Bidi* | A small, inexpensive cigarette, locally produced usually from cut tobacco hand-rolled in leaf. |

| Chana | A savory snack made from flattened chickpeas sprinkled with dry spices. |
|---|---|
| Chanya choli | Traditional Indian clothing consisting of a long, full skirt, blouse, and scarf. |
| Chole bhature | A dish from the northern region of India. It is a combination of spicy white chickpeas (*chole*) to be eaten with fried bread (*bhature*). |
| Dahi | Indian yogurt. |
| Dal bhath | *Dal* in the context of this book is used to describe a lentil or split pigeon pea soup normally consumed with *bhath* (rice) or *naan*. |
| Dal dhokli | A dish prepared by simmering whole wheat flour bits in a lentil-based soup perked with spices. |
| Desi | A person of South Asian (Indian, Pakistani, Bangladeshi, Sri Lankan, etc.) birth or descent who lives abroad. |
| Dhobi | Clothes washer. In the context of this book, it also refers to someone who irons clothes for a living. |
| Diwali | A Hindu festival of lights held in the period from October to November. It is particularly associated with Lakshmi, the goddess of prosperity, and marks the beginning of the fiscal year in India. It is a time of year when people often take vacations, go shopping, and have big celebrations. |
| Diya | An oil lamp used in the Indian subcontinent, notably India and Nepal, usually made from clay with a cotton wick dipped in ghee or vegetable oils. |

| | |
|---|---|
| *Dupattas* | A shawl-like scarf; women's traditionally essential clothing from the Indian subcontinent. |
| *Garam masala* | Mixture of spices commonly used in Indian cooking. |
| *Gathia* | Deep-fried chickpea flour. |
| *Gori* | A light-skinned person; often slang for a foreigner from the Western world. |
| *Jai Shri Krishna* | A salutation in place of "hello," "good morning," "good night," or in place of short prayers. It is intended to not only remember God, but to attract and send positive vibes. Its literal translation in the simplest form is "victory to Lord Shree Krishna." |
| *Jalebi* | An Indian sweet made by deep-frying flour batter in pretzel or circular shapes, which are then soaked in sugar syrup. |
| *Kaka* | Refers to your father's brother. The English equivalent is "uncle." It is also commonly added as a suffix to first names as a sign of respect or used on its own for anyone you wish to refer to with the respect of an uncle/elder. |
| *Kala khata baraf ka gola* | A snowball shaved from ice with black currant syrup. |
| *Kanyadaan* | The literal translation of the term is *kanya* = "maiden" and *daan* = "donation," which may be seen as the Donation of a Maiden. Essentially, it is the giving away of the bride by her parents to the groom, entrusting him with her future well-being. |

| Kem cho | Means "How are you?" in Gujarati. |
|---|---|
| Khaman | A food common in the Gujarat state that is prepared from soaked and freshly ground chickpea flour. |
| Kundan | A traditional form of Indian gemstone jewelry involving a gem set with gold foil between the stones and its mount, usually for elaborate necklaces. |
| Kurta | A loose collarless shirt, usually worn by men. In this context, it refers to the traditional white linens commonly worn at Hindu funerals. |
| Lenga | A form of full ankle-length skirt worn by women, which is long, embroidered, and pleated. It is worn as the bottom portion of an outfit with a blouse. In this context, it refers to the whole outfit worn for a special occasion. |
| Maa | Used to refer to one's own mother. |
| Maharaj | A reference to a Hindu priest. |
| Mandap | A covered structure with pillars temporarily erected for the purpose of a Hindu or Jain wedding. The main wedding ceremony takes place under the structure. It is traditionally made of wood and decorated with flowers. |
| Mandir | A Hindu temple or shrine. |
| Mangalsutra | A necklace placed on a bride by the groom during a Hindu wedding ceremony sanctifying their nuptials. Women continue to wear this throughout their lives to signify that they are married. |

| | |
|---|---|
| *Mausi/Masi* | Refers to one's mother's sister, so its English equivalent is "aunt." It is also commonly added as a suffix to first names as a sign of respect or used on its own for anyone you wish to give the respect of an aunt. |
| *Mehndi* | Another word for henna. |
| *Mela* | A carnival; festival. |
| *Munsi* | The village money lender / loan shark. |
| *Paan* | A pod combining betel leaf with areca nut widely consumed throughout India. It is chewed for its stimulant and psychoactive effects. |
| *Panchayat* | Village town council, usually made up of five people. The word *panch* translates to five. |
| *Papad* | Wafer-like thin, crisp, round flatbread. |
| *Pav bhaji* | A dish that consists of a thick vegetable curry served with a soft bread roll. |
| *Poha* | Dish with rice flattened into light, dry flakes. It is prepared in different ways throughout India with a combination of spices. |
| *Pooja* | Ritual of worship; often a formal ceremony performed by a priest. |
| *Rangoli* | An art form in which patterns are created on the floor or the ground using materials such as colored sand, rice, dry flour, or flower petals. It is usually made during festivals, such as Diwali. |
| *Rasmalia* | A dessert originating from the eastern regions of India. |

| Roti/Rotli | Bread, especially a flat round bread cooked on a griddle. It is found in various forms throughout India. |
| Rozi roti | Daily bread (and butter). |
| Salwar kameez | A long tunic worn over a pair of baggy trousers, usually found on women. |
| Sangeet | Literally translates to "music." It is often used as a term to describe a celebratory event during an Indian wedding, in which case it translates to "music night" or "musical party" and usually held a day before the wedding. |
| Sari | A garment consisting of a length of cotton or silk elaborately draped around the body, traditionally worn by women from South Asia. |
| Shenhai | While it refers to a musical instrument made of wood, with a double reed at one end and a metal or wooden flared bell at the other end, *shenhai* also generally refers to music traditionally played during weddings. |
| Sherwani | A knee-length coat buttoning to the neck, often worn by the groom and other males at a wedding. |
| Subzi | Any kind of vegetable prepared with a combination of spices. |
| Yaar | Friend, usually with an inference of "my friend." |
| Zari | A type of gold or silver thread used to decorate Indian clothing. |

# Book Club Questions

1. Aanya's childhood bond with Ayaan and their immigrant upbringing along with their parents' immigrant experiences are central to the story. Could you relate to their stories?

2. What perceptions do you have of both modern India and America? Does this narrative change or alter those perceptions?

3. The American Dream and the concept of an embryonic Indian Dream are central to the book. How were these themes addressed/discussed throughout the narrative?

4. There are two key historical events in the book. Where were you during these events? Have either one or both events shaped or affected your life in any way?

5. From the three main characters, Aanya, Ayaan, and Abhi, who did you like, appreciate or empathize with the most and why?

6. Aside from Aanya, Ayaan, and Abhi, what secondary characters did you appreciate, relate to or empathize with the most and why?

7. How did Aanya's relationship with her mother (Shalu), father (Raman), Ayaan's sister (Aditi), and his parents (Kishore and Leela) evolve throughout the book? Was it relatable or realistic?

8. Reflect on Aanya's resilience and how she copes with emotional challenges. What strategies does she use to move forward? How does her journey resonate with universal themes of loss and healing and is it relatable and/or realistic?

# Acknowledgments

Call it a midlife crisis or perhaps a midlife success (thanks, internet, for the positive spin on everything): One morning, I woke up with a desire to pursue a long-shelved dream—I wanted to write a novel. I turned to my husband, Amit, and shared the themes I gravitated toward. He began plotting, there was some back and forth, and before we knew it a story had materialized. The next year was spent writing, the next several more editing, pitching, and revising. All told, almost seven years of simmering and endless support from friends and family took place before this book came to fruition.

To my forever firsts, my family: Amit, though I may not readily confess it (insert subtle cough) and sure, I put up a good fight, your counsel and advice form the backbone of every decision I make in my life. Thank you for being a part of this process since the morning I woke up wishing to write a novel. You are a true partner and anchor. I can give you no greater compliment than to let you know that you are both Ayaan and Abhi, all in one package. I honestly could not have written either one of these characters if it were not for your love and solidarity in my life. To Ayushi, your passion for reading and ruminations for days on end about character developments/arcs, dialogue, and plot twists are admirable. You genuinely embody the power of books, proving that stories have the capacity to build a more empathic, compassionate, and just world. One day, I hope to fall for one of your characters as much as you have fallen for Ayaan. To Alisha, I could not ask for a better or bigger cheerleader and cuddle bug than you. Thank you for always being up for anything as long as it is with "Mama"; from organizing the pantry to grocery shopping, you make every mundane mommy task an adventure I treasure. The three of you truly make the sun shine in my life, and I am grateful for us!

To my parents, Satish and Niru Shah: This story is an homage to your generation for making brave moves, sacrificing for your children, and forging unbreakable bonds along the way. Dad, your love and mastery of oral storytelling are the inspiration behind this book. I hope you recognize your voice and fragments of yourself throughout this tale. Mom, I extend my heartfelt gratitude for always standing by my side and defending me a hundred percent, no matter the situation—even when I am unequivocally in the wrong. Your resolute support of your daughters is the trait I am most proud to inherit as a mother of two of my own.

To Mansi Shah, my sister, confidante, on-demand therapist, and everything in between: Dissecting the daily grind with you is the highlight of my day. I deeply appreciate the bond we have built over long walks and talks.

To my in-laws, Ashwin and Lata Thakkar: Your unparalleled kindness, generosity, and selflessness are a standard I can only hope to aspire to. Thank you for all you continue to do for us.

To Kruti Parikh and Mita Harivallabhdas (and Mansi): Thank you for enduring not only this roller coaster but also so many more. From navigating being kids to raising our own kids, I truly treasure our lifelong friendship, full of chatter, laughter, and blackmail-worthy Lemon Zest moments.

To Salwa Ammar: Reading your work "The Wrath of Wednesday" was the spark that ignited this story. I am grateful for your mentorship in my professional life, your encouragement regarding this book, and, most importantly, our friendship.

To my very first readers—Urvee Bhathela, Jignasha Iyengar, Aashka Parikh, Amie Shah, Payal Shah, Prarthi Shah, Rajat Shah, Monica Teixtera, Akash Thakkar, and Anjana Virdi—thank you for indulging me and being kind about my naïve early drafts. Your encouragement and excitement about this project are sincerely appreciated. Thank you, Janet Rovenpor, for never missing a grammatical beat and the three-day turnaround.

To everyone else in my very, very, very big extended family: I am grateful for you all. I thrive on the love and chaos of building memories at all our gatherings through both good and challenging times.

To my Writing Sisters, near and far: You remain steadfast in this process. Slow and steady, we are getting there. Thank you Alicia Blando, Melissa DeSa, Robyn Fisher, Kate Jackson, Pia Kealey, Delphine Ledesma, Marti Mattia, Lisa Rayner, and Victoria Sams.

To Zoe Quinton, my editor, thank you for polishing this story into its best version. To Brooke Warner, my publisher, and Addison Gallegos, my project manager for your guidance, and especially for the fall 2024 fiction cohort, whose camaraderie transformed this daunting journey into a surprisingly pleasant sisterhood.

. . . And, of course, to you, my readers. Thank you for making it this far. I would love to hear your thoughts. Come find me at https:// shahgrishma.com/

# About the Author

**G**rishma Shah was inspired to write this story not only as a daughter of Indian immigrants who spent part of her childhood growing up in motels/convenience stores but also as an expert on culture and globalization. After years as an academic in New York City, publishing, researching, traveling, and teaching, she believes that nothing educates, enlightens, informs, or propels us forward like a good story. Consequently, she has been moonlighting as a storyteller, working in New York City and living in Monroe Township, New Jersey, with her husband and two daughters.

## Looking for your next great read?

We can help!

Visit www.gosparkpress.com/next-read
or scan the QR code below for a list
of our recommended titles.

SparkPress is an independent boutique publisher
delivering high-quality, entertaining, and engaging
content that enhances readers' lives, with a special
focus on commercial and genre fiction.